AYŞE'S TRAIL

Atulya K Bingham

'Ayşe's Trail is a stunning work of bravery and honesty. It is a marvel of storytelling that the vivid unveiling of one woman's journey has the power to illuminate our own very different journeys across the world. The effect of Bingham's words resound long after the last page.'

Claire Raciborska, *Smoke of Spirits*

'For those in the 21st century who understand the curvature of space and the folding of time, Ayşe's story will come as a welcome glimpse into histories that overlap. This is a story of the journey of one modern Turkish woman who does not draw on the lessons of history, but reaches deeply into its spirit and thereby finds within herself the resources to create that journey.'

Brian Crocker, *Walks in Turkey*

AYŞE'S TRAIL

Atulya K Bingham

Mudhouse Publishing

AYŞE'S TRAIL
A MUDHOUSE BOOK

First edition published in the UK in 2013
Copyright © Atulya K Bingham 2013

ISBN 9781849144438
Reproduced, printed and bound in the UK by MUDHOUSE

Acknowledgements

Just like the Lycian Way itself, this book has been a long winding hike, and without the help of many people it would never have reached the printing press. I'd like to express my sincere appreciation of all those who assisted me, motivated me and supported me during this process.

My sincere gratitude goes to Ayşe Metin for her inspiring friendship, and for taking the time to share her story with me.

I'm extremely grateful to Claire Raciborska and Seth Falconer for starting me out on my writer's journey, and Claire for her close final edit of the text. Without their comments and support I wouldn't have made it past the first draft.

Many thanks also go to Allison Orr for her thoughtful read and intelligent feedback in the early stages of this novel.

Vinzent Enro's reading of the book in its early stages was invaluable. He immediately grasped 'the soul' of the story and helped develop many of its themes. His positive attitude to all my creations has always been a lifeline for me. Thank you.

I'm very much indebted to Brian Crocker for his meticulous edit, as well as his excellent insights on the philosophy of time and the Lycian Way. His belief in the story and his efforts for bringing it to fruition are deeply appreciated.

Much appreciation goes to Yvonne Bartfeld for her honest comments on chapter one, and her stimulating friendship over the years.

Thank you to Melissa Maples for her close edit of chapter one, to Sarah Juckes at Completely Novel for typesetting Ayşe's Trail, and to the Completely Novel team for their numerous tips and overall excellent support for writers.

Elif Aysan, Birgit Sabinsky, Feryal Özdemir, Baykal Solmaz, and Nilay Eryener Tan are acknowledged for their patient support, both physical and motivational, throughout this long adventure.

Many thanks to Betty Rampling for her advice on the first chapter, and her ongoing interest in the book.

And of course, where would any of this be without Dad? I thank him for his stoic acceptance of my peculiarities, being there for me, and also his practical and crucial advice regarding the structure of the book.

To the many Ayşes in Turkey,

and to Gran.

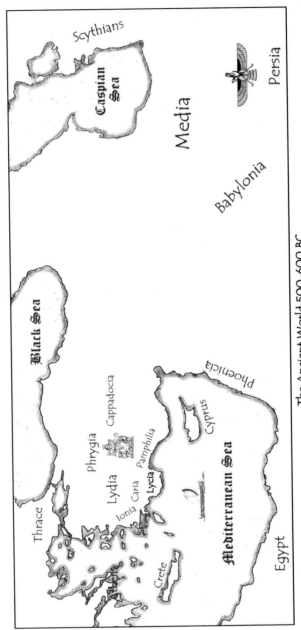

The Ancient World 500–600 BC

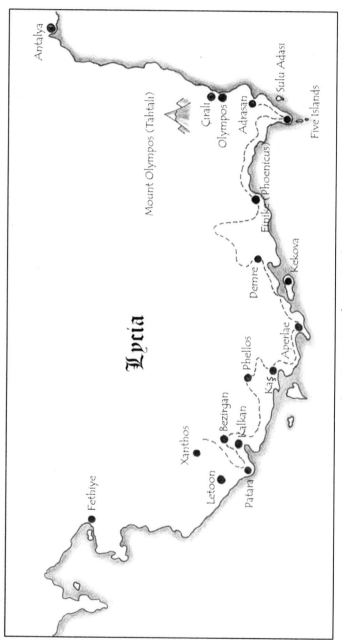

Lycia in Modern Turkey

'For me, nothing is more important than freedom in every sense of the word.'

Ayşe Metin 2010

Let me just say this: When one is about to die, all sorts of thoughts pop up. The mind turns into a busy street with anything from a dolmuş to a truck full of watermelons cutting in. Some thoughts circle round and round like taxis looking for a customer. My apartment in Istanbul, for example, seemed to take more than its fair share of my very mortal attention, and I hope my husband and son don't take that personally.

Obviously, I had never considered that dying might constitute a part of my adventure. Well, not really dying. I did, I suppose, entertain a few romantic notions about parts of my ego shrivelling off, and then another me, the real me, rising from the ashes like a hiking-boot-wearing phoenix. But actual fatality? The kind where one turns green and then purple before intestinal bacteria eat the rest from the inside out. No. It never crossed my mind. If it had, I daresay the hike would never have started. Death was something vague and distant like Mars, a place only other people older and wiser than I went. Well, I had more important things to do, didn't I? Things like reaching the town of Xanthos and then all the lights flicking on, after which I'd murmur in wonder: Aha, that's who I am, and why I'm here.

I wasn't in Istanbul, of course. I was loping through a smoking pine forest in the southern hills in a futile attempt to outrun a forest fire. The fire had whipped itself into an orange lather. It was like a restless creature that the mountain back was trying to shrug off, and it was gaining ground. As I stumbled pell-mell over stones, I heard it licking the pines behind me with its horrible orange tongues. One by I one, it scorched off each layer of their fragile branches. The trees screamed when it torched them; trees do scream, I heard them. And then my

11

bathroom interjected. What was in the dirty laundry basket? Was there toothpaste on the sink? *I think I just wanted to tidy up all the loose ends.*

Forest fires are conscienceless monsters, and they devour anything in their path. Scorpions, vipers, guileless hedgehogs, wild boar, one ingenuous hiker, it was taking us all without so much as flinching. To be honest, the only reason I kept on running was that I just couldn't think of anything else to do.

In the end I ran out of breath, and that was why I paused. I looked back one last time. The peak was a skyward beacon the tourist schooners floating below would soon see. As I hunched over and gasped for air, I kicked myself. Why the hell had I taken on the pilgrimage hike of the Lycian Way in the first place? My great dream could so easily have been singing on television or winning the lottery, instead. I mean, I'd expected a lot more than this for my pain; a snippet of enlightenment say, or perhaps the odd shamanic power, or a profound insight into myself that would make all the unattractive parts of my personality melt away like one of our fluffy Pişmaniye sweets in an old lady's mouth. At the very least, I would have hoped to be living carefree in the Now, the worries of the world no more than motes of pollen or dandelion clocks that I blew gaily out of my face. Well, that's why we do these things, isn't it? Self-improvement. And I must say, I felt seriously short changed

A violent crack interrupted my thoughts. A large pine, perhaps a century old, burst into flames not a hundred metres from me. Finally, I realised. It didn't matter, did it? Nothing mattered. Not the trail, not the position of the bathroom mat, I didn't matter. From the burning flank of the mountains, my aspirations looked no more than vapid blips in a universe of greater things. My

12

trail wound directly back into the forest fire. It was annihilated by it. And when I realised that, I felt so glum I just couldn't find it in me to keep going. I was finally getting my comeuppance for abandoning the herd of normality, for striking out alone and doing exactly what I wanted to do.

Well, that's what they'd have you believe, the ones who've never walked on their own, isn't it? That's definitely what they'd like you to think.

Day One

Thirst

Olympos - July 2008

It started in Olympos. Things had always started there, and no doubt they always would. When I say Olympos, you may think I mean the mountain in Greece. But I don't. There was more than one Olympos in the ancient world. The Gods had many homes. The Olympos of this story is squashed into a chasm on the south coast of modern day Turkey in an area known as Lycia. It has seen it all in its long, convoluted history: money, pirates, democracy, tyranny, tourism and debauchery (not necessarily in that order). Everyone who is anyone has been there. I remember Odysseus stopping by. Both Julius Caesar and Hadrian called in on their way to other places. Perhaps there was even an apostle or two. Ayşe Metin visited many times. It was her favourite holiday spot in the world until that hike. After that, everything changed. Spots were no longer single points in space and time. They became long strings of elastic that you could loop, coil and stretch at will.

Now, as chief storyteller of these parts, I've heard a number of yarns in the long, hard span of my life. Gossip and conspiracy are like fresh air to me. But the tale of how Ayşe walked Lycia is one of those that wormed right under my mottled, old skin. When she first set off, we were complete strangers. We've grown close over the years. But back then it was different. Yes, everything was different. It was different from the moment she put one foot in front of the other.

As I said, it began in Olympos. The trail. Well, her trail at least. It was one of those roads people have in their heads. They think it's going one place, but it ends up taking them somewhere else. Ayşe didn't know any of this. All she knew was that it was a midsummer morning in 2008, and she was about to set off. But before she took that all important first step, she decided to have one last glass of tea. Well, she would. She was Turkish, and no mission, however small, was ever undertaken without the aftertaste of tannin on the tongue.

She was wilting in a *köşk* – the wooden platform so many Turks wiled away the summer hours on. The air stuck to her in heavy, damp wads. The sky was holocaust white. Turkey's southern coast, as any local will tell you, is murderously hot by July. The heat has its own colour and shape in these parts. It's not the clinging, grey steam of an Asian city, nor the fruity swelter of a tropical island. This is the neck of the Middle East and it doesn't deal in pleasantries. The Turkish sky is a wide, open eye, and it rolls white and furious in its heavenly socket. It's the eye of a dominant woman. A Medusa even. The lid never lowers. The eye glares. It fixes the Earth under its neutron gaze, and makes the rivers shrivel, the pine trees crack, and the rocks splinter in resentment.

Ayşe's *köşk* squatted in a shady orange garden. It was surrounded by five or six similar platforms. Holidaymakers sprawled in most of them fanning themselves or finishing their breakfasts. For some reason or no reason, everyone in the garden looked like a rock star from the 1970s; A swarthy Dave Gilmore slouched in the lap of a cigarette-puffing Janis Joplin, Cher – prior to her forays into plastic surgery – lounged in a corner reading something by Ayn Rand, Elton John was the cook, and there were numerous Freddie Mercurys milling about– men with moustaches of such body and gloss you could have used them to apply make-up or emulsion. Most of the Freddies weren't homosexual. This was the 'other' Olympos. The valley not the mountain. Like a negative of a photo, or a parallel reality, things were often back to front.

'Any tea left, Sami?' Ayşe called out. She didn't look like a rock star. She looked like someone you might take home to your mother. This in itself was strange, because she was a mother in her own right, someone other pleasant looking girls would be taken home to. She held up an empty glass between her index finger and thumb. Her nails weren't polished, but they were spotless and well-manicured.

Elton John the chef, whose real name was Sami, was leaning in the doorway of the wooden kitchen. Sweat ran in rivulets from every inch of his face. His T-shirt stuck patchily to his paunch like a badly pasted hoarding. 'As this is probably the last *çay* of your life, I'll do you a favour my dear and bring it out to you.'

Ayşe let a smile slip across her face. Everything about her was carefully put together, from her lime green vest top to her hiking boots. Even her socks were immaculate. She was someone from whom the words 'slump' or 'slouch' would have scuttled away yelping. She sat on a pile of cushions, one long leg crossed neatly over the other. It might have been forty degrees, but she refused to do anything more than lightly perspire. Taking a wet tissue sachet from her pocket, she gently wiped her throat. It was baffling. Even to me. How could such a woman consider hiking? She just looked too brittle. Too clean.

That morning, as every morning, the mountains pressed against the sides of the small Olympos guesthouse. They were so high Medusa's eye could only peer into the valley between ten and four. Even so, the rocks loped down the mountain backs in shattered regiments. They were broken men turned to stone mid-step. Ayşe felt the steep banks squeezing her out. The stone mountain men were rushing at her, hounding her to move.

The road to the beach wound in front of her deck, and it seethed with a motley snarl of tourists. Heads bulged

17

with dreadlocks, overgrown beards hung from jowls, sweaty flesh fell out of bikinis. Every now and again a headscarf bobbed up and down like a buoy in a turbulent sea. Yet, as divergent as they appeared, each one of the crowd plodded on in the same direction. Everyone followed everyone else. It was a snake without a head.

As she watched the beach-goers, Ayşe quietly sat on her secrets; her age (thirty-eight), her marriage (second one), her son (eighteen years old and not seen for three years). Destiny could have moved many ways at that point. She could have stayed drinking tea all morning. She could have done what everyone else was doing; lounge on the pebbly seashore, bury her nose a self-help book, and insulate against the gnawing sensation that deep down she was a bit lost. A bit bewildered.

But she'd done all that before.

Instead she turned to the map. It was concertinaed on the cushion next to her like a jack-in-the-box poised to leap. A tiny gulp, barely visible, made its way down her throat, because this wasn't an ordinary piece of cartography. It was neither designed for motorists, nor the average tourist. It was a trail map. The kind only a slender wedge of humanity would ever open – the bandana-wearing, staff-bearing oddities otherwise known as hikers.

Ayşe tugged at the cover. A mysterious, green world unfolded. It was a wrinkled wonderland of fluted peninsulas and forgotten histories. Lycia. A red dotted line dug in and out of the map folds. It squirmed over three hundred kilometres in front of her to places she couldn't yet see, pushing through legions of fir, teetering along precipices, and creeping through the shells of ghost cities.

'Here you go, one glass of çay for her ladyship.'

Sami the chef folded his pudgy fingers over the railing of the platform. He thrust his head inside and stared hard at her. 'Really dear, are you going to camp? Up there?' He swivelled his eyes meaningfully to the towering slope in front of the *pansiyon*. The stone men stared down with thickset faces. The peak was out of view. The cook's eyes bulged. 'It looks *horribly* uncomfortable.' He wrinkled his nose up. It gave him the air of a very flushed, completely furless pug. 'All those nasty little bugs everywhere. And what will you do if you see a reptile, heaven *forbid*?'

Ayşe eyed his belly and grinned. 'Well, why don't you join me? Be my chaperone. I mean, let's be honest, you could do with a bit of a hike.' She pulled at the glass ashtray on the squat wooden console in front of her.

Sami patted his tubby belly proudly. 'I'm a *chef*! Corpulence is part of the job description, dear.' He pushed his nose into the sky, and turned briskly from the platform. As he walked back towards the kitchen he called behind him, 'Pah! Fitness freaks! You'll be laughing on the other side of your face this time tomorrow, you just wait!'

Pulling her straw-gold thatch into an elastic, Ayşe meticulously checked each strand was secured. She stretched supine, her arms extending along the wooden railing like a pair of well-maintained grape vines. A cigarette sprouted from between her lips. The last before she set off. She lit it. A stem of smoke stretched upward forming a twisting, nebulous pathway to God only knew where.

It was something of a miracle, because as she closed her eyes she managed to wholly overlook the slew of danger she was stepping into. No one attempted the Lycian Way in summer. Not even those with grubby socks, unkempt hair and stubble-invaded faces. It was madness. Hazard crouched under every ancient rock. It gloated at you from behind every juniper tree – dehydration, crumbling precipices, big cats, vipers, scorpions, Abdullah the goatherd who hadn't seen a woman in months. And then there were the other things. The things no one quite understood. Shadows from other times. Other places.

The cigarette was folded into the ashtray. Ayşe dusted herself down, and pulled herself from the platform. Her boots were by her pack, and they gaped between the heels and the tongues. She stuffed her feet inside the hungry boot-mouths. Next she stooped, pushed an arm through each strap of her rucksack and levered herself upright. She swayed a little and bent over to cope with the load. Then she put one foot. In front. Of the other.

ಬು◯ಜ

In those days, I was utterly green when it came to long-distance hiking. Yes, a complete novice. I had hardly spent a night in the wilds and most definitely had never camped alone. I have no idea what came over me; the entire mission was a leap into the vacuity of ill-conceived folly. The trouble with me is, when I'm infected with an idea, I have to go through with it right to the bitter end.

Naturally, before setting off, I had studied the map quite intensely. Maps are wonderful things, aren't they? Pretty crochets of lines and dots superimposed upon a dappled unknown. The Lycian Way was a ribbon of enticing place names, things like Zeytin *(Olive),* Beymelek *(Archangel) and* Kalamar *(Squid). Then there were what I assumed were ancient Greek cities. They paraded under myth-coated labels like Oracle, Xanthos and Letoon. That last name sounded so good I said it a few times, rolling it round my mouth like an exotic boiled sweet; Letoon, Letooooon.*

It would of course soon become apparent how little information a map can impart about a trail. When terrain is squashed flat upon a piece of paper, all of the most important details are left out. Things such as the potential charm of a town, or how sun-baked a given incline is, or whether an Ottoman viper is lurking in a certain field are simply beyond the scope and scale of two dimensions. I can tell you now: Beymelek, for example, far from embodying any sort of angelic atmosphere, is quite the most unheavenly blot on the landscape you are ever likely to traipse through; a strip of dusty, motorised misery.

Anyway, from the vantage point of the map, I had decided to try and walk as far as Fethiye. It was nearly 300 kilometres away, but I didn't care about that. The map marked kilometres off in tidy little squares, not with a skull and crossbones or an icon of a collapsed hiker, as it should have done. I ought to have considered what 300 kilometres really means, I suppose, but as soon as I heard of the Lycian Way it was as if the physical practicalities of walking the thing evaporated into the pink fluff of daydream.

That first morning I didn't actually start walking from Olympos. I had taken a lift to the neighbouring village of Adrasan, because I wanted to start the hike from somewhere new. The car was now behind me, and I found myself on a quiet beach. I looked about. Adrasan was pretty. It still demurred before the ghastly concrete hand of mass tourism, and a miscellany of ramshackle guesthouses and eateries were scattered along the seashore. It wasn't much past ten, but the heat was already closing in, so I stopped dithering and set to it.

I was terribly excited on that opening leg of my trail. It was a dream come true, you see. At last, I was hiking the Lycian Way! I trotted along the bay, hands on backpack straps, brimmed hat pulled over my forehead. I didn't whistle or sing, but I'd be fibbing if I said I hadn't considered at least a little humming. The going was easy at

21

that point, and the surroundings inspiring. The sea was as flat and clear as a mirror, with the mountains scooped up on all sides. But even then, after not much more than ten minutes of hiking, I realised I had made a fatal error, and that mistake was strapped onto me in the bulging oblong form of my twenty kilogram rucksack.

Twenty kilograms is a ridiculous burden for a trek of such length, and it was a fact I came to understand intimately over the course of the next ten days. Ordinary folk flinch at carrying twenty kilograms to an airport for God's sake! But what was I to do about it? The tent – a simple recreational affair – weighed at least five kilograms, the sleeping bag an additional three. All I had packed seemed such a necessity. Well, almost all. It is true, I was carrying more than a sensible amount of toiletries. I'd had only family-sized flagons of shower gel and body lotion in my Olympos tree house, as opposed to the handy travel packs a more experienced traveller might appropriate. There were no supermarkets in the valley from where I could restock. Had anyone suggested I leave anything behind, I expect I simply would have brushed them off, because I had no idea of the damage I was inflicting on myself, nor how unnecessary body lotion would be.

Now, you might suppose with all that baggage, I was awfully well-prepared. Ha! A list of the essentials I had blithely omitted included; a camping stove, compass, proper hiking boots, distress flares, GPS equipment and one of those very handy Swiss army knives with the knife and spoon and whatnot attached. In retrospect, the only truly life-saving thing in my rucksack was water. With every person I conferred with warning me of dried up springs and parched devastation, I had packed four-and-a-half kilograms of liquid survival, and yes, I felt naively safe with it lodged upon my back in that way; a hump of fodder and beverage, camel-like in my independence.

Finally, I arrived at the end of the beach. I was now just beginning to perspire. The trail swerved to the right here and disappeared up a slope coated in thick pine trees. I braced myself for my first plod up an incline. Just for a moment I hesitated. I could have turned back from that point quite easily and returned to Olympos, to the beach and the security of the familiar, to that soft, spongy place otherwise known as the comfort zone. It could have all ended there and then.

It was strange, but I never thought to question why I was attempting this, now of all times. I was a city woman after all, an Istanbulian mother with a dark, but far from unusual past. Two days earlier, I had been happily relaxing on the beach with the rest of Olympos, soaking up rays and paddling in the water with no inkling I'd be walking The Trail. Yes, it was peculiar how the idea had snuck into my head. Most peculiar.

ᛯᛯOᚳ

I doubt Ayşe ever really knew the true reason. But I do. She started hiking the Lycian Way because of Olympos. The old city told her to. It was the rocks that did the talking. The whispers slid from their cool, grey bodies and wriggled right into her head.

Anyone who walks through Olympos knows magic is afoot. It's obvious. You can't miss it. The seashore will stop you in your tracks. The crawlway through the great rock at the river end is the door to another world. The clear blue pane of the Mediterranean is the window. And Mount Olympos, the giant, stares over both from under its cloud-wreathed crown. You are watching. And you are watched.

But it is the ancient city in the valley which holds the deeper secrets. The ruins of the houses, two millennia old, reek of them. The temples are squatting on the gas of the past. Its vapour leeks from the cracks in the walls diffusing plumes of myth and legend as it rises. Visitors unwittingly breathe in those tales. But few are those who hear anything.

The day before she started her hike, the Lycian Way wasn't much more than a pipe dream. Ayşe had been heading for the beach, just as she always did. She added her blonde head and gravity-mocking physique to the snake of beach-goers and 1970s rock stars. It slid through the valley, past the agora and the ancient baths.

Wooden shacks, small pansiyons and stalls choked the two-thousand-year-old track. Their open fronts were cluttered with wares spilling onto the road like the overflow from too many gluttonous mouths. Their vendors harassed the people as they squirmed on their way to the seaside.

'Chiz Pankek!'

'Toorkish Viagra! You try, you try! Five times in the night guarantee.'

'Hello lady, you wanna kayak to the next bay? See a turtle. Or a big shark. Next year they build big five star there and you never see again.'

Ayşe pretended she hadn't heard. She carried on her way. The touts soon became quiet. The timber ghettos of the guesthouses disappeared. The forest and the river joined forces. They sheltered the trail in their cool, quiet company. The beach serpent moved onward into the dusky shadows with Ayşe still wrapped in its scales.

The Olympos mountains were great Gods of mottled limestone, beards of pine trailing the length of their rocky chins. The mountains pressed against the sides of the path. They squeezed the track so tightly the stones, old and new, popped out. An ancient wall appeared. It was as high as a

24

man and as long as a train. The old, grey stones pinched together to keep the tourists out of antiquity. Or could it have been vice-versa? A creaking wilderness had entwined itself about the ruins strewn left and right along the way. A crumbling agora, a temple lost to a swamp, pathways winding to nowhere in particular. Here was the original Olympos. The far off home of the Lycian ancestors. Who would have guessed this is where it would all happen? Where it all happened? Where it's all happening?

Tourists visiting Turkey's south coast were often baffled by the ruins they encountered. With educations speaking only of ancient Greece and Rome, what was Lycia? Unbeknown to many, the ancient world hadn't ended at Athens. Between the old empires of the ancient Greeks and Persia, there were other kingdoms. Other civilisations. Other people.

'Meral! Stop a minute will you, love! I want to have a quick look inside.' A young man wearing nothing but shorts and a ponytail, pulled himself from the caravan of beach pilgrims. His bikini-clad girlfriend extracted herself too. She paused beside him which caused Ayşe to almost run into the back of her.

Ayşe swallowed a scowl. She tried to circumnavigate the pair but found herself blocked by the wall. Oblivious, the couple gazed into the remains of the city, and through the thick laurels that devoured it.

'Aw, I wish I could go back in time, and see how it was back then. Do you think they were happier than us?' It was the young woman who asked. She ran two fingers into her cleavage and dabbed at the sweat.

The man scratched his chin. 'Nah, it would have sucked. No telly. No internet. *iPad MyPad yok yani!* The only good thing would have been the free dope.' He paused and thought for a moment, eyebrows rising like a pair of

25

thick, black flying carpets. 'Come to think of it . . . Fuck yeah! Can you *imagine?*'

Ayşe, still wedged behind them, cocked her head to one side. Then she peered with them up an ancient water channel. It disappeared into an alternate world of inky pathways and brindled stones.

A large metal sign at the mouth claimed Olympos dated back to the second century BC. But the city's early life was shrouded in mystery, secrets hidden deep in the Lycian dirt. Archaeologists sensed the ruins were older. Every day new artefacts crawled out of the rubble, clues veiled by the dust of time. Who would dare to say what would emerge next? Or which tools were needed to understand what was found? The past was resting in the future just as the future rested in the past.

'Erm, can I get past please?'

The man turned. 'Oh sorry!' He grabbed his girlfriend by the arm and dragged her back a step. The woman smiled weakly. Ayşe stepped by.

Evening was almost here. The tourist snake had now divided into two, as those returning from the beach formed a lane in their own right. Ayşe was momentarily stranded between the two streams; those coming and those going. This wasn't unusual. Ayşe often felt caught between the for and the against. As she stood in the centre of the path, she looked like a one-woman island. The returners kept clipping her left arm while the beach goers were egging her forwards.

Medusa's harsh eye had long since pulled out of the valley. Evening now hung heavy in the mid-summer air. It was the time of day when strange things happen, things which cause transformation. It was exactly at that point of limbo and in that dimming light, that Ayşe spotted something on the hillside opposite. An arch. It was poking over a carob tree. In the daytime the sun would have fried the colour out of it. But now, as day's eyelid closed, all kinds of new tones appeared. The stones were luminescent gnomes. The trees writhed quietly about their trunks. The arch glowed orange against the green wall of Moses Mountain. It was then, in a single instant, Ayşe changed her mind. Without any more of ado, she peeled herself from the coils of the beach monster and went her own way.

The mountains Gods watched. The broken stone men hanging from their beards blinked in rocky silence. The eye of the sky slowly began to darken. Veering right, Ayşe crossed the dry riverbed, its cobbles knocking together under her feet like a trench of chattering teeth. The pink lips of the oleanders swayed in the breeze. A pine-speckled shoulder of rock blocked her path. It took ten minutes to shin the silent, crack-filled bulge. It stood like a watchtower from antiquity. This was the necropolis, Olympos' garden of the dead.

Ayşe found a usable boulder to sit on – a boulder no doubt chiselled by a Lycian artisan two millennia prior. It was a stone which by chance or design lay at the edge of a tomb. She dusted its surface down with her fingers and then folded a sarong and placed it on the top. Then, she took out a bottle of water and washed her hands. Finally, she perched on the grey slab.

Shadows yawned in the ancient arches, and a light breeze picked up, whispering over the stones, making the bushes skittish. Lycia. Every rock has had the hands of ancestors on it. Every track has been trodden by ghosts. There's so much past lying about, people are tripping over it. Myths ooze out of the crevices. Yesteryear pushes through the cracks. The light drained away. The air thickened darkly in the temple remains. Ayşe was impervious to the gloom. She stared out over the valley, over the clandestine neighbourhoods of backpacker shacks. Lights flicked on one

27

by one. They turned the pine thickets and citrus groves into a forty-watt wonderland, a land throbbing gently to a reggae beat.

She closed her eyes and left her thoughts for a moment. The ancient hulk of rock pulsed gently beneath. Warm from a day of sun-lounging, it was now pumping its heat back into her. She wondered what else it had absorbed as the centuries had rolled through it. A lump of limestone. A bunch of molecules. A city of atoms. A universe of quarks and bosons. She wondered what was absorbed now as she laid her hands on the hard, craggy skin feeling something palpable move between them. It doesn't take much to sense life flowing. Just a little awareness. A little quiet. A little care.

The lights fell away. Bob Marley petered out. The backpackers gathering expectantly about the trays of aubergine and spinach below turned translucent and disappeared. Two-and-a-half thousand years deep in those rocks, other lives were being lived. Other paths walked. Other choices made. As night enveloped the valley, the ancient city stirred.

ಬO෫

Olympos 545 BC

'The Persians are coming!' the boy hollered. He stood in the middle of the small square spluttering. His face had turned the colour of a ripe plum.

Stall holders stopped mid-haggle, children stopped mid-whine, and beggar boys stopped mid-fig-theft. Even the donkeys and goats thought twice before defecating on the flagstones. The town's agora had become so quiet you could hear an oregano stalk drop. A crowd of Lycians, fish, figs, and milk perched precariously in their arms, had all turned to stare at the stringy, rat-haired lad. He was puffing and wheezing, his eyes bloodshot from the strain.

'The Persians . . . they've got Xanthos . . . they're coming!'

An older man strode forward. Not many realised, but even two-and-a-half thousand years before, the Olympians still looked like 1970s rock stars. It was one of the many temporal anomalies the valley was subject to. The man's crown was bald, but a long silvery mane edged about the hairless circle like rays around a full moon. His purple robe was finely tailored. The hem almost dragged on the steps as he climbed up to the square to meet the adolescent. Milky columns lined the agora, their chiselled ridges running in dark lines the length of their pure white bodies.

'Are you sure, absolutely sure?'

The boy blinked. 'Harpagos. He's . . . he's in Phoenicus already. I saw him.'

A murmur of horror spread through the crowd. General Harpagos, commander of the Persian forces. His name had been whispered the length of the Lycian coast for weeks now. He was infamous. Unstoppable. Even the largest, state-of-the-art fortresses collapsed like rattletrap goat sheds in the face of his army.

'You *saw* him? You actually saw Harpagos?' The nobleman Licinius stared intently at the boy. He was thirteen years old but his skinny frame made him look younger. The lad nodded solemnly. His small mouth was puckered like a walnut as he peered up. It was the face of a child. He didn't even have the fluff of adolescence yet.

'Good grief! Well, what did he look like, then?'

'Like a rock.'

'A rock? What kind of rock?'

29

'One of those big, flat rocks at the side of the river with the grumpy faces.'

Licinius screwed down the front of his eyebrows. The bridge of his bulbous nose splintered into wrinkles. He let out a quiet sigh. The boy thought everyone looked like a rock. He was obsessed with them.

'Apart from his rockiness, can you tell us anything else? Try to describe his face.'

The boy pushed his irises up under his lids and thought for a moment.

'It was hairy with a big pine cone nose in the middle. And his mouth went down at the ends like this . . .' The boy put a grubby index finger into each mouth corner and pulled downwards until he bore the same expression as a tragedy mask.

The leader of Olympos lowered his head. He was a thoughtful man, not prone to acts of wild impetuosity. But, it didn't get any worse than this. He had to speak. He turned to the on-looking crowd. Very slowly and deliberately, he addressed the dumbfounded citizens of Olympos. 'It is as we feared, Lycia has fallen to Persia!'

The words fell onto the stones of the town in cold, hard spatters. Licinius gathered his robe about him. The lad noticed the chief's hand tremble as he fumbled with the folds. Lycia had never, since he or his mother or his mother's mother had been alive, belonged to anyone but herself. The Olympian nobleman stared out blankly. He wasn't sure if he believed in the end of time, but if there were such a thing, this could well be it.

Resting his hand on the smooth curve of a column, he looked up to the necropolis, to the beds of the ancestors. Then he turned to the crowd one more time. 'Go home. Everyone go home and get ready. Proceed as we have arranged.'

Slowly, reluctantly, the women and men of Olympos trailed out of the town square, a murmuring river of distress.

Licinius walked too. He stumbled over the large, smooth stones to the outskirts of his small precinct. And as he walked he lamented. The Persians, the hordes from the East with their despotic monarchs and their arbitrary barbarism, had finally breeched his beloved Lycia. Keeping the Greeks out of their hair had been work enough, at least the Athenians feigned democracy. But the fire-worshipping Persians? And that land-hungry maniac, Harpagos? It was the end of civilisation as they knew it. Probably the end of the world.

Huffing slightly, the leader increased his stride. His feet slipped in the tan leather straps of his sandals as he clambered clumsily up the hillside. He pushed heavily at the rocky steps in the earth. The necropolis. All about him, white stone shone in the dusk like the surface of the moon. The graves lay quiet. Silent. They showed no trace of the impending disaster, no sign of the chaos building on the horizon. They slept as though the future of Lycia was already assured.

The nobleman turned to look at his home. Everywhere he saw busy rivulets of humanity hurrying into their houses. Grief moved over his heart like a dark cloud. He hesitated for a moment. Only a moment. Then he knelt and prayed. Now, Licinius didn't pray to the almighty king of the gods, Zeus. Nor did he pray to Athena, Apollo or any of the great names in the Olympian Gods-sphere. The Lycians never did anything like their neighbours. The deity he called out to was a little-known slip of a divinity called Leto. The goddess of Lycia.

'Mother, where are you?' he whispered. The tombs said nothing. The mouths of the stone slab caskets remained

31

closed, and Licinius stayed on his knees. He screwed his fists closed and then stretched them open. Once. Twice. Three times.

'What do I do? You who have walked these mountains a thousand times, *help* us.' Still there was silence. Nothing moved, not even the sprigs of sage sprouting from between the rocks. The crickets had become quiet too. Everything was waiting for an answer. Even the dead. Licinius stretched out his hand and touched the flat surface of the tombstone in front of him. It was rough, but surprisingly warm, as if there was a heart and blood inside. The sensation of the stone calmed him. It was solid and refreshingly steadfast. It was then he became aware of two words circulating in his head. They were quiet yet persistent.

'Move on.'

The nobleman lowered his eyes. He nodded. It wasn't what he wanted to hear, but it was the truth. The citizens of Olympos would have to abandon their beautiful city and take to the hills. They were refugees. Licinius' hand was still palm-down on the rock. 'So be it,' he said. He paused. A heaviness filled the necropolis. It felt as though the graves were sinking under the weight of the future, a future even Leto couldn't lift. Licinius took a deep breath and turned his head to the sky. Then he shouted into the darkness, '*But walk with us!*'

His voice reverberated through the valley. *Walk with us, walk with us . . . with us . . . us.* Such was the force of those words, such was the emotion pulsating through them, as the sounds hit the rocks they impregnated them. Their meaning drove farther and deeper than the meaning of any words spoken there before or since.

As night sank its teeth into the valley, the huge, fir covered mountains were swallowed into the pitch. Before anyone so much as blinked, the ancients were gone.

ᘓᗝᘗ

Ayşe started. She opened her eyes. Night had wound silkily through the graveyard. The eye of the sky was black and endless. It no longer turned men to stone and left them clinging onto mountainsides. It was the Goddess Aphrodite who stared into the valley now, and her eye was deep and full of diamonds. Velvety. Seductive. Her gaze made the necropolis open its mouth and sigh. Arches and tombs pushed through the gums of the darkness like wonky giant's teeth.

Now, it might have been coincidence. It might not. I'm not the one to ask about the whys and wherefores of it all. The only thing I can say for sure is, this was the exact moment the Idea of walking the Lycian Way occurred to Ayşe. If you had asked her what had convinced her to go for it, she probably wouldn't have known what to say. But she sensed an urgency as she sat there, as if time was running out.

She straightened her back and uncrossed her legs. Then she cleared her throat. What was the harm in trying? She'd coveted the dream for long enough. She muttered to herself to change. Move on. Do something new. Finally, she grinned. The black eye of the night saw that smile and winked in starlit approval. Walk. Yes Ayşe would walk the Lycian Way. And there was no time like the present.

ᘓᗝᘗ

I think it all boiled down to Carlos Castaneda, the Peruvian-American anthropologist back in the sixties who returned to nature and found himself (or lost himself, depending on how you look at it). Yes, in retrospect I'd probably blame him. I'd been reading about his vision quests, and retreats of self-discovery out in the wild, you see, and that's why I decided to walk the Lycian Way. I don't know quite what I expected it to do for me, but anyway. I practiced yoga and meditation on and off, as well. I was a spiritual seeker, I suppose, though I was lacking any sort of path. It was ironic. I was sallying forth upon the Lycian Way, when the point in question was, I didn't know the way.

It might come as a surprise to a Westerner that I had a penchant for Carlos Castaneda and yoga. Aren't we Turks Muslims after all? Well yes, we are, but we don't use that term in quite the same way a Westerner might use the word 'Christian'. Certainly, it says Muslim on my identity card, as it does with 95% of the country, including many of the atheists, but that label doesn't preclude any of us from the variety of old and new age spirituality traversing our intercontinental roads.

I was mulling on all of this as I walked. And that is one of the most fantastic things about hiking; the amount of thinking time it affords you. Thoughts bloom like exotic flowers when you are surrounded by nothing but hills and trees, and I was surrounded by trees, hundreds of towering pine trees with thick, husky trunks. They were wooden chimneys pumping out clouds of green needles.

The dirt track snaked through the forest until it reached the old camel farm above Adrasan. I think the place had been a tourist attraction once upon a time. There weren't any camels now though, just a grassy plateau with a handful of shacks and a large wooden barn. I stopped

34

and filled up my water. My shoulders were aching already. Perching on a stone wall, I unfolded the map and briefly wondered why there wasn't a health warning on the front cover to caution people against freighting themselves with too much baggage. I mean, I can't have been the only greenhorn to set foot in the Lycian hills. As I have said before, and will probably say many times, maps are frustratingly limited in their capacity to convey the reality of a footpath. I thought perhaps I should design my own, one with kilometres marked in blisters and gradients colour-coded for simplicity like temperatures on a weather map (green = pleasantly flat, amber = adequately tones the thighs and tests knee joints, red = vertical death, and so on). Yes, I know there are these things called contour lines, but they just don't give the same impression of the challenge ahead.

One thing a map can usually inform about, however, is one's next destination. I saw from the dotted line; my first target was a lighthouse known as Gelidonya. It perched upon a wind-torn outcrop and from the photograph looked quite desolate. A bank of steep hills separated me from that side of the coast at present. From where I stood, all I could see was an evergreen forest rising in front of me, and a carpet of dry pine needles.

I slid the map back into my pack. Carefully, eyes scouring for the red and white trail markers, I started to climb in a rocky zigzag, up and along the mountain side.

Considering the amount I was carrying, I reached the crest of the first bluff in quite good time. But as I trotted over the lip of the hill, I was brought to a sudden halt. The slope crashed abruptly down into the sea, perhaps two hundred metres below. And there, bursting out of the blue was a place I had never seen before. It was an island, an abnormally red, steeply rugged island. It looked to be uninhabited.

Stretching my hand backwards, I reached into the side pocket of my rucksack and pulled out the map once again. The isle was easy to locate; yet on the map it was nothing but a green blot with 'Sulu Adası' typed above it. One would never suppose it was the dramatic, fish-shaped protrusion in front of me. Sulu Adası. I thought for a moment. Sulu Adası means 'Water Island' in English.

I was thirsty, and the view from the ridge was impressive, so I took a few moments to enjoy it, drinking as I did so. As I pressed the water bottle to my lips, I noted it was my penultimate bottle, not that I was unduly concerned at that point. I assumed there would be a natural spring somewhere along the path, and so I slid the water bottle back into a side pocket and carried on. An extensive pine forest flanked my right, the Mediterranean extended in a dark, blue pool on the left, and all the while the red peak of Sulu Adası was there. The Water Island. The way it blushed, well, it looked embarrassed, as if it were sitting on some scandalous secret. Unfortunately, at this initial phase of Lycia I was very much an amateur. I had no idea Lycia was something you read like a novel, which was why I neglected the signs.

ಬಂಂಂ

Carlos Castaneda. Magic, vision quests, and the places where spirits and humans meet. Did Ayşe know what she was letting herself in for? It was a wonder she couldn't see the other world already. The world of ghosts that was Lycia.

The belief in ghosts is a cultural universal. Any anthropologist will tell you that. Where ever you are in the world you are never alone, because the supernatural is there

36

with you. Cultural universals are not easy to find. Even God doesn't enjoy universal status. The Buddhists have no deities, the Hindus a pantheon, and the Lycians of old were goddess worshippers. Yet, far and wide across the globe, spirits have been peeping through the gauze of reality since humans could stifle screams and quiver about it – from the Aborigines in Australia to the Mayans in South America, from the druids of Old England to the Native Americans, from the Zulus to the Chinese.

In Ayşe's day, the moderns had long since turned their back on the realm of ghosts. Some nodded sagely as they slouched in the comfort of their armchairs. Others raised a skeptical eyebrow and tutted as they supped a coffee in a favourite metropolitan café. But would they have felt so self-assured wading through the Lycian wilderness as night fell, solitude licking their heels, swathes of pitch engulfing the path? Their confidence in three-dimensional rationality might well have failed them as they picked past the vestiges of an agora on their left, a raided tomb on their right. Yes, their arms would have pricked like the overhead branches of pine needles, as they remembered: if they folded back a couple of loops of time in the spiralling coil of progress, the ancient Persians were stamping along that very route, at that very moment.

Stomp. Stomp. Stomp.

Just two-and-a-half folds of time.

೫೦Oಅ

Lycia 545 BC

'Find a place to dock, now! I'll be damned if I have to spend another night lurching about on water!' General Harpagos blinked his wide mahogany eyes open and closed. They were the owl eyes typical of a Persian, both wise and sad all at once. If he had been a 1970s rock star, I'd be hard-pressed to say which one. The eyes were John Lennon. The rest? Frank Zappa.

Harpagos drew his lips together and scowled at the curling sea below. His right hand gripped the curling horns of his drinking rhyton. The thumb was at the base of the chalice and pressed firmly over its tip to stop the wine from leaking out between gulps.

'We're stoppin' here Commander, alright?' the lookout said. He was an ugly devil with a face cluttered with boils and decomposing teeth. He shuffled along the stern of the ship in greaves.

'It's land, isn't it?' Harpagos rolled his eyes to the sky wondering briefly about the relationship between brains and appearance. Then he nodded to the helmsman. It was fairly hard to nod with the weight of an iron military helmet pressing on to his head. But he did it anyway. The crew jangled and scraped into their positions, and the great blue eye at the bow of the galley turned slowly towards the bay.

The Persians had sailed in from the Lycian port of Phoenicus, less than half a day back along the coast. Lycia was on the cusp of becoming Harpagos' own personal empire. Only a couple more obstacles stood in front of him, and one of them was Olympos. She was hardly a big name among the Lycian townships, but she was strategic.

The seashore was drawing into view. The boats were wooden snails crawling over a lake of steel. They left glistening tracks on the surface, tracks that would disappear before they reached their destination. Harpagos, commander in chief of the Persian forces, looked out to the Lycian coast before him. It was consumed by a dense wood of juniper and pine. The forest led directly to Olympos. The valley of the Gods. The place where so many stories began and ended.

Peering through the whorls of his silver-black hair, he surveyed the shadowed thickets, the sheer, rocky slopes, the looming razor peaks. He felt the darkness weigh on him. What was he doing here in this wild, wolf-infested terrain of goddess worshippers? What the hell was he doing?

What Harpagos was doing was following orders. That was Harpagos' trail. His fate. Absorbing the demands of the Persian emperor, upholding The Empire, and scrapping his way up a hierarchy.

Lycia, however, had another way.

Alone. Independent.

She moved like the wind and the sea and the rocks.

Time folds back on itself.

One. Two. And a half.

ଓ○ଓ

Like an awful lot of people, I had never really understood the history of the Lycian Way. Who had been here? When? And why? No. I was pretty ignorant about it. It was all something of a mystery, a rather irrelevant mystery. Well, what has any of it got to do with us now? I mean, history never seems to concern anything but gangs of men fighting over this place or that, does it? As if we don't have enough of that going on as it is! I was more interested in finding the present moment and staying in it, because that's what everyone seemed to think was the answer to everything at the time. From my yoga teacher to Cosmopolitan, everyone was telling me it was Now or never. So to be honest, at that point, I hardly considered who might have walked the Lycian Way before me. My quest was to disentangle myself from the past, not sink deeper into it.

I turned to the path. It slid to and from the edge of the mountainside, the forest and the sea grabbing at it intermittently. By now, my walking had changed from an enthusiastic trot to a subdued amble. The sun was beating steadily, the overhead branches incapable of scattering the heat. Then my water ran out.

I remember how I savoured that last tiny pearl of aqua. It quenched my thirst for a moment, but only a moment. The empty water bottle gave a hollow crackle as I thrust it back into my pack, and I wondered where water would be. I started to hike faster. If I could just get to Gelidonya lighthouse, there would be a tap, I was sure. Gelidonya, however, seemed ill-disposed to appear.

The day forged on, and with each step the heat intensified. It was sheer idiocy to walk in it. Back in Olympos, folk would be flopping about in sweaty heaps by now, most of them struggling to find the willpower to even light a cigarette. Their efforts would be concentrated on small thirst-quenching missions like buying ice-lollies or opening cans of soft drinks. And here I was trekking under the afternoon sun with a pack most budget airlines would have charged me extra to carry. The Water Island was still on my heels as well, and it refused to fall back. It was like a red stray dog desperate for an owner. I seemed to be making no progress whatsoever, but there wasn't really anything I could do about it, so I just told myself to get there, not to think about anything else. Well, that had always worked until now, hadn't it? You know, one uses one's mind to create a plan, and perseveres until one achieves it.

Planning is all very well, but I can tell you, where thirst is involved, one doesn't have a hope. Breath, thirst, hunger are the first three rungs of human striving, and they are solid rungs, probably made of cedar or something, which is why they don't bend under the paltry weight of positive thinking schemes. But it wasn't just water I was thirsty for. I'd been thirsty for years; thirsty for a little danger. Yes, I wanted to test myself, didn't I? Why? Because how could I know who I was if I didn't know where I ended? And how could I know how deep my resources went, unless I fell from the cliff of the known? And so, as my throat dried out, and taps, springs or other water dispensers failed to sprout from the dust, I did indeed plummet from the ledge of the tried-and-tested. Well, it was more of an unhappy droop, really.

I wasn't the only one on a downward turn though. The sun was sinking fast. I started to become a little frantic. There remained an hour or so until darkness, and I had no idea how far away the elusive Gelidonya was. I was wandering in a desert of pine prickles, quickly dehydrating, crippled under a cumbrous and entirely waterless hump. As I trudged, slowly making ground on the Water Island, I started to feel so horribly parched I almost considered popping open one of those shampoo bottles. Soon thirst consumed everything. I was unaware of the path, the forest or the stones; all I could perceive was a dusty, dry basin where water ought to have been. I prayed aloud. I willed water to appear. I visualised springs gushing forth from secret, rocky enclaves. I think I utilised pretty much every positive thinking technique I could remember. Nothing. It was unbelievable. And this was only day one. But the worst part of it wasn't the lack of water, it was that I was incapable of generating water. I took it as a failure.

The light faded, and the air became muggy. I now caught the occasional glimpse of the five-island cluster ahead, but there was still no Gelidonya lighthouse. Each descent seemed to trick me into false hope leading not *down the bank of the hill, as I invariably anticipated, but into a cleft only to lead up again.*

I'm not particularly histrionic, and that's probably a good thing, because otherwise I'd have been crawling on hands and knees by then, or perhaps even considering nasty survival tricks involving my own evacuations (honestly, if it came to that, I should hope I would still have the dignity to simply sit on a rock and pass away). But I was very fed up, and starting to feel frightened too. I thought a number of times, I should never have begun this ridiculous pursuit. I had been foolish, ill-informed and incompetent. The thought of all those people who had shaken their heads condescendingly at my single-handed adventure, the great throng of common-sense, possibly being right . . . Well, it wasn't pleasant at all.

In the end, I called a halt. None of this looked like a good idea anymore, so I decided to call for help. Sliding my arms out of the straps, I let my pack go. It thudded on to the ground, a concrete obelisk in a wilderness. Feeling the various distended bulges of my rucksack, I found the phone and wrenched it from one of the pockets. But when I stared at the small screen at the top, the fateful truth dawned. There was no reception here, not even a bar flicking tentatively on and off. Oh dear. That was when it occurred to me, death wasn't entirely outside the realms of possibility. It was a sickening thought, one I had never truly considered at the outset; not one person had passed me on this path, not one sign of life, not even so much as a miserly goat. I hadn't drunk a drop for hours.

The horizon was flat and lifeless, the sea and the sky fading in the progression towards evening. As I stood staring along the iron sheet of the sea, I took a deep breath. I needed to take myself into hand, because one way or another I had to get out of this mess. I stooped and pulled

*on my rucksack. Then I stuck out my chin and stumbled off
again. Well, what else could I do?*

∞O𝕮

The tall pines were a creaky wooden army. The trees stared
bleakly down at the woman on her lonesome and thirst-
ridden journey. She stood bowed under her load looking off
into the bushes. Something had caught her eye. The shadow
of a moving branch perhaps, or a fox or a stoat.

The first stage of human dehydration is
characterised by fatigue and confusion. If water isn't drunk
the second stage begins. Grim side-effects like sunken eyes,
seizures, and delirium follow. Ayşe was dehydrating. Her
body was sending distress signals through her, warning
lights in a dark storm. So it was hardly any wonder she was
seeing things. And no wonder she soon forgot about them,
either.

It was probably just as well, because she was
treading in someone else's footsteps. The forest all about her
remembered it only too well. Two-and-a-half thousand
years earlier a Persian had been stamping along this very
pathway. He had moved in the opposite direction, from
West to East, from Gelidonya back towards Olympos. And
the imprints he left were spots of dark intensity,
commander-sized depressions in the earth.

∞O𝕮

'Cut the wooden hag down!'

Harpagos was astride a white Nisean horse, and the
poor beast's knees must have ached under its burden of
metal and man. Harpagos, just like many in his army, was

struggling under pounds and pounds of chainmail. He had never got used it. In winter it froze him turning his chest into a shivering iron cage. In summer it baked him. At that moment, he was so excruciatingly hot he began to think his organs had stewed inside him.

'Chop the damn thing down, I said!'

Ahead of Harpagos ten infantrymen danced around a sprawling mess of brambles. They waved their axes and scythes like iron flags. Every time the bush was dealt a blow, her dozens of arms convulsed. To Harpagos it looked as though the tree was laughing. Laughing at him.

'This place hates us, do you know that?' Harpagos whispered the words to no one in particular. But the word 'hate' lingered in the air. The black holes between the pines absorbed that word and held on to it. The general screwed his eyes up. Over the years the sun had beaten his face into a sweaty brown pulp. It had sketched deep contours on his skin, as though mapping his destiny.

The outside world was oblivious to the discomfort of the commander of the Persian forces. Who wouldn't have wanted to be Harpagos? Wasn't fame and fortune the dream of every man in the world? And credit where credit is due, Harpagos looked the part. He postured in a gold-trimmed purple tunic. He was laden with beads and bracelets and rings. But what really made the world at large admire him was the thousands of people just itching to do his bidding. He only had to nod or wink or raise his hand and a henchman would come running, or a beautiful girl would smile and move closer.

'Out of the way boys! She's acoming down,' an infantryman called out.

There was a colossal rustling and shaking. The tree was felled. A flock of men huddled around the prickly, green octopus and set about dragging it out of the way.

Soon enough the Persian army continued onward. The convoy slid through the forest like a deadly, fat viper. It didn't bother to hide itself. It flaunted its colours, red, saffron, and indigo, as a warning.

As Harpagos trotted on, he caught glimpses of the sea. Here and now it was as clear and smooth as a child's skin. But he knew. Just around the corner behind him, past the five-islands, a plan bobbed and ducked. His plan. Because one cove back, a dark swarm of fifty or more galleys was gathered on the film of the Mediterranean, every one of them flying the Persian flag.

Harpagos had learned from his spies, Olympos would be a devil to penetrate. The scrawny, rock-lined channel leading from the sea to her walls could prove tricky if the Olympians resisted. And he had seen enough resistance from the Lycians already. God yes! This was why he had decided to take half his army over the hills to enter through the back door of the Olympos valley, while the other half cruised round the peninsula by ship. It was a neat strategy. The general was an old hand.

The Lycian conquest had hardly been challenging in the traditional sense. He'd lost no more than a handful of men. Yet Harpagos gulped at the thought of it. It was a dry saliva-less swallow. He blinked hard too. If he stretched his eyelids back with enough force would the pictures shift into the background? Or would they remain? Ghosts from another time and another place, ruining his day, scuffing the fine surface of his victory. At the other end of Lycia, two weeks back down the trail, stood a place called Xanthos. To the Lycians it was their capital city. To Harpagos is had been a turning point, a place in time and space where right and wrong switched sides. It was the exact spot he had finally and conclusively lost his way.

He bent down and muttered in his horse's ear. 'Will the future be any less wretched? Will people still be at the mercy of despots hundreds of years from now? Pah! Idiots, the lot of them.'

He gripped the reins of the steed a little tighter. As he studied the sharp slope to the sea, he found himself wondering how it would look centuries from now.

The crusty, old pine trunks ratcheted past him like the spokes of a massive wooden wheel. The shadows within them beckoned. Harpagos began to feel sick. He realised he was succumbing to heat stroke, so he raised the index finger on his right hand.

'Water sir?' An indigo-swathed attendant stretched on tiptoe and held a silver jug up to him. Harpagos' eyelids hung heavy. His head was spinning in circles, the trees whirling about him in a cyclone of bark and needles. The noise of the cicadas was cranking up with the heat turning the forest into a pulsating cacophony.

He wanted to take off his helmet, but he didn't dare. Who knew what was sneaking about the shadows? His temples throbbed. His head was a drum the forest was thumping on, each vibration a painful explosion shaking dark webs out of dark corners. He closed his eyes and then opened them again. It was at that moment, something caught his eye. There was agitation in the trees. Something was moving through the bushes a little way off.

The general became very still, so still he almost disappeared. Dread moved artfully out from its pit. It hit him like a well-placed blow in the gut. And then he saw it. The flash of fair hair. And a lumbering gait. Something akin to a hunchback.

He jumped, pinched himself, and peered closer. But whatever it was, had already vanished.

ଽଠଓ

I'm not quite sure where I went for those moments between Adrasan and Gelidonya. Everything became a little muddled as I fought my way over the rocks and through the bushes. I wandered like a mad woman. The trees, the topography of the earth, and the eerie shadows they cast confused me. Was I walking? Drowning? Floating? Was the sun up or down? Was I dead or alive? Was I alone?

I'm not entirely certain how I kept up the momentum. It was as though someone else were rambling for me while I flailed pathetically about behind. How long it all went on is another unknown. It seemed like hours, but in all honesty, given the sun's position, it can't have been particularly long. The pine trunks started to look like timber bars in an endless wooden jail. There were trees everywhere, row upon row. And where the trees stopped, the cliffs to the sea began. I had foregone thinking things couldn't get any worse, because they inevitably did. Soon enough, I collapsed on a spiky lump of rock and gave up. I was doomed. Night was stalking me. I had no place to pitch a tent, no energy to pitch it with, and no water. How insignificant I felt as I squatted there. Was that it? The sum worth of my life, death by stupidity? I wouldn't be the first or the last to have their life extinguished by lack of foresight, but it seemed so insulting, so horribly ignoble. I mean, I could at least have made it past the first day!

The sun had long turned fat and red. It sank managing a good gloat before it went under. And then I surprised myself. Yes, really. Because this was the point I expected to throw in the towel and cry myself to oblivion. But another part of me must have had other plans. Small zesty sprigs of anger began to flourish inside me. I shouted and kicked a rock in frustration. Nothing was going my way, so to hell with it! To hell with maps and trails and all

47

of that! I mean what use were they anyway, if they lead you on a merry, waterless dance to nowhere but dehydration? I stopped caring about what I ought to be doing, and started to mutiny. I'm not entirely sure what I was mutinying against, but it seemed to be any sort of rule – natural, logical, or otherwise. It made no sense to go on, I was only losing energy, but I refused to heed reason. Die there? Languish on a rock all night waiting for some animal to take me? Like hell! If I was going to expire, it may as well be up on my feet mid-stumble. I may as well keel over making an effort and give the know-it-alls of the world something to talk about. With that, I pulled up my God-awful rucksack once again, wheezed under the weight of it, and set off in the direction of the sun, somehow managing a haughty 'I'll-show-you!' strut, as well. Which just goes to show, it's amazing what you can do when you're cross.

Now, there are some ideologies (perhaps issue from yoga, or Buddhism, or certain interpretations of these Eastern philosophies) that posit emotions such as joy and peace to be good, while frowning upon things like anger and fear. 'Ah, you are holding anger in your pelvis, perhaps you can work on that,' *says the yoga teacher with disguised condescension, as if anger were a disease one should take care to prevent, like the emotional equivalent of syphilis. Hmph. Alright, granted, I was exasperated with the Lycian Way and nature and all of it, for what felt absolutely like a betrayal, which was, of course, ridiculous. But, I can say without any hesitation, it was anger and pride which fuelled those final bursts of energy and kept me going. My fury might well have saved my life.*

Anyway, I continued, though my feet could hardly find the pathway and fell into every hole in the ground. Despite my head-held-high stomping, I was actually inordinately slow; each step was a mission in itself. Long, crooked pine tree stalks dangled over the path as if they were drunk. Sometimes I had to duck under them, the pack inevitably catching on the bark and snaring me like a parachutist caught in a power line, other times I'd clamber over or around the trunks, and my knees were now screaming in resentment.

Finally, the trail veered a corner. I couldn't believe my poor dust-filled eyes, because there in front of me was Gelidonya lighthouse. Just like that. She stood on the cliff top, white and welcoming, as though she had been waiting all afternoon for me to pop in for tea. There was something I didn't realise, though. Gelidonya held no hope at all, because for reasons I simply cannot even begin to entertain, the lighthouse housed no water. Happily, I wasn't acquainted with that knowledge as I pushed towards the white tower.

Then, a man appeared upon the scene, quite unexpectedly. He strode through the battered wire fence enclosing the lighthouse; a muscular fellow with a billowing scarlet cape tied over his shoulders. I recall thinking at the time that he bore an absurd resemblance to Superman. What's more he was carrying an inordinately large and fortuitously full bottle of mineral water.

As with so many of the mysterious folk that appeared in the coming two weeks, I never learned the man's name, and I never saw him again, either. It was as if once I set foot on the Lycian trail, nature concealed a secret supply of angels that would only appear when one was utterly desperate. These helpers were singular in their altruism. They never seemed to want anything. They offered only what one needed, not a gram more, not a gram less. That perfect balance became a measuring stick, a way to know everything was in order.

Superman, as he shall hence be known, immediately grasped my situation. He held his water out to me. I lunged for the plastic and sank upon the hot rocky ground, not even caring what I sat on. Never have I been so grateful for refreshment.

I had envisaged camping on the Gelidonya peninsula, but the lack of water now rendered that plan defunct. What would have happened had Superman not appeared? I shuddered.

'Have you any idea where I could camp tonight? I need somewhere with water.' I held the bottle in both hands like a crystal ball.

'Korsan Koyu, There's a spring there, I know. I've just been,' he said, exhibiting a perfect row of Kent Clarke teeth.

Korsan Koyu; The Pirate's Cove. Nice name. Just the place a lost adventurer might sojourn, eh?

'I'll walk back down and show you, if you like.'

Fine by me. After I'd guzzled a good part of his water, we set off. Unfortunately, as I stumbled the length of that last rocky slope, I felt my knees buckle. It was too much. I had endured twenty kilometres of climbing and descending in that merciless heat, with a pack on my back which by now felt the size and weight of a house. I was at my physical nadir.

Superman gave my pack a long stare. 'I've got a car at the bottom. I'll give you a lift.' He didn't exactly pull his shirt open and display a silky unitard with a giant red S on the front, but he may as well have done. I was, by then, quite prepared to bring the back of my hand to my forehead and swoon, if need be.

'A car? But there isn't even a road here!'

50

'Looks like it's your lucky day then, doesn't it?' The Kent Clarke teeth were back on show.

Five minutes later, I had squashed myself into his Tofaş. Well, no other car would have survived that track without losing a wheel or the front axle, that's for sure.

I was soon at the Pirate's Cove. It was a jewel of a beach, immaculate in its seclusion. There wasn't a soul about. At least that's what I thought at the time, anyway.

Day Two

Waymarking

Evening had come and gone. Aphrodite blinked above. As diva of sex and procreation, the hot, steamy nights were hers. Anyone who stared into her come-hither eye saw a thick soup of stars, asteroids and planets swirling inside. Whether that soup was stirred by an almighty hand, or whether it rotated of its own accord, was anyone's guess. Yet turn the heavens did, their glittery, black broth pouring into the bay.

The dome tent was a womb piercing the surface of the sand. Ayşe was a foetus curled into the scarlet quilting of the sleeping bag. Night rested heavily on the tent membrane. It coaxed out all manner of skeletons in all manner of closets.

Beneath the groundsheet of that tent suffered the sand, sand hiding a million secrets, sand that had seen empires come and go. As Ayşe twisted in her sleep, the grains rocked beneath her. Each grain of sand was an entity in its own right. Each granule attempted to remain whole. Sometimes the sands were shaped by the elements outside, other times it was they who did the shaping. That morning it was a human pressing down on them, shifting them, shaping them, changing them. A human. A body of bone and flesh. A concourse of emotions. A world of thoughts and memories. The sand drew on Ayşe's body heat, slowly absorbing her presence. Was that all it absorbed? For as darkness stole away the shroud of normality, and Ayşe's eyelids fluttered, other things began to seep out into the obscurity.

Other worlds. Other times. Other realities.

಄ಂಂ

Istanbul 1990

Nereden nereye? From God knows where to God knows where. It was a modern Turkish expression denoting surprise at the gaping ravine between where we start out and where we end up. Not so long back it had all looked very different. Single-handed treks into the wilds of Lycia were not even thinking about being thought. It was Istanbul, 1990, and Ayşe, who was just twenty, had just learned she was pregnant.

She stared about the bathroom. The white tiles were a porcelain mesh covering the walls. She spied the mould flowering like metastatic cells all over the grouting. Her heart lay quiet and heavy in her chest. Damn! It wasn't supposed to be this way. She was supposed to feel at least happy, wasn't she?

'Hey! Where's breakfast? I'm late! Allah Allah! Even the fucking *çay's* not on. Agh forget it! I'll get it on my way,' Murat was in the living room. Noises jostled intimidatingly outside the bathroom door. The swish-swish of slipper-clad feet hustled along with thuds, thumps, furious rustlings and janglings. Then silence. Ayşe wasn't keen on those silences. They were noiseless holes of unknown reaction, voids of catastrophic potential. *Bang!* Rattle, rattle. He was out the door.

Ayşe had known she and her husband were a poor match from day one. He was attractive and brash, and an insurance salesman to boot. Enough said you might think. But it had been 1989. Turkey had barely opened up to tourism or satellite TV, and an unmarried woman of eighteen was always regarded with suspicion. Her colleagues in the German security systems company – in between touching up their lipstick and the interminable thud, thud, scribble, stamp and sign of Turkish bureaucracy – convinced her she was on the brink of spinsterdom. Find some bloke and marry him, or an eternity of passionless nights watching old *Yeşilçam* repeats with your mother sagged long and heavy before you. The hunt was on for every working girl in the firm. It was now or never! Dog eat dog, or may be bitch eat bitch.

When you looked at it, Murat's credentials were impeccable. He owned a car. (A car? Oh Ayşe, what a catch! Reel him in my dear. *Reel him in!*) He managed his own business (envying nods while the girls puffed on their Marlboros and supped their tea). Mum liked him too. (He had a job and money, what more did she want?) So it was, Ayşe appeased society's piety police and wed Murat. That had been all of a month ago. Now the two of them, already tottering ungainly on the tightrope of coupledom, were about to have a new-born to contend with.

Ayşe walked into the living room, and grabbed at the half-empty packet of Parliament on the table. She pulled at the ashtray too. It was rammed full of butts, and bristled like a white hedgehog. She tapped the soft-box on her hand until one of the sticks slid out. Pushing it between her lips, young Ayşe sat on the sofa bed in front of the jabbering TV.

The supermodel news presenter, flawless in her caked-on beauty, crooned about how the economy was booming. It always was, even during a recession. Meanwhile, a parade of photographs flicked along in the background. President Turgut Özal, captain of the Motherland Party, was waving to a crowd, shaking a European leader's hand, addressing a mob of grey, moustached parliamentarians.

The part-Kurdish leader of the Turks grinned, his large teeth visible under his thick brown whiskers. And he had a lot to grin about. Turkey was changing. Gates were opening. Colourful foreign goods, sun-tanned foreign bodies and stable foreign cash were now forming a steady trickle across the Bosphorus as Turkey's answer to Margaret Thatcher waved his liberal economic wand.

The transformation of the Republic had begun. It turned from a place with adequately filled pockets and nothing to buy, into a land of shelves heaving with goods but nothing to buy them with. The Motherland had taken her first shaky steps on a brand new path.

⅋

A few months later Ayşe, now heavily pregnant, huffed and puffed her way up the hill to the local mosque. The spindly pale turrets of the minarets pierced the Istanbul sky. It was the colour of mercury. The air was stodgy and dull. There was no Medusa or Aphrodite in Istanbul. It was as if the Goddesses were snoring behind an eiderdown of cloud.

As she reached the gates she paused to catch her breath. She wasn't here to pray. She wasn't here to speak to God either, though she had plenty to say. Like a million other Istanbul dwellers she was here to collect water. For reasons best known to the powers ruling the land, that year Turkey's largest city was perpetually in drought. There was water in the sky. There was water all over the country. The trouble was, it didn't flow through the pipes or run out of the taps.

On good days (or rather nights) water would tentatively dribble out between two and three in the morning turning the city into a land of nocturnal hoarders. In the dead of night, in every flat all over the metropolis, you could hear the slow drumming of liquid filling plastic tankards. On bad days, the only aqua rich sources in Istanbul were the mosques.

Ayşe stood at the rectangular tiled sink, blue and green flowers twisting over the ceramic squares. She turned the tap. Water churned sluggishly into her plastic pail. For a moment she stared down at the protuberance of her belly. There had been a time back then, back at the beginning, when she'd considered an abortion. Funny how things had worked out. She had confided in her sister. Her sister had said even though the marriage was miserable, the baby had come from Allah. Back in those days Ayşe had listened to her family. Back then she'd heeded the words of others, and trodden along their well-travelled paths. Turning to face the gaping space between the open mosque doors, she wondered. Was it from Allah? Or was it from her? Or was it from somewhere else?

Perhaps it really didn't matter. Despite everything, she had always wanted a child. And now despite everything, she had one.

ಬ೦ೞ

Back in the Pirate's Cove, the first slivers of light slipped guerrilla-like over the horizon. They slunk across the sand, steadily decimating the night as they went. The cool morning air rushed in from the sea taking the beach by surprise.

Dawn deftly struck the roof of Ayşe's tent, and she began to stir. Memories slipped back into the darkness, the past receding underground. The present moment was here. It crawled through the cloudy warrens of Ayşe's mind, hauling itself through manholes and up into the light. She woke slowly, and remembered. The Lycian Way. Her trail. It was waiting the other side of her mosquito net.

ഔ◯ങ

I felt quite the survivor as I crawled from my tent. Alright, I can't say I was particularly keen on the small heaps of sand in the corners of the groundsheet, nor the strings of ants I noticed congregating around my bag of dried apricots. I spent a good ten minutes brushing the dirt out of the tent. But if this was the worst thing I'd face, then I could live with it. I felt a wave of satisfaction when I pulled out my neatly packed collection of zip-lock bags and found a toothbrush, comb, wet tissues, soap, deodorant and various other delights of modern hygiene. Ha! I'd done it. I'd managed to overnight in the middle of nowhere, all by myself, without disintegrating into a blabbering wreck and calling a taxi home. But then, there are far more frightening things than being alone, I can tell you that without any hesitation. That is one thing my past has taught me. The past. In many ways it isn't past at all, is it?

Anyway, I tugged back the tent flap and crawled out into the bay. Now, it's not often one manages to appreciate dawn in the countryside, and that, I have realised, is a sorry loss for humankind, because unusual things happen when one rises early. The Pirate's Cove was bathed in shadow at that hour, and the sun still crouched behind the mountains I'd struggled over the previous day. I trod through the champagne sand relishing the feeling of the cool grains between my toes. Then I stretched in front of the water. I noticed how light I felt, despite my lack of sleep and the soreness caused by my pack. I suppose all those who camp in the wilds feel the same way, don't they? It's as though the ground sucks out one's troubles leaving a vacuum for daybreak to fill with good feeling.

It was idyllic there; not a human in sight, the sea lapping at the skirting of the cove. I swam, and then washed off the salt with water from the spring. I felt clean, capable and smug (ha, who says you need to wallow in grot and grime to hike, eh? You don't need to be a stinking brute. You can be pretty and tidy and even braid your hair). I could have stayed all day, really, but I was impatient. There was a future yonder and destinations to reach, which was why, without further ado, I packed up my belongings. Within half an hour I was back on the trail.

It was a dusty little track. Hundreds of pines stretched upwards about it like ancient columns, their cracked old trunks creating a maze of avenues. I walked with birds (don't ask me which ones, I'm as badly informed about ornithology as I am archaeology) trilling in ludicrous exuberance. Small reptiles scuttled out of sight as I passed. And then I spotted something. Someone was approaching. I could see a gleaming bald patch bobbing up and down. The figure was a little way ahead, and as he drew closer I realised it was a jogger, middle-aged and male.

On spotting me, the man's eyes popped. He pulled aside to catch his breath. Hunching over, back heaving, his hands rested on his knees.

'What are you doing here?' he spluttered.

'Erm, hiking?'

'No, I meant how on Earth did you find this place? We're in the middle of nowhere.' He was puffing so hard, I began to wonder if we were on the edge of a medical situation.

I pointed to a fading red and white pair of stripes painted upon a rock almost ten metres from where we were standing. His eyes narrowed somewhat as he focussed on the line of my finger.

'Allah Allah! I run this trail every day, but never once noticed there were marks!' He was still gulping the air down. Good Lord, if the man ran like that every day, he was on a one-way jog to a heart attack, I'd say. I wondered briefly where he had appeared from, and then I remembered: ahead was the rather unexciting resort of Karaöz. The jogger saluted. Then he lunged off into the darkness of the pine thicket still wheezing like the foot pump of a camping mattress I didn't have.

I shrugged and ambled on. Waymarking. Hmm. Back in the days when I was first trying my hand at the walking business, I had also passed Lycian Way trail markers, yet it was a year or more before I noticed them. But if I we couldn't so much as spot a splash of red and white paint, what else were we failing to see? What exactly was out there?

I turned a corner. The trees parted and the Mediterranean yawned before me. I squinted and stared off into the distance, to the faraway place between sky and earth where the thousands of waves puckering the water's skin converged. In fact, what was out there was a place beyond time, only I hadn't quite worked that out at this nascent stage of my trekker development. I've come to the conclusion the roads of the Lycian Way are temporal corridors. It's a pilgrimage really, but not in the traditional sense, because no one knows anything about where they're going to. One presumes one is walking in the now, but one soon finds oneself carried off elsewhere to other times. It's mystifying.

The trail followed the cliffs at the sea's edge. I could almost see Finike town through the haze, and I wondered if I'd make it there before the day was out. The Mediterranean slid between here and there, a twinkling bridge between worlds.

The past. It was so close I could almost hear it. And then I saw it surface approximately fifty metres from the shore. It was so beautiful, I almost yelled.

'Turtle!'

The call came from an anonymous oarsman lodged on the outrigger of the massive wooden galley. It was a hi-tech trireme vessel with three lines of grimacing rowers on either side shunting the ship along. A couple of Persian officers shuffled over to the gunwale, armour clanking as they went. Harpagos peered half-heartedly out as well. He was draped over the gunwale like a discarded suit of armour, his face as robbed of colour as a limestone slab left too long in the sun.

For a moment she was visible. The leathery head of a Caretta Caretta turtle bobbed in her salty, aquatic home. She inspected the leviathan in front of her, her pre-historic eyes reeling in apprehension. She breathed in the Mediterranean air, just as her ancestors had done forty million years earlier, just as her children would do long after the Persians left the coast of Lycia. The web of patterns etched on to her mahogany skin entranced the Persian soldiers. These were men who had spent little time on the sea, having waged most of their invasions on horseback or camel, over steppe lands, and through forests. Even these war-hardened warriors were silenced for a moment. Just a moment. Then the Caretta Caretta dove under, parading the spellbinding geometry carved on her shell as she sank.

'Sir, are you alright?'

The general pulled his head up. His assistant was cantering along the hull towards him. From the expression on the man's face, Harpagos surmised he looked just as bad as he felt. The galley was pitching from side to side, and his guts were sliding with it. Too late. He leaned over the side and endured another deep wretch.

He hung there, lurching up and down. Phoenicus was behind him, Olympos in front. And he was in the middle, neither here nor there. Two huge square sails flapped behind him, and somewhere behind those sails the sun was journeying home.

Harpagos drew every scrap of power he could find and raised his head. 'Tell the berk in charge of this contraption to find land NOW, or I swear I'll send him back to Xanthos!'

The assistant shuddered. He gulped, and teetered quickly back to the helmsman.

Harpagos found himself looking at the wooden planks of the deck. They'd been washed orange by the sinking sun. Then he closed his eyes. He would have preferred not to remember, yet ever since he had arrived in this Godforsaken Lycia, no matter what he did, the past barged its way into him. Or had he always contained it? He was coming to the conclusion his memories were engraved somewhere inside him, some place in his head or his bones, or under his skin. Was that why he couldn't shake them off? Who'd ever heard of shaking off bones or fingerprints? They were with you for life whether you liked it or not.

He gritted his teeth and lifted his eyes again. As he surveyed the craggy face of Lycia drifting by, his mind floated alongside. It was getting to the warlord. It was as though this place had found the loose thread in the tight-knit weave of his self-invention. Lycia's jagged fingers plucked and pulled at that thread, unravelling all kinds of forgotten deceptions. For even though Harpagos was commander of the Persian army, even though he was one of the most powerful men in the Persian Empire, Cyrus' right-hand man more or less, Harpagos wasn't Persian at all.

They say it's the first killing that changes a man, and once you've crossed that line it's easy. Harpagos would have agreed. He remembered that killing well. But it wasn't a murder executed by his own hand. It had been even more heinous than that. It was inscribed on his soul, and would be until he went to his grave. Because Harpagos hadn't always been this wrangled old warlord. No, not at all.

The great galley ploughed through the water. Three rows of oarsmen huffed and puffed as the wooden poles hit the blue and shattered it. Their arms shone with sweat like boulders in a stream. Their hair was plastered to their brows. Harpagos was oblivious to their effort, though, because he was deep in a struggle of his own. Not only the struggle to keep his dinner down, but the struggle to forget the day. The day they had murdered his only son.

ഃO�cരദ

The years rolled through the sea and along the Lycian Coast, one thousand, two thousand, and more. The oarsmen faded. The galleys disappeared. The Persians were no more than a memory. But there was one thing that had survived. She was old and wrinkled and coated in barnacles. The Mediterranean loggerhead turtle, otherwise known as Caretta Caretta. She was there, surfacing and diving, just as she always had been.

A woman stood up on the cliff. She watched as the she-turtle's head poked though the Mediterranean's blue film. Then she turned, stooped slightly and carried on along the trail.

ഃO�cരദ

I couldn't believe it! I'd seen a Caretta Caretta, and it was like bumping into a stegosaurus ambling through the

63

forest, or treading on a woolly mammoth's tusk. Even from my distance the creature had looked, well, other-worldly! But exciting as this was, something else was chewing at my attention with ever increasing intensity. The heat. I was horrified at how fast the sun was racing up the sky, so I moved quickly on. The track girdled the mountains. It wound along the sea like a dusty elastic band. I followed it marching with the kind of naïve enthusiasm only someone at the beginning of a day, at the beginning of an adventure, is able to muster. Before long, I reached the huddle of white boxes that is Karaöz.

Now, I can't say I'm partial to Karaöz. The 'village', for want of a better word, is all but a ghost town. Row after row of small concrete villas stretch along the bay, all in various states of lacklustre abandonment. It's a resort for the retired; the purpose-built dream future of our government workers, and I suppose it was that image of the 9 to 5 memur and his or her neat and tidy, pre-packaged box of second-hand dreams that triggered the memory. Because years ago, when I had been working as a PA in Istanbul, I too had cemented plans for my future. Oh yes, and look how well that turned out.

Now, planning is not something which has, by and large, come naturally to the Turkish mind, and if you ask me, if something doesn't come naturally, it's best not to bother with it. Nevertheless, in the Istanbul office of my twenties, for a time the words 'goal', 'target' and 'agenda' became rather fashionable. My boss was one of these personal development fanatics, and one day, he arranged a training for the staff, the title of which was, 'Finding Your Life Purpose'. It was this I remembered, as I walked through the empty grid of passageways of Karaöz, Ha ha! Well, honestly, can you imagine trying to sit twenty Turks, people who have survived military coups, earthquakes, and annual economic collapses, and asking them to plan, not a year ahead, but ten!

The life coach was German, and he wore shorts, which in itself was reasonably shocking for the office. He flaunted tanned, orange legs – actually, they were the colour of persimmons, rather oily persimmons. He kicked off by asking us what the words 'Life Purpose' meant to us. I remember how we had shifted in our seats about the conference table. Well, what sort of purpose does one require for life? One gets up and enjoys breakfast, goes to work and comes home again. Was this what he meant? What else could there be? Apparently there could be an awful lot more, clear life goals for one thing. And then came the plans we had to write; I remember how anxious I'd felt. Well, I hadn't realised a life aim was of such importance, had I? Now suddenly, here was this European explaining I had been misapplying my time, and that without some sort of a project my life would be a complete waste and nothing would ever happen!

In those days, we wanted to be like Europeans (mainly because we didn't want any more coups or yearly economic collapses, and it seemed like Europeans had a knack of avoiding them), thus we dutifully racked our brains and tried to come up with our aims. Half the table was at a complete loss, and a few got their neighbours to fill in the plans on their behalf. By the end of the day, Persimmon Legs' hair had turned from neatly gelled to a mane of wild, overextended curls. What sort of goals had I jotted down? What sort of dreams had I harboured? Marriage? The perfect family? A nice job, nice clothes, nice husband?

As I trotted through the concrete alleyways of the seaside resort, paint peeling from the walls of the half-empty plastered crates, I saw pink flowers dropping from *the overgrown trails of bougainvillea. They clustered on the floor in browning heaps. Within minutes the sporadic gusts of wind dispersed them. And then I began to feel queasy. The past, the dark days of Istanbul, always left me with a nasty taste in my mouth. I turned to the sea hoping the horizon might offer some solace, but the waves were spinning like wheels, churning the sand and stones in dirty, brown circles.*

৪০Oও

Did the sea know how Ayşe felt? Was it separate from the human observing it? Or was it in some way connected? There were those who were convinced water was more than it appeared, its molecular structure changing in the atmosphere of human thought. Not everyone believed that story. Many thought it was baloney. Yet in the end, however the world was interpreted, they were all stories, stories based on patterns and feelings and various lines of reasoning.

The sea churned on. The sunlight marked the backs of the waves. It illuminated irregular undulations of twinkling dots. Ayşe's shadow cut a human shape into the foam as the waves broke by her feet. Whether the water sensed Ayşe's trepidation, or whether it simply reflected back anything that fell upon it, is not for me to say. But reflect it did. And the reflection Ayşe saw wasn't that of a grown woman with a backpack and hiking boots. It was the watery, ripple-broken picture of a young mother.

৪০Oও

It was August 1990. It was Istanbul. Ayşe gave birth to a baby boy.

Smack. Slap. Wallop. Domestic disharmony amplified. The war began in earnest now as the noose of marriage tightened. But did the world feel Ayşe's trouble? Could it reflect it, if it did? Was the outside connected in some way to the inside in ways no one understood? Because it just so happened, that very same month, unrest had begun kicking up the dust elsewhere. The world wasn't watching Ayşe. Its eyes were on the other side of the Turkish border. A man called Saddam Hussein was on a mission, and Iraqi troops had filed into Kuwait. It wouldn't be long before the US responded. The Iraqi 'Mother of all Wars' had begun.

At home, abroad, inside, outside, discontent and rage ricocheted around, leaving their casualties flailing in their wake. And war disorients humans. It throws them into worlds of chaos where the bearings of right and wrong are in a state of constant flux. Sometimes it's hard to see just where the enemy is. Within? Without? You? Me? Evenings spent so squashed into corners your back develops a right angle. Choices whittled down to the bare bones of 'survive' or 'don't survive'. You're looking just one inch in front of your big toe. Everywhere the fear is so fat it's pouring out of the windows and onto the balcony while the bruises spread over your skin. It's a wonder the neighbours can't see it.

Ayşe was damned if she stayed. Damned if she didn't. Damned. Completely up the creek. Or so it appeared.

It was then something unexpected happened. And the unexpected was an Idea. It started as a renegade seed buried under ground. 'Divorce'. The thought pushed through the tarmac of Ayşe's mind and began soaking up the sunlight of her attention. How it took root is a mystery. There were millions of women like Ayşe in Istanbul stuck in unhappy or abusive marriages. Why didn't the Idea germinate in their minds? Or if it did, why didn't it grow? And the Idea did grow. Every day, it became more than it had been the day before. It moved quietly, slowly, from inside to outside, from the realm of thought out into the world of action.

When Ayşe's baby son reached five months of age, she went back to work. She began secretly saving money. And even this tiny act of insurrection was revolutionary. Women didn't get divorced in Turkey at that time. It was a type of social suicide. It could have been a physical one too. All over the country women were shot, or knifed, or attacked for wanting to leave a marriage. Ayşe didn't have the support of an enlightened family. Her husband was never going to understand. Whatever his façade of modernity, deep down he believed she was his property. The only things she had going for her were a salary and a deep vein of quiet obstinacy.

Apparently that was enough. Ayşe Metin focussed hard on a spot some distance ahead. Then she stealthily trod the line of survival. Waiting. Waiting for the day.

৪৩

Months later, the family moved into a lofty apartment in the Istanbul neighbourhood of Bakırköy. Here, the sea breeze would rattle the windows and sneak in the wall cracks, stirring the air. The days clicked on, one by one. Her baby boy Umut was growing; nails, bones and skin gradually hardening. A friend of a friend acted as baby-carer. She came and went. Umut started crèche, was out of nappies. Did he know his mother's freedom hinged on his independence, incremental as it was? Clickety click, clickety

68

click. Time inched by. Never stopping. Never pausing. Until one day the future arrived.

ଔ

The flat was cool despite the temperate summer air outside. The lounge seemed vast and empty, shadows deepening along the skirting and the poorly whitewashed corners. Ayşe was chewing on a cigarette by the window. She was waiting for Murat. The light slunk steadily out of the room. Night burgeoned on the horizon in smoky, dark plumes. Eventually, the metallic rattling of a key in the door brought Ayşe to her senses. She knew exactly what was coming next.

Murat shoved his way through the door, dark hair flopping over his brow. Sliding off his shoes, he padded his way into the lounge and took up residence on the sofa.

Ayşe opened and closed her mouth like a mackerel on the end of a submerged hook. It felt as though someone had stuck a hand down her throat and snatched away her breath.

'What's going on? Isn't there any food tonight?' Murat grabbed the remote control and lounged back into the cushions. Slotting a *Tekel 2000* between his lips, he aimed the remote at the television.

And then she said it. Somehow the words tumbled out into the open. 'Murat, I want a divorce.'

Fifteen minutes later Ayşe was hunched over nursing a split lip. Baby Umut was screaming next door. The bawling sawed through anything it touched like the jagged blade of a hacksaw.

'You want a divorce? You want a fucking *divorce*? Sure! Get the *fuck* out! But I keep my boy! I'm telling you now I'll *never* let you have him! Bitch!'

69

The words roared around the room. They shook the mortar in the walls. Murat was loping about like a bullet-struck bear. Drawing himself up for another round, he pounded in Ayşe's direction. She curled over in anticipation realising just how much she hated this man. She hated him with her whole heart, mind and body. One day she would sock it to him. One day.

That night she dreamed. She dreamed she turned into an enormous bloodthirsty beast. It was a monstrous being with fangs and claws and power. That beast leapt on the sleeping body of her husband. Then it murdered him, ripping him up bit by bloody bit. Through the pitch of Slumberland, through the realm of dreams, Ayşe touched something sacred, something as ancient as life itself. It was the raw, unapologetic force of self-preservation. The force of life, and death. And everything in between.

ဩ O 03

I pulled away from the sea. The air was salty and damp, the seaside disturbingly dark, as though I'd tainted it. I turned to face those sorry little concrete houses in Karaöz. They had been erected with the precision of post-orthodontist smiles, the smiles one might drop on to a curriculum vitae, the vacant smiles of the lost. Funny to think they were lost because they adhered to the pre-ordained path, rather than transgress it.

I walked and left Karaöz to fade behind me. Gradually, the gnashing sound of the waves grinding against the pebbles quietened. Cicadas strummed the air instead. And then I put a bit of a spurt on, because I was determined to see something new and inspiring before the day was out. Hmph. It wasn't long before I reached the neck of a road. There is no ancient trail from Mavikent to

Finike, as the sea was a more accessible transportation route for the merchants of old, so the Lycian Way stretches flat and monotonous in the form of a trunk road. Most trekkers avoid hiking on the asphalt by taking the bus and re-joining the trail further along the coast. I reached the same conclusion.

I stopped and waited on the banks of the tarmac hoping to spot a vehicle. The road basked oilily in the morning sunshine, an obsidian snake of the civilised world. I wondered how I would ever happen on a bus in such a place. The sun burned. The asphalt perspired. I waited. I wondered.

Suddenly, there was a terrible screech. A white and rather battered Fiat came to a skidding halt beside me projecting a spray of gravel into the cooking air. I peered inside the car.

'Where you off to yenge?'

The driver was a local lad. He grinned, revealing two rows of large, tannin-stained teeth. Assessing the risk, I concluded his most threatening characteristic would no doubt transpire to be his driving (not that bad driving is a hazard to be taken lightly. I live in a country where a significant proportion of those unfortunate to board an ambulance are crushed on the road before they even reach the emergency room). But although the passenger seat of any Turkish car is not for the faint of heart, from where I was standing, in the middle of nowhere, it looked preferable to walking on sticky tarmac for the next few hours.

'I'm trying to get to the main road,' I said.

The lad nodded at me to climb in. I disentangled myself from my accursed back pack, pushing it like a dead body onto the rear seat. Then, I slid into the passenger side.

71

The *Tofaş* Fiat rumbled and shook over the slipshod attempts at asphalt. Ayşe gazed at the concrete disfigurement of Mavikent. Mavikent translates as Blue Town. Yet there wasn't much blue about the place other than the sense of despondency it evoked. Two-story apartment blocks lined the unswerving road. This was small-town Turkey's lunge after modernity; tacky petrol stations, run-down car-mechanic workshops and some of the most poorly constructed apartment blocks this side of Baghdad. The mess gradually shrunk from the rear window. Meanwhile, Ayşe's driver took up the conversation with the zeal of a government agent.

'My name's Ahmet. Pleased to meet you. And you are? Ayşe. Oh right. So where are you from then? Istanbul? And what are you doing around here? On holiday? Olympos? Ah right, of course you are. Are you married? Well, where's your husband then?'

She parried the relentless volley of interrogation, while Ahmet tested the shocks on his aging Fiat by taking the road humps in fourth gear. Despite the *Tofaş'* decrepit appearance (the poor old girl was more advanced in years than its driver), it hurtled onwards. Stray chickens were avoided, large dustbins circumnavigated, and somehow the multitude of insubordinate motorists that reversed, U-turned or parked arbitrarily in the middle of the pot-holed street lived to see another day.

୫Oଓ

While Ayşe was driven westwards, in another time, in another world, someone else was moving in the opposite direction. Two dots on a line. Two particles on a wave. Each one assuming the other had nothing to do with it. That they were walking alone on a one-way trail to death. But whether they knew it or not, the further forward Ayşe trekked, the further back into Harpagos' conquest of Lycia she reached. And every step meant something.

The road opened up long, straight and grey, while the dented white *Tofaş* spluttered on. Ayşe rocked forwards and backwards, her backpack still lolling unconscious on the backseat. Now, the blue fabric of the Mediterranean spread before her. The gulf of Finike, or Phoenicus as it had once been known. The sea at the centre of the ancient world. Thin ripples snaked along the surface. An oily light danced on their folds. As the haze of mid-summer devoured the horizon, shadows moved hauntingly through the depths. Water. Two parts hydrogen, one part oxygen. Atoms. Particles. Bonded in time. Bringing life to other lives.

A hot, misty curtain hung over the blue, while speckles of light on the waves scurried for cover. Down, down in the depths, where the light of day rarely encroached, caskets of ancient past lay strewn about the rolling silence of the seabed. Amphorae, anchors, tombs and trinkets. They were all there, all humming with suppressed stories that itched to be told. The past had its own meter, and its own time. It pulsed beneath the surface like a discarded transmitter, ancient dots and dashes echoing through the water. As those oscillations moved outwards and upwards, they would break the surface, spilling their confidences as they did so.

ഇO౮

"Sir, we ain't got enough oil. Four of the amphorae got smashed by a fella who tripped on the gangplank."

"So, we'll grill the fish then. Get a *move* on yer little tyke! Get that fire going! The rate you're working the embers won't be ready till Tyre!"

Harpagos listened to the cook and one of the cabin boys as they made a meal out of making a meal. He loitered at the stern of the ship watching Phoenicus shrink into the hills. The galley was below him.

"And you! Get a knife and *gut* 'em! I want two hundred fish with their innards *out* by the time the sun's arse hits the sea!"

Harpagos was standing completely still. He was encased from head to foot in armour. Neither the sea air nor the rocking of the boat made any impression on it. He was an iron monument. Yet, underneath the metal, the flesh and blood man flinched.

"Gut 'em. Innards out." Those words shouldn't have even grazed him. Harpagos had spent most of his life at war. But here in Lycia, for one reason or another, those words were deeply troubling. Perhaps it was because, just as they had been preparing the fleet in Phoenicus, he had seen that boy . . .

It had only been an hour earlier. Harpagos had been in his war wagon at the time, overseeing the loading of the boats before they departed for Olympos. The Persian war wagons were a cross between chariots and mobile wooden fortresses, and they stood about four men's height from the ground. It gave the general an unequalled vantage point. He had been scanning the habour-side market from his perch. It was then he'd seen a scraggy local lad. He'd noticed the urchin because of the way he was carefully counting the galleys in the Persian fleet. *Why would a street urchin care about ship numbers?* Harpagos had wondered.

74

The boy must have sensed someone was scrutinising him. He'd flipped his rat-tailed head up and peered at the war wagon. When he saw Harpagos dressed to the hilt, and bearing down on him, his eyes had widened like apples. The lad had promptly backed away. Harpagos had seen him run, his bare feet kicking up small puffs of dirt as he went. It had been a long time since he'd seen a kid run that fast, not since his own boy had . . .

Harpagos turned from the view of Phoenicus and began to move heavily from the stern to the bow. The great painted eyes of the galley pointed eastwards, towards Olympos. But it was beyond there they were ultimately headed, to Phoenicia and Babylon – the places the Persians were really interested in.

Harpagos now stood at the bow staring towards his destination. It was then it occurred to him. He was staring east, to the place from where this entire journey had begun. It was as though he was going right back to the beginning. To his youth, and the great old kingdom of Media. To the day. *That* day.

And then it happened. Harpagos grabbed onto the gunwale to steady himself. But it was too late. He had buried that day so deep, he was sure it would never be found. How the hell had it wormed its way out? That day. It was a speck on the horizon which was growing alarmingly fast. It was coming back. And he had to get out of here before it did.

As he lurched over the side of the trireme, he found himself face to face with the sea. Only there was no water. No blue. Only wave upon wave of hot, white sand, and it rolled on and on without end.

ℬ

Harpagos was deep in the desert of Ancient Media. It was twenty years earlier, back in the days when Persia hadn't been that much to rave about. Media had been Persia's powerful, big brother, and Harpagos was working for its crackpot king, Astyages, as commander in chief of the Median army. As I said, Media was the place to be back then. It was the ancient world nexus of art and culture. What? You haven't heard of Media? Well, what do you expect me to do about it? Is it my fault your school history books are packed with partiality and selective information? I'm telling you what I know. And I was there. Back in those days, there was only one spot more happening than Media, and that was Babylon with its Hanging Gardens. Media seemed to have it made. There was just one cloud in her wide, unrumpled sky, and that was King Astyages who was as mad as a box of frogs.

Anyway, in those days, Media's heyday, young Harpagos was Astyages' right-hand man. He had it all; the position, the house and servants, access to the royal gardens, even concubines here and there. He was trusted and influential. And that night he was curled up next to his wife snoring with the contentment of a man who has everything. That night. That day. And then all the nights and days which followed.

The citadel was snuggled in a divan of sand, dunes rising and falling about the walls like wind-blown linen. The tall, ribbed stalks of the palm trees arced along the perimeter of the city walls. They were spiked night-watchmen. But even they couldn't spot the danger, because it lurked somewhere deep within. Harpagos was unaware. He breathed into his wife's neck as though it exuded pure oxygen. His arm flopped over her belly. His nose was lost in her hair. But over in the palace, trouble was brewing. King Astyages of Media wasn't having the best of nights.

The king's chamber was a large rectangle of decorated drapes and rugs. The walls were alive with torches. Instead of bedposts, figurines of gold looked over the bed; a snake, a fish, an eagle and a boar, with spinels and emeralds for eyes. But none of it soothed King Astyage's soul. A nightmare had slipped through the many cracks that fragmented his delicate mind.

The royal eyelids were flickering like dying candles. Astyages twitched and jerked. Through the murk of sleep, he was watching his grandson overthrowing him, and the sight gripped him with terror. He woke up. A cold sweat glazed his brow. He threw back his clammy, cotton sheets, and swung his legs out. Then he pulled himself up and bellowed, 'bring me the magi, *forthwith!*' He pushed the curly, grey hedge of his hair out of his face and began to pant like a hound. The manservant ran out of the room.

Ah the magi. Part-priest, part-wizard, part psycho-therapist. It was the dubious honour of this coven of mystery-gurus to steer the monarchy through the hazards of the unknown, and unknowable. With their star maps and alchemy, their swirling capes and their high hats, they foresaw, forecast and foretold. And woe betide them if they misread the constellations.

The three men, ripped from their own slumbers, ran through the corridors of the palace, the flames of their torches throwing a hissing, snaky light over the stone floor and the walls. Entering the royal chamber, they hastily bowed before the bed. Astyages fumbled with the sheets and babbled. They nodded gravely. It was a most portentous dream.

Now, just as everywhere, Media was spiritually confused. Perhaps so were the Magi. There was a pagan past of stars and spirits over which was laid a newer religious system: Zoroastrianism, the first monotheistic religion in the world. The Zoroastrian God was called Ahura Mazda; it was a god of light and truth, but not a God of retribution. In Zoroastrianism, it wasn't a deity that avenged the wronged, it was life, and any victory or ruin a Zoroastrian experienced was the result of their previous actions. It was with this in mind that the magi studied the nightmare of Astyages. Because the king had been generating a lot to atone for over the years.

The magi meditated. They studied the position of the sun and the North Star. They lit a fire for Ahura Mazda and whispered into the flames until they heard the embers speak. Finally, an interpretation wove a path out of the smoke.

That afternoon, the three wise men gathered about the throne in the royal hall. Astyages was clutching the throne-arms as though they might slide away from him. The magi bowed. They wrung their hands. They tugged at their beards. 'The dream will come true,' they said, solemnly shaking their heads.

Mad King Astyages gaped at them, his eyes whirling like sandstorms. He groped for his goblet of wine.

'What's your council?

'Do away with the boy!' They chorused.

Tiny bubbles of saliva collected in the corners of the king's mouth. He began to sway on his throne. 'Get the general. *Now!*' He screamed at the darkening walls, and anyone within earshot within them. The magi slowly but surely backed out of the hall.

Enter our General Harpagos. Unwitting. Smiling. Still young. Time hadn't yet had chance to turn his face into a map. It looked like any other day for the commander of the Median forces. King Astyages was squatting high on his

78

throne. His eyes flitted left and right about the hall as Harpagos approached. The monarch fiddled with the rings on his fingers. He mumbled a little. He smirked. Then he issued Harpagos with the directive:

'Kill the baby!'

Harpagos eyes lowered briefly, yet he made no comment. He nodded his assent before bowing and retreating from the hall. But that night in his quarters, he didn't snore like the man who had it all. He didn't breathe the life coming out of his wife's neck, nor lose his nose in her hair. He didn't sleep a wink. He might have been a warlord. He had slaughtered many a man on the battlefield. But slaying a new-born? He would be crossing a line, snapping the flimsy thread that held decent folk separate from fiends. As he stared up at the ceiling, he paced along every lane of strategy he could find. Each path was a cul-de-sac. There was no way out. But that didn't make any difference, because, as far as Harpagos was concerned, there was always a plan. There had to be. And he would think all night until he engineered one.

The next day, he woke at the crack of dawn. And dawn did crack in Media. There was scant grey between night and day in the desert. But before the sun blazed its morning trail over the sand, Harpagos had slid out of his quarters and lost himself in the shadows. As he left his home with the glorious rugs and the bowing servants, the buckets of jewellery and the open courtyards, he turned once. For the first time, he understood how nothing was really his. He was a slave. A rich, pampered slave. Everything and everyone belonged to Astyages, and Astyages was barking mad.

When he arrived at the grandchild's house, he found the boy's mother still asleep. She was holding onto the babe as though he was the future king of the world. And that was fitting, because he was. The infant was none other than Cyrus the Great, future founder of the Persian Empire. Harpagos was about to save his life. Though he would pay dearly for it, very dearly indeed. He didn't know that yet, though. He was sure he had covered all his bases. Without waking the woman, he stole the baby and hid it with some peasant folk. It was just like the story of Moses. Or was it Snow White?

Ten years passed. Ten pleats in the concertina of chronology. Everyone became older. Everyone became wiser. Media was still powerful, and Persia still hunched in its shadow. Then, one way or another, King Astyages discovered the terrible truth; his grandson Cyrus was still alive.

On *that day*, advisors congregated about the throne. No one knew where to look. The walls of the grand hall had disappeared into the late afternoon shadows so it looked as though it went on without end. Only the great golden urns were visible, their necks and shoulders caught by wayward rays of sun. Astyages opened his mouth and wailed. He jumped from his throne and hammered on the floor with his fists. After that he stood up and took to hurling pots. He gnashed his teeth and screamed, beating anything and anyone he could find.

The king was quick to devise a punishment for the general who'd betrayed him. Within hours Harpagos' only son was murdered. The ill-omened boy had his throat slit, was sliced up into hunks and barbequed. Or was he cut into pieces before he took his last breath? Harpagos would always wonder about that, because these things happened back then. The ancient world seemed like one prolonged atrocity. But in whichever order, and however cruelly the murder happened, the boy's meat was finally grilled. Then, it was served up at a banquet at which the guest of honour was none other than Harpagos himself.

It was the night Harpagos would never forget. The nobles half-drunk on Median wine lolled about the royal dining hall, the table heaving with luxuries – golden platters and finely crafted finger bowls, glass goblets Europeans wouldn't see for centuries, stuffed fowl, roasted oxen, fatted calves, freshly baked unleavened breads, cheeses, yoghurt, dates, figs, nuts – apricots were yet to come, when the Persians took over the world. The grand hall was lit with hundreds of oil lamps and torches, the air sweetened with incenses and perfumes burning in ornate golden censers. It was with just such a backdrop that Astyages gleefully revealed to Harpagos the true contents of the dish of the day.

All about the table guests' eyes widened. One or two reached for their napkins. Three or four blanched. But gradually, a hall full of dark heads and midnight eyes turned to stare at Harpagos. And they were surprised by what they saw.

There was no wrath. No cry of grief from the Mede. Not one shiver of emotion passed over his face. Harpagos sat silently on his anguish. And he would sit on it for years to come. His eyes glazed slightly. Then he stood, collected the left-overs of his son for burial, and thanked the king for the dinner.

Astyages should have seen his demise lurking ominously behind the passive-aggressive smile. But he didn't. Once the banquet was over, he consulted his magi once more. Perhaps in a bid to rid themselves of their wicked ruler, perhaps because the wheels of Zoroastrian justice were now turning, or perhaps because they really were spectacularly hopeless at their job, the magi assured the king his grandson Cyrus was no longer a threat. Astyages took their word for it.

⁝O⁞

The haze still hovered over the Gulf of Finike. It clouded the line between the sky and the sea. Ahmet's voice whirred in the background while the yammer of the Tofaş' engine competed for sound-space. The sea lolled impassively within its deep blue crypt, holding its treasure, safekeeping it.

'*Abla*, this is far as I go,' said the young driver as he stamped on the brake and ran down two gears with one quick flick of the wrist. The *Tofaş* grumbled and rattled as it dragged itself to a stop just before Finike harbour. Ayşe snapped out of the past.

'Good luck with your walk and all that. Don't know how you dare, I wouldn't. Who knows what's out there eh? Who knows? I mean aren't you, like, well . . . shit scared? You must be some kind of athlete, right? Training and all that? How far do you reckon you'll get? *Vallahi,* I wouldn't do it if you paid me a million. No frigging way *abla*. My auntie told me there's stuff out there, like . . . well mountain monsters and stuff, big cats, big dogs, ghosts. *Allah Allah ya* . . . you're out of your mind. Got to be. But good luck there anyway eh? Good luck!'

Ayşe grinned at the young driver. The car had halted in front of a steeply banked river. Here apartments were more polished than those Ayşe had seen shunting past the window in Mavikent or Kumluca. Their walls were white-washed to perfection. A strip of gleaming blue was clearly visible across the road. The Mediterranean. High brown peaks cut sharp isosceles triangles out of the sky. They closed off the distant plateaus like a circle of pointed hats.

It was time to get out. Time to walk.

༄ O ༃

By some benevolent quirk of destiny, Ahmet had brought me all the way to Finike. I clambered from the vehicle. Struggling somewhat, I extracted my belongings from the backseat before pushing the door frame, slightly buckled as it was, closed. He tooted and launched himself into the road with a symphony of spinning wheels. Honestly, these young men of ours, it's a wonder they ever live past thirty.

The dust settled, and I cupped my hands over my forehead to assess my surroundings. A tarmac road stretched from the sea and ploughed straight up into the mountains. All of the buildings were clustered at the seaside end of that road, one of the last of which was a small bus station. I headed towards it. I had no idea, at the time, but I was on the verge of encountering the Lycian hiker's most notorious demon. I was on the brink of losing my way.

But before all of that, I ought to say a word or two about Finike. Yes, because unfortunately the town doesn't have an awful lot to say for itself. It could have become a tourist magnet such as Marmaris, or perhaps a yachter's haven in the vein of Göçek. Instead it skulks upon the fringes of all too many things. Not quite conservative, yet not quite modern, not quite town and not quite rural. Finike has suffered at the hands of a thousand well-intentioned buffoons, all attempting to transform her into something and not quite managing. Well, what is Finike? I expect she herself hardly knows.

No matter. It was from Finike that I set about the Lycian Way in earnest. There was, however, already something of an annoyance. The trail was nowhere to be

83

found. I struck out from the bus station in the direction of the hills behind searching this way and that for red and white stripes. The sun was now climbing and gathering strength as it soared. I hoped whatever else might happen, there would at least prove to be some sort of potable ahead.

Eventually, I spied a dirt track ascending steeply the length of the mountainside. It seemed to stretch towards a cluster of tall spiky landmarks: television and radio receivers. Not really knowing what else to do, I pursued them. The track squirmed in blistering discomfort beneath the heat, and without so much as a fig tree or jutting ledge to hide momentarily under, I was soon rasping. But I kept plodding on, step by step. In the end I made it to the top.

I was now in front of the giant metallic transmission rods I had spotted from below. They were contraptions from science-fiction in this otherwise primitive landscape. I took a few minutes to absorb the view. The hilltop was a muddle of scrawny rocks that receded into slopes of sun-bleached scree. Now I think about that moment, I wonder again at that first mission. Why was I there, at all? What on Earth was I doing? I was propelled by some sort of drive I didn't understand. It was as though there were a chest of treasure, or a long-lost enigma or something, buried ahead. It's always like that with hiking, and I've never worked out why.

Pulling my arms out of the straps, I let my rucksack thud to the ground. Then, I took up my search for the red and white paint of the waymarkers. On closer inspection, I discovered a disused well behind the antennae. It might have been a cistern from antiquity, but honestly, my knowledge about these things is so limited it could have been a wine cellar for all I knew. Nobbled, whitened stones had wrested themselves loose in places as though they had grappled for their freedom and won, and the circular cobbled wall was left pock-marked and immersed in goat droppings.

Eventually, I was forced to conclude I had no idea where the trail was. This way and that, left and right, down and up. Not a splash of paint was to be found. How could I guess where to go? I circled the peak. There was no water and I was already thirsty, horribly thirsty actually. Oh no. Was I going to have to climb back down all the way to Finike and start again? Agh!

Nowadays, I rarely find myself in such predicaments, because one has GPS and the like, but I was such a novice back then. I'm not certain I even knew what GPS was. I began to feel cross again, and I daresay a little panicked. Day one, I had all but parched to death. Day two, and I was astray, expending limited time and energy reserves in what appeared to be a futile effort to stay on the path.

I started to grope for a plan. This was absurd, because I didn't have a plan, did I? So I squatted on a rock for a moment sensing an utter lack of strategy. This wasn't the first time in my life I had acted impetuously and subsequently lost my way. No it definitely wasn't. But, that other time there had been fewer options at my disposal, so my rash escape seems altogether more reasonable. Though not without its price. Everything always has a price.

ಬಿ◯ಚ

The sun was a white disc, and its incandescence was too intense to watch. Yet if anyone could have stared at it, they would have noticed; passing in front of the disc was a black dot. The speck moved quickly. It changed size as it drew concentric rings over the sky. It sank. It rose. And every now

85

and again it fell just low enough to make its speckled wings visible. The two glorious fans splayed as the bird dove through the air. Common Kestrel. He was master of the Lycian skyways.

Now, I said Kestrel looked like a dot from Ayşe's position on the mountaintop. But that's not how Ayşe looked to Kestrel. He could clearly see her perched on her rock in all her humanness, in fact he could easily make out the small lizard behind her as well. Kestrel's eyesight was at least twice as powerful as Ayşe's, so for him the world was a different place altogether. He would have understood nothing about why she was lost. The creamy vein of the Lycian Way wormed along the coast for any bird of prey to see, along with a web of alternative routes. Goatherd's trails. Village pathways. There were footpaths everywhere. Ayşe could have gone anywhere she wanted to.

But Kestrel wasn't interested in hiking trails. He was excited by trails of another kind. Perspective is everything. And perspective is filtered by the lenses of need and want. Lycia – her hills, rocks, forests and grassy banks – was no more than an insipid background on which Kestrel searched for light. Ultraviolet light. Because voles left tracks of urine that shone ultraviolet in the sun. Kestrel could see those silvery threads from thirty of forty metres up. And when he did, he knew he was close to lunch.

Kestrel looped around the slope scanning Ayşe's point of disorientation. Who knows what he made of the woman on the rock? Did he even know she was female or human? But whatever the objective truth (if indeed such a thing exists), it looked as though Kestrel took note of Ayşe, as she stared over the cracked lip of the hill. If he concluded anything at all, he would have probably inferred she was scouring the ground for food. That's what he'd have been doing in her shoes.

As it happened, Ayşe didn't even see the ground, although she was looking straight at it. Perspective is everything, and her perspective had shifted. She had slipped onto another timeline altogether. The mountain peak and the Kestrel became faded two-dimensional images of their present selves. Lycia disappeared. In its place another world materialised in the viewfinder. An urban world of unhappy marriages and difficult choices.

Ayşe was looking at her past, and she was seeing the early nineteen-nineties.

೫Оരു

There had been no sun in Istanbul that day. A drab sky hung overhead like the bed sheets of a budget hotel. Ayşe was alone in the apartment standing in front of a steam belching teapot. Murat had left for work. She poured herself another glass of tea, rubbed her eyes and picked up the phone on the spotless kitchen counter. This was her last shred of hope. Mum and Dad.

Ten minutes later the receiver was back on the hook. Ayşe was wiping her eyes. It didn't help, the tears kept coming. They ran like rain along a street-side gutter. Ayşe's parents, a full generation behind her, hadn't seen her point of view at all. Marriages weren't there to make you happy. They were there to save face.

'Belt up and be done with it,' her mother had told her.

It was a tunnel without lights or ends. All she had was this life, the wrong life, with the wrong man. But that's never all we have in truth, is it? Because every day that passes we turn into something new. Sometimes it's we who change our environment. Sometimes it's the outside that changes us. Yet either way, we are no longer the same.

Trouble had transformed Ayşe into something which, ironically, could transform the very same trouble. It was already too late, because an Idea had attached itself and was growing. Life force was making a move. There was no way out. No way to win. And the pressure from all sides forged a diamond moment of potential.

Days passed. Weeks passed. Despair upped the ante in daily accretions. Then one day, a day which from the outside looked to be just like any other of the gruelling rotations on Earth's axis that serve to fill a year, survival dragged itself out of the primal swamp of Ayşe's life. It saw the thin film of the surface beckoning and made a lunge for the open air. Ayşe ran.

No one saw it coming. A moment, that's all it took, and Ayşe was sprinting from Istanbul, from the tedious prattle of the bourgeoisie, from the fighting, the crying, the darkness. On that day she left a world behind her. Her son, her marriage, her parents, her home and her job; all of them fell away as she ran for her life. It was an impossible move. Leaps of such desperation often entail catastrophic somersaults from non-stick shallow-fry directly into the flames of the gas hob.

Hours later Ayşe could be found huddled into a poorly upholstered seat, bobbing up and down. The aging Mercedes coach carved its way ruthlessly through the Anatolian countryside. As it lurched to and fro in the darkness, it belched smoky clouds of exhaust into the air. The pollution wound far back behind the bus almost masking the road.

Gradually, the bald moonlit steppe lands grew grassy pelts. As she jolted closer south these pulled back and the heavies of the Taurus Mountains drew themselves up. They bristled in dark furs of pine and cedar. Other worlds. Other roads. They were out there.

With every kilometre of tarmac that churned under the tyres, the shackles of Ayşe's life slackened. She'd left them all. Ha! Now here she was on her own personal survival mission. It was a chorus that played again and again in her life; the lyrics of leaving sung to the tune of being alone. As the bus shunted down the gears heaving itself over the final ridge of peaks, the sun rose pink over the Mediterranean city of Antalya. Sleek, white apartments lounged nonchalantly in the wide plain. They winked in the auburn glow. And beyond them the sea was a silver mirror extending to the end of the world.

An hour later, twenty-four-year-old Ayşe stretched her aching legs. She shook her hair out and hobbled off the bus. She leaned on an upright supporting a small square of welcome shade and pulled out a cigarette. It was barely eight in the morning, but the heat of the day had already staked its claim on the city. Now what? Now where?

The touts in the bus station, a greasy, hairy crew with spare tyre a plenty and body odour to boot, screamed themselves hoarse.

'Alanya Alanya *Alanyaaaa!*'

'Side, anyone for Side! Side is ready to go. *Si deeee!*'

'Kemer. Ke *merr*. Going to Kemer *yenge?*'

Ayşe exhaled a layer of thick, grey stratus and watched it dissolve into nothing. Kemer. She vaguely remembered the place. It was a pretty little village clustering around the ubiquitous blue Mediterranean bay. Flicking the butt onto the floor, she squashed it with the heel of her pump. Then she picked up her bags and followed the frantic hollering of the bus-firm ticket-seller. She caught up with him noticing the flaky detritus of dandruff skirting around the edge of his bald patch. A dark splodge of sweat spread over his pale, blue shirt as it strained across his bulging torso. Averting her eyes, she pulled herself onto the half-empty bus.

ও○গ

Perspective is everything, and Ayşe's perspective began to move. Her eye – not the organs of sight placed at the front of her face, I mean the other eye, the invisible eye of her inner world – twitched. It rolled from Antalya and its buses and touts. It rolled at such speed it was a wonder no one felt giddy. That great oculus turned until it fell in sync with its two physical counterparts. It widened. The present moment flooded gratefully in.

Ayşe looked up. The mountain peak reappeared. Rocks and scrub sprang to life. The blue camber of the sky was curved over the summit. It was an archway leading to another world. She was still crouched on a boulder. Lost. In the middle of nowhere in the heart of the Lycian hills.

It was strange but Ayşe thought nothing of her journey through time. Humans in those days never did. They zipped back and forth over decades as lightly as if they were changing their television channels.

Istanbul, Antalya, Lycia. They were as near as the bat of an eyelid.

ও○গ

So there I was, perched upon the wrong mountain peak, lost with a vague sense of misgiving gnawing at me. But, as usual, I didn't really know what to do about any of it.

I tilted my head upwards and stared into the sweeping emptiness above. Sky, there was nothing but sky, open and spacious and blue. I noticed a species of bird of prey above me. A buzzard? A hawk? I watched as the raptor plunged towards the ground, a dark arrow searching out its target. It made me think. Well, obviously the bird didn't possess a map or GPS coordinates. I doubt it spent much time contemplating its route either. After a little reflection, I concluded, to move at such speed and with such decisiveness the bird must have had another approach. Perhaps it held a desired location in its mind, and the rest, how it arrived there, was some sort of instinctive, or even intuitive, orientation.

This was all well and good, but how does a hapless modern human access this long-forgotten instinct? From where exactly does one pull these gut feelings out? I had really no idea. Yet I needed to know. I needed to know which way something in the region of twenty minutes ago.

And then, without any warning whatsoever, I heard a sound.

'Helloooo!'

I almost jumped out of my skin! It was a woman's voice, though God only knows where she had come from. I soon saw her. She was swaying towards me in rural regalia; şalvar pants, a flowery cotton shirt, and a headscarf tucked loosely about her hair. The little old lady even bore a long stave upon her shoulder with a handkerchief tied to its tip. I breathed deeply. It appeared I was saved.

Unlike the jogger of the morning, my gnarled lady-friend knew about the red and white painted stripes and the Lycian Way, and this in itself was quite a stroke of serendipity, as the chances of meeting human life in these parts were otherwise negligible. I stood up and put on my pack, my knees straining under the weight.

'Teze, do you know where I can get some water?' I adopted a pleading expression and hoped she'd point me to a spring only locals knew about.

She grinned, and I saw she had a gap in her teeth. It looked like a keyhole. 'Follow me!' she said, and carried on in the direction she had already been heading. Aha. I was in luck!

We walked into the forest. The pine trees were tall, woody parasols, and I wallowed in their regularity and their quiet upright cool. We continued a while until we reached a shaded thicket. There were bushes and bracken everywhere, and in one corner was a mountain hut in such disrepair it stretched the word dilapidated to the outer reaches of a definition about to collapse on its struts; some of the slats were missing, the roof was sinking in various places, and the windows looked like they'd been pieced together from any pane of glass available. Which poor devil lives there? I wondered. I hoped for her sake, it wasn't the woman.

But as we approached the hovel, a peasant couple hobbled out. The gate, which hung desperately from one hinge, whined like a cat in labour when they opened it. The four of us congregated in front it. I looked at the couple a bit more closely. Both the man and woman had skin as crusty and corrugated as pine tree bark. There were lines all over them and going in every direction you could think of, as if they'd been laughing with every inch of their faces, for years on end.

'Get the girl some water, poor thing's dying of thirst,' said my little lady friend, the keyhole appearing in her mouth again.

The tree-bark couple cackled, and each line on their faces became four. They pointed to a wellspring at the end of their garden.

'Goornangetchaselfsomewater,' said the woman.

I blinked.

'Getchaselfsomewaterissdownairatbottomagarden.'

I tried inconspicuously to pull apart the words and piece together some sort of meaning. They may as well been speaking a lesser known dialect of Nepalese. The man looked at me as though I was some kind of half-wit.

'Sdownair!'

'Oh, down there, I see.' Grinning semi-inanely, I hastily trudged down to the well. When I peered in, I saw there wasn't a chain and pitcher as I had expected, but a number of ropes suspended into the hole. Shrugging, I tugged on one of them. Slowly, up from the depths rose a five-litre plastic bottle full of water. Well, that was a relief! Apparently, in summertime many wells' water becomes dirty and undrinkable, but the temperature remains cool. This couple had filled up bottles from their home and were cleverly using the hole as a fridge.

How that pair survived up there, I have no idea. There was no power that I could see, and no shops to buy supplies, no doctors or pharmacies. But then, my Grandparents had lived the same way for most of their lives, hadn't they? And they had plenty of laugh lines too, now I think about it.

It might have been a little rude, but a) I wanted to be getting on again and b) I needed a translator, so I said my goodbyes and left the three bumpkins there chortling, breeding wrinkles and competing for words per minute.

I strode from the forest, walking out of the shade and into the white heat of the sun. I walked about ridges and through woods, over rocks and along dust, always on the move. As the trail rumbled beneath my feet, the sun arced gracefully over the lapis bowl of the sky. Ha ha! I was walking, I had water and I knew the way. What more could a hiker want?

Actually, a good night's sleep, and that's harder to come by than one might expect when one is out in the wilds.

Evening arrived. It was then I stumbled upon the tiny hamlet of Beloş, the place I would spend my second night. Because I was determined to camp alone, I ignored the shepherd couple who invited me to stay in their cottage. This was my adventure after all, wasn't it? Perhaps I'd have a mystical dream in the night, or a vision, like Carlos. Hmph! Dreams. I'd be lucky to get forty winks.

After ambling another kilometre further along, I dropped my 'hump'. When I let it go, I almost floated off into the ether. I remember looking at the pack slumped there with its straps and pockets, and its obese immobility. In all honesty, I wasn't quite sure whether it was my friend or my enemy. Still, there was a reason I was carrying it, wasn't there? Untying the drawstrings, I reached for my tent. Within minutes, the roll of tarp had transformed into a bottle-green cupola. It looked as irregular and lonely on that slope as the transmission towers I had seen earlier in the day.

As the final glimmers of daylight seeped beneath the horizon, I bent down to peer inside my shelter. Somewhere over the brow of the hill I heard the ripple of whoops and laughter. A few of Beloş' children appeared. Curious, twitchy and giggly they squashed in front of my makeshift home. They huddled about me until darkness pressed down upon the mountains, and then they scampered off home. All of a sudden, it became exceptionally quiet.

It never ceases to amaze me how something as simple as taking away light transforms a previously unintimidating landscape into the stuff of nightmares. As I

94

rolled and fidgeted upon my camping mat, noises creaked and rustled through the grass all around. There were haunting cries, scamperings, rattlings, hissings. I was adrift in a squirming sea of nocturnal ingurgitation. I have to be frank, I was petrified. Blinking, twitching and sighing, I awaited the dawn.

ജാO౪

Ayşe was curled up in the tent-womb again. It was an odd reality in there. Time shifted gears, the minutes opening and closing like valves. The outside and the inside no longer moved in unison. Was it the Earth had slowed down? Or had she sped up? Time. There was something wrong with it. It just wasn't consistent, was it?

Ayşe wasn't the only one to have pondered on the nature of time. It had baffled many great minds from the ancient world right up to modernity. Future civilisations would wonder how humanity could have ever existed in such a botch of temporal ignorance. And how did it ever get from here to there?

It's not my job to comment on all of that. I do what I do, so don't expect miracles. I'm a witness. So, I'll describe what I saw and heard, and no more.

Back in Ayşe's day, time looked fairly straight forward. There was a past, a present and a future. And that was that. It was a one-way train journey from birth to death on a non-stop locomotive. The future was ahead, but never reached. The past was behind, dead and buried. And passengers spent the entire train ride trapped in tiny carriages of the present moment. Because they were stuck in those boxes of Now, they began to think only the Now was real. It looked like humanity was consigned to a fate of powerlessness. The past and the future were nothing but

95

figments, while the present was too miniscule to do anything constructive with.

Still, even back then, there were few who didn't doubt the railroad of time, or the dubious impression of time flowing. A shift began. Slowly but surely, physicists and philosophers started disembarking from the train of linear time. And as they did, the world was altered. For when they stepped out, their feet sank into an endless undulating fabric. It was a weird and wonderful place they called the block universe.

The block universe was a multiverse of infinite states which the human brain separated out into the occurred, occurring, and going to occur. It was a timescape that looked like a landscape. Everything in it existed simultaneously. If any given state wasn't visible to the human eye, it was because it had been overshadowed by another. Like a village the far side of a mountain, or a sea hidden behind a ridge, invisibility didn't mean something didn't exist. It just meant from your perspective, it was currently out of sight.

Some physicists and philosophers bought into the block universe. Everyone else folded their arms over their chests. They looked on skeptically. For if this block universe was real, why were they still stuck in their train carriages, worrying about the future, regretting their past mistakes, and being born only to get old and die?

There were many theories, and there was much confusion. It was a shift in thinking as radical as when some bright spark had declared the Earth to be round and not flat. Just as those in ancient times had feared falling off the planet, the moderns were wondering what would happen if they jumped from their temporal train. Would they be thrown into a parallel time-verse? Or would they plummet headlong through the gloop of eternity? And if they did, what would they hang on to? From where would they get their bearings? This 'block time' was all very well, but it didn't bear any relation to day to day 'reality'.

Unless you were in Lycia. For when anyone trod the bygone roads of the Lycian Way and into the cities of old, there could be no doubt. The conventional view of time scurried back into the dust, while the block universe sprouted plausible foliage. As people wandered through two thousand-year-old town squares (colonnades flanking the agorae, mosaics peering out under rimples of sand), as they popped their heads into a temple of Artemis, or settled down in a perfectly preserved amphitheatre to munch on a fig, the past seemed so near they could touch it.

Was it wishful thinking? Was it a temporal anomaly? Perhaps it didn't matter. Because as the stones lounged warm and cratered under skin, and the earth spilled through fingers, everyone sensed the ancient life radiating from within. It was as if the atoms themselves held the light of lost time.

Time.

It moves. It slides forwards. It slides backwards. Or it doesn't.

Time is happening. The past is now and the future is over. Or it isn't. Who could be sure?

Day Three

Destinations

Back in Olympos, it was a sticky tar of a night. The pitch was pulled down over the Lycians like the canopy of an executioner's hood. Aphrodite's eye was firmly closed, and the only light was a smattering of stars that jabbed stubbornly through the blackened forest.

The nobleman Licinius peered over his shoulder. The long, sorry train of Olympians was just about visible in the darkness. Only a few held torches, and they floated overhead illuminating yellow patches of heads and shoulders. People had taken whatever they could carry. Bearded men struggled under terracotta amphorae of oil and wine. Middle-aged women held bunches of chickens by the legs as though they were stalks of wheat. A goat bleated as a young girl tried to yank it along behind her. Some people had dressed themselves in essentials; old crones donned strings of garlic around their necks, and their pockets were stuffed with carobs. Young ladies clutched small decorated pyxides boxes, each brimming with their favourite bangles, brooches and earrings, or powders and creams, or perfumes. The men were there with axes, knives and chisels suspended from their thick leather belts. Their hair trailed over their shoulders. These men were used to strife and trouble. They weren't used to fleeing.

Some cried, others were silent, shocked by the loss of their cherished homes and their beautiful town. Olympos was impressive, even back then in its early days, with a small public bath, a Leto temple, and an agora. It was a city with a continuous supply of fresh spring water, fresh fish, fresh fruit and vegetables. Everyone agreed, Olympos was Eden. Two-and-a-half-thousand years later the moderns (who by and large assumed themselves to be far advanced of these ancient cultures) would marvel at the workmanship; the artistic precision of the mosaics, the sub-floor heating of the public baths installed only a couple of hundred years later, and the beauty of the valley. The Olympians had chosen their home well. Who in their right mind wouldn't want to live in such a place?

These were desperate times, however. The Persians were crawling over Asia Minor like a bad bout of hives. Harpagos was knocking at their door, and the Olympians were on the run. They would flee to the place they always went, in the past, the future and now. The hills. And there they would wait until the Persians were defeated by someone else, or the Earth shook them out of the cities, or the mosquitos infected them with malaria. Leto would save them in the end. She always did. The only hitch was, to move up to the plateaus, the Lycians had to walk in the direction of something which had haunted them for as long as anyone could remember. The dreaded Chimera.

Everyone had heard of the Chimera. Sailors from Athens to Phoenicia would gape at its rampant fire-breath as they fared along the Lycian coast. But, even to lay eyes on the thing was to invite misfortune. She could bring on fierce storms, sink ships, and even burst volcanoes. Chimera was a hideous fire-breathing she-monster with the head of a goat, the body of a lion, and a writhing serpent tail. She lived a stone's throw from Olympos, and it was one of the reasons the Olympians survived as long as they did. No one ventured near.

According to Greek myth, a monster-slayer called Bellerophon had once rode on the winged horse Pegasus and killed the Chimera by thrusting a stick of lead into its mouth. The Olympians, though, had little faith in that legend. They lived skipping distance from the Chimera and saw her flames rearing through the earth any time they ventured to the seashore after dark. If there really had been a Bellerophon, and he had indeed slayed the Chimera, then he hadn't done a very thorough job of it, because she was definitely still breathing fire up there on the hill. And woe to all those who saw her. For the Lycians, the story was no more than Greek propaganda; a convenient way for Athens to maintain a fictitious image of its superiority.

'This way!' Licinius' wife whispered, and beckoned him on. Her robe rippled indigo under an inky sky.

Licinius turned and waved his people over the first ridge out of the valley. He looked as though he was scooping the air up into both arms as he dug his hands out and over his shoulders. His wife Aurelia was one step ahead of him. She clutched at a soft goatskin purse filled with silver and gold coins. Aurelia, like many Lycian women, was in charge of the purse-strings. In her other hand was her eight-year-old daughter. The girl who would carry on their name. Their future.

As she picked through the tall thickets of aromatic laurels, Aurelia thought about her home back in the valley. Image after image dashed to the forefront of her mind. They jostled for attention like a band of vainglorious dramatists after a tragedy performance. She remembered her fashionable black-figure vases, her marble hallway lined with oil lamps, her superbly stocked kitchen with its huge amphorae of oil and wine, dried fruits and herbs. And then she envisaged Harpagos' army breaking in and ransacking the place, their grubby Persian hands pulling off her bed sheets, their hammers shattering her imported terracotta lydions, their torches blackening her milky limestone walls. It made her mouth ache from teeth-gritting, and she had half a mind to turn back and give the whole mercenary lot of them what for. But facts were facts. If Xanthos had fallen in such a bloodthirsty and wicked manner, and if Patara had surrendered too, a small up-and-coming town like Olympos didn't stand a chance.

They reached the top of the ridge. Night steamed from the ground up, rather than down from the sky. It misted out the stars. It was then they saw the orange flickers of the Chimera. The flames charged at the darkness like burning wolves.

The citizens of Olympos came to a halt. They bunched up, eyes expanding, hearts pounding. Over a thousand heads turned to look at the blazing mountain in front. A thousand mouths fell open as they gawked at their fate. Aurelia scanned those night-blackened faces. She was looking for one in particular. It was a face that would have stood out, being smaller and dirtier than the rest.

After a few moments she turned, braids twisting about her neck as she did so, and tapped her husband on the shoulder. Through the stifling sludge of that dark hour she whispered, 'Licinius! Where's Jason?'

Jason, the small rat-haired boy who had brought them the news of the Persian invasion, the orphan and the Olympos scout, where *was* he?

ຂ◯ດ

About a hundred kilometres west of Olympos, and the far side of a time-ridge two-and-a-half thousand years high, was Ayşe's tent. It clung to the hillside in Beloş like a barnacle in a sea of midnight. A sliver of a moon sliced an opening in the darkness, while all about Ayşe nocturnal creatures awoke. One of them was a camel spider.

The camel spider can be an intimidating critter. In fact, it's not an arachnid at all, and belongs to another class of wildlife altogether. But it looks like a spider. An enormous, hairy spider. The kind you might have nightmares about. And it can gallop up to sixteen kilometres an hour too, so if you're running away, you'd better be in shape. For all these reasons and more, you probably wouldn't want to spot one at the edge of your groundsheet. A groundsheet full of holes. Holes large enough for a tortoise to crawl through.

Ayşe was asleep, and thus saw nothing. She turned absently onto her side and let out a dream-filled sigh. Meanwhile the camel spider reconnoitred the tarp. It snuck through one of the gaps. Suddenly, it was plunged into a strange new world. It was a world without earth and stones, a world with a smooth floor and a huge, silk-encased beast. It crawled with eight-legged stealth on to the sleeping bag, over the neatly folded clothes that formed a make-shift pillow, finally resting on the top of the beast's head.

Like most people back in those days, Ayşe thought her mind sat in her skull, her thoughts whirling inside like moths looking for light. She believed she suffered her troubles alone too, huddled inside her tiny fleshy cage. Her joys, her sorrows and her awakenings were only hers to feel. None of this was the case. Things moved from inside to outside. Things were drawn from the outside within. There were waves and colours and vibrations rippling all about her other beings could read like books. As for her thoughts, they comprised no physical space to ever get trapped within anything. It was an odd fable of atomisation, and it was even odder the moderns believed it. Yet, if enough people believe in anything, it acquires an almost impenetrable facade of reality.

The bristly pads of the camel spider's feet pressed gently on Ayşe's scalp; feet that could perceive the electrical field surrounding them, something like an EEG machine. Who knew whether or not the critter had the capability to interpret what it sensed? Yet had it understood, had it been able to correlate the electrical pulse with images and words, this is what the camel spider would have reported . . .

ಏ☉ಚ

Ayşe runs through the fields, the grass scratching her legs. She's on a mission, an important mission to feed Grandpa. As she trots through the plots, one by one, past the swelling tomatoes, the cucumbers, and the rose-bushes all thorny and sweet, she's gripping Grandpa's lunch. The little girl clutches it with the resolution of a messenger crossing battle-lines. The summer sun pounds infernally onto the top of her head as she winds through the melons lying plump and yellow on the earth. Finally, she spots him, or at least his boots and legs. He's up on a ladder propped against a plum tree. Ayşe stares up at Grandpa in his baggy *şalvar* trousers and chequered shirt. The sweat makes his face look as waxy as a polished hazelnut.

He grins as he sees his granddaughter, his teeth an on-off affair in his curling mouth. Then, he hops down the rungs. 'Where've you been? My stomach's been growling for a good half-hour.'

Ayşe holds out the box full of home-made goat's cheese, Grandma's unleavened wafer-thin village bread, and fresh tomatoes.

'Ah! You little angel.'

Grandpa sits down to chomp his lunch with his four-year-old, straw-haired granddaughter. It's a scene they re-enact every day. Ayşe likes feeling the stony earth under her feet as she perches on a rock. She watches Grandpa rolling the cubes of feta and tomato slices in the bread. Grandpa works hard out here. It's a never-ending job. He's struggling single-handedly with what is basically a farm.

Before long, the little girl is scampering the three kilometres back through the burgeoning farmland to the house. Her duty is over. But, today when she arrives at the cottage, something is wrong.

She walks in to find her seven-year-old brother crouching on the living room carpet. Both Grandma and her brother are stuffing belongings into a holdall. Grandma tucks a lock of grey hair back into her headscarf. She snorts as she looks up at Ayşe. 'Malik's off to join your ma 'n' pa. *Yurtdışında.*'

Yurtdışında. Abroad. Grandma's chewing over the word like a rotten olive. 'He's gonna be reading at a foreign school. Oof! What good will come of it, who's to say? What business have any of them got over there? Never saw nothing in it meself. Pah!'

Granny's bottom sticks out round and fat in her flower-patterned cotton *şalvar* trousers. She pulls her woollen cardigan tighter over her floppy bosom, despite the soaring mid-summer heat. Ayşe stares forlornly at the holdall. Why are they always leaving? Where is this mysterious *Yurtdışı* place her family are sucked into? And why is she always left behind?

Night comes soon enough. Grandma lights the gas lamp. The family kneel in a circle on the floor, with the gas flame turning their faces white. The rug is warm and soft under their legs. This is the only room in this house where they all sleep, eat, and pray. Grandma brings a large tablecloth everyone pulls over their knees. Plates of food appear. Chickpea stew, steaming risotto rice, a large plate of home-made yoghurt, fried aubergines, sliced cucumbers and tomatoes. Almost every thing in the spread before them was either grown by Grandpa, or made by Grandma.

Ripping off sheets of papery, white bread, everyone tucks in. Soon Grandma sets the teapot heavily on a wooden stand next to her. She begins the ritual of tea-pouring. First, she warms each tulip-shaped glass with hot water. Then, she pours both tea and hot water into their transparent bellies. Ayşe brings the glass to her lips smelling the sweet tannin-brew as she inhales the steam. This is home.

Two years pass in Sultanköy. Two more ploughings and harvestings. Two more summers in the fields with the bugs and scorpions. Two winters all squashed up in one little room listening to the chug-chug-chug of the wood burner. That room is like a train going nowhere in the cold months. Six-year-old Ayşe feels exiled. She wonders if the station guard will ever blow the whistle.

Then, one day it happens. The shriek of steel grinding against steel wakes her. The wheels are finally turning.

'Ah, there you are! I've got news for you. It's your turn now, love!' Grandma is in what passes for the kitchen, rolling out dough into impossibly thin circles. She is holding the long wooden finger of a rolling pin up and waving it in the air like a baker's magic wand. 'You're six so you're going to one of them foreign nursery schools like your brother. Don't cry! You've gotta go!'

She isn't crying. She can't wait. Ayşe runs out into the garden making the chickens panic and flap about stupidly. She hides out behind the cow shed hatching pictures of what *yürtdışı* looks like.

Two days later, Mum and Dad arrive. After a week or so, they bundle their girl into their car and take off for a foreign land. Ayşe sits in the back, bobbing up and down on the seat. She twists her head behind her and watches Grandma and Grandpa wave her off. Ah, *this* is more like it! No one is leaving her now. She is the one off on an adventure. She is the one with a life. The car is a carnival. A magical mystery tour.

A month down the line things are looking different. Germany isn't the fairytale city her imagination had conjured up. The roads are not paved with *helva*, the houses not coated in icing sugar. No one is ever around. Her mother and father both work all hours, and her siblings are at school. Ayşe is homesick. Here in this miserable, grey desert where the people, colder than the weather, don't know of laughter, Ayşe struggles to find her place. She isn't special. She isn't an angel either. Loneliness crawls out from tiny, doubting holes in her heart. It draws icy rings around her, rings that become thicker and tighter with time. Before people abandoned her, now they don't include her. Perhaps there is a reason. Perhaps it is her. She wonders if she should try to get better in everything, so they see she is really OK. But there again, perhaps it is a good idea not to need them, just in case she doesn't quite make the bar.

Years go by, they fold one on top of the other, their outlines always showing through. Ayşe gets used to the cold, grey desert, the church-like triangular houses, the unbridgeable gulf between her life and the life of her German peers. She grows up a teenager in a strange Gomorrah world. Her make-up-smeared school chums are outrageous. They sullenly pout at their teachers, bark rudely at their parents, and cavort in discos kissing their boyfriends openly, as if they were proud. She watches from the cloister of her six pm curfew. The unthinkable taunts her from every corner while her parents guard her assiduously from the perils of Western life.

Then one day it ends, just as abruptly as it started. Nine years after arriving in Germany, Ayşe's mother takes a call from Sultanköy. Grandpa is dying. It is decided by the family someone should accompany Mother. That someone is Ayşe.

Little does she know as she boards the Turkish Airlines flight to Istanbul, this is the end of her life in Germany.

૤○ଃ

Back in Lycia, in a tent-barnacle glued to a mountainside, Ayşe scratched her head. She let out a long sigh and rolled over.

The camel spider lifted. Had it had eyelids it might have blinked a few of its eight eyes at this point. Camel spiders don't have eyelids. How they keep their eyes moist is a mystery. Slowly, feeling somewhat over-stimulated, it crept from Ayşe's scalp. It crawled onto the polypropylene floor, that useless hole-ridden groundsheet. Soon enough it found a tear. Thus, out it wandered, out onto the earth of Lycia, taking Ayşe's story with it as it went.

Outside, the lid of the heavens had been thrown wide open. The eye of the night sky was peeled. It watched over the rocks and the bugs through the holes the stars punched into the stratosphere. It watched until that other eye appeared on the horizon. The eye of the sun. The eye of Medusa.

૤○ଃ

I crawled from my tent, a sleep-deprived wreck. My head itched on the outside and ached on the inside. I felt like I'd lived through two other lives in the course of the night. There was none of the previous day's self-satisfied grooming, and I was already what you might call 'over it.'

Pouring a little water on my toothbrush, I crouched over a rock and cleaned my teeth. I'm afraid that pretty much constituted the extent of my efforts at personal hygiene. I tried to comb my hair but it was already becoming knotty. I ran my fingers over my face. My skin was thickened with unwashed secretions. I might even have begun to smell a little too. I think it was the first time in my life I had plunged to such depths of squalor, and it had taken no more than two nights. There were only two consolations; the first was no one could see me. The second was my zip-lock bags. Each evening, I would pull out those little plastic wallets and arrange them in my tent. Then the next morning, I'd pack them up again. I derived a perverse pleasure from their smooth, four-sided regularity, and lovingly opened and closed the 'zip' at the top that kept all the grot of reality out. They were small pockets of orderly sanitation in a wild and dangerous world.

Anyway, the bags were in my rucksack now. I had packed up the camp. Before I left, I stood holding the map open in front of me like a morning newspaper. I studied the red dotted line almost as if I knew what I was doing. The path charged up contours that were marked in deceptively peaceful hues like olive green and brown. But I wasn't fooled. It was plain as day that I was about to start climbing a substantial mountain. I followed the line as it burrowed through some wonderful place names: Forty steps (would there really be forty and where would they lead to?) Alakilise (The Church of the Angel Gabriel), Gavur yolu (Infidel's road). My eye moved along the trail. Where was my destination of the day? I set my sights on the village of Zeytin because there was an icon of a tap there which meant water.

Now there's a lot of talk these days about destinations and journeys and the like, so I'll add my two-penneth worth, because so many of these adages are

109

horribly culture-specific. Westerners tend to be quite destination oriented, and therefore that 'it's-the-journey-not-the-destination' cliché is presumably relevant. But what about the rest of us? I can tell you now, destinations are vague entities in Turkey. It's all one endless meandering journey with no arrival here. Think about how many times one is asked to stop for tea, or a chat, or asked to come home and meet the family! And the result of an all-journey-no-destination policy is that so very often you never actually get anywhere. At all. Ever. Nothing improves. Nothing is completed. Projects evaporate in the steam of a thousand brewing teapots. No, in my experience one needs journeys and destinations in equal measure, just to ensure some sort of propulsion.

Anyway, finally I put away the map and heaved my rucksack upon my shoulders readying myself for another day on the road. The unease of the night still pulled at my bones, the leaden weight of the pack only making matters worse. I left the camp spot on the Beloş hill side and ploughed upwards and onwards. Occasionally, I lost my way, but then I would find it again. And this was how I walked; losing, finding, losing, finding, until finally I stumbled into an odd highland thicket.

Since the previous day at sea level, I'd been steadily ascending. According to the map I was now at about 1600 metres, or thereabouts. The summit air moved in cool frissons over my arms and cheeks, though the wide lip of the sky remained aloof on the far side of the treetops. Things were changing, turning stranger and wilder. I was entering another world (though I admit, when you are viewing the world through two hours of sleep, it's only natural for it to take on a surreal slant).

Huffing somewhat, I picked and pulled my way through the maze of light-hungry hollows of the woodland.

And then I stumbled upon something quite odd. Up there, in the middle of nowhere, strewn amidst a weald, were a number of rambling homesteads. They were slapdash assemblages of brick, wood, and weather-torn plastic, spattered onto a mottled incline.

No sooner had I reached the huts than a huddle of puckered faces encircled me; men and women with some of the most shrunken faces I've ever seen. They all looked like they'd sat in a pickling jar for too long. Weirder still, these were the sole inhabitants of this isolated hilltop 'no place'. There were no middle-aged people, no children, no one under about seventy. As I stared around the circle of white hair and toothless gums, I started to hear the tremulous chords of any manner of horror films in the background.

'Eh, what's the hurry? Come and 'ave a glass of tea love.' It was one of the biddies who asked. She had sun spots as well as wrinkles, and they peppered her face like tiny, brown continents. At that moment, the sunlight was cutting crisp lines into the branches of the trees and the rocks. Everything started to look superimposed. It became a land of figment, an excerpt from a fairytale. But which one was it? Hansel and Gretel? I remembered how that ended from my primary school in Germany.

'C'mon love, stop for a minute. Have a rest.'

'I'm sorry, I have to keep going.'

The crowd of old dears couldn't comprehend my hurry at all. Well, they had all day, all week and all year, didn't they? I could have drunk a glass and asked where the young had disappeared to, I suppose (Did you boil them in a pot and eat them, Grandma? And what nice teeth you've got, too) but to be honest, I was starting to think it might be the place itself that turned everybody into fossils; once you entered, you were doomed to terminal old age.

'Aw, where you rushing to anyways?'

111

'I really have to be going, I've got to get to . . .'

Well, where did I have to go, in truth? On the one hand, I didn't want to be like Persimmon Legs and his five-year-plans with my head so far in the future I had no time for civility in the present. On the other hand, I felt there had to be more important ways of passing the time than just sitting around and chatting about whether or not I was married, and if so, where my husband was. This last consideration settled it. I quickly pulled my rucksack on and strode off waving good bye as I marched. The old dears were left gaping after me like a drove of silver-haired cattle.

From then on, I roved along the parapet of the world feeling quite the happiest person alive. It was a dominion of woody, root-covered earth and cool, dark canopies. Occasionally, the sky would make a stab for the inner sanctum of the forest, but by and large, shadows cast by the spires of the pine trunks were the rulers here. Ha ha! I was progressing. But I was also thirsty. And that was annoying.

Now, I daresay I could write a book about thirst, I've known it so intimately as a result of that walk. It matters little how much water one imbibes, the sheer heat and murderous descents and ascents of the trail in summer deplete one's every cell. I was perpetually dehydrated, and every time my water finished, I'd flash back to my Gelidonya experience on the first day; the dizziness, the panic, and then the gradual loss of power. So imagine my elation when at last I spotted a well. It was a stone ring huddled on the forest floor and almost lost in bracken. It looked like a benediction, but I'm sorry to say, it wasn't. Not in the slightest.

As I approached it, thousands of fallen pine needles snapped under my feet. The needles created traps. My right foot sank into a buried hole, and I panicked for moment wondering if it was a snake pit or something. I yanked my leg out and at last reached the well. But when I peered over the edge of the stone rim, my stomach lurched. There in the darkness lay a baby wild boar. The poor creature was dead. Its eyes had vanished, presumably devoured by another animal, and the small pig's body was bloated. It had fallen down the shaft and drowned. I imagined what must have been last moments of misery – the struggle of the baby boar as it attempted to remain eternally afloat, the desperate scraping at the unforgiving stone walls – and I thought there and then, perhaps one should refrain from romanticising too much about nature, as she can be altogether quite unsentimental.

I shuddered as I took in the sight of the boar. What did it mean? What did any of this peculiar day mean? That deep at the heart of nature anarchy reigns? That plans, and road-maps, and painted red-and-white stripes, are merely the bare scaffolding tacked upon the awesome and terrifying edifice of creation? Perhaps there was no meaning at all, just me drawing nonsensical conclusions from a random, dank hole.

Now, when one is alone in a hilltop Lycian forest without so much as a whir of civilisation nearby, and the nearest community one is aware of comprises a dozen mad geriatrics living in hutches, small events have a tendency to appear big. I pulled back from the well and prepared to move on, but I was unnerved by it. I surveyed my surroundings. The trees thickened darkly. Hints of trails slithered this way and that with unhelpful rocks and deep layers of dusty pine-needles rendering them difficult to negotiate. Hell! I was lost again; lost with thirst now clawing at my throat. And it's no trifle to be lost in the Lycian hills. I felt a prickle between my shoulder blades as I remembered a story a mountaineer friend of mine had *told me before I left. Two Israeli tourists had wandered off track in Lycia a year earlier. They called for help but had no idea where they were. In the end, all that had been found of them was a shoe . . .*

I gulped. I wanted my trail back, but now there were so many paths. From the spot I was standing on, passages crawled out in every direction. How could I possibly divine which was mine? How could I find the damn way?

ഇO ഄ

I know that spot in the forest. It's like the Olympos valley. Medusa's eye barely touches the topsoil there. Her rancour is absorbed by some old, stalwart pine trees. They form a scrum over the floor, wooden arms intertwined. And where the sky can't probe, the Earth has her way.

Ayşe wasn't the only one to sense something amiss in that space. Travellers have been shuddering through those shadows for thousands and thousands of years. Some of them were Turks, some Greeks, some Lycians. And one of them was a Mede turned Persian.

You might not believe me. A fair few don't. Many historians have studied my home, but none could ever agree how Harpagos and the Persian army crossed Lycia. East to West? West to East? North to South? By boat? The fact is no one knows. No one can prove it. I can't prove it either. But I know because I was there. Unknown to the historians and the archaeologists, unknown even to the ancient Lycians until he descended on them, General Harpagos was storming through the forests of Lycia like an impromptu winter deluge.

'Do you know where we are?'

'Ain't got a frigging clue. Can't see the sun or nuffink from 'ere. It's all just trees init. This place is giving me the heeber jeebers, I'll tell you'

'We'd better tell him, then.'

'What, that we're lost? Not likely. Smore than my jobs worth that is.'

'Well, we can't just keep them following us like this without a destination!'

'We've got destinations. Phoenicus and then that Olympos place. We're just not sure if we're going to them or not.'

'Oh you're genius, you are!'

'Look mate, if we tell him we're lost, our head's in the wicker basket before you can say *scary Lycian forest*. At least this way, we might just wind up at the right place by mistake, eh?'

The two scouts were hacking through brambles and holly bushes. Both were short and wiry with faces that demanded double takes. One had florets of curly black hair erupting from his ears like ebony trumpets. The other had a squint and no front teeth. Both stopped their trail beating for a minute and gaped through the shrubs behind them. Fifty metres back, a cohort of over five hundred men were clearing a wide track through the forest. They were breathtakingly destructive. Bushes flew left and right, branches snapped like ears of wheat, and every so often a great pine crashed to the ground. Behind this forest-devouring military spider, the Persian army stretched into the shadows; a force of sixty thousand or more. It was like a fantastic, multi-coloured bird of prey. The ochre and pomegranate-clad infantry with their wicker shields and spears, were pushing through the trees. Meanwhile the cavalry, robed in its peacock blue livery, swayed ahead on dromedaries and horses. Lions slunk hastily out of view, leopards lay low and quiet, great brown bears ambled off into various caves as the mighty Persian war machine came crashing fearlessly through.

But why would the Persian army trudge over Lycian rubble and rocks when they had the Carian or Xanthian fleet at their disposal? Harpagos could have simply kicked back in a trireme and sailed the length of Lycian Riviera, enjoying fine seafood dinners on deck under a setting sun as he went. The reason was this: Harpagos was a master at ambush, his men trained for mass attacks on open plains or in the steppes. He had driven his army through the kingdoms of Anatolia – Phrygia, Lydia, Ionia – at breath-taking speed. Now, here he was at the trembling lip of the western world, the Mediterranean lapping at his sandals. He had never set foot on a ship up to that point, and had no experience of naval warfare. The Lycians, on the other hand, had plenty. That is why the great General Harpagos chose the tried and tested. Land. Earth. Rolling under his feet, sucking out all the trouble and woe as it went. But he might have been regretting it.

'This has got to be the worst Goddamn drive of my life.' Harpagos muttered. He was standing and hanging onto the front of his chariot. The wheels sank into holes, struck rocks and stalled at tree roots, throwing Harpagos into the air every time. The floor was shuddering so violently under his feet his armour rattled. He sounded not dissimilar to a tinker's cart. He gritted his teeth and tightened his grip on the rail before leaning over towards one of the horseback captains beside him.

'I've had enough of this preposterous dance. Once we get to Phoenicus, we're sailing!'

116

The captain nodded, and his saffron cap continued nodding for minute after he'd stopped.

'The sea is stuffed full of pirates, and the forests are impossible. How do these Lycians ever go anywhere?'

'I don't think they do, sir. They don't seem interested in expansion,' the captain offered. Then the horses' right foot hit a rock, and both beast and rider lurched forwards. Harpagos threw the heavens a cursory glance, but all he saw was leaves and pine needles.

'Whoa!' Called someone up front. 'Obstruction!'

And then, by the mercy of the Gods, the chariot drew to a halt and the shaking abated. The great Persian bird of prey had been stopped mid-flight.

A hundred yards ahead, the two scouts were staring up. The object of their gawking was a woman on horseback.

'Oi! Getcha pretty little arse out the way, *now*!' It was the man with the squint who tried to hustle her along.

'Hey. She's good-looking. Tell the general to come and have a look,' said the scout with the black, hairy ear-trumpets.

'Good point. Might just save our bacon.' The squinter turned round, scratched his groin and yelled, 'Oi! Iss a girl, and she's hot!'

The team of path-wideners behind murmured and a runner sprinted from them to the front of the war train. Harpagos was now cooling himself under the shade of two large pine trees. He was somewhere near the front of the convoy, flanked by his own personal bodyguard unit known as the Companions. Later storytellers would mistakenly call them 'Immortals'. Where another language goes, confusion often follows. It was a translation error. The Persian bodyguard elite were a formidable sight. They wore fine saffron tunics. Underneath those was scale armour. Each man held a golden-tipped spear, a large silver dagger, a bow and arrow, and a shield.

'Sir. It's a woman on horseback. She's not budging,' said the runner, bowing and huffing in alternate movements.

Harpagos stood up and strained his eyes. He could just about see her ahead. Deciding to investigate, he raised his arm. Instantaneously, the sea of yellow parted. Next, the four white Nisaean horses pulling his chariot trotted amiably forwards. Hundreds of the Companions bowed as their commander rumbled before them. The chariot bounced over the rocks and broken twigs below, until it finally came to a standstill a mere few feet away from her. Gloaming was now sliding through the openings in the trees. The boulders here and there were adopting their ritual, eventide colours.

She sat on a chestnut horse stacked with firewood. Her eyes were as deep and green as river whirlpools. The maiden raised those eyes and stared directly at Harpagos. For some reason, the back of his scalp suddenly felt unseasonably cold.

Harpagos spoke no Lycian, and he presumed this strange young woman didn't speak Elamite, the official language of the Persian Empire, either. But he had to make some kind of contact with her. He was curious. How could such a creature possibly posture in such self-possessed calm before his almighty army? Struggling a little in his heavy iron greaves, the satrap pulled himself down from the chariot and clanked towards her. There wasn't a scrap of fear in her face, nor a hint of suspicion either. As he stood by the side of the horse, he held out his leather-clad hand. He might have been getting on a little, but as warlord

118

extraordinaire of the Persian conquest he was confident he still had something of the debonair in him.

The young woman sat motionless while that most important of Persian hands remained hanging in mid-air. She did nothing. The hand began to look marginally ridiculous. Finally, she raised her arm and indicated back in the direction the Persians had come from. And then she opened her mouth. She only said one word, but the word was more than enough. 'Xanthos.'

Harpagos just stopped himself from staggering. In a flash, the Persian satrap felt every ounce of his iron scale armour. He feared the weight of it might drag him to the floor.

'Look here, we're not going to Xanthos. We've . . . we've already . . .'

He pulled back his outstretched hand and tried to stare her out. But, all he saw were those unnerving eyes. They bored right through his armour, through the facade of his self-image, ripping apart the flimsy skin of his beliefs and justifications. Xanthos. The Lycian capital. It was only days ago they had been there. The Persians had routed the citadel quickly, but that didn't improve things. Harpagos had always thought nothing could have come close to losing his son. The Xanthians had proven him wrong.

The horseback beauty patted the neck of the chestnut mare and swung her about-face. She promptly galloped into the enveloping safety of the forest. Within seconds, her silhouette had disappeared into the myriad of blackened voids between the trees. Harpagos said nothing. He stamped on the magma of perturbation inside, turned and clanked wordlessly back to his chariot. Yet with every step, his mind chewed on what he had seen. The sun had just set, and the forest had become a labyrinth of passageways. The curled fingers of the surrounding oaks clawed at every opening.

'Damn Lycians and their spooks,' he grumbled to himself as he hauled himself back into his chariot. It could have been a forest nymph, or one of those weird she-demons, or even the night Goddess Nyx for all he knew. From his dealings with the Ionians and the Carians, Harpagos was only too aware of the exorbitance of unearthly existence these people gave credence to. There was no room for such superstitious balderdash in Zoroastrianism. Still, there was no doubt about it. No doubt at all. Lycia was slowly but surely getting under the Persian's war-hardened skin.

Ahead, the two scouts looked at each other, eyes bulging.

'Phew! That was lucky!' The squinting man grinned flaunting the full extent of his dental devastation. There were more gaps than teeth.

'If Xanthos is *that* way . . . '

'Phoenicus is *this* way. Told yer, didn't I? Problems always sort themselves if you leave 'em alone.'

꙰Oꙮ

That space in Lycia became darker and darker. Aphrodite could see no more than Medusa. The eye of the sky was blind here. The shadows gnawed at the tree trunks. The peat underfoot rose in a pitchy smoke. Slowly but surely, the space disappeared. God only knew where.

A train approached from nowhere. The train of time. It was a calibrated locomotive, and it sped at such a rate, anyone who saw it felt giddy. It chugged out of the ancient world, shields and spears flicking past the windows like

120

stills in a kinetoscope. The forest grew taller, older, wiser. The bark on the pines thickened with every passing year. There were no more Persians or Lycians, no more chariots and chainmail. Harpagos disappeared. The only thing remaining was the rocks, and the ghosts hiding inside them.

The train rumbled on over the centuries, until it arrived at southern Turkey. At the Lycian Way. At a woman hiker in the 21st century called Ayşe.

؃

Ayşe stood at a junction of tiny forest pathways. From above, the scene looked like a star, thin lines radiating out from the wayward hiker. She was standing in the middle of nowhere with not an inkling which way to go. She was stuck. Unmoving. And she hated that. She'd always hated that. Because whenever she stopped, she found herself reversing. Sometimes she went back to Istanbul. Sometimes other places. Places she'd run away to.

⁊O؃

It was 1990. It was Kemer. The word meant belt in modern Turkish. That's what Kemer had been back then, a quiet belt of honey-coloured sand looping along the base of a steep evergreen slope. In those days, newly awakened to a tentative tourist industry, the resort of Kemer boasted no more than a handful of hotels. They squatted hotchpotch on the beach like random teeth along a sweet-lover's gums. Ayşe was soon offered a post at one of them. The hotel owner, a toad of a man with buck teeth and a beach ball of a stomach, handed her a room key.

'Speak German? Very good. Start tomorrow in reception, nine in the morning. That's what we need. A nice young blonde to snare the tourists.'

The receptionist job progressed well for two weeks. Guests came and went, and were impressed with Ayşe's German. Papers were filed in the correct place under the pinewood reception counter. The phone was answered in three languages. And everybody found their way to the beach and the nomadic park. Unfortunately, the hotel owner wasn't interested. That's not why he had hired her.

Ayşe was a refugee fleeing the war of marriage. The Kemer hotel was a way station on her escape route. It looked like a decent rest-stop, though, with clean bathrooms and a pay packet to boot. Then sixteen days in, something happened to burst the shiny, new bubble of independence. It was the middle of the night. Ayşe was fast asleep in the staff quarters on the top floor. There was a knock at the door.

She started and opened her eyes. Her room was a crate of darkness. Only the street lamp down the road threw a strand of light onto her bed. She blinked and pushed her head up to listen. A second knock at the door, this time with some urgency behind it, convinced her she hadn't been dreaming. Being young and not yet having learned the lessons all woman eventually do, she didn't question the knock. There had to be an emergency in the hotel. Perhaps a guest wanted help. May be someone needed a translator.

'Just a minute!'

Ayşe got out of bed and quickly threw on the bathrobe hanging on the door hook. She clicked the lock and opened the door. The hotel owner was there with his buck teeth and his flabby belly. Only, there was something disturbing about the belly. It wasn't covered up as it should have been. It protruded in front of the man like a mutant, hairy pregnancy. Ayşe stood stock still. Her skin bristled with static. But, not yet having learned the lessons all woman eventually do, she followed the rules of social etiquette and smiled politely.

'İyi akşamlar,' she said.

Buck teeth-hairy-belly stretched one arm onto the door post. He grinned, and as he did his moustache crawled to the ends of his upper lip. His eyes were like a pair of starving ferrets. They scurried all over the pretty, young blonde sniffing for carnal pleasure.

'Can I come in?'

Ayşe's heart had grown the size of a basketball. It banged about inside her so furiously she couldn't hear herself think. She didn't know what to do. This was her boss. He held her pay. But not yet having learned the lessons all woman eventually do, she followed the rules and tried to be polite. Later she would learn, just as all women do, that politeness and social convention are evil's most obliging accomplices.

'Erm. Well it's late. And I'm sorry, I'm very tired,' she murmured.

Buck teeth-hairy-belly lurched forward and kissed Ayşe. He reached for her breast with his left hand and managed a grope. It took two seconds too long, but she grasped the lesson all women eventually do. She pushed the hotel owner away and slammed the door in his face. Back in her room, the walls had turned to slime. The floor was a rug of roaches and the bed a nest of rats. There was trembling. Shaking. There was a cold, numb feeling. She lit a cigarette. Then she packed her bags. By sunrise she was gone.

ଔଠଓଃ

I think there are places in forests which, one way or another, are haunted, places where one could become interminably stuck, places that make your skin crawl and

123

your knees shake. I might have been in such a place and it occurred to me, I had been standing there for some time. My heart was pounding, but I had no idea why. Perhaps I'd been daydreaming, or just gazing into space, and dehydration was coming for me, as well. I could tell, because things were starting to look not exactly as they should.

The wizened pine trunks were great crusty serpents rearing from the depths of the forest floor. A sunless silence pervaded. It was punctuated only by the unhappy cries of nearby birds. I had to choose a path and move, otherwise I'd be mired at this point forever, wouldn't I? Without thinking, I set off into one of the forest alleys. But if I thought I'd had my fair share of oddity that day, I was wrong.

The trail moved in and out of the shadows with bushes and boulders altering its shape. Pine needles covered bracken and creepers transforming them into spindly scarecrows. Then I turned a corner. I was brought to an abrupt halt. I think I might have squealed. Well, I hadn't expected to see such a thing, had I? Where could she possibly have come from? You see, directly in front of me and sitting squarely astride a chestnut horse was one of the most beautiful girls I've ever seen.

We stared at each other for a moment. She had green eyes, peculiar eyes actually, but there was something else, only I couldn't quite work it out. It looked as though she had been on an errand collecting wood for the family, yet she commanded such grace and presence I was taken aback. She was a bit like a mythical goddess, I suppose, not that I'd know what one of those looked like, but anyway. Then she smiled and indicated the way. And do you know what? For the first time in quite a while, I was certain it was the way.

124

One of the *wonderful* things about bumping into women on the trail is that one knows they will do you no harm. The most they will ever want from you is a chat. If that girl had been a man would I have connected in the same way? I doubt it. One's guard is always up, isn't it?

Anyway, I thanked her for her assistance, and she smiled again. Something shuddered inside me. Slowly, I was starting to grasp it; losing the way was showing me the way, every wrong turn had its oracles, and every missed marker was a chance. I turned and walked on. I heard the horse and the girl clipping off into the distance.

I left the strange snake trees and their shadows, the spooky dark holes and the crying birds. I continued on my way. I lost count of the times I went astray that afternoon, though. It seemed impossible to stay on the path, almost as if the Lycian Way were alive and wriggling about on her own. I kept referring obsessively to the map, but Lycia refused to conform to any sort of regularity. It was all very infuriating. And I was nowhere near the village of Zeytin, my destination of the day with its lovely little icon of a tap.

I was also a little frustrated because although things were slightly surreal, nothing particularly earth-shattering had happened to me. I had hoped I might meet my spiritual guide up here. You know, a real *other-worldly* being. I wondered why I didn't have these experiences when all these mystics do. What was wrong with me?

The sky was steadily losing its pallor, darkness crouching beneath the rim of the horizon. It was just then that I reached Alakilise and The Church of Gabriel, and spirit guides or not, that was a relief. There just had to be water here somewhere, and a half reasonable spot to camp on. I must admit, following the sleeplessness of the previous night, I had begun to fantasise on the subject of soft beds and solid walls. I had another week at least of

125

rough ground and terrifying night ordeals to contend with, combined with the uninspiring prospect of one more dreary meal of dry biscuits and nuts. I don't know what I wouldn't have traded a home-cooked dinner for.

What happened next was the queerest, most convoluted sequence of events, and it led me, if somewhat indirectly, exactly to the place I wanted to be. I was still parched, in fact, I was nearly crawling by this point, so when a young shepherdess appeared, swanning through her bleating rabble of goats, I jumped on her, immediately.

'I'm so thirsty, can you help?' I was nearly hoarse. Now, as an aside, shepherds and shepherdesses have since transpired to be my unsung heroes, the genuine gurus, the enlightened ones. They are neither villagers, nor urban, and when I look into their eyes, I see them burning with something we 'civilised' folk have completely mislaid. You will never see such eyes in a city; the intellectuals are too arrogant, the conservatives too bound by their duty to traditions. I wonder what they experience as they roam the mountains alone, day after day. Anyway, this shepherdess straightaway pointed me to her well. Stooping, I reached into it and hauled up the tin canister inside. But, when I tipped it into my plastic bottle, I was horrified to see it trickling in dirty, red rivulets. It appeared to be liquid mud. Looking up, I stared at the girl 'You drink this?'

She nodded shyly. I recoiled. See? This would never happen in a self-discovery book, would it? Every guide leads the protagonist to exactly where they ought to be, like the numbers on a dot-to-dot picture. They don't manifest with duff information and substandard water supplies!

I continued on a bit, starting to feel stressed. Where was the drinking water? It had to be here somewhere. A little above the path, a simple shepherd's hut was visible. A cloud of sheep drifted about it in whinnying wafts, and there was a small lad loitering in front. Waving, he called out, 'Sister! You can go to your friends' house! It's just over there.'

Friends? Which friends? Right then, the only friend I wanted to meet was a transparent liquid called H2O. And anyway, who could I possibly know up here in what was essentially no more than a summer retreat for wool-growing mammals? I made my way to the house, first and foremost to quench my thirst, but also because I was wondering what on Earth the boy was crowing about.

It was a typical mountain-village hut, bricks and wood tacked together with a poor spread of cement. Sliding my feet out of my boots, I entered the open door and felt the soft wool of a hand-made rug beneath me. I squeezed myself and my hump into the main room, embarrassed about the awful smell I was certain was emanating from my feet. The family didn't seem too worried though. They clucked and cooed about me. It was as though they were witnessing a festival reunion. Huffing, sticky, and feeling horribly unclean, I shed my pack with a groan. I turned rubbing my burning shoulders, to spy three young foreigners grinning at me. Aha, my 'friends'.

Two of the male hikers moved to one side, and I sat cross-legged on the floor next to them. A gaggle of fleshy bottoms and bosoms set down a cloth and a sini in front of us. The metal tray was heaving with food and drink. One of the lads reached for the sheet bread and ripped off a sizeable corner.

'Whoa! This is great, eh?' He began cramming the bread in his mouth.

'Ya, I'll say. Where are you from, then?' It was the young woman with the bleached blonde hair who asked.

'Istanbul. And you?'

127

The group were South African. They had started the route in Fethiye, exactly the place I was heading for. Thus, like passing merchants at a Silk Road kervansaray, we spent the evening exchanging tales of the journey.

'Xanthos, now that was a really creepy place, like the creepiest place I've ever seen. There has to be ghosts in that amphitheatre, just has to be.' It was the second lad who spoke. He had a goatie that no longer was, so it had become a two-layered beard.

'Ya. Really. Do you know what happened there?' Asked the woman.

I felt a fool. This was my country and no, I didn't have the tiniest idea. I'm not sure I'd even heard of Xanthos until I'd looked at the map a week ago.

'A lot of people died there,' said the bread gobbler between mouthfuls.

'Badly.' Added the two-layered beard.

I tried to listen to the rest. But it was in English and I was so tired that I just couldn't follow who had killed who or why. With leaden eyelids, my mind wandered to other things. I began to worry about where I was going to sleep, because I simply couldn't drum up the motivation to erect my tent.

But someone was looking down on me. Hatice, the host, who I had now begun to think was a Lycian angel in disguise, had prepared beds for us in the barn next door. And that, quite frankly, was the best news I'd heard all day. Despite the pungent stench of the sheep, I lay down on the cotton sheets smiling. I couldn't believe how benevolent everything was, or how luxurious simplicity can be.

The 3rd Night

Circles

Modern Turkey. If the country had been a roof, it would have been a dome – a wide and star-filled arcade. And a medley of folk huddled under it. There were Turks and Armenians, Kurds, Jews, Greeks, northern Europeans, Russians and many more, all of them living in the garrulous house of The Republic. It was a gateway in time and space, a place forever in between.

So who were the Turks? Where had they come from? And what were they doing vacillating on the edge of Europe in such an ambivalent fashion? The Turks were part of the Turkic people, a group stretching from Siberia through parts of Russia, China, Mongolia and Central Asia, with Turkey its nethermost tip. These nomadic people had wandered, or more often galloped, over the Urals, along the Indus, and around the Caspian Sea. Originally, they had been shamans, and many still were. Even the English word 'shaman' had been loaned from the Turkic word *şaman*.

The ancient Turkic people had been sky-worshippers. For these people, the meaning of life was intimately wrapped up in a culture of harmony with the environment. Even the modern Turkish flag, with its star and moon, evoked Tengri the sky god. Islam arrived later from neighbours in the Arab world. Even so there were Turks who still harked back to their earthy spiritual origins. Perhaps that was why Ayşe was intrigued by Carlos Castaneda and his forays into natural magic. What she saw burning in the wild eyes of the shepherdess was the fire of the shaman. And when she heard the footsteps of the shepherd, it was the deep thud of the shamanic drum she was reminded of.

Down in Turkey's south-west, in the hills of Lycia, shamanism was everywhere, though no one seemed to realise it. The landscape was streaked with wish trees,

130

healing herbs and cairns. The villages bubbled with fortune-tellers and dream-readers. The rural folk still clutched the lost secrets of the Earth within their tightly curled, henna-stained fingers. And now the moderns, foreigners and Turks alike, had come to seek those secrets out.

ะ๑Oભ

Hatice brimmed with delight as she pulled the rotten plywood door closed on her visitors. Guests! And foreigners among them. Who would have ever thought a nothing little blip on the landscape like Alakilise would see the likes of tourists? Did this mean the price of her land would increase? Could she begin a *pansiyon*, just like they did down on the coast? Ah what an evening it had been! And they'd all definitely enjoyed her food. But good gracious, how had that lonesome blonde lady carried her rucksack all this way? Is this what foreigners thought of as *fun*? (In her eyes Ayşe was as much a foreigner as the other three. She wasn't from Alakilise, and she spoke with a hoity-toity accent as well).

Hatice shrugged her shoulders, for like many Turkish villagers, she had seen a wide variety of oddity in her bumpy life. She followed the philosophy of the majority of Mediterranean rural folk, namely, it took all sorts. Hatice's husband had turned in for the night. The sixty-year-old woman was alone and began to rinse the white, plastic dinner plates. Her kitchen was simple. Planks were nailed unevenly onto the crumbling walls and functioned as her shelves. Rusty nails hammered into them served as hangers for spoons, utensils and the like. The kitchen cupboards were concrete cubby holes with stopgap wooden doors banged onto them. An outsider might have thought the entire place could have done with a lick of paint, but Hatice didn't. Kitchens had always looked the way hers did around these parts. She had lived in Alakilise all her life, as had her parents and her parents' parents. She was as part of the landscape as an oak tree, a sprig of oregano, or those old limestone arches crumbling over on the hill, the ones foreigners called the Church of Gabriel.

The small village woman opened the back door. 'Hadi Kaya. Come here. Here! Here! Oof come on you big ol' lump!' She filled a metal bowl with the leftovers from dinner. Her huge dog Kaya turned his head. He was a Kangal, or Anatolian shepherd, the favourite guardian of many a villager. He pushed his long back legs up and sidled over to the bowl. With his thick sandy coat, he was almost the size of an adolescent lion.

It took him less than a minute to polish off the food. Then he flopped onto the barn floor letting his big dog head sink into the dust. Pity Kaya. He was so lamentably hot he could hardly bear to prick up his ears. As he slumped there his wet snout twitched, just as it always did. And what a snout that was! It was one of the most refined organs of smell in the animal kingdom. It was a nose that could detect an endless rainbow of odours, a nose that was a staggering one hundred thousand times more discerning than its owners'.

Kaya's head pressed flat against the barn floor, and he smelled worlds upon worlds: the sheep, a number of bats, a couple of house mice, an Anatolian rock lizard, the woodlice in the barn doorpost, a turtle dove perched in the rafters, the cigarette end dropped by the neighbour, the remnants of dinner (tomato, yoghurt, rice, cucumber, garlic), the neighbour's donkey, the outside toilet, and much more. He was also aware of the four new odours emanating from the other side of the flimsy barn partition. The newcomers.

Kaya shifted his huge brown eyes left and then right, before pulling himself up onto his haunches and inhaling again. He knew just from the smell of them, three of the newbies were together, and one of them was alone. He knew the loner was a female too.

Kaya pushed up his back legs and lazily wandered over to the wooden partition housing Ayşe. His big, black nose scanned the air as millions of information-clad odour drops raced towards his snout. Oh, there were all kinds of things on the female human. Kaya smelt the cotton of her T-shirt, the fresh mint of toothpaste, her sweat. Her body odour read like an entire novel. He smelt wafts of happiness, splashes of fear and excitement. She was sleeping, but Kaya sniffed out waves of feelings. They crashed over him, a multi-coloured sea of sense.

But there was one emotion that rang out clearer and louder than any other. Kaya took another sniff. Hmm, yes. It was the unmistakable smell of deep-seated, slow-burning anger. The smell of a survivor. The old canine might not have cognised it in terms of such sophistication, yet he knew instinctively what was happening. Dreaming was something dogs and humans shared. Ayşe's dreaming mind was bringing things back from before. And by the smell of things 'before' had really roiled her.

ಬಿOಇ

Ayşe ran from Kemer. She escaped eastwards along the coast in a sweltering minibus packed with tourists and no spare seats. The driver, unfazed by the *capacity 20 people* sign screwed above the dashboard, yanked out a red plastic stool. He motioned her to sit down. She huddled there clutching her bag under her chin.

The bus accepted three more people before it heaved off along the road. As it trundled up to the highway, its

133

bumper was no more than two inches from the ground. Every time the driver braked, Ayşe skidded nearer to the front of the bus. And whenever she rocked too violently so that the stool legs came off the floor, the chubby village woman on her right grabbed her arm to steady her. The huge Bey Mountains watched the bus as it ploughed along the tarmac. Their stark, rocky faces were both proud and disapproving at the same time.

Two hours later, Ayşe found herself, yet again, in Antalya bus station with the sweaty touts and the bawling ticket vendors. Yet again, she wondered where to go. For some reason or no reason, she chose Alanya.

Alanya became a city. In its youth however, it had been a beautiful seaside getaway. Two prime arcs of saffron sand swept gloriously up to a rocky peninsula. Battered yellow taxis would career up the crag at terrifying speeds. They would spin their wailing passengers along the vertiginous terracotta ridge, all the way up to the fortress at the top. From here the tourists could wander almost alone along the ancient ramparts with the Mediterranean air gusting in from over the blue.

It was here in Alanya, Ayşe landed another job in a hotel. It was a sleek, white cube of a place a few streets behind the main seaside strip. The front was lined with baby palm trees resembling giant pineapples, and there was a small square of turquoise in the courtyard that half-naked Scandinavians would leap into and shatter at regular intervals.

Yet again, Ayşe worked on reception. And yet again, it was no more than a few weeks before The Patriarch intervened. It was a scorching summer morning, and she was standing behind the reception counter hanging up the returned room keys. A blonde child scampered past in swimming trunks dragging a pool noodle behind him.

'Rollo! Rollo! *Warte mal!*' A Teutonic female voice called after him.

Then the phone rang. Ayşe answered it, just as she always did. 'Hello, Turquoise Paradise Hotel, how can I help you?'

'Can I speak to Ayşe Metin?' The voice sounded like a steel spike being dragged through a bed of stones.

Ayşe's hand went cold as it held the phone. The receiver felt like a human bone, a femur from an autopsy. She inhaled, but forgot to exhale again. The breath just hovered in her lungs waiting for someone to tell it what to do. She had been found. What should she do now? Put the phone down? Hide under the counter? Come clean?

'Who's speaking please?'

'Ayşe, this is your husband's lawyer. I've got something important to say, and you might want to hear it.'

How had the lawyer found her here in deepest, sunniest, Turquoise-Paradise-Touristland? That was sadly very easy. As soon as anyone had an over-the-table job in the Republic, the local *Jandarma* would be provided with their ID card details. The concept of confidentiality was a hazy one in modern Turkey. Doctors, lawyers, your gynaecologist and your local police station could and would divulge anything to anyone, at any given time. If banknotes crossed palms, then the information was yours. Thus, in a land of seventy million people and three hundred thousand square miles, Ayşe had been hunted down.

So here was Murat's lawyer, and apparently he had something important to say. But what did *that* mean? Was she in more trouble? Was Murat burning a trail of revenge in her wake? Ayşe pictured him sitting in his Ford Cortina, left arm dangling out of an open window, puffing smoke through his rakish, black hair.

It's better not to judge the hand of fate, however. It's a conjurer's hand, and there are trap doors and invisible threads hidden all over. Ayşe put the receiver back to her ear. The lawyer spoke. And what he said opened her eyes as wide as freshly-baked *simits*. Apparently, after a few weeks of reality, Murat had decided he wasn't too keen on bringing up a two-year-old boy single-handed. And a boy should be with his mother. He had changed his mind. He wanted her back to take care of their son. Well, well. Ayşe sat and stared in bewilderment as divine justice walloped down an ace and scooped up the cards. The phone kept ringing. Next came calls from her ex-boss and her uncle, both offering to support her if she returned. Ayşe's immediate family remained conspicuously silent. It was this which still stirred ire as she snored in a makeshift bed in the Lycian hills. It was this, Kaya the dog smelled.

After chain-smoking for a day and brooding over the options, Ayşe decided to return. She endured another fourteen-hour bus ride back to Istanbul. She'd lost everything; her son, her home, and her job. What she gained in return was something granted only to those who have nothing left to lose. Freedom. Once again, power had suddenly taken to the floor, shaken her booty and shimmied over to the other side. Arbitrarily. Spontaneously.

When she arrived back in Istanbul, Ayşe realised how desperate Murat was. And she would leverage that desperation to be rid of him forever. No matter how she felt inside about having her son back, she played it cool. Ayşe made a deal; she would take care of their son on the condition he gave her a divorce as soon as possible.

Life resumed in the burgeoning continent-crossing metropolis of Istanbul. She began working at the same company as before. But, Ayşe's parents didn't budge in their mind set. They refused to acknowledge the impending break-up, or assist their daughter. Despite winning back her son, Ayşe could sense her aloneness stretching in front of her. That solitude was a thin, cracked road on an isolated, wind-torn brow. How would she do it? Work, take care of her son, and pay for a flat? And then, in 1993, it happened. The divorce came through. Reality kicked in.

ಏ⃝ಜ

Back in Alakilise, midsummer glided eerily through the night sky. A sallow moon simpered on the horizon. Kaya the Kangal turned and mooched back to the doorstep. Hatice *teze* was still there. She was staring out at the profile of the mountains. Broken stone men hung from them here too, clusters of limestone leering from their blackened faces. The old lady looked along the trail coiling back in the direction of Beloş. The road was immured in darkness. She shivered.

The reason for her trepidation, and the reason she couldn't help but look, was now and again, Hatice heard things that went bump in the night. Things she didn't understand. And she wasn't the only one. The women of Alakilise would gossip about the shadows they saw drift over the rocks. The strange noises. The grinding creak echoing through the darkness made many a local shudder. It sounded like a giant millstone. Or a mammoth horse-drawn cart.

As the silence of the dark hours grew heavier, Hatice's mouth set into a tense line. She turned away from the mountains and quickly shut the door.

ಏ⃝ಜ

She hadn't seen him, but out there in the darkness, far off in the distance, was a man. He was staring into the night, brooding. His saffron tunic rippled slightly in the breeze, the gold trimming gleaming every now and again. From the purple and gold tiara on his head, it was clear he was worth a fortune. Not that it helped one iota.

137

The man surveyed the triangular mountain tops silhouetted against an indigo sky. The stars held their positions unwaveringly – a celestial map in a world of darkness. He stood alone in his enormous war chariot. It towered over the epidemic of Persian tents that now colonised the hill. An army of sixty thousand or more snored, drank, or chatted in those tents. Every one of them knew what they were doing. They followed orders and received salaries in return. No responsibility. No difficult choices. They just worked for someone else. They didn't ask where their life paths were going, or even if they were on the right one. If they had they wouldn't have stayed soldiers. They'd have been someone more like the general in the war chariot.

But how had Harpagos got where he was? How had he become the greatest Persian general of all time?

Harpagos gripped the banister, but the wooden rail gave him little comfort. As he surveyed the constellations, he began to look more and more like a deserted sea captain. There was no best buddy by his side. No wife waiting for him either. She had long ago died of sorrow. He closed his eyes. The darkness on the inside and the outside met. The years went by. They folded one on top of another, until yesterday became today. Harpagos was back in Media. He was always back in Media no matter where he travelled. That day was still inside him. He was living it over and over again.

'Send this to Cyrus. It's *very* important.'

'A dead hare? What's so important about that? I'll shoot ten more if you like.'

Harpagos pulled the Persian courier up by the lapels until they were face to face.

'If it gets to Cyrus you'll be rewarded. If it doesn't, I'll kill you.'

The courier nodded and didn't stop moving his head until his feet were back on the ground.

It was nearly twenty years since the day. *That day.* For years, the poker-faced Harpagos had duped mad King Astyages into believing he was still his loyal aide. But he had remained strategically in contact with Cyrus, the baby boy he had saved by losing his own son. By now, Cyrus had become a strapping great warrior in his own right, general of the Persian army no less.

Revenge was coming. Harpagos could smell it riding on the hot desert air, kicking up the sand as it went. He breathed as he watched the courier's cart disappear out of sight. The sky was as white and implacable as stone. The cart tracks stretched into the horizon splitting the desert in two. Harpagos had waited long and hard for this day. Inside the belly of a hare now bouncing on a cart bound for Persia was a message. And it was telling Cyrus to invade Media.

A week later, Cyrus gathered his troops. An unwitting Astyages sent Harpagos out to meet him. The fight was over before it began. Media was invaded. Cyrus was emperor. And Harpagos was looking at promotion.

Circles. Round and round and round they went, those mighty wheels of consequence. Humans punished others. Others punished them, and life creaked round on its axle. Until something changed. Or evolved. Until someone somewhere decided to get off the cart and carve a brand new trail.

Harpagos drifted slowly out of the Media of years gone by and returned to his war chariot. The Lycian sky spread over him, a diamond-filled new world. The tip of a fattening moon poked over the brow of a distant hill. He watched it snag the black velvet above.

Harpagos thought he was alone. He was mistaken. Someone else was there. He was being watched. A few metres away, a woman stood inside a ring of large rocks. The limestone hunks pushed through the ground almost as though they were growing. It might have been a coincidence. It might not. This ring of rocks turned into the very place the Church of Gabriel was built a few hundred years later. The woman turned. The eruption of her hair glinted. The locks were lit up by the moon and shone like twisting silver snakes. She held her hands out in front of her with the palms facing upwards. It looked as though she was feeling for rain. Or perhaps she was saying, 'what do you want?' What was the woman doing? Praying? Sorcery? Whatever it was, she was focussed unwaveringly on Harpagos.

He was oblivious up there in his pulpit. The summer pitch clung to his forehead and his neck. His beard itched as well. As the satrap drank in the Lycian night, the thoughts looped and swirled in his head; Xanthos, fires, roasted flesh . . . his boy. It was buggered. The whole damn, ugly world was buggered.

Wearily, Harpagos climbed down from the chariot. When he reached the ground, he tilted his head to look at his mobile fortress scored onto the midnight skyline. The wooden rollers were so colossal he would have had to stand on tiptoe to see over them. The general glanced down instead. The grooves in the soil were barely visible, but once you became accustomed to the light, two great furrows snaking through the tents and into the distance were obvious. He put one foot into one of the chariot tracks. It just fitted. Then the other. And he followed those channels, step by step, back in the direction of his tent.

The woman standing inside the rock circle watched Harpagos on his slow homeward journey. Once he was out of sight she closed her eyes and inhaled.

Day Four

Gateways

Those who haven't taken on a hiking expedition will never know the unparalleled joy of washing in a proper sink with running water and a mirror. That, after three days on the road, is all the hiker requires to feel their every wish has come true. In Hatice's house in Alakilise, after the best sleep in days, I walked out of my barn. I stood at her cracked little porcelain wash basin and sighed a long, contented sigh. I brushed my teeth (twice), I combed my hair (and plaited it), I stared into the mirror and pulled at my features trying to see if I'd aged in the past three days, or not. I cleansed. I toned. I moisturised. Bottles that hadn't seen the light of day since I left Olympos, now perched behind the tap in a cheerful line of polyethylene. Oh toiletries, you were missed.

Nevertheless, I was in a hurry that morning. I'd got it into my head, the more kilometres I covered, the more I would have achieved, and the closer to some sort of epiphany I'd be (because I was still after a life-changing flash of spiritual awakening, and I was sure it was out here somewhere. In fact, I think I'd have marked the spot on the map, probably about two-thirds of the way along the trail, and I'd have indicated it with a Buddha sitting on a cushion of cloud and smiling in heavenly ecstasy). It was then that I remembered my conversation with the South Africans in the evening. I quickly pulled out my map turning it this way and that until I found what I was looking for: Xanthos. Was this the place? My holy grail? But the lad had talked about people dying there, and ghosts and some sort of nastiness, hadn't he? Hmph. It was then that I noticed the other historical site exactly next to Xanthos. Letoon. A name to inspire, if ever there was one. I drew a ring round it. It was near enough to the end of the *trail to constitute a decent enlightenment point. Who knew eh?*

Anyway, after that, I bid Hatice teze and the South Africans farewell and continued on my way. Outside the heat had already become quite difficult. This was my fourth day in Lycia, however, my pack couldn't be said to be getting any lighter, nor was I adjusting to the load. It was an awful lot like shouldering a wounded soldier, a soldier obstinately refusing to recover. It was in this hunched and hobbling manner I descended from the hills. The slope bumped and joggled all the way down to Demre town.

Having descended from such unpopulated and peaceful heights, Demre was a plunge into commotion. I was all but knocked out by it. Car horns, drills and saws, the shriek of dolmuş brakes, squealing children, slamming doors, school bells, dustcart anthems, the holler of watermelon salesmen, gates in need of oil . . . it was as though all the world's noise had convened in that dusty seaside town. And it didn't look a lot better than it sounded, either. As one of the larger plastic-coated pistons in the national agricultural engine, Demre has become disfigured by a pipeline of greenhouses. Row after row of synthetic arches corrupt the landscape. One wonders how this sort of thing is possibly allowed to manifest in a place of such rare, natural exquisiteness.

I wended my way through the baking streets. I simply wanted to get out of the place. The walking was hot and tiresome, and I was becoming exasperated enough to mutter at the state of the pavements (either non-existent so one was forced to leap out of the way in the face of every lunatic motorist hell-bent on mowing down pedestrians, or so high one required crampons and ropes just to climb up them). I think it must have been then, a wasp of a moped

144

sped up behind me. Once the cumulus of dust had settled, I noticed the rider, a village girl, all spunk and chatter.

'The Lycian Way signs have worn off, abla.'

'Typical! Do you know the way?'

'Get to the campsite at the end of the main road and go from there,' she said.

I looked at her a little unimpressed. Well, I had no desire to lumber on a busy carriageway, had I?

'Hop on the back, if you like. I'll take you!'

I raised an eyebrow. It looked improbable. This little scamp, me, and my pack, all toppled upon a moped? But I hated Demre enough by then, not to care. I clambered behind her, and the motorbike wobbled. She steadied it. Then we were off. The engine whirred hysterically, while my rucksack lurched precariously behind me like a drunk. My tiny, tan-skinned driver gripped the handle-bars and grinned, as happy-go-lucky as you please. That was the last thing I saw, because after that, I decided to screw my eyes shut.

We arrived at a river mouth. As I climbed off the bike, my pack-casualty almost toppled me. The girl eyed it dubiously, and I felt my face prickle in embarrassment. Well it was embarrassing! This great hump of unsightly baggage hampering my every move. For a moment, I imagined how much easier it might have been if my husband was with me, because at least I could have dumped some of it on him.

After a goodbye smile and wave, I began to walk again. The path started at a reed-filled flatland by a beach. As I advanced upwards into the hills, I noticed, the waterway wasn't so much one channel, as a tangle of unruly streams winding in various directions out to sea – a small delta. The road wound upwards, along rocky cliff edges and dappled hilltops. The sun climbed alongside me. While I ambulated, I heard my mind. It was making nearly

145

as much racket as Demre, the thoughts clanking through like machinery. I realised four days had passed, and in that time I had met not one ill-disposed human being, encountered not one peril, not one intimidation. Rather, people seemed to be springing out of every crevice to assist me. They escorted me to places they had otherwise no intention of going, housed me with no thought of repayment, they shared their resources, their knowledge, and their time. I simply hadn't ever noticed, or considered such a thing possible. Ever. I had always assumed I was alone, and it was inevitable people wanted something; relationship necessarily entailed some sort of agenda.

Alright, I daresay there will be those who insist the girl on the bike did want something, if only a little excitement, but I think they are confusing agenda with exchange, and it is thanks to Lycia I have learned the difference. Exchange has a spontaneous quality to it, a sense of balance and beauty, while agenda involves a covert plan in which balance is usurped by an attempt at exploitation. Agenda always leaves at least one party with a sense of dissatisfaction.

So I was walking. Stunted shrubs guarded the path edges in prickly regiments. For the duration of the afternoon, I went astray just once. At that point, a shepherd popped fortuitously out of nowhere, a muddle of goats bleating and chewing about him. I watched the slit-eyed heads reaching up to clip small twigs off in their teeth, while their tail-ends defecated where they stood and provided the trees with fresh compost.

'Do you know where the Lycian Way is?' I threw the question out half-heartedly, not expecting much of an answer.

'Aye. Ooer there!' The goatherd was chewing on a stick as he pointed. I was surprised. I mean, shepherds are *free spirits and hardly use waymarked trails. Why should he know where it was?*

For two hours, I marched onward and upward inhaling the extraordinary panorama about and below. The veins of reed-lined waterways wriggled into dark, blue welts out at sea. The lumpy backs of peninsulas were stencilled one upon the other out to the edge of the Earth, and the twisted fingers of olive groves curled sourly like neglected bonsais. I progressed step by step, breath by breath, until I was lost again, lost upon a spot of flat, stony ground.

Yet was I really astray? Or was this the exact spot I was supposed to be? Aha, perhaps a little bit of shamanic wisdom was finally seeping into me, after all. You see, there in a place which appeared to be nowhere at all, I had suddenly stumbled upon what I can only describe as ancient treasure. I stopped in my tracks. Well, I had little choice. Directly before me towered an enormous wall of rock, and fashioned into it was a row of the most incredible Lycian tombs I had ever seen.

As I mentioned earlier, when one resides in a country such as mine, where the clutter of ancient history spills out from every nook and cranny, where two-thousand-years-old is recent history . . . well, one tends to become a little blasé regarding old stones. But by day four, with nothing else but nature and antique ruins to amuse me, even I found myself wondering about all the feet walking my walk, all the lives lived on this tiny spot of earth, all the words spoken, all the births and deaths and tears and laughter. Well, where do they go? Are they sort of stacked up one upon the other? Are we the only living beings to hold the past inside us? Or are there others?

Evening was now lurking in the lengthening shadows. It stole into the cracks and holes. I swung my *rucksack onto the ground and trod carefully up to the large carvings. They were almost perfect, as if no one had touched them since the grave robbers. Presumably, they had belonged to someone rich and . . . Lycian? Ahem. Yes. That was, I'm chagrined to say, the best I could do.*

I put my hands in the hollows which had housed the corpses, and my scalp immediately prickled like a cactus. The apertures were cool and dark, and very eerie. It was then, something occurred to me. I turned to my backpack and fumbled for my map. Perhaps I could glean some sort of a clue regarding my location – a site of this quality simply had to be marked, didn't it? I scanned the length of the Lycian Way tracing my finger along the dotted red line; Demre, Kaş, Kalkan, Xanthos. In each quadrant, I earnestly hunted the three dots denoting historical remains. Nothing. Not a peep. It was inexplicable. How could this place have evaded the map? There and then, I made a note to add ghosts, angels, creepy forests, and haunted tombs to my 'real feel' map for the novice hiker. One needs to know these things before one sets off, don't you think?

I folded the map back up. And then things turned very untoward indeed. You may think I make this up, but I swear the rock-face changed. Obviously, I was seeing things, because the tombs seemed to be awake, or even stirring, and clearly tombs are not alive so can neither wake nor stir. Finally, to add a little 'atmosphere' to the proceedings, dusk turned the dimmer switch. It looked as though the vaults were receding deeper and deeper into the rock, and – well how should I put this, without qualifying myself here and now for certification? – it felt as though parts of me fell into those tombs, as well. I closed my eyes. Oh dear. The black holes in my past were here, too. The past and its troubles. Those pockets of resentment had been waiting, waiting for a time and a place to clamber out and breathe.

Inhale. Exhale. Breathe.

ೞ⃝ೲ

The shadowy grave-beds of the mid-nineteen nineties were here. Their ghosts whispered on the back of biting winter winds. With a chaotic skyline of minarets, construction sites, and the clutter of red-tiled roofs as her backdrop, Ayşe finally won her divorce. She was twenty-four.

She dug deep. Work. Struggle. Survive. She rented an apartment and sent her son to a kindergarten, while she won the bread. The edges of her soul hardened as she pitted herself against life. A life that crawled relentlessly on. A life that felt like someone else's. Ayşe was alone, and it would probably never be different. She was a single mum in a country which had never heard of the concept. Even her ID card proclaimed she was *dul* – a widow.

Perhaps the only saving grace was Ayşe lived in Istanbul. Ah, and despite all its woes, who didn't want to be there? It was a city like no other. Unmanageable. Incompliant. A civic jumble. It sprawled along estuaries. Cuboid apartments and lavish domes agglomerated the length of the Bosphorus. In which other city could you board a ferry to get to work for the price of a sandwich? In which other city did you arrange to meet your friends for coffee in Europe, or Asia, or both in one day? Where else did you drive at midnight over suspension bridges feeling the breeze of the West flutter through your hair, while dulcet eastern melodies wafted in through your windows?

That's, at least, how Istanbul should have been. But, things were changing. By the mid nineteen-nineties,

149

Istanbul stoically accepted her fate as she bloated beyond all recognition. Every week, thousands from the eastern provinces were swarming towards her. The silken hems of the city's multi-layered skirts began to fray. All about her periphery, *gecekondus* latched on – neighbourhoods of poor housing built overnight to evade planning permission regulations. Suddenly, new faces began to appear, faces hungry for that forbidden paradise, Europe. But also faces of desperation. Faces of people on the run. For no matter how much the authorities tried to hide it, everyone knew, nightfall was once again stealing through Turkey.

Thousands of kilometres away in the east, a war was going on. The PKK and the Turkish army were slogging it out in the hills and caves. Mothers and fathers wailed as both sides sent thousands of their children to die in a fight whose only outcome was to flatter the egos of their leaders, and line the pockets of arms manufacturers.

The refugees from the war were plenty. Political fear and instability trickled down. Your average Turkish person was dealing with hyper-inflation, an absurdly expensive and unreliable electricity supply, and corruption on every stratum of government officialdom. Road blocks were commonplace. Your vehicle, your *dolmuş* or your coach could be spot-checked at any given time. This was a very bad time to mislay your identity card.

Shadows.
Buried deep.
In
side
Under
ground.

150

Where Turkey went, Ayşe necessarily followed. She had her own shadows to bury. It was all about hacking through the joyless sedge of days feeling the hard, wet rock face of her existence slipping beneath her fingers. There had to be more to it than this. There had to be something better.

One day, she was wandering the length of Bakırköy high street with a female friend from work. The shop fronts were cluttered with plastic mannequins wearing bell-bottom trousers and tight woollen sweaters. The paved street was crammed with pedestrians of all shapes and sizes. Roly-poly middle-aged women in long coats and shawls pushed past sleek young ladies sporting impossible hairstyles. Short, thin men in flat caps loitered in shop fronts alongside Al Capone lookalikes sucking Camel cigarettes. Young, blonde women from any number of ex-Soviet states clipped along in raffish heels, eyed by fat swarthy fellows with too much facial hair.

Ayşe and her friend circumnavigated a *tulumba* seller. His wheeled glass box displayed an aluminium plate laden with syrupy creations. The winter sun flecked the Bosphorus with tiny gold ingots.

The pair reached the harbour. Gulls squawked about the concrete waterfront as fishermen huddled around their lines, rods arcing optimistically into the waves. The two women inserted their *jetons* into the metal turnstile. They pushed their way towards the waiting ferry.

'I've had enough of it Sevim. I'm going nowhere living hand to mouth like this. I want something for my future. And Umut's future.' Ayşe shouted to her friend through the swarm of folk surging to board.

'You need to get yourself on the property ladder, girl.'

'Tell me something I don't know. But how?'

151

The women stepped onto the gang-plank. They made their way to a couple of wooden seats. A *çay* seller was zipping nimbly about the rows of passengers, his circular tray sprouting a garden of tulip glasses, all rooted in red and white plastic saucers. Ayşe and her friend reached out for a glass of tea as the ferry sounded its horn. It was then, amidst the smell of sea salt and fish, and with Bakırköy harbour receding behind them, the friend mentioned a new cooperative project.

'It's quite a good deal Ayşe. My brother did it, and now he's sitting pretty. You buy the apartment cheaper if you contribute to the building costs before the construction ends.'

Ayşe gulped her tea down. She watched a entrepreneurial gull sweep down and peck a piece of simit from a passenger's hand. It was a reasonable idea. The only trouble was, the block of flats in question was currently nothing but a few foundation channels dug into the Turkish soil.

That night, back in her rented apartment, Ayşe mulled it all over. She was dying to get off the treadmill of travail. It would be wise to grab this chance by the throat before it scampered off into the wilderness of a new construction law. But there was no getting away from it. No matter how much she trimmed the edges of her budget, she couldn't afford to pay rent, pay her son's childcare, and put up the house instalments. Chewing anxiously over calculations, she eventually realised there was only one exit open to her. Her parents.

The next day, she gritted her teeth, dialled the numbers, and asked if she could live with them until the flat was built. After five years of denying their daughter's situation, mum and dad accepted this new proposal. Ayşe submerged herself a little deeper. She left her apartment and her independence. She stuffed her soul into a box she hid in a cubby hole, faraway in the future.

ಬಂOಀ

Istanbul receded. The Bosphorus, the gulls, her parents' house, all sped away. Ayşe saw the streaked walls of tombs appearing. She felt the evening breeze warm on her cheeks. The Lycian sun had set leaving the sky as grey as a slate miner's dream.

Standing in front of the ancient tombs, she leaned her forehead on the warm limestone. The stark outlines of the tombs dissolved into the dusk. It was the time of day strange things happen. Things that cause transformation.

It all began with the air. It began to press heavily against the lone hiker thickening about her like a glutinous resin. She felt stuck. As she stood there with her palms laid on the intricate grooves in the rock, she gradually became aware of something else. Someone was behind her, she was sure. She could feel their eyes on her back, studying her. Who was it? What the . . . ? She whipped about scanning the twilight and seeing no one. Nothing. Not a single thing she could put her now filthy, scratched finger on.

ಬಂOಀ

The lands of Lycia are a treasure trail, precious gems of truth buried somewhere below. Within forests. Under sand. Beneath sea. There they lay waiting. Waiting for the day. The day when someone, somewhere, lays a hand on them. Touches them. For it's through connection the stones tell their stories. It's through feeling real messages are conveyed.

153

Tombs. Graves. The beds of the dead. What tales might they have to tell? All about the world, folk have their ideas about what happens to the dead. Some say they return to Earth in other bodies. Others say their souls go to heaven or hell. The yogis of India claim human spirits are stuck to their physical bodies by something called prana – an astral glue holding the physical to the non-physical. When they die, this glue abandons the body, and as soon as it does they are corpses. The Taoists call this same stuff 'Qi'. The Turks have another word 'can'. 'Can' is your life force, the power of your soul to keep 'you' in the world. Pity the native speakers of English. With their inadequate language for such matters, they are left fumbling with the amorphous term 'energy'.

Even so, one thread runs through every tradition. Humans are not just physical matter. There are pieces of them that are invisible, pieces that wriggle through spaces, pieces that sneak far beyond them.

The tomb Ayşe had stumbled on to, had seen very well what happened to the dead. It towered there quietly holding its knowledge. That hulk of limestone remembered the collision of two dimensions. For, once upon a time, the cold corpse of a man had entered its gaping mouth. Drained of its *can*, the body had been as stiff and unyielding as stone. The spirit was there too, and yet not there, pulling and biting at the matter it could no longer inhabit. That conflict – the struggle between the physical and the not, between the corporeal and astral – tore secret passages in the atoms of the rock, deep rifts in the flow of space and time.

Those great slabs of limestone appeared impenetrable, yet were they? For unbeknown to anyone but the rocks themselves, things were sliding. Like water through a crack in a dyke, the past was dripping into the present, while the present leaked steadily back into the past. Somewhere, an opening which spanned millennia had manifested. While Ayşe stood at one end staring at a tomb, two-and-a-half-thousand years back along the tunnel of time, someone else was approaching. He was initially nothing but a speck in the distance, his silhouette gradually taking human form. But sure enough, that 'someone' was closing in. And that 'someone' was General Harpagos, commander in chief of the Achaemenid army.

ೞО೮ಽ

The iron of Harpagos' helmet was clearly visible, and it bounced and shook as his chariot proceeded up the slope. His army trailed beside and behind him, a fan-tail of spears and men. Xanthos – poor Xanthos – was no more than two weeks behind them.

The general trundled along the track with the sun plump and heavy in the sky. The sea was dark and moody beneath a crest of bronze waves. The wooden wheels of Harpagos' chariot were turning, while the massive manpower of the Persian army muscled its way upwards into the hills. An eagle soared overhead, its wings silhouetted against the reddening sky. The great bird arced and looped looking remarkably similar to the winged Faravahar crest on Harpagos' armour, the icon of the Persians. The satrap shielded his eyes from the sun's glare and watched the creature drawing its wide, predatory circles.

The Persians finally reached a place to rest. By chance or design, this was the exact spot, two-and-a-half thousand years in the future, Ayşe was stumbling on to those ancient Lycian tombs. This side of time's billowing curtain the small plateau was empty. The rock face stood unetched and smooth.

The general stroked the mesh of his beard and inhaled the warm dry air. Then he raised his arm. Tens of thousands of men clanked and scuffed to a halt. The last flickers of light were playing on the rocks, making them turn and shimmer. One more night was approaching in this bizarre country; a country of freaks, and spooks, and bewitching landscapes. But before darkness had its say, the sun bade Lycia a spectacular farewell. The entire vista burst into life. All around the stones quivered and rippled gold, russet, and violet. As they performed their sunset dance, they seemed to be reaching out, calling. Even Harpagos had to admit, Lycia was one of the most beautiful places he had ever seen. And he'd seen a few.

It was 545 BC. Back in those days, folk were further from their minds and closer to the nature of things. Back then, they saw spirits and angels and banshees. They heard the whispers of muses and the commands of the gods. Perhaps they glimpsed the staggered vistas of the block universe every now and again. Perhaps this was what they had always been seeing.

Harpagos leaned his back on the smooth rock of the promontory. He felt its crust somewhere beneath his purple smock and his armour. A swarm of images swirled in his mind. They stuck their hooks into his mood, dragging him further into his gloom. He wondered if there was a place the past didn't exist. A place he could run away too. A place with no memories or images or words. Harpagos' owl eyes lowered. The grizzled fleece of his beard hid the grim line of his mouth. He stood up, ambled a little forward and turned round to consider the sheerness of the rock. Then he stretched out his hand and touched its limestone flank. He wondered whether a rock could know anything of pain, or hate, or anger. He wondered if it was less wretched than him.

And then it all became quiet. No one would have believed it possible (least of all Harpagos himself) but his mind was finally, if briefly, silenced. For once, it couldn't find a respectable answer to the question. And it was in this small pocket of unexpected peace, something saw a gap.

The occurrence was so fleeting, Harpagos was never completely sure if he had seen anything, or not. It could have been the sun, or . . . or his mind. He saw it as he was staring absently at the rock face. He saw *her*. A figure at the rock. A woman. Fair-haired. He tried to move his feet, but some idiot had glued his sandals to the ground. And for some reason, he couldn't close his bottom lip. It hung there like a gaping satchel. That was before 'she' turned around and looked straight at him. The Persian commander blinked. What the . . . ? But the strange vision had already vanished before he could finish the question.

General Harpagos whirled about. He scanned the field of helmets, tunics, and spears swarming around him. Had anyone else seen her? He saw one of his officers chewing absently on a carob in front of him. The rest of his attendants were staring in disinterest about them, scuffing the dust with their sandals.

Harpagos beckoned a short beady-eyed man in his entourage to follow him. He walked past the rock face, towards an olivine patch of trees. The man touched the apogee of his hat, and strode out in pursuit. This was the Zoroastrian priest. It had been a long time since Harpagos had bothered with religion. His contempt for the magi was as large and wide as the lands of Persia herself. But, he had seen more things he didn't understand in the last fortnight, than he had in the rest of his life. Who knew? May be a man of spirit could shed some light.

The two men came to a standstill beneath the ample boughs of an oak. As they turned to face each other, the

157

priest bowed, as was the Persian custom. Evening was stroking the branches. It rustled quietly through the leaves. It was a simple question Harpagos asked, one children everywhere ask all the time. 'Do you believe in ghosts?'

The priest's eyes narrowed very slightly gauging the exact distance between his beliefs, and the precariousness of his political position. He reached tentatively into the dark and parried the question with an inquisitive look. The way he tilted his head indicated he was expecting more in the way of details.

'I thought I saw a woman here in front of that rock, did you see her?' Harpagos was half-whispering, half-spitting as he glared at the clergyman.

The small black eyes widened, just a little too much, a little too quickly. A flush rose to the priest's cheeks, and he lowered his gaze to collect his thoughts. For this man of religion had seen nothing, and if anyone here were to witness a spirit, then surely it had to be him.

'My lord, there are no ghosts here. There is but one God. Ahura Mazda. The rest can only be lies!' The eyes were now tiny darts.

Without further ado, the priest summoned his acolytes and sent them off to find wood. A fire had to be built, a worship led, and superstition forever banished. Harpagos said nothing. He let the priest have his limelight and complete his ritual. As the flames licked and teased the dry sticks, he watched the vain, orange tips prancing in the darkening air, all vying for supremacy. And he concluded once again, as he had concluded many times in his life, ultimately a true leader is accountable only to himself. He must follow his own gut. There surely lay the only pure truth.

The only trouble was, Harpagos' gut was telling him something he didn't want to hear. Lycia was haunted. More to the point, it was haunting him.

ɞ

The woman stood behind the large ring of fire worshippers. Her hair had been brought to life by the flames, and the curls cavorted in the glow. It was the wildest head of hair anyone had seen this side of the Aegean. It might have been an entity in its own right. The woman's big black eyes rested on Harpagos. She wasn't praying or weaving magic tonight. No need. The woman smiled. It was an all-knowing smile. Because Harpagos wasn't the only one who had seen Leto in the rock. No, not at all.

Day Five

New Territory

The previous evening, I had scrambled as far away as I could from the tombs and ended up erecting my tent in a thicket nearby. That night, I endured hours of racing thoughts, heart palpitations and abject fear. I'd like to say I awoke the next day, but that would imply I slept.

In the morning, I pulled back my flysheet door to find the trees bristling, oak and pine limbs scratching at the morning sky. I just wanted to get out of there. The entire place spooked me half to death. As it happened, the crypts would haunt me for a long time. Over future years, I would walk the Lycian Way more than eight times, yet no matter how hard I looked, I was never to rediscover them. Do you know what? It was as though they had disappeared into the rocks.

But creepy, laws-of-physics-defying burial chambers aside, I had by now settled into the hike. I'd grown accustomed to the semi-permanent grime which coated me, and even my 'fruity' smell. Well, alright, that is a slight exaggeration. Smelling was actually a source of constant worry. Whenever I saw water, I was washing in it, not that it helped. Less than ten paces later, I would be perspiring, and then ten paces after that I'd be covered in dust, or burrs, or pine needles. Even so, I had at least half-heartedly accepted my appearance was beyond my control. The thing I was more concerned about was, although it was day five, I felt I hadn't made much progress. I don't mean in terms of kilometres, I mean internal progress. In many ways, I was just the same person as when I started. Yes, I was hiking. Yes, I was proving people wrong, but so what? I was still rehashing my past in my mind, over and over again. I was still far from living in the hallowed present moment I had heard so much about. I wasn't enlightened, I hadn't become a *shaman, and the only visions I was having were flashbacks I'd have rather forgotten.*

I restarted the trail, half of me hoping something would happen, half of me hoping it wouldn't. Despite my proximity to the sea, the coastal road was non-negotiable. It was blocked by unfriendly thickets of hispid shrubs, true vegetative goblins they were. Although the Mediterranean must have been all about me, it was invisible, concealed behind a bas-relief of sun-scorched mountain tops, the peaks holding back heaven like a line of jagged temples.

Almost unconsciously, I drifted on to a goatherd's path uphill and found myself battling against a slope of rubble and scrub. The sheer intensity of the sunlight, and the blinding whiteness it drove out of the stones, forced me to squint, even beneath sunglasses and brimmed canvas hat.

Eventually, after an awful lot of sliding and scuffing of shoes, I reached yet another mountain hamlet; humble, remote, and yes, as usual, deserted. Silence wafted about the forsaken homes like a humanless mist. The usually garrulous mouths of the wooden doorways were firmly closed and bolted. I stopped and wondered for a moment. What could have happened this time?

It was then I spied a sign of life. In front of one of the houses a little way off, an elderly couple was perched upon a makeshift timber balcony. The two of them were sharing breakfast, and I could tell from the silver spouts curling from the steel teapot.

'Hello there! Hello!'

Unfortunately, the old dears were somewhat hard of hearing, and they remained hunched in their rickety chairs, unheeding.

Shrugging, I trotted over. The old man wore a crocheted white skullcap, while his wife peered out from a lilac gauze headscarf. When they saw me saddled like a workhorse, the two of them guffawed. The woman thrust the teapot in my direction.

'For Godsake put that bag down and have a cup of tea! You'll cripple yerself!'

'Well, the trouble is teze, if I put it down, I can't get it back on again.' I grinned. 'Anyway, where is everyone? Every village I pass through is empty?'

'Ah, they've all gone up to the yayla,' the man said. His face poked out from the skullcap like a little brown acorn. Ah the yayla. This is a high-level plateau with cooler air that villagers move to in summer when the heat becomes too much. What a life, eh? They could simply up and leave, migrating like geese. There were no bosses to negotiate with, no mortgages to be paid, the entanglements we take for granted elsewhere simply didn't exist for them. Did such people have paths? I wondered. Or were they wandering aimlessly like herds of wayward goats?

For reasons I will never understand, the couple knew all about the trail; its high points and low points, its starts and stops. They seemed to view it all as an amusing sideshow, a wandering circus bringing troops of foolhardy foreigners all waving strange concertinas of paper to file past their door. After a little hand-waving, gesticulating and shouting from them, I gathered I ought to turn right.

I was now on my way to Kekova. Now, Kekova is an untainted treasure on what is fast becoming a rather spoiled coastline. Stringent building laws have allowed the village to remain much as it always has been; a string of cosy fish restaurants perched upon a wooden jetty, a handful of quaint stone houses rendered pansiyons, a cove of water transparent enough to reveal sunken Lycian cities. If ever a place inspired one to consider the possibility of Atlantis, Kekova would be it.

Kekova was a way off yet though. As the tiny hamlet disappeared behind me, my road emerged as a torrid, black line of tarmac. It wended its way over a landscape of saffron-coloured fields and tawny peaks. But the view couldn't hide the fact, this was a trunk road, and my heart sank at the dispiriting sight of near on a blister's worth of asphalt. Tarmac is the hiker's equivalent of gruel, something one chomps through out of bare necessity. Personally, I'd prefer to walk twice as far on a meandering mountain track than trudge upon an automobile road. Perhaps it's the uncompromising functionality of it; its slick delivery of us from A to B. Perhaps deep down we don't really want to go from A to B at all, we'd rather loop, and swirl, and get thoroughly lost.

ༀ○ཚ

The tarmac sizzled. It sweated and snarled. But it couldn't read Ayşe. It couldn't communicate with her at all. This was because it was soulless. It hadn't been through the Earth's heart and back again like the rocks. It comprised no bodies of the once-living, like the soil. It wouldn't have known what life force was, if vitality had surged forth and driven straight over it. Tarmac was in purgatory. But luckily not forever. One day Gaia would break it down, and sculpt it into something new.

Ayşe carried on walking. Or trudging. The predictability of the straight road dulled her senses. She moved back inside her head. This is why she didn't see one of the rocks at the roadside wobble. It moved slightly to the right, stopped, and then moved again.

Very slowly, four legs pushed out from the blotchy grey lump, followed by a scraggy thumb-sized head. The eyes peered out from their wrinkly beds. They peered left

164

and right to see where the strange vibrations had come from. Those eyes fell on Ayşe. Tortoise stayed very still. He'd been around a while. Experience had taught him invisibility was often the best policy.

Despite their lumbering gait, tortoises are survivors. On average, they live roughly as long as human beings. And sometimes much longer. Tortoise was forty-seven, nearly a decade older than Ayşe. You could tell by the concentric rings on his shell. Like a tree, he carried his age and his story inscribed for all to see. All in all, it made you wonder. How could an animal as primitive as Tortoise be as adept at surviving as a human? Weren't humans the pinnacle of evolutionary complexity? Weren't they supposed to be more accomplished in the art of prolonging life, compared to something further back along the evolutionary trail, something as unimpressive as a small reptile in a shell?

Tortoise waited until the thud of Ayşe's boots could be heard no more. He was by necessity a patient creature, always trying get somewhere, step by heavy step. He moved so laggardly, it could take hours to advance a few metres. By the time he arrived, had he forgotten why he had set out in the first place? Or was it that by then, it didn't matter anyway?

The ground eventually stopped its thumping. All became still at the roadside. Then Tortoise rose. He put one foot in front of the other. One. In front. Of the other. And shuffled in the direction of the tarmac. The sun beat down on his shell. The soil beneath him was a baking desert. It was just as Tortoise's right foot touched the asphalt, he heard a terrifying din.

The earth was trembling. Shaking. And this time it wasn't in a tone he liked. He was too slow to move. All he could do was freeze and retract inside his shell. And there he sat. Waiting. Waiting for the moment. The moment silence would come again, and he would live another day.

It was strange, but despite his longevity, Tortoise had never pondered whether there might be more to life than just surviving. That wasn't Tortoise's job.

ଔ○ଓ

A noise brought me to my senses. It was a coarse squealing in the distance, and it seemed to be approaching at speed. The squeal soon turned into a roar, and I whisked around to see a motorbike rushing in my direction. The bike drew closer and closer. Then to my dismay, it pulled over directly next to me. I took a guarded step backwards and surveyed the rider; a middle-aged man, rather thin and with bushy eyebrows. He grinned and offered me a lift.

Now as an aside, it's not a custom of mine to hop upon the motorbikes of unfamiliar men. Certainly, it's not an activity I would particularly recommend to anybody else either. There was, after all, the horrible story of the Italian woman who decided to hitchhike across the world dressed in a bridal gown. She was being sponsored for charity, as I recall, which only makes the outcome seem worse. The story was an embarrassment for the country, and a headache for the tourist board, as well. The poor girl was raped and murdered by a truck driver in the south east.

It is at this juncture, I'd like to utter a word or two regarding what I refer to as the power of discrimination, and the value of understanding the culture you are in before throwing your life into the hands of any given maniac in charge of a vehicle. Now, it might appear to the outsider that I would throw caution to the wind and run any manner of risks when in search of a dream, as if

166

dreamers were peculiarly impervious to the hazards of real life. If this is the impression I have given, it's an inaccurate one, because caution is always at the forefront of my mind when I walk alone. And a great many troubles are so easily avoided with a little background knowledge.

First, the Turkish tourist industry has long held a vested interest in projecting an image of our land as a place where anything goes, where one can stroll to the market in a thong, or make love on a beach, or ride a bicycle with preposterous amounts of bottom flesh hanging out. Certainly, while there are plenty of opportunities for all the above, it is nonetheless crucial to recognise, those opportunities present themselves in tourist resorts, and even 5 km away from such a spot, another more traditional culture prevails, one where tottering about in a bikini is tantamount to pole dancing naked in a church.

Second, is the benefit of heeding first impressions. I think one knows from the first instant all one needs to about strangers. We sense immediately whether someone is a generally decent soul, or that there's something not quite right. And we must act upon these hunches! When a shepherd or a taxi driver spends more than five minutes conversing with one's chest, it's no good reasoning this away as a cultural difference, and therefore that everything will be alright. No Turkish woman thinks this is alright. Such behaviour is the height of rudeness, and deserves a response in kind. The fact five out of ten men you meet might lose control of their eye focus in this way, isn't an indication of its acceptability. In such situations, a brisk and haughty 'no thank you', a withering look, or simply stalking off with your nose in the air can go a long way to preventing an escalation in unpleasantness.

Anyway, back on the Kekova road, the man on the motorbike had offered me a lift, and he had possessed the decency to voice the offer to my face rather than any other part of my anatomy. Thus, I abandoned the trail and that dreary cable of tarmac, and clambered aboard the bike. Off we sped. The hot wind rushed over my skin as I watched grassy domes and khaki blips of brush flick by.

We soon arrived in Kekova. The bike driver cruised through a dirt road lined with pretty stone and mud buildings. He left me at the jetty. From there, I perambulated past tables with white napkins and wine glasses surrounded by a dozen or so foreign tourists supping cold beer. I started to feel a little out of place. Everyone turned to stare at me, presumably, because I was caked in a thin layer of dust, strands of hair poking out at various angles, and tottering under my backpack. I lowered my head. Suddenly, my appearance mattered again, and to be honest I didn't like it.

Then, just before I left the village proper, I decided to buy a watermelon from one of the grocers. Now, you might well wonder why any sensible mountain-walker with a pack the size of a dead body would buy a watermelon. And you'd be right. It is, presumably, the most cumbersome fruit in all creation. But for reasons that remain elusive, when I saw it, I suddenly experienced a bout of weight amnesia. Outside the small shop, I severed a slice from the green basketball, its pink innards yielding their delicious juice as I bit into the flesh. The remainder I slid into a plastic bag which in turn I squeezed into the top of my backpack. This brought my total load to nearly twenty-five kilograms. Oh yes, I would pay for this injudicious decision the following day.

Off I went again; me and my pack and a watermelon. My next target was a spot called Aperlae, a place I had never visited, or even heard of. The path was a winding, looping labyrinth crawling with rough tangled bushes, none of which respected the trail at all. Thorns twisted out haphazardly. They dragged relentlessly on my rucksack. Eventually, the bushes receded, and then the drought commenced in earnest. On either side, a desert of flat earth stretched as far as the eye could see. It was a dusty sea devoid of both trees and wells. I began to wilt.

On the trail to Aperlae, not one drop of water was to be found. All I had was my watermelon. But I felt rather proud of myself, because I didn't panic, nor did I attempt to force water out of dry rock using sheer willpower. Instead, I began to wait with a certain curiosity as to when, and from where, my next drink would arise. I think this might be what people call 'acceptance', isn't it?

It was then, I hobbled into the stony olive-strewn cove of Aperlae. By this time, I was both parched and exhausted. The bay comprised a small disc of water. It could almost have passed for a lake, except for the pudgy fingers of land opening at one end. A wide channel of blue pulsed in and out. At the far end of the bay was a cobbled stone house, the masonry of which was a work of art; white limestone chunks slotted together in a composition that was at once mosaic and jigsaw. There were forget-me-not blue shutters lying flat against the windows, and a shaded terrace. A small motorboat was tethered from the wooden jetty and bobbed graciously upon the tiny rippling waves.

Yet there was something not quite right about Aperlae. Apart from this one building it was completely deserted. Unlike the other villages I'd passed through, this wasn't a recent abandonment. I could see the crumbling skeletons of other stone houses all about. There had been life here once upon a time. But what had happened to it?

Then I spotted something unexpected; a facility next to the house. On closer inspection, it transpired to be a café,

169

though who its clientele could have been is hard for me to say. It reminded me of those lonesome gas stations one sees on long empty highways in American horror films. I half expected a door to creak on its hinges and a crazed hillbilly with a shotgun to lumber out of it. But I was thirsty, so I dropped my hideous pack to the ground, pulled out a chair and slumped into it.

A woman popped out in jeans and a pink T shirt, conspicuously shotgun-free. It was somewhat bizarre in this lonely place, but I ordered a drink. A steaming glass of Nescafe appeared in front of me, but that wasn't all. The woman smiled and placed a small, white shell next to the coffee cup. I looked at it. It was a hole-riddled excuse for a shell, and I wondered why she'd left it there. I held it in one hand while I sipped my drink.

How difficult it is for me to convey the joy of sitting on that terrace. There I was, experiencing the adventure of my life, all alone yet surviving. No, it wasn't simply surviving at all. I was sleeping rough, scavenging for sustenance, my socks were so filthy I hardly dared to look at them, I was exhausted, and parts of my body ached I had no idea housed muscles, yet had I ever felt this content before? Ha!

I was starting to believe I could do almost anything, and I had been hoodwinked into playing it safe, that life was secretly on my side. I had also long realised Persimmon Legs was an idiot and didn't know what he was talking about. I mean, never mind earthquakes and the economy, how can you possibly plan five years ahead when you have no idea who you will be by then, or what on Earth you will want?

৪Оෆ

Ayşe held the shell between her thumb and her index finger. She turned it around and around. It looked like she was twisting a dial, or turning the volume up. The shell was a spiral. It coiled down like a staircase in an ancient house. Each whorl went to a different floor. Each turn told a different story. Once upon a time that shell had been a snail. A very special snail. A murex sea snail. And two thousand years ago it had been murdered, all for its purple mucus. But though the body had vanished, the shell still held onto the past. It remembered Aperlae. It remembered it very well.

It might have been difficult for the moderns to believe. All that was left of her by then was a single house. At one time though, the harbour had bustled with folk; merchants, fishermen, and murex snail snatchers. Aperlae had been teeming with those little snails – they were worth more than their weight in gold – and just like at Phoenicia, the dye made from their tiny bodies turned the wealthy an exclusive shade of violet.

Nothing lasts forever, though. Aperlae held on for a good thousand years or more. But it was the Lycian soil that cut her down to size. The town was near a fault-line, a fissure that plunged through the Earth's crust to God only knew where. Was it karma? Was it a case of Zoroastrian justice? Whatever the cause, over time the rocky crust sank. The waterfront edged over the land. The Mediterranean – home of the murex – slowly but surely began to gulp down districts of Aperlae.

I can still see Ayşe sitting on that terrace drinking her coffee. Did she know, hidden under the shivering, blue skin of the sea in front of her, fortunes had been made, ships had docked, and millions upon millions of snails had been decimated? If she had rolled back the shoreline of time and listened to the waves and the wind, what would they have

171

told her? She may have heard tales from Aperlae in her heyday. Or then again, she may not. Because there was a stronger connection elsewhere. Another apparitional intersection on the quirky Möbius strip of time. As she inhaled the timeless Lycian air, and turned the shell of the Murex in her hand, the past began to relay its special message. Quietly. Softly. Almost imperceptibly. Ayşe closed her eyes, breathed deeply and smiled. Did she hear it? Or didn't she? The voices still echoing about the bay. For there, two-and-a-half thousand years beyond her, Aperlae was moving. Her waters were swirling with other times.

ಶ౦ಌ

'Hold her steady, will yer?'

'I'm tryin' me hardest. Lawd. We're all over the place!'

'Oi! hang on. What's that?'

'What the bleedin' Nora?'

'Bloody hell! Are they soldiers?'

'Whoa! Oh God! We're buggered! We're all bloody dead!'

'What do we do?'

'Get back there and help 'em. Get the oars!'

'Who are they? *What* are they?'

'How the hell should I know? Just grab them oars, *now!*'

A couple of local fishermen were pitching in a small wooden rowing boat tugging at a fishing net. There was a racket. Yammering. Yawping. Clattering. The mouths of the two fishers fell agape as the trickle of soldiers turned into a river of colour. It flooded into the cove. The Persians had reached Aperlae.

In a matter of minutes, sixty thousand men shattered the tranquillity of the fishing village. One of the fishermen cursed. The other squinted and pinched himself. Then, for no sensible reason whatsoever, the pair of them began to yank frantically at the submerged rope net sending their little boat into a frenzy of lurches. Next, they abandoned their net. They grabbed their oars, and took to speed rowing. It was futile. The Persians were all over their little village before they could even get close to the shore.

Harpagos' chariot drove deep furrows into the sand. It soon came to a squeaky standstill. Shielding his helmet-clad face from the glare of the sun, the warlord stepped down onto the small beach. He removed one of his leather gloves and stooped to run his fingers through the wet sand. Before long, his hand came upon a small, white creature. He picked up the shimmering snail and surveyed it. 'Crazy Lycians,' he muttered to himself, shaking his sweaty head. 'They're sitting on a damn gold-mine, and they haven't a clue!'

He replaced the snail at the water's edge. Then he marched off in the direction of the villagers. Most of them were cowering in front of their homes, or staring out from behind tiny, rundown doorways. As the Persian general reached what was presumably the centre of this hamlet, an old man stepped forward.

The elder's knotty grey hair fell below his shoulders. He tottered on bandy legs. He was 'dressed' in a grotty smock, and when he opened his mouth Harpagos was greeted by a broken fence of teeth. The old man dropped to his knees in front of the Persian. He babbled frantically in Lycian. Harpagos had no idea what the chap was talking about. He turned to his convoy and waved for his translator.

173

The grand white orb of the sun was gently curving to the west now. The sea was ripening into a golden pasture of waves. Aperlae's fifty residents gawked as that other yellow sea of soldiers – the Companions – rippled. Twenty or thirty of Persia's finest warriors trod forwards. They wended their way to Harpagos.

As the deadly team approached, it was clear they were guarding someone. The saffron-clad bodyguards fell back. A small hooded figure stepped forward. Harpagos turned to the mysterious cloaked personage, lifted his helmet a little and extended his arm towards the prostrating villager before him.

The figure pushed the hood back. Fifty Aperlae folk promptly gasped. The woman was draped in a white tunic. She curtly bowed her head in greeting. She was good-looking, though her hair had no sense of decorum. It erupted from her head in an unruly black torrent. Hanging from her neck was a large bubble of turquoise, while a cobra of gold coiled around her arm. Harpagos surveyed the weathered clan of fishermen with their uncomely wives, and puffed up a little.

The villagers of Aperlae, most of whom had never set foot out of their bay, would not have recognised the woman. Nor would they have understood the implications of her adornments. But other Lycians would have known. The cobra was the symbol of the great Goddess Leto. This woman was a Lycian priestess. She was from no other place than the sacred Letoon, the one and only shrine-city of Leto in the ancient world.

Yet, there were two questions very few could have answered. What was a Lycian priestess doing travelling in a Persian war convoy? And why was she translating for Harpagos?

'Now, tell me, what the devil is this old fellow yelling about?' Harpagos had to squint the sun's rage was so intense.

The priestess looked at the general. She pushed a few frizzy coils out of her face and pouted. 'Well, obviously, they don't want to be killed, do they? How would you feel if sixty thousand armed foreigners suddenly crashed into your home? They say they're just a band of fishermen, nothing more, so spare them,' she said.

Harpagos' eyes drew closer together. He put a couple of fingers under his helmet and scratched his baking scalp. Lines of exasperation stretched over his face as he scanned the decrepit huddle of villagers. 'Why the hell would I slaughter them? For God's sake, what good would that do any of us right now? Tell the man I require but one thing of him, his allegiance to Cyrus and the unhampered use of his harbour.'

The priestess turned to the folk of Aperlae and translated. All around sighs of relief could be heard. Some fell to the floor and wailed in gratitude.

'And tell them all something else,' Harpagos said. 'Tell them Cyrus shall turn this insignificant hamlet into the most prosperous centre of trade in Lycia. Tell them their children will be wealthier than any Aperlae person before them. Tell them Persia shall make them rich and civilised!'

The priestess turned to Harpagos and raised an eyebrow. 'Civilised? You call yourself rich and civilised?'

A few Companions overheard that. They widened their eyes, rolled their eyeballs from left to right, and swallowed hard.

Harpagos folded his arms over his armour-hardened chest. He funnelled a glare in her direction. 'Well yes! As a matter of fact I do. Look at this rabble! You'd think they'd all been left to rot in one of their crab baskets. I'd be surprised

175

if there's more than one tooth between the lot of them. How do they eat? Does one of them chew on behalf of the rest?'

The ragged folk of Aperlae strained to work out what was happening. The only thing they understood was, a conflict was going on, and conflicts were always juicy, even if you didn't have a clue what they were about.

The priestess blinked and muttered, 'A slave can never be rich.' Her right eyebrow arched toward the bridge of her nose. 'Anyway, have you seen Leto yet?'

Harpagos turned. He looked the woman dourly in the eye. It was too hot for all this, it really was. The sweat was trickling from the tip of his nose. 'For God's sake don't get me onto that! Agh the Letoon! I should have had you all strung up. Why me, when I have plenty of other superstitious berks here paid to dabble in the dubious? Gods? Goddesses? For heaven's sake! I'm off to find some shade.'

The priestess put her hands on her hips. Her head fell backwards. She laughed. The laughter rocked from inside her to the outside. It made the air full and joyous. Harpagos could feel her laughter echoing in him, rattling him. As she chortled, the priestess' tunic rippled and swayed. Harpagos watched the curves of her body through the fabric, and then turned briskly away.

'Listen! Can't you hear her murmuring along the water's edge?' She called after him. 'That's Leto. She's here.'

Harpagos remained facing in the opposite direction thinking it was a good job the Zoroastrian priest was a long way back and out of earshot. Then, he briefly twisted his head back towards her. 'I don't know what the hell you're talking about, and neither do you, if the truth be told.' He stabbed the sky with his index finger as he spoke. 'There is one thing I do know, though. I'm going to conquer Phoenicia, and the sooner I get there the better.'

The priestess cocked her head to one side. 'Ah the great Phoenicia. Hmm, we'll see about that. We'll see.'

Harpagos ignored her. 'Companions! Set up camp. I need some shade *now*!' Then he stomped off in the direction of the village, armour squeaking.

For her part, the priestess began to walk in the opposite direction towards the sea. She was tailed by a score of Companions. She was barefoot and left small prints in the sand, prints soon eradicated by the ploughing sandals of her new Persian bodyguards. When she reached the water's edge, she knelt. The sea soaked her white tunic to mid-thigh level. She placed her hands into the cool blue, closed her eyes, and whispered. The sea lapped ever so gently about her outstretched fingers. It moved over her knuckles, under her palms, around her fingertips. Meanwhile, twenty iron-clad Companions stood perspiring in a line behind her. What she was whispering no one knew. Neither did they know why a subtle wind picked up, nor why a foamy hem of waves began to collect about the whispering woman. Yet these things happened. Quietly. Almost imperceptibly. How long the priestess knelt there is anyone's guess. But the Companions would have said, 'all Goddamn day'.

After the sun had shifted a fraction, throwing her shadow a little to the east, the woman opened her eyes. The ritual was over. Leaning forwards a little, she brought some sea water up in cupped palms and splashed it over her face. Then she raised herself up on her feet, bowed to the bowl of the Mediterranean, and turned around.

℘Oʒ

I finished my Nescafe and took one last look at the bay. My gaze caught the dark blue tips of the waves. The sea was shimmering frantically as though it might break apart and reveal some hitherto concealed world. I don't know why, but just there I felt connected, in touch, in the right place.

Finally, after much procrastination, I pushed my chair back and stood up. Then, I readied myself to leave. Though my baggage was only getting heavier, I was, at least, mastering the art of putting it on. I had learned that trying to lift it from the ground and 'swing' it over my shoulder was somewhat lethal, as the momentum of the thing would flatten me. Instead, I would set the pack on a rock, or in this case the chair, then I'd squat in front of it, push my arms though the straps and lever myself up. This was not only faster, but it meant the brunt of the weight was accommodated by my strongest muscles (my thighs) rather than my poor old back and arms. Once I was standing, I'd tighten the straps. Finally, I'd push my torso forwards for balance and set off.

I left Aperlae. After an hour or so of picking my way over rocky ground, I entered a stretch of flat land. The path here was easy to navigate. Two banks of rough stones lined its edges like nubbly buffers with olive trees dotting the landscape. They were crooked little pigmies harrowed by the winter winds roving the open fields. Marvelling at their tenacity, I stumbled on.

Before long, I was happily lost once more within a cluster of homesteads called Kılıçlı. The lapis arc of the sky cradled the tiny village as it clung to the yellowing hillside. And yet again, as if it were a theme of the Lycian Way, there seemed to be no one in the vicinity. The squat uneven cottages stood silent. They were medieval witches' hovels, their blackened windows gaping like gouged eyes.

There was a mosque too. By contrast, it was sleek and orderly. As luck would have it, it housed a perfect wooden köşk upon which I could pitch my tent. As it was a mosque, it provided washing facilities for the ritual pre-prayer-cleansing, so I could bathe and wash my laundry which was altogether very convenient.

I had hardly erected my tent before I heard someone call out to me. The village wasn't as abandoned as I had imagined, and I felt a stab of trepidation about my choice of campsite. I looked up. A round village woman was leaning out of her door.

'Hey! Fancy a bit of dinner dear?'

I laughed. Why was I hauling this colossal food pack everywhere, again?

'I'd love some! Thanks so much for the invite!' I called out.

'Well get a move on then! It's ready, all you got to do is eat it,' she barked. Her cheeks were two pudgy aubergines when she smiled.

I scrambled from the wooden platform and scurried inside her house. Her husband was there, her son and, believe it or not, the village imam, who far from expressing perturbation was fine with my camping under his minaret. I considered the world 'down there'. In that world, an imam would be herded into one political pen, and I would be herded into another; he a man of religion, myself a secularist, or hippy feminist, or some other such nonsense. But the truth is, sometimes an irreligious hiker has more in common with a village imam than with a city-dwelling secularist.

We chatted and gorged until darkness. I strolled back to my camp, the night a stew of domes, minarets and canvas. I sank onto my sleeping bag. Ah, life was good.

৪০০৩

Just above Ayşe, strutting on the stout branch of a mature plum tree, was a tawny owl. She ruffled her mottled feathers before spinning her head one hundred and eighty degrees, and back again. Then, she fixed her eyes – eyes whose retinas consisted of about fifty-six thousand light sensitive rods – on a spot at the perimeter of Ayşe's tent. There those eyes remained focussed, blinking every now and again. The mammoth brown irises absorbed little colour. They didn't need to. Tawny had no use for it. She was a creature of the night and could pick up the subtlest traces of light, even in the moonless pitch of a mountain hamlet.

A small common toad had leapt onto the platform. He loitered at the edge of Ayşe's tarp. Warty. Squatting. Two yellow eyes bulged out of his cool, rubbery head searching the night air for mosquitos. There were plenty tonight. They were rushing at the mesh of Ayşe's door panel. The toad's tongue darted in and out. His toad tummy bulged. Too bad his eyes weren't scanning backwards for trouble. Too bad his neck didn't rotate half-way round his head so he could gawk what was behind him.

Did toads know of well-being? Did they have little epiphanies like humans? Did they, in their own amphibian way, sense pockets of positive vibrations? Did they gravitate towards them? The moderns had no idea, after all they knew no toad language by which to ask them, no way of reading their salientian thoughts – should they have had them. But then, how did they know of the inner world of any other being? They searched for clues in language, in gesture, in action. They hunted for some hint the other was behaving as they would have done, was feeling as they did. When they reached out like this to one of their own kind, they termed it positively, as empathy. Yet strangely, irrationally even, when they did this for any other being in nature, it was coolly dismissed as anthropomorphism.

180

In truth, no one knew what toad was thinking or sensing, except for toad himself. Yet for some reason or no reason, he was happy to hang about the edge of Ayşe's groundsheet. His belly was full. The first pearly rays of a youthful moon were wafting through the trees. Toad was alive. For now.

Back on the plum tree, Tawny shifted from one foot to the other. She opened her wings. In one deft leap she silently struck out into the black air, a fabulous white-feathered missile. She extended her talons and swooped. Was it luck? Or was it fate? Or was it something neither human nor animal understood? For at that precise moment, toad happened to shuffle under Ayşe's groundsheet. He waddled just enough to become uncatchable. And there toad stayed enjoying the warm cover above him and the moist wood beneath him. All in blissful ignorance.

Tawny came to land a metre from Ayşe's makeshift home. If owls could mutter profanities, she would have done. She flapped her wings a little and stomped her scrawny bird feet, feet that protruded from white, downy knickerbockers. Tawny didn't possess the stern plumed eyebrows of the great-horned owl or the eagle owl. Her eyes were surrounded by a large ring of creamy feathers instead. All in all, she looked fairly benevolent for a bird of prey, more like a tiny speckled granny.

Tawny toddled closer to Ayşe's green dome. Watching. Waiting. She saw the light fluttering on the backs of leaves and tracing the furrows of tree bark. She saw light everywhere moving in magical and unnatural ways, illuminating God only knew what. What *were* those other things? To a modern day human, Tawny was seeing the soft shine of the canvas, the twinkling of a peg, the light gliding over tent poles. She was looking at the large cupola of the mosque too, soft silvery fronds of moonlight slipping over the arcs. The owl stayed like this for quite some time. Blinking. Head swivelling. For despite her rumbling belly, there was something exciting about this corner of the Earth. Something in the air made everything as potent as could be.

The other side of the canvas, Ayşe was lying on her sleeping bag staring into the black above her. Unlike Tawny, she couldn't see a thing. But she could *hear* one hell of a lot; the mosquitos surging at her door flap, the owl's call, the medley of rustling outside. God only knew what *that* was! Nonetheless, in spite of her fatigue, the trekker couldn't help but notice the atmosphere of wonder. Her tent was charged with it. She had no idea whether it came from outside her or from inside. Yet it was there, and it was delectable. It had been a while since Ayşe had tasted this particular flavour of emotion. It was the flavour of optimism, of impassioned youth. It was the exact emotional zest she had known in her salad days. The distinct smack of the late 1990s.

Before she could so much as raise a mental finger to flip through her inner memory closets, Istanbul – dressed somewhat flamboyantly for a change – pranced merrily out on stage. For the city between two continents, the end of the twentieth century was nothing to mourn. Anticipation sparkled in the estuaries. It glittered through the Golden Horn and under the Galata Bridge.

Past times. Good times. Very good times indeed.

ೞ‍O‍ೞ

Heavy fat plumes of cigarette smoke burgeoned throughout the large Istanbul office, while a catchy *Sezen Aksu* number lightly rattled the windows. The winter night pressed on the panes. Cheering and festivity in the street below was audible four floors up. Ayşe stood clutching a wine glass. She was giggling with a circle of colleagues. They were all dressed for the occasion, the men in sharp suits and polished shoes, the women painstakingly coiffed and parading their latest outfits. Everyone was tipsy. Nearly everyone was shouting. It was New Year's Eve and 1998 was twenty minutes away. In this more industrious corner of Istanbul, did anyone realise Turkey's renaissance was imminent? Perhaps they did, in a foggy, subliminal way. People were already beginning to do strange things, things they would never have done three or four years ago.

Ayşe had good reason to party this year. Her apartment was now ready, and she had moved in with her son, Umut. After seven years of struggle, she was on the brink of her own life, a spanking new life of liberation and independence. Her motherland was following suit. The tight conformity of Turkish family tradition slackened here and there. Freedom of expression and the lifestyle of individualism oozed in. Individualism. It had become a dirty word in the West. It was a breathe-hole in the ice elsewhere.

No one saw it coming. As the Earth spun into a new millennium, Turkey pirouetted through change. Radical social change. The kind of change which cleaves one generation from another with such force, bridge-building becomes a formidable engineering project.

The bohemian quarters of Istanbul were the epicentre; the backstreet music venues wriggling out from İstiklal caddesı, the hip street cafés crowding through Nişantaşı, and the multi-ethnic hang-outs of Cihangir, where Turkey's intellectual youth, in pleasingly sixties fashion, took to challenging the moral codes of the past.

In time, this shifting of tectonic plates in Istanbul's underground sent tremors throughout the European side of the city. And then the shockwaves, building in strength and volume with each kilometre, rumbled into the western edge of Anatolia. Change pounded down the Aegean and along

183

the Mediterranean. Istanbul, Ankara, Izmir and Antalya, all shook and pulsed with the movement.

Did the outside reflect the inside? Did the body mirror the soul? Because, at that very point in space and time, another earthquake happened. It was July 1999, when the crust under Izmit waxed restless. And when Mother Earth stomps her feet, you'd best run for cover. The ground from Sakarya to Istanbul rolled and shook cataclysmically. Tarmac ripped like paper. Streets crumpled as if whacked by a slew of Titan hammers. Hundreds of thousands of homes were razed to the ground in one fell swoop. The concrete carcasses of apartment buildings lurched over the boulevards like huge slain dinosaurs. Sixty thousand people were killed from one day to the next.

There have been bigger earthquakes in the world. And, there was no doubt, the death toll was largely a result of poorly-built apartments, and construction engineers on the make. But the earthquake rocked the whole nation. Nearly any Turkish person you would meet in the next twenty years knew of someone who had died on that day. For some, entire families vanished into the Earth.

The intellectual hub of Istanbul exploded as terrified residents sold up and moved elsewhere. Thus, the spores of Turkey's elite took to the wind and spread into Anatolia.

Within five years the western half of Turkey had become a different place. Suddenly, you could cohabit with a partner without being married. The bars and cafés were no longer seedy, dark holes full of twitching moustaches and furtive eyes. They were playing jazz or Turco-Western fusion and had begun to teem with women. And, as was the inevitable consequence of women getting a pay packet, the divorce rate was now soaring.

But I'm charging ahead on the chronological freeway. Let's pull over and reverse to junction 1998. What?

You can't reverse on a motorway? Ha! You haven't driven in Turkey.

It was New Year's Eve. Ayşe was working in a small German company as PA to the chairman. Tonight was the office party. Music blared, glasses clattered and the chairman, who was now beside her, cracked a particularly bad joke. The surrounding ring of colleagues promptly swayed and bent double in cahoots. Ayşe sucked on her cigarette and gazed around the room. A few feet away through the dinge, she caught the eye of a young man. He grinned shyly. Ayşe grinned back.

The young man had shown more than a passing interest in Ayşe lately. The only trouble was, he was nineteen. But, there were other powers at work. Beneath the surface, the unquantifiable was moving, drop by tiny drop, from one side to another. She might have been eleven years his senior, but Ayşe was attracted.

Amidst the laughter and the flowing *rakı*, she slipped away from her colleagues. The darker corners of the room did their best to hide the twinkling of eyes. The smoke tried its utmost to veil the proximity of the figures. As the evening spun excitedly forward, and 1997 collapsed willingly into 1998, Ayşe scampered after her heart. She began a relationship with the young man, the man who was to be the great love of her life. He was nineteen. And Sex and the City wouldn't air in Turkey for another two years. It was bad enough to be a divorcee, but a divorcee dating a teenager?

The coming months tried her patience. Her colleagues archly disapproved. The workplace became hostile territory. Narrow-eyed glances whizzed like sniper shots over the photocopier. Snide remarks ricocheted from monitor to monitor. The insidious chemical warfare of poisonous gossip leaked all over the office. It choked Ayşe to the point where she resigned.

It didn't matter. Ayşe returned to her former company as assistant to the board of directors. More money. Higher status. Promotion.

Too good to be true? Too darn lucky for words? Karma. Or Zoroastrian ethics. You reap what you sow – at least that's what they say.

Individuals have karmas, groups have karmas, countries have karmas, even a rock has a karma. And there has always been a karma connecting each human to his or her life. When someone treats their life as a quest, when they scoop out the detritus of fear and hack through the choking creepers of social opinion, when they dive headlong after their dreams, something dramatic has to happen. One way or another, they've made a stand and sent their lives a sign. The sign they are in the business of transformation. Life will transform in return. She owes and she has to pay. Sooner or later.

But if folk aren't prepared to go the distance, if they care more what the neighbours think than they do about their life, if they refuse to dig out the energy to live it, or they bury it, shun it or curse at it every morning as they fumble for the shower head . . . then, no one should be surprised to find that same life slouching on its backside in front of the television leaving half-eaten slices of pizza on the sofa arms and cigarette butts in the sink. What you give is what you get. Thus spoke Zoroaster, along with quite a few others.

By the summer of 1999, Ayşe was driving her first new car, living in her own home, and spending some of the most thrilling moments of her life thus far with the young man. A plump, tender-skinned relationship was born. It was a relationship based on love, trust and freedom. This was something new. Completely and utterly.

ಐಔಣ

Ayşe rolled over in her sleeping bag. As her body switched sides, her mind followed suit. Her back was now to the past. Her face, peaceful and smooth, met the present.

Night slunk out of Kılıçlı like the prowling shadow of a God-sized puma. His creatures gathered at the edges of his silhouette. They made last-minute haste to finish their nocturnal gorging. Then, the gong of aurora rang out from the east and sent them scattering into their holes.

Was it a scrambling, squawking or flapping? Was it a squelch or a thud or a croak? Whatever it was, the kerfuffle woke Ayşe. Through the muddy grog of half-awakeness, she started. Sitting bolt upright for a moment, she searched the tent for trouble, checked the door panel was firmly zipped, and then lay back down waiting for more.

There was no more. Whatever had gone on the other side of her canvas would remain a dark secret of the early hours. Finally, night slipped into the wings, giving dawn her brief spot on the stage of the sky. Ayşe rolled over and pulled the sleeping bag from under her. She hardly ever bothered to zip it up at night. It was simply too stifling. Instead, she left it by her side, so she could pull it over her if the temperature dropped.

As the first shaft of sunlight sped over the rim of the Earth, it skimmed over mountain peaks and tree tops. It beamed onto minarets, and roofs. It hit Ayşe's *köşk* too, and by the time it did, Ayşe was packed. She put her backpack on the edge of the platform, slid her arms through the straps and stood up. She didn't notice Tawny overhead, owl head now sunk into her feathered neck. Tawny paid no attention to Ayşe either. Her belly was full, her eyes shut fast. It was bedtime.

Day Six

Trails of Destruction

Ayşe had never heard of the goddess Leto. She wasn't the only one. If you had travelled from Fethiye to Antalya, you'd be hard pushed to find more than a score of people who had. Villagers, city folk, men, women, tourists, hikers, religious people or atheists; none of them realised Lycia was Goddess territory. They bumbled on through their days as though their latter-day myths were the only ones ever to exist.

Archaeologists knew about Lycia's best kept secret. They dug up the rocks and studied them like huge, stone cryptograms. They tried to unlock their stories. They would unearth tablets with strange codes scratched on them, or broken statues, chipped busts. Occasionally, a temple, or even a whole city, would emerge. They were assisted, and sometimes hampered, by the historians. Armed with their libraries of ancient literature, the scholars would interpret and re-interpret, taking this angle and that in an effort to weed out some facts. Homer, Hesiod, Hyginus and Ovid had all contributed to the lore of Leto. And this is roughly what they said.

Leto was the daughter of the Titans, Coeus and Phoebe. She was beautiful, but for reasons unknown, no one ever saw her. She was known as 'the hidden one'. Zeus, still managed to find her though, and Leto soon wound up pregnant by him. Hera learned the story. She chased the unseen goddess from Mount Olympos, banishing her from all fixed lands of the Earth. Without a place to rest, Leto couldn't give birth. She fled to Delos, a floating island, squatting inside a loophole in Hera's law.

Leto gave birth to twins on Delos; Artemis the huntress and Apollo the god of the sun. But from that day forth, the primordial single mum was on the move. She roamed the lands of Asia Minor, always seeking shelter. No one would take her in. Everyone feared Hera's retribution. Where would she rest? Would she ever know home?

Then one day she found herself in Lycia. At first, it was as hostile as anywhere else. It is said, when local peasants met Leto, they refused to let her drink from their pond, stirring up the mud at the bottom. Leto, now at the end of her celestial tether, turned them into frogs. So, perhaps it's no coincidence post-Hellenistic Lycia offers such a grand reception to its guests, particularly to lone-wandering women. Perhaps the country folk remember. Or the vibrations inside the stones remind them.

Yet in the end, despite the shaky start, it was Lycia that became Leto's refuge. A band of Lycian wolves protected her. The wolves became her chosen animals. The Lycians her people.

Legends are legends. They wind on like twisting forest trails, and who ever knows to what end? Then there are the facts, or the clues the archaeologists discovered carved into Apennine limestone. Because Lycia wasn't the only land to have formed a cult of Leto. Though it was the only place where the belief took on such a powerful shape. It was potent soil, a rocky garden where Greek myth was fused with the mother worship of central Anatolia.

Long before Ayşe, long before Harpagos too, even a while before Leto – eight, seven, six creases ago in time's undulating fabric – the central Anatolians were bowing low before the Earth Mother Kybele. Her influence spread far and wide, to the Carians and Lycians, over to Athens, and even as far as Egypt. Such had been the mania for all things feminine back then, weird and wonderful doctrines sprouted. There were sects of raving mother worshippers. Many a researcher blinked as he read about the orgies and mutilations, whereby, according to the sources, men would gamely castrate themselves in ecstatic rituals to the grand She.

Leto was a hybrid goddess, half Kybele, half Hellene. Who knew exactly when the transmutation occurred? All anyone could say was, by the time Harpagos and the Ancient Persians were on the scene, it was long over. Lycia was Leto Land.

As goes the soul, so goes the body, the inside always finding its expression on the out. By the sixth century BC, Lycian society and politics mirrored their choice of patron. It was democratic, semi-matriarchal, and staunchly independent.

'Their customs are partly Cretan, partly Carian. They have, however, one singular custom in which they differ from every other nation in the world. They take the mother's and not the father's name. Ask a Lycian who he is, and he answers by giving his own name, that of his mother, and so on in the female line. Moreover, if a free woman marry a man who is a slave, their children are full citizens; but if a free man marry a foreign woman, or live with a concubine, even though he be the first person in the State, the children forfeit all the rights of citizenship,[1] explained the ancient Greek historyteller, Herodotus.

As if remembering the plight of the Great Goddess and her banishment from Mount Olympos, the Lycians took on her struggle for solitary survival. And they gave everything to retain their sovereignty, as the events at Xanthos proved. Twice.

Xanthos, Lycia's beleaguered capital. She fought tooth and nail to the bitter end. Was Leto looking down on her? Did she see the flames and the tears, and the suffering of her people? That's something I can't comment on. I have

---

[1] *Herodotus, 'The Histories'*

no access to the realm of the gods. My stories come from here on Earth, and they are all too human. But, even if Leto was disinterested in the fate of her devoted subjects, someone else was losing sleep. He saw the flames every day. They followed him everywhere he went. Even the word 'Xanthos' brought him out in a cold sweat.

༺❍༻

If General Harpagos could have banned the word Xanthos, he would have done. Not that he was anywhere near the Lycian capital now. The Persians were stationed in the hills, in a place which two-and-a-half thousand years later would be known as Kılıçlı. It was the same place Ayşe was camped, not that Harpagos could see her. Her tent was the other side of a temporal hill and out of his line of sight.

It was day break, only rather than cracking apart the sky, day was oozing into being. A grey wave spread sluggishly over the horizon. Thousands of tents rose out of the earth in unison, giant toadstools erupting through a forest floor.

Harpagos had left the camp and was pacing through the grand old pines and cedars. He hadn't slept a wink. It felt as though someone had forgotten to light the torches in his head. His mind was a dark pit. God only knew what was in there. Pine cones and twigs fractured under his sandals, and every now and again, his tunic snagged on a spiky offshoot. When it did, Harpagos would stop and throw the offending bush a glare, before disentangling himself and trudging off again. He was tailed, as always, by a small band of Companions. It was one of the many curses of his rank. He was never alone.

He had walked for about fifteen minutes when he was brought to a halt. There in front of him was a tree so immense, no other tree could draw near for a good thirty metres. The girth of the trunk could have fit ten men inside, and the branches were like a full-sized Hydra.

Harpagos stepped closer. It was then he had the uncomfortable feeling he was being watched. There was a rustling up in the boughs.

'Let it go!'

The words came from somewhere above. Harpagos jerked his head upwards. His eyes immediately popped. There, lounging within the branches a way up the tree was the translator-priestess. Her white robe was trailing over the woody arms. She looked like something pulled from an Athenian myth.

'Let Xanthos go. What's done is done,' she said. She was scrutinising him from above. A well-formed leg dangled from the branch. It swung to and fro like a pendulum.

Harpagos scowled. He didn't want to have this conversation now, not with his bodyguards eavesdropping every damn word. But the truisms kept coming. They rained down on him, a well-intentioned deluge of unwanted advice.

'Guilt has never helped anyone. You'll spend your life blaming everyone else to justify why you did it. Hmph. That's sort of what you're doing already, isn't it?' The corner of her mouth and her eyebrow drew together, so that the right side of her face lifted sardonically. Harpagos had met a few smuggler women in his time, but not many. Even so, she was attractive. It was a nonconformist sort of beauty; fabulous olive skin, breasts like a pair of ripe apples, and that maniacal *hair*. This was no doubt why he was tolerating her.

Harpagos stared down at the floor. There was no breeze. Everything was eerily still. Morning had begun to pierce the oak leaves. It scattered spots of sunlight over the bracken-littered earth. A few silent moments passed. Finally, he tilted his head back to speak. When he did, he

193

almost fell backwards. A bolt of terror zipped from his head to his feet. It crackled the length of his spine like static. Good God! How had he failed to notice the thing before? It must have been camouflaged in the dappled canopy of the tree. Now the sun was making a concerted swipe at the shadows, it was clearly visible. There slumped next to the translator, huge spotted head raised, ears pricked in attentive listening, was a leopard. The beast stared directly at Harpagos, sniffed, and turned her nose in the opposite direction.

'What the . . . Are you out of your tiny *mind?*' Harpagos threw a hand in the direction of the cat. The leopard swiftly turned her head back to face him, yellow eyes flashing.

The translator put her index finger to her lips. But Harpagos wasn't to be shut up.

'So that's it, is it? You think we should abandon conscience, and let the law of the jungle reign. It's only natural the strong pulverise the weak, eh? Who cares? Let the frail be annihilated.'

'Oh come on! Stop being so melodramatic. There are no weak,' she said. 'Only those that think they're weak and surrender their power to those who think they're stronger. It's an illusion.'

'Pur-lease, *spare* me!' Harpagos screwed his mouth up and spat on to the forest floor. He craned his neck back again. 'I have a hundred and one priests spouting this sort of tripe at me every day. *"You create your own reality, sire, Zoroaster said so."* For God's sake, haven't any of you got something original to say?' Harpagos turned his head from the translator to the leopard. He looked at it distastefully and pointed. 'Power is an illusion eh? Ha! Tell that to the next deer to find itself wedged between the jaws of that thing!'

The cat raised its head a little and stared hard at Harpagos. He dug his heels in and glared back. The two of them stayed locked in a battle of wills until the translator stretched her hand towards the head of the leopard. She scratched between the creature's ears. The leopard closed her magnificent feline eyes and purred.

Harpagos lifted his eyes to the sky and silently mouthed the word 'barmy'.

The translator ignored him. 'The Great Mother favours none of her children above the others. Sometimes the deer wins, sometimes the cat. But no being ever wins all the time, except perhaps the one who sees through the ruse. But, even then . . . '

Harpagos raised one bushy eyebrow, then the next. He pulled his tiara down, and huffed. Then he nodded sharply and turned on his heel. As he strode away, he stole a sideways glance at the leopard. He distinctly saw it bare its teeth. He hoped the translator had the thing under control. He didn't fancy its claws in his back just before breakfast.

As the warlord picked his way back to the Persian camp, he muttered to the shrubs and the creepers. 'Witch. She's a goddamn witch. I knew it!'

ဆ O ಚ

In exactly the same place a couple of thousand years down time's rolling slope was Ayşe. She was looking about a large empty glade. It was peaceful. Her feet hugged the ground and it felt fantastic, as though the soil itself was secreting balm. She was standing on the grave of the great oak tree. Nothing wins all the time. The oak had been felled a thousand years earlier for ship building. But the soil held the broken down magic in its roots. The area would stay special for a long time to come.

༄ O ༄

It was now the sixth day, and I was optimistic, perhaps even a little cocky. I thought I had cracked the art of trekking in the wild, you see. I'd screwed up a decent-sized tranche of my plans by now (I think I might have thrown them in the wastepaper basket of that café in Aperlae). I was spontaneous, intuitive even, and suitably dishevelled to boot. My hair was a nest of wayward grot, and I can say with some surprise, I didn't care in the slightest, because I was a happy, carefree hiker. The early light seemed to concur with my mood. It crashed auburn over the hillsides in euphoric torrents. Hmph! Why is it always at such moments of over-confidence things conspire to go awry?

Before I took off, I sat on the ground in front of my tent for breakfast. Well, that's what I called it, at least. I munched on a handful of dried chickpeas, almonds, and sunflower seeds. It was a meal that would have barely satiated a squirrel. This was the sustenance which was supposed to transport me over ten kilometres of terrain until lunch, when inevitably I'd pick at a little more of the same squirrel-food. Honestly! No wonder the day ended as it did.

Anyway, after 'breakfast', I tottered along the cliff top track in the direction of a place called Limanağzı. This section of the trail is at once one of the most beautiful, and equally one of the most exacting. It's a path of continual ascents and descents over rocks and boulders, with very little shade. As I stumbled, I gaped at the buff-coloured land taking voracious bites out of the enormous, blue mousse of the Mediterranean Sea.

The trouble was, there wasn't a trickle of water to be found along the entire stretch. Before long, my head was

196

spinning. I suppose it could have been dehydration that allowed me to have my little 'experience', though the silence and solitude certainly played their part, as well. You see, it's only when one is far from humanity, far from any form of civilisation, one hears nature speak. And this sort of expedition is, I realise, something one must undertake alone. To go beyond common reality, there must be no chatter, no distracting discussions about this way or that, no compromise. One must be utterly submerged in one's inner world.

I stopped to stare at the coastline. The warm, rocky ground pressed against the soles of my feet shouldering me like Atlas. It was then I felt it. My perception had shifted. Now, what do I mean by that? And how do I go about describing it? Well, to begin with nothing looked or felt as it had before. It was as though everything had another dimension to it, or my eyes had grown accustomed to that dimension. Let's take the sea as an example. It was no longer simply a distant expanse of water, but an enormous blue being, writhing and dancing and the like.

What I was seeing is both inherently obvious, and nevertheless almost always overlooked. Nature is alive. The Earth is alive. Everything from the dust to the trees to the sunlight stroking the leaves is alive. What's more, this essence is more enchanting than any of the grosser superficial pleasures we humans have devised to entertain ourselves. Well, is this not what we are all ultimately thirsty for? Life? And the ridiculous thing is, it's everywhere, and it comes without a price tag, or a tummy tuck.

I walked on and up, higher and deeper into Lycia. With each step the separation between my inner and outer worlds became less and less palpable. I noticed I wasn't stuck inside my body at all. I was everywhere, sort of connected. *And it felt so good! Like coming home. Now, people have laughed at me when I have told them this. Some said I must have eaten the wrong kind of mushroom, or ingested a mildly poisonous herb by mistake. I don't know about any of that, I'm simply explaining what happened, that's all. Was this it? My lotus position? Could I mark this spot on the map with a Buddha on a cloud? Was I now liberated from all suffering and an angel to boot? Apparently not. Nothing lasts forever, not even enlightenment. I really don't know why, but my old world returned almost by stealth. I didn't deviate from the Lycian Way once, yet it happened, nonetheless. And then, there I was, slap bang in misery again.*

Inevitably, morning had receded into the ever decreasing shadows leaving noon to take a firm, fiery hold on the day. The heat was thick and heavy. All at once, I felt a frightening thirst creeping upon me. Thus my sixth day on the Lycian Way unravelled, feverishly and somewhat stickily, and I unravelled with it. Remember the watermelon I had so foolishly acquired the previous day? Well, my back had no chance to forget. I'm sorry to say, despite my flirt with 'higher consciousness', and the village hospitality of the past days, I was physically coming apart.

With hindsight of course, my predicament was unsurprising. Each day I spent twelve to thirteen hours a day ascending and descending sheer slopes, an endeavour accomplished mostly undernourished and dehydrated, all while bearing my twenty kilogram burden. Nor were the nights any sort of improvement. Rather than recuperating, I languished during the dark hours in a state of perpetual terror, nerves braced for a tent breech. Was that wild boar about to skewer me? What was that terrible wailing sound? Was there someone out there? Spooks? Ghosts? Attackers? It all but drove me to the brink of insanity.

Thus, sleep-deprived and debilitated, this sixth trudge of fire proved to be the death blow.

My pack was by now intolerable, and I was staggering rather than walking. I began to wonder whether I would make it. There were rocks and stones everywhere, and the cussed bumpiness of the trail slowly but surely broke my knees. I was hiking upon a razor-backed monster. I was also horribly hot. The combination of pain, exhaustion and dehydration was ruinous.

The sun sank. Evening had arrived. Slipping and tripping the length of the headland, I inched towards the sea. I couldn't go on, I knew it, and felt my body entirely give up. My limbs were useless lumps of flesh attached to an aching torso. I propped myself up against a tree and decided to smoke a cigarette (which will seem counter-intuitive to anyone except fellow smokers). Then, just as I took my first therapeutic puff, I spotted people in the distance; a knot of holiday folk lounging on a remote half-moon of sand. Limanağzı. I had made it.

I hobbled to the beach, but I'd had enough. I decided to camp right there in the seaside restaurant, only as it happened, I was unable even to manage that. Discovering a hammock, I collapsed within it and drifted to sleep with a cloud of mosquitos feeding upon what little was left of me.

೮ठⱨ

The mosquito. With its blood-sucking, disease-transmitting antics, it's the bane of humanity, happily ruining any warm summer night outdoors. The buzzing squadrons that zipped about Ayşe that night had one thing in common. They were all female. Only the mothers-to-be of the gnat world have the special skin-piercing proboscis custom-built to suck out mammalian blood.

As the Mediterranean night wrapped Ayşe in its arms, she barely stirred. A faint breath of salty air licked her sleep-soothed face. The winged hordes plunged in.

Blood. Thick and red. Looking like the force of life itself. Red cells, white cells, platelets, plasma, proteins, glucose, mineral ions, hormones, carbon-dioxide, oxygen, water. Humans carry on average about five litres of this elixir, and it moves on and on, round and round, from their hearts to their brains to their toes. It transports a bounty of goods; heat, haemoglobin, waste. But what about the things unseen? What else might move through those viscous crimson corridors? What could blood tell about the human condition, if only it could speak?

Ayşe was now at the heart of Lycia, the land of myth and magic. The moon was steadily rising, her ivory smile lighting a twinkling boulevard out into the sea. The olive trees sighed. The crickets trilled. The trees and the rocks looked on. No one saw it and no one knew, but as the female mosquitos drank from Ayşe, things were moving from A to B. Cyphers were being transferred. The heart squeezed the blood round and round and round. But it wasn't the only thing on a loop. Ayşe's mind was plugged in wherever she was. Even in unconsciousness the memories were on permanent shuffle. Who could say why? Was it random or was there an order to the selection? But that night in Limanağzı it was the year 2001's turn for attention.

Some might have said it was claustrophobic being trapped in this inescapable loop of time. But the stories of the personality didn't care. Like everything they wanted to survive. They wanted to be heard.

ಏ Ο ಐ

The cars were everywhere. They moved in great swarms through Istanbul, a squawking, honking river of transportation. The Bosphorus Bridge all but bowed under the weight of the 180 000 vehicles ploughing from Asia to Europe and back again every day. Its brother, the Fatih Sultan Mehmet suspension bridge, was equally varicose. Many were the tales of full-bladdered Istanbulian wayfarers stranded in traffic snarls half-way between the two continents.

'I simply couldn't hold on until Europe,' they would wail, before expounding their innovative ways of relieving themselves inter-continentally. Inevitably, their stories would end with plaintive cries of *'Ne yapayım yaa?'*

'Ne yapayım?' It was another golden gallstone straight from the belly of colloquial Turkish. Directly translating as 'What can *I* do?' it also had subtle shades of 'It's not my fault' and 'Well, what do you want me to do about it now?' thrown in. Usually accompanied by a small shrug and a victimised expression, it was a fabulous, get-out-of-jail-free sort of a phrase. And it mysteriously absolved the utterer of all manner of crimes. From peeing in the middle of a four-lane highway, to failing to construct a public toilet on the Bosphorus Bridge, from arriving at work half-an-hour late to forgetting a date, all could be justified by *'Ne yapayım'*.

In central Istanbul it looked like evening rose from the streets, as if night were a black gas the government pumped out of the gutters. Ayşe was weaving her way home. She steered from the great car-stuffed arteries of Istanbul proper and through the cluttered capillaries fanning back to her house. The young man would be waiting for her. She was in a hurry. As she reached her neighbourhood, she scoured the street for a parking spot. There wasn't one to speak of, so she pulled into a small space under a no-parking sign instead. (*Ne yapayım?*)

Stepping outside, she yanked her shopping from the passenger seat. The air was steamy and almost a little too rich in the seaside neighbourhood of *Avcılar* that evening. Various tempting dinner odours wafted from a multitude of apartment windows. Her neighbours on the right were obviously having *kızartma* tonight. The sweet smell of frying aubergines made her unsure whether she was hungry or nauseous.

Five minutes later, Ayşe was in her small apartment emptying her bags. Even here in deepest urban Istanbul traditional bazaars were still the place most residents bought their groceries. The colour, sociability, freshness of produce and sheer convenience of Turkish street markets, meant they would win the competition with the multi-national supermarket chains long into the twenty first century. It was an efficient system. The bazaars moved about cities like herbaceous satellites. Each morning, the nomadic grocers would drive to the next neighbourhood, erect their tarps and create their comestible masterpieces. At dusk they vanished leaving a trail of vegetative destruction in their wake. Then, from out of the darkness, fleets of dust-carts sent by the borough council would appear and swiftly eradicate the hills of detritus. By morning it was as if nothing had happened.

Once Ayşe had finished unpacking, her small kitchen worktop held a loaf of fresh white bread, a kilo of tomatoes, a small plastic bag full of thick home-made yogurt, some feta cheese, wild cherries, apricots, florets of fresh dill and parsley, large bundles of earthy spinach, and the long pale green fingers of capsicum.

There was someone else in the kitchen too. He perched uneasily on a barstool about the breakfast bar. The young man. He had quit his job a while back and was now studying at university. For two years he and Ayşe had lived apart yet together in freedom, space and respect. It seemed they'd found the key. The way. The road to that elusive goal – the happy relationship. Yet is anything ever what it seems? Do we ever know the truth? The young man was, after all, still young.

Seagulls squawked and shrieked in the shadowy air, while the merry tinkling of the gas cylinder cart grated on the nerves of the whole street. Ayşe stood in the small kitchen of her flat stirring a pot of homemade lentil soup. The steam curled out from the pan in salty wafts. The young man's eyes drooped so low they were all but lolling on the floor. 'I'm sorry' he mumbled.

Ayşe spooned the soup carefully into two small bowls without spilling a drop, before she silently placed them on the table. Not a muscle twitched on her face. 'You'd better sleep on the couch tonight.'

He closed his eyes for a moment, and sighed. She wiped the work surface clean and slid onto the stool opposite him. 'I'm not surprised' she continued. 'I've been expecting this day. Nothing could ever go *this* well.' But inside she splintered, the hairlines zigzagging wildly, ripping her into a million tiny pieces.

The next morning Ayşe woke up, sent the young man away and told him not to call or come back. As he closed the door behind him, she stared about her living room. Cushions were tucked tidily into the sofa. The dog tooth of the parquet flooring was a grainy polished jigsaw. Fallen in love with someone else? What the hell did that mean? And what did it say about how he'd felt about her? Had there ever been anything real? Had it all been a lie?

Some buffoon had just gone and trounced her beautiful trail, slapped black paint over all the markers, ripped up her map. She had walked into the wilderness only to get lost half-way. Stuck and alone in the middle of nowhere.

She walked over to the window and stared out. A *simit* seller and his two-wheeled cart squatted on the corner with a cluster of hornet pedestrians hovering about his wares. Her home suddenly was too lofty, too far removed. The life of the street was a million miles away.

Two days came and went. Two long days in the lovers' dungeon of disillusionment. The phone rang. She didn't answer. Messages came. She didn't read them. And then he was standing in front of her, vowing it had all been a mistake. Ayşe was the one he loved. Perhaps he even added a desperate '*Ne yapayım?*'

Ayşe wondered what to do. The path of her heart hadn't exactly led her to the place she thought she was going. Would her mind make a better navigator? Questions buzzed and flapped like crazed female mosquitos around a sleeping body. What did those four letters l-o-v-e really mean?

୫୦Oୠ

The *simit* sellers quietened. The flat dimmed. The young man was sucked backwards until he became no more than a speck in the distance. Istanbul evaporated into the night. All that was left was the buzzing.

It looked like Ayşe would be eaten alive that night. And the gnats would never be satiated. But something saved Ayşe in her swinging rope-bed, there on the sand of Limanağzı. It was something which couldn't be seen, but it moved mountains from time to time. Because nothing deters a mosquito like a good gust of wind. Ayşe's saving grace was Lycia's respiration. Her breath travelled in soft whirls all over her magnificent lands. Now here it was at the coast, a north-westerly blowing gently through the beach-side eatery.

Everything has a trail, and the Lycian wind was no exception. Were we to have followed those flurries back – tracing the loops and swirls of their journey – where would we have ended up? I've no idea of the exact starting point. But I can say where it had come from before it touched Ayşe. It had blown in from across the Xanthos plain and over the Esen river.

Hours earlier, the wind had been in the ancient city of Xanthos. It had swept over every lichen-eaten stone, and into every yawning crevice. The moving air had pried into the city's most hushed corners. It had danced in the large silent amphitheatre eddying over the empty seats. Xanthos had touched the wind, just as she touched all those who saw her, and the air sang out the words of her sorrow as it rushed along the earth.

Xanthos
Lost
Stones bestrewn,
She collapses
Upon her knoll.
  Walls
  Sunken,
Columns crumbled,
Tombs toppled in disarray.
  Broken
    Burned

And

Unredeemed.

All castaway bones in a common grave.

Not one did they save. [2]

ଅଠ O ଔଃ

No. Not one did they save. I know that story well, the sorry story of Xanthos. It rings inside me. And the ringing may never stop. It was the time and place destinies were changed. People changed tracks. States changed hands. And nothing was ever the same again. And I shall tell you that story. Because I'm sick of holding it. My time has come. It always does in the end . . .

General Harpagos, commander in chief of the Persian army, was flanked by men, thousands of them, shields and armour glinting like rows and rows of sharp polished teeth. It was a formidable horde of warriors primed for a whitewash. The serpent necks of the dromedaries twisted and turned. Their riders, a sleek crew of some of the deadliest archers in the ancient world pulled back their bowstrings in anticipation. The sun was taking no prisoners that day. It hurled down its molten white heat, broiling the entire plain.

The Xanthian army marched out to meet the fighting force of an empire. They comprised a modest bunch of men, but their ardour more than made up for their lack in numbers. Lycia had been independent for centuries. These were the children of Leto, and they trusted no one. As they

---

[2] See *Notes for the historically interested.*

lined up, a wall of flesh ready to protect a wall of stone, they growled and spat.

'Lycia is free. Xanthos is independent. The Persians can go to hell!'

Both sides stabbed the sky with their swords and roared. It had begun. Moments yawned open. Swarms of arrows filled the heavens, swelling and swaying like a hideous black creature. The creature swooped, driving down into the Xanthians, clawing into their shields and bodies. No one ran. No one deserted. Freedom was worth a lot more than that. In the slither of time it took the archers to reload, the Xanthians pushed forwards. It made no sense to stall. The Persian archers would decimate them. And sure enough, the troops of Harpagos bristling with the confidence of a thousand victories drove in to meet them. The sky was dark with arrows. The ground was a forest of iron. Arrow tips thundered into the home side, while Harpagos gathered the cavalry.

On it went. The Xanthians mustered all the gall they could find and launched themselves into the oncoming droves. They slashed and hacked dealing an onslaught of blows, slicing into the guts of Harpagos' army. Sword blades streaked the air silver, and the domes of shields smirked as the sun hit them. The stony earth soaked up the sweat and blood, recording how each man fought, not for his life, but for his sovereignty.

But, as the sun rolled westwards, the Xanthians were, slowly but surely, squashed back within their city walls. Defeat weighed heavily in the tenebrous air. The might of The Empire was now well and truly on their doorstep. Thus, the Xanthian men, in an act of incomprehensible desperation, gathered their wives and children, their treasures and their cattle. They locked them in the citadel. Then, they took a match to the lot, and proceeded to burn their cherished home to the ground. This is exactly how much liberty meant to them, and how sure they were life under the Persians wasn't worth living.

The fire began to roar as it ripped through the life and soul of Xanthos. Harpagos gripped the edge his chariot. He stared in horror as the screams and smoke spiralled out of the Lycian capital. The distinct smell of roasting flesh made him nauseous. It took him places he didn't want to go. He was at a loss. Cyrus had never had any intention of crushing the Lycians. All he wanted was allegiance, and a gateway to Phoenicia. He didn't even care if they worshipped Leto or Ahura Mazda. The Persian Empire wasn't about that.

As the atmosphere grew ever more sinister, smoke and dusk wove shadowy bands through the sky. The city drawbridge creaked and groaned open, a huge wailing mouth in a dying face of stone. Suddenly, the Xanthian men appeared. Half-crazed and roaring oaths to the likes of burning in hell before bowing to Persia, they charged, swords aloft, into the midst of the enemy.

'They . . . died sword in hand, not one surviving.'[3]

Not one. That's how Xanthos fell to Harpagos, and he took the memory to his grave. Though perhaps he shouldn't have taken it as personally as all that. The Xanthians were to repeat this madness almost exactly five hundred years later when Brutus attacked them for not paying their taxes.

For centuries the story was considered a myth. Then one day modern archaeologists discovered something. As they picked and scraped at the Xanthos earth, they uncovered a distinct layer of ash dating back to roughly the same time as Harpagos' invasion. Legend or truth? Some

---

[3] Herodotus, *The Histories.*

said the ash was coincidence. Other's claimed it was slightly the wrong date. But I know. I was there.

Day Seven

Rest-stop

Night left Limanağzı. The wind, which sensed the eye of Medusa, rushed on out to sea. It pulled its invisible train from the restaurant, from the olive trees and the lone woman slumped in the hammock beneath them. Some of its stories it left scattered about the dust. Others it stole. The wind journeyed out over the waves, whirling and winding on its way. Sometimes it followed a pattern, as though its path was already marked out. Other times it shot off haphazardly, for no clear reason at all. When it did, a new story was born. A new picture drawn.

The timeless witness in Ayşe rose. It swum through the years. Lightly. Silently. Like a monk seal gliding through the Mediterranean. Chronological ripples skimmed it as it went. It saw the light of the present moment above it. It surfaced. The sleeping woman felt the change. The darkness thinning. The light taking its place.

And she lifted her eyelids to see.

಄Оಇ

The moment I woke up, I sank into a strange bout of melancholy. Presumably, my physical condition (which was pitiable) had something to do with it. I was lumpy and itchy from an insect pillage, stiff, fatigued, and in pain. Where my pack had pulled on my shoulders, there were now unsightly chafed patches beneath my arms. I had long ago removed the sleeves from a sweatshirt and used them as underarm protection pads. My lower back was in a worse state. I could feel the injured muscles hardening into bands of chronic pain. Lower down my body, my feet had become an unsightly pickle of wounds, and I'm afraid my walking boots had all but disintegrated. You have to wonder at us hikers really, don't you? I'm sure any sensible person would have abandoned the mission at this point and caught the next bus home for a hot shower and a few days in bed watching romantic comedies, yet nothing could have been further from my mind. The Lycian Way had buried its way under my skin and was now a part of me. I just had to see more of it.

The good news was, the tourist village of Kaş was quite close. I soon hobbled off on the path and, within an hour, found myself navigating the narrow, Greek style streets. I headed for a campsite within an olive grove I knew from a previous visit. As I trudged wearily through the entrance, a garden of seaside terraces descended in front of me. The earthen steps were dotted with coloured canvas shelters, all of which looked out onto salt-sprayed rocks with the Greek isle of Meis huddled opposite.

Having pitched my tent, my next task was to stagger back to the small town, because there could be little doubt, I needed medical assistance. When I located the hospital, I turned myself in feeling both silly and guilty, a little like a suicide-attempt survivor. The doctors punctiliously patched me up with cream and bandages and whatnot.

'Go home and rest. You are absolutely not to walk for at least three days!' The doctor, a good looking young fellow with full lips and a dimple, waved a plastic pouch of medicine under my nose as he spoke.

'Yes, yes, I'll do that.' I said, with no obvious conviction.

The dimple twitched.

'Allah Allah. You athletes are as bad as smokers. You won't be happy until it kills you.'

I looked up, pushed the front of my eyebrows into my forehead and buried my head in my shoulders by way of apology. He was right. Once one starts, one just can't stop.

My next port of call was the cobbler, a hunched little man with skin that caricatured the attributes of his work material. Gingerly, he turned the remains of my footwear over and over in his hand. He studied the boots with the concentration of a man taking on a significant challenge. I thought he was going to throw them back at me. Finally, he lifted his head. His eyes puckered into sceptical slits. 'Tomorrow!' he barked.

And off I went. I heeded the doctors and rested. Pulling out some of the literature that had contributed to my backache, I passed the day in a hammock. Swinging. Breathing. Thinking. I ruminated on and on. As much as I was walking Lycia, she was walking me. My body might have been receiving something of a battering, but my mind was surprising me. I realised it was both as tough as iron, and as malleable as clay. As the land rolled and bumped under my feet, my attitude was changing, and I sensed I was being cleansed. Even so, I was far from resolving my relationship with the past. I staggered under my memories refusing to put them down, as though they were my home, or my refuge or something. Yes, I know this has all been said many times already, but has it actually been done? Has anyone really put the past down and walked free?

From my shaded hammock, I stared over at my backpack. It slumped in weary inutility on the inside of my tent awning. The pockets were bulging like over-stuffed cheeks, and its pot-belly was sagging. As I rocked to and fro in the hammock, I began to run through the contents in my mind. Could I could get rid of some of it and walk a bit lighter? One by one I evaluated each item.

The tent: this was impossible to leave, I needed shelter.

The sleeping bag: technically I could have survived without it, but it was incredibly handy. Its function as a bed was the least of its benefits. I could roll it up as a cushion, use it as a yoga mat, put it under my head as a pillow. No, I didn't want to say goodbye to that, and anyway, I'd borrowed it, so it wasn't really mine to throw out.

The camping mat: It was the lightest thing in the pack, so it made no sense to leave it. And again it wasn't mine.

My clothes: The only way I could have reduced the clothes I'd packed was to become even more objectionably filthy than I already was. It would mean having no spare socks or underwear, or shorts to sleep in. No, that wasn't acceptable.

Water: Unthinkable. I was forever thirsty as it was.

Food: I did have a couple of cans of tuna fish, a tomato, some bread, apricots, nuts and sunflower seeds. Could I throw my fate entirely out to the elements and walk without provisions?

Books (Being in Dreaming by Florinda Donner, Leyla's House by Zülfü Livaneli, The Power of Now by Eckhart Tolle: I was half-way through Leyla's House, so that was staying, Being in Dreaming was my favourite book in the world, and I wasn't going to part with it even if it left me with kyphosis. That left The Power of Now. Hmm.

Notebook and pen: Nope, I wasn't parting with either of those. They weighed nothing anyway.

Torch: Staying, no questions asked.

Hat and sunglasses: As above.

214

Wallet, cards, money and telephone: Obviously staying.

Cigarettes and lighter: Don't be ridiculous.

Toiletries: Ah, now this was an area where I could potentially shed a few pounds. I had soap, shampoo, conditioner, a hair brush, cleanser, moisturiser, toner, eye cream, toothpaste, a toothbrush, dental floss, wipes, tissues, body lotion, nail clippers, a nail file, cotton buds, cotton wool, a wash cloth, hair bands, hair clips and quite a lot more; however, the only thing was, when I examined each individual item, a) it was so small as to make little difference on its own, b) some of it was quite pricey so I didn't feel like wasting it, c) I wasn't prepared to spend days with no soap or toothpaste.

ஐO௦

Ayşe lolled in the hammock. A T-shirt was rolled into a pillow under her head, and a golden confetti of sunlight fell through the olive trees about her. She pulled the Lycian Way map out from under her and unfolded it. Then she held it above her face to shade her eyes. The red ribbon of the trail wriggled and squirmed over the green outlines of Lycia. It knotted together a bunch of places she was yet to see. She traced her finger along the crimson vein. Kaş. It was well over half-way. Phellos was coming next, then Kalkan and Patara. And soon after, Xanthos and the arcane-sounding Letoon.

Ayşe's finger rested on the Letoon yet again. She flipped to the back of the map and studied the photograph of Lycia's most sacred space. It had been the name which had drawn her, a name, unbeknown to the hiker, derived from the great Goddess Leto herself. Is that why it had attracted her? Were the syllables imbued with ancient diva magic? Did even the name Letoon vibrate with the forgotten mysticism of another time?

The walker's eyes fell on to the photograph. It showed the remains of two mighty rows of bone-white columns. All were snapped off a short way up from the base. The columns were semi-submerged in a swamp clouded by green algae. They surfaced like the heads and shoulders of a long-lost marble army. Beneath the water's piebald skin, cadavers of stone walls and floors glistened faintly. In one corner a mottled cuboid of a tomb rose eerily out of the deep. Letoon. Mysterious indeed. A quiet, yet persistent voice began to tap away at Ayşe. What was the Letoon hiding? Because there just had to be something down there in that mire.

It was hot, very hot. The lids of her eyes capitulated, and the map fluttered to the ground. Ayşe breathed. In and out. She sank into the mesh of the hammock falling slowly, gently, into another place altogether. The hammock barely moved. The air was still. Nothing was stirring at all. Yet, in the invisible world hiding within and beyond the visible, something roused. It was rare anyone ever pondered on the Letoon. Rarer still, they considered her mysteries. Her truth was largely forgotten. By the modern age the place had not much more than a handful of visitors a year. Somewhere, some when, in a time beyond all times, something trembled in anticipation. The dust, the wind, and the sea all gawked as Lycia's manifold rocky ears pricked up.

Further along the trail, over in the Letoon, that most secret of secrets stirred. Slowly, the eyelids of an entombed enigma pulled open, as they did from time to time. The eyes rolled from left to right, seeking, searching. Was someone coming at long last? Was daylight in sight? For the past had been buried a long, long time in the Letoon. Waiting.

Waiting for the day. It was waiting to tell its tale. Waiting to shout it at anyone who'd hear.

ഇ○ദ

'Keep them moving, for God's sake,' Harpagos told one of his officers.

He was finding it hard to stand in his chariot as the horses faltered on the track. The Persians were trudging away from Xanthos, and the smoking hillock was receding behind them. They followed the Xanthos River southwards heading for the port of Patara.

Armour clanked along the stone roads. Camels lurched to and fro, their riders rocking and rolling with every step. A shroud of silence had descended over these war-spattered battalions. If they marched with any speed, it had more to do with distancing themselves from the horrors they had seen than any lust for future conquest. 'Pity the divisions left behind,' sixty-odd thousand minds were thinking. And they sweated from their swathed heads down to their dusty, open toes.

Harpagos was desperate for solitude, but it was hard to come by. The sweltering, late-morning air was drifting so slowly he could hardly feel it move. The grass stalks were all but motionless. But his grump was interrupted. Because there, bursting from the sun-parched hill in front of him, was something he had never seen before. He sat up sharp in his chariot. The thing moved closer. And as it approached it grew. Harpagos craned his neck to get a better look. It was a huge sarcophagus mounted on a high pillar. It soared in the air like a massive stork's nest, or a sky-borne treasure chest.

The general promptly slumped back onto his seat. His head hung low under his helmet, his shoulders rounding. Rather than intrigue him, the sight spooked him. Despite every indication to the contrary, Harpagos had always harboured the suspicion he was an unlucky sort, that life was just biding its time before it brought its axe of tribulation down on him. He wondered if that time was approaching.

As usual, the chariot was girded by a thick belt of Companions, and the vivid fields of indigo and saffron headdresses bobbed in unison. The convoy slowed. Everyone stared up in bewilderment at the mighty overhead casket. They hoped it would go away. But it didn't. And there was more to come. Before long, a white marble temple rose in front of them. It was stuffed with scores of huge carved columns. It was spanking clean, and shone eerily. The whiteness was almost blinding.

They marched on. There was another temple. And another. Everywhere tombs protruded from the ground. It was as though Gaia had refused to hold the dead within her any longer and had spewed the coffins out onto the hillside. An enormous statue of Leto towered at the entrance of the main site. It was flanked by Artemis and Apollo. Their chilly marble eyes followed the Persians as they passed. The Letoon. Not one home was to be seen. Not even a shack. No people or noise either, just silent mausoleums and temples, and ice-white marble. Sixty thousand men grew ever more subdued as the Lycian sun climbed higher and higher above them.

As far as Harpagos had heard, no one lived at the Letoon. It was the sacred worship site of the Lycians. The house of the Goddess Leto. Still, he was curious. He also sensed the cloud of doom which pervaded. He knew only too well how superstitious men of war could be. They were all of them beginning to wonder. Had they been cursed? Had the Lycians jinxed them? Harpagos was one of the few generals in history to understand the relative insignificance of numbers. Sixty thousand men or one thousand, it only took a seed of doubt to spread the poison ivy of defeat. He had to pull himself together, find that seed and eradicate it. He would face the Letoon and her demons. And he would damn well overcome the lot!

In the future, some would say this had been his destiny all along. Others would claim it was the whimsical nudge of chance. Whatever the cause, it was a decision which altered the path of both his history and Lycia's.

At the perimeter of the Letoon, the Persian army set up its vast, rambling camp. A multitude of tents rose along the dry grass bank. They twisted skywards like the pointed hats of the magi. It was an ethnic medley of a war caravan. The highly trained regiments of the Persians were supplemented by throngs of conscripts reaped from the various conquered kingdoms. Then there were the Achaemenid Empire's fearless paid assassins too. These were either Greek hoplites or Scythians. Throw in the masses of camp followers tagging along to cook for the soldiers or care for the wounded, and the wives and concubines the Companions were allowed to bring along, and even on a day as dark and ominous as this one, the Persian camp was something of a motley rainbow.

Harpagos' plush circular tent was the first to grace the skyline. It had all the splendour of a palace. There were silverware-laden royal trays, two sumptuous red divans and some of the finest rugs from Persia unrolled over the Lycian dirt. The Greeks could say what they liked, but the Persians certainly travelled in style. An assistant removed Harpagos' sandals, and he bathed his feet in the silver tureen of water by the tent door. As he entered, the smell of perfumed oils burning in censers wafted over him. The inside of his tent was a wonderland of embroidered colour, pomegranate, saffron, ochre, indigo, gold.

Harpagos plopped down onto the divan, pulled off his helmet and rubbed his temples. An attendant entered with a silver jug of lemon water. The general took the refreshment and then waved the man away,

'Close the door,' he said. 'Under no circumstances disturb me.'

Inside it was a shadowy cotton cave – a fabric womb offering shelter from the gross reality of the outside. The cool darkness was a comfort, of sorts. Harpagos lowered his head into his hands, tightened his bottom lip and stared hard at the deep red rug under his feet. Finally, silently, a tear which had taken years to swell, rolled the length of his face. Another followed. It traced a glassy track along the bridge of his nose before dripping onto the carpet below. No one saw him weep. No one ever had. Most thought he had a heart of stone.

The reasons Harpagos cried were as manifold as all the stones in Lycia. Somehow, despite all the tragedy and blood he had seen, it was Xanthos which cracked him. Two hundred years later it would crack Brutus too for exactly the same reason. Never had Harpagos been witness to such a futile waste of life. Never had he felt so misunderstood. And is this not the most painful fate of the outcast? Being misinterpreted? Misconstrued?

This conquest, this battle on behalf of Persia, had always been for Harpagos a kind of healing, albeit a convoluted, spiralling type of remedy. He had suffered, so he wanted justice. He knew all about the fickle hand of power, the hand which sliced through his son's throat and served him the remains on a plate. He believed in Cyrus the Great. He believed in his magnanimity. When he held aloft his sword in Cyrus' name, he fought for the idea of his son's freedom. Perhaps he even fought for the carcass of his own. Now it was as worthless as desert dust. As pointless as a footpath in a sandy dune. Xanthos had swallowed up all the goodness in his war.

Harpagos screwed his eyes tight shut. 'To hell with Lycia!' He spat at the floor. Anger that had been quashed for years and years snuck up from behind and ambushed him. This all had to be somebody's fault. Someone should pay. It was then, Harpagos saw the Lycians as his enemy. They were the progenitor of all his woe. And he decided to wreak his revenge. He beat down on the earth. On and on. The ground of Lycia received his blows without judgement, the dust particles holding the vibrations.

ಬಂ೦ಜ

Two-and-a-half thousand years in the future, a hundred kilometres away, the ground shuddered ever so slightly. No one noticed the tremor other than a couple of academics hunched over seismographs. But the trees did. And the small reptiles within them did too. Just outside the small town of Kaş, a woman was rocking under one such tree. A map lay half-open on the dusty ground beneath her hammock. The woman snoozed on. A light breeze picked up whipping the sea into an arras of royal blue folds. The rocks tumbled white and jagged into the water. The thin hard leaves of the olive trees rattled lightly in the moving air. They were a terrace of giant deformed maracas.

No one saw what crouched above the woman hanging onto a twist of dry olive branch by its quirky pincer-toes. This was entirely by design. Fused toes were only one of the chameleon's idiosyncrasies. What with its novel rotating eyes, its protracted tongue, and its unorthodox habit of changing colour, it was easy to assume the

221

chameleon was from another planet altogether. But it's when a chameleon starts walking, it comes into its own.

This chameleon was on the move. He swayed from side to side as he stalked along the branch, shoulder blades protruding, back lowered, little cleft feet opening and closing around the knurled dry wood. The movement was half panther, half gloved-magician, and it would have caused even the most disinterested human to stop and stare. No one so much as blinked an eye, however. Chameleon was a master of camouflaged stealth. One of his eyes pointed forwards. The other covered his rear. And every now and again they would swap, or move from side to side instead. Those eyes were good at long-range focussing. They could spot a mosquito up to ten metres away. But that's not what this chameleon was after. He had noticed an attractive female skulking about a cactus plant a little way off, and he was aiming to grab her attention.

Chameleon was wandering in a peopled minefield. Hulking great humans loped about under the trees, or flopped in hammocks like the one just below. Still, it was a manageable feat as far as he was concerned, and he took on the challenge without so much as a second thought.

As it happens, chameleons don't use their colour-changing ability primarily for camouflage at all. Its most important function is communication with other chameleons. They can turn black and ugly to warn, or neutral to appease, or even light multi-colours if they're out to seduce. As our chameleon reached the nether tip of his olive branch, his dilemma was this. How do I stand out without standing out? He stepped carefully from the knotty brown wood into a clump of olive leaves. There he stayed, adjusting his daywear, getting lighter and brighter all the while. His colour was similar enough to the leaves, a predator was unlikely to spot him. Another chameleon on the other hand would have no trouble. And should another of his kind see him there, dressed in his new green-blue speckled suit, they would know exactly what was on his mind.

Down below the olive tree, a few metres away from him over by the cactus plant, the female chameleon sat quite still. She gradually turned yellow and light green. Up in his tree, chameleon rocked a little. He would, slowly but surely, have to creep down from his perch. Only then he heard a sound. One of his eyes rotated swiftly backwards. He stayed deadly still. Because there was movement. It was coming from down below . . .

Ayşe had woken up. She put her middle fingers into the corners of her eyes and tried to rub away the sleep. She was still groggy, the nap clinging onto her like the slime of a muggy day. Stretching her arms and her back, she lazed for a while and let the present moment find its way back to her. The trouble was, as always after a daytime snooze, the present had some difficulty staying on the path. As Ayşe inhaled the warm sea air and pushed her hammock to and fro, other times sabotaged the Now by pushing it off the track. She stared out along the coast. Her mind wandered back to where she had come from. Across the bay lay Limanağzı, and behind that outcrop the Lycian Way was crawling back east, back to the Olympos valley.

How had she, an Istanbul city lass, ever found herself there to begin with? She, with her nice clean apartment and her weekends shopping, her VW Golf and her office job. Ayşe remembered how, and why, and it made her both wince and smile all at once.

ೞ O ೞ

Istanbul 2001.

Months had gone by. Four, five, six. Eventually, Ayşe and the young man were a pair again. Now, it was a union built on different foundations, hoisted as it was on struts of dented trust. Not that the love had died. It was facing the darkness within it. Freedom and respect remained the cornerstones. Time would tell the rest. The tender-skinned innocence born between them was inevitably growing tougher.

Meanwhile, the other man in her life was also changing. Her son, Umut.

The door slammed so hard the plates rattled, and the teenager marched in hurling his rucksack onto the floor. He'd just returned from a weekend with his dad and was primed for a fight.

'How was your trip?' Ayşe peered out from the bathroom, her hair in a towel.

'Right, like you care!' Umut strode past her and into his room. Ayşe heard him kick the door shut. She unwrapped her hair, leaned against the wall and let her eyelids drop shut. She loved Umut, and at this point in his life he couldn't understand it. He thought love was need or control or sacrifice. He thought, like most people, love meant giving up who you were for someone else. Ayşe knew this because she observed how he always came home with an empty wallet no matter how much money she gave him. He spent it on his friends. They probably threw their arms around his shoulders and crooned about what a sport he was. Until the day he didn't have anything to give them. Until he was as empty and dry as a cleaned goat carcass.

Eventually, the door of his room opened. Umut sauntered into the lounge, slumped into the sofa and folded his arms.

'He's not back yet then.'

Ah. He was talking about the young man. This was the *real* issue. She wasn't behaving how a mother should, far from it! According to the rules of this land, she was behaving like a 'bad woman' and bad meant not complying, not fitting in, not changing your colours to blend in with the rest. Bad always means that. In every society since the beginning of communal living, bad has equalled not being controllable. Because we think we need each other. Because we think we can't stand alone. So it is we tie those nearest to us in knots, until we squeeze the very life out of them.

Yet, there was one door open, a pocket of bad where no one lived up to anything. A place where her unconventional colours synthesised with the rest. The valley of outcasts.

It had been a couple of years earlier, a friend had introduced her to Olympos. She'd loved it on sight; the window pane of the sea, the crown of beach pebbles, the slopes with the broken stone men falling down them, and the white peak of Mount Olympos – home of the Gods – presiding over it all. She loved Medusa's summer glare and Aphrodite's night eye. But most of all, she loved the anti-culture germinating under Olympos' topsoil. The alternate Godverse hiding in the cracks. Because it had started in Olympos, even if it ended somewhere else.

Days Eight and Nine

Arriving

It was a stiff and grumbled awakening. I was still exhausted, my legs ached, and my feet were beyond what one would normally consider usable, the blister to flesh ratio was simply too high. My back was raw, as well. To be honest, it felt as though I'd spent the night being flogged. I consoled myself with a proper breakfast in Kaş (no squirrel food, or nuts, but luxuries like hot tea, simits and cheese). Next, I made my way to the cobbler. My poor shoes were clinging to life as a man might cling to a tree root in a torrent. I smiled at the emotions this pair of dilapidated footwear was able to evoke in me. They were long-lost friends, possibly the only things in the vicinity to look as thoroughly pulverised as I did.

By afternoon, I was preparing to move on. I packed up my rucksack vetting each item as I did so. Anything I was getting rid of, I put to one side. At the end, I looked at the throwaway pile. It was no bigger than a small anthill. I managed to say goodbye to a bottle of body lotion, one pair of murdered socks, half a loaf of bread and 'The Power of Now' which I left on the basis I could find it anywhere. I couldn't see the sum of these parts making too many inroads into my twenty kilogram cargo, though.

I had waited until this late, because a fellow back in Limanağzı had cautioned me to not to walk in the day due to the difficulty of the climb. He was right. I set off as the sun was releasing the shore, but the road was, nonetheless, gruellingly steep; an incline deserving of a crimson colour-code. As I huffed my way up the hill (honestly, the pack felt exactly the same; I was already regretting leaving 'The Power of Now' behind) the stunted rock-side shrubs winked amber in the twilight. The humpbacked curve of Kaş prevailed beneath me. Eventually, it got to the point where

I was so tired I couldn't feel the pain any more. And to think, people call hiking a hobby.

I reached a dusty plateau. It was as flat as a table top, a peculiarly red table top. The soil there was the colour of rust, and it spread far and wide – a sort of Mediterranean outback. I trudged over it until I reached a modest, yet unusually well-maintained, mountain village. Still lumbering under my pack, I had a quick look around. I could see some exemplary, old stone houses scattered amongst almond trees. But most were empty. It pained me to observe this yet again. All over, villagers are enticed by ridiculous television series and commercials to evacuate their land and move to the city. What awaits them there? Well, plenty of debt for a start, exorbitant electricity bills, pollution, transportation costs, unemployment, rent, and a severing of connection with the Earth, the significance of which I was only now comprehending.

Evening was here already, and it stretched across the sky in violet ribbons. I started to search a place to pitch my tent. Spying a mosque, I trotted towards it. At the rear of the simple domed structure was a public hydrant. Two charming antique bronze taps had been set into a concrete headstone. I decided this would be a convenient spot to overnight.

Dragging my backpack to the rear of the tap, I investigated the surroundings. Everything looked just perfect, and for the first time in eight days, I anticipated a peaceful sleep. But one should anticipate nothing in life. From the outset of the trek people had warned me of the many hazards. Wasn't I afraid? What if a man broke in to my tent? What would I do? What if I was bitten by a snake or a dog? How would I get help? These warnings scurried in the back of my mind like worrisome house mice. I would hear nothing of them until the middle of the night when they'd scuttle about and wake me up. But after a week without incident, I had started to dismiss the black worry-mice as exaggerations. I suppose, I was feeling a little hiker hubris again.

The light began to fade, so I went to drink from the hydrant and brush my teeth and whatnot. Hunching over, I reached for the tap, but when I twisted it open, I froze. Suddenly, it was as though my feet had grown stalks; the soles turned into tap roots burrowing into the ground. For there, no more than two inches from my face, was the scaled head of an exotically patterned water snake.

I'd never been in such close proximity to a snake before. Why these creatures evoke such dread in us is a mystery to me, but they do, as though they are the living embodiment of our darkest nightmares. Is it the Garden of Eden revisited? Is it a long, lost instinct inherited from hairier ancestors? Or is it the chilling trails they trace over the earth, their bodies forming circles, 'S' shapes and figure-eights as no other animal can?

The water chortled out from the spigot in silvery fronds while the snake and I eyed each other in mutual repulsion. I shivered. The snake gulped (well I imagine it did). Both of us remained there for an exceptionally long moment. Then, we simultaneously scrambled off on our separate ways.

I tried not to dwell too much on the encounter. The simple fact was I couldn't. I had to camp somewhere after all, and here was all I had, snakes, scorpions, wild boar or not. But, had I dared to consider it, would I have spotted the omen camouflaged amidst the beautifully patterned scales? Things are often never what they appear, are they? Just as help and kindness can arise deep in the heart of jeopardy, danger often hides in the places we assume to be safest, the spaces in time where we relinquish our guard *and become, well a little complacent. The trouble starts, I think, when we assume we 'know'.*

The sky snatched away the light. My tent was up, and I was washed and lying horizontal. But I was far from comfortable, in fact I was all but nailed to my mat in apprehension. I prayed that night, to whomever or whatever might be interested, that I be spared a nocturnal reptile visit. Hmph. One should be extremely careful for what one wishes, because more often than not one gets exactly that, not a gram more and not a gram less. It was going to be 'one of those nights'.

It took less than an hour. All at once, my ears pricked up. There was noise, a loud, rumbling sound. I pulled myself up on one elbow and paid better attention. It was the sound of an engine, of what must have been a four-wheel drive (what else could have made it up the rough boulder-filled track?) And it was moving closer. Good grief! Someone was pulling up at my little, spring-side camping spot! Suddenly, my snake encounter seemed altogether innocuous, as I heard one, two, three gruff male voices approaching my tent zipper. Their boots scuffed noisily through the rocky dirt. They stopped. A torch-beam flipped wildly over my canvas. I'm afraid the word fear does little justice to the emotional havoc being wreaked inside me.

I read somewhere, a few years later, instinct with its instantaneous surge of heightened awareness and explosive energy, is triggered when the reptile brain is activated. Was that a coincidence? I had never realised the mechanism was so efficient. This is the power that pulls cement walls from the legs of loved-ones, the power to fight and kill for your life. I have no idea how it happened, but before I knew it, I found myself crouched by my tent door, holding a switch-blade knife in my hand! There I sat awaiting my imminent fate, not even daring a tremor such was my abject terror. I can't quite believe I'm saying this, but I was poised to launch the knife straight at the first head I saw.

The canvas rustled and rippled as one of the men 'knocked' on my door. I chewed my lip. Every sinew in my body was braced for the coming attack.

'Open up! This is an army patrol!'

The army? Was this good or bad? I didn't know whether to sigh with relief or remain vigilant. What right had they to disturb me like this in the dead of night? And then it occurred to me: they could hardly suppose I was female, or alone. All they saw was a tent parked 'suspiciously' in the middle of nowhere. So, I spoke up to make it quite clear, just in case I unzipped the tarp and found myself face to face with the barrel of a rifle.

'Certainly, Officer!'

From the murmuring and shuffling outside, I gathered I wasn't the only one to sigh in relief. Hmm, be it snakes or grown men or lone hikers, everyone is petrified of a stranger. Stifling a chuckle, I hid my knife under my sleeping bag before unsealing the flap to pass my identity card through.

Shaking their heads in confusion, the men in khaki held their flashlight over the laminated orange square. Then they grunted and bid me goodnight. Oh, the threads of ignorance, and the webs of terror we weave out of them.

It was time for a cigarette.

ৠ〇৫

As the smoke snaked out of her mouth, Ayşe's heartbeat slowed. She had left her tent and was perched on a boulder nearby. It was beautiful out there. The night wound about the hilltop in silky, black loops. The half-moon soared overhead. Ayşe watched the moon. It was hard not to find her shimmer alluring. Her light fell over Lycia like silver rain. It dripped over the rocks and trickled into the earth.

The evening's drama filled Ayşe's head. Her mind blabbered on. She finished her cigarette and carefully tucked the butt into her portable cigarette-box ashtray. Sleep would never come, she was sure. And that was why she folded her legs on the large boulder, closed her eyes and began to try and meditate. She watched her breath. It moved in and out, just like everything, swinging from being to non-being and back again.

Before long, the night air breathed with her, as did the stone beneath her. An agama lizard sensed the specialness of the space and tip-toed closer. He crawled half-under the rock and remained there with his prehistoric dragon-head raised. He sniffed the air, drinking in the white glow from above. As the moonlight flowed, all over Lycia things stirred. The blackness squashed itself into holes. It shrunk from the magic waking up. Long-buried secrets from a bygone time felt the moondrops on their hides. And when they did, their timeworn eyes flicked open.

The moon reached her apex. Half of her existed. The other half was engulfed by night. The wide expanse of Lycia gaped up, for the moon was her beacon, her signal. Ayşe sensed it too, the glitter of night on her skin. It sank into her pores, calling out to the primeval in her, to the ancestors, to all that had created her since the beginning of time. It doesn't take too much to feel your primordial essence. Just a little space. A free mind. Some fresh air. As the life inside Ayşe flexed its ageless muscles, Lycia quivered. For unbeknown to anyone at all, that awakening was a powerful sign. A flare in the darkness of wayward modernity.

A little way over to the west, over the nobbled vertebrae of the Ak mountains, beat Lycia's sacred heart. The Letoon. The pulse had now quickened. It shook the stones and the dust sending shivers along her ancient, rock-ribbed skin. She was waiting. Still. Waiting for the day. The day when she could unlock her knowledge, unfurl the pure, white sails of truth. Could the day be approaching? Were the moderns finally coming back home? For Lycia's message had been entombed for thousands of years. It was interred within her lithic flesh. On sensing the aura of Ayşe, Lycia was reminded of exactly who had buried that knowledge, and why. Two-and-a-half thousand years under her skin, the beasts of the past called out. Persistently. Plaintively. Their cries haunted the night.

The Letoon-545 BC

Harpagos left his palatial yurt at eventide. He beckoned twenty bodyguards, and they came swiftly hither, jangling and rustling as they did so. The general climbed onto his steed, perching on the saffron and purple embroidered saddle-cloth. The chosen Companions followed, half on foot, half on horse-back. The splendid formation moved through the war caravan, picking through the various encampments on their way. Harpagos' large band of Companions, currently mostly Medes and Persians, were situated closest to him. As he passed their carnival of tents, he watched them. They were all trying to drown their woes in good food, good wine and plenty of fine-looking women and men, all courtesy of the great Achaemenid Empire.

Next, he ambled past the well-to-do Hoplite division from Ionia. This lot rubbed slightly on Harpagos' nerves. They generally fancied themselves to be superior to the rest of the warriors. The Hoplites owned their equipment and armour. They took the business of war very seriously. As the sun sank below the Lycian skyline, they were busy polishing their customised, round shields and their tell-tale plumed helmets.

A little further on were the regiments of Lydian conscripts with plenty of Phrygians among them. A slightly cantankerous crew, they could usually be found squatting in huddles, bemoaning their lot. Whenever Harpagos or the Companions were thought to be out of earshot, the topic of campfire discussion circumnavigated the well-worn terrain of whether it had been worse under their previous king Croesus, or now ruled as they were by Cyrus.

Finally, Harpagos found himself amidst the Scythian clan. He groaned inwardly and tried not to see the obvious. As usual, they were sprawled over the grass, women warriors among them, all stoned out of their tiny minds. For the Scythians were notorious for their love of marijuana and lugged sacks full of the weed on campaign. Harpagos often wondered how this rabble of hairy, tattoo-daubed layabouts ever managed to so much as stagger onto the battlefield. Yet, the Scythians were the nonpareil of the Persian machine – mercenaries of guts and skill. Everyone respected them. Harpagos would usually give them pride of place right in the centre of the field, something that irked the Ionians considerably.

The Persian commander-in-chief hadn't embarked on this evening jaunt to observe his troops, however. He was headed somewhere altogether different, somewhere which was bothering him more than he cared to admit. It nagged at him like a torn nail, or a scrap of date-skin trapped between his teeth. He stared across at the field of smooth, white columns ahead and decided to get to the bottom of it. The Letoon. Perhaps this was the place to come to terms with these damn Lycians. Perhaps he could make a peace offering to their Goddess. It would be a nice diplomatic touch, one Cyrus would definitely approve of.

Minutes later, the convoy was picking its way through the maze of tombs to the main temple. It was deserted. Not a soul was to be seen. Adjacent, stood two other temples. Parts of their facades were covered in webs of indecipherable inscriptions. Only a tiny sliver of sun remained. It hung on to the skyline for as long as it could before it was sucked unceremoniously into the belly of the underworld. Harpagos realised he should have begun this reconnaissance mission far sooner. Shadows began to creep up the successions of tall columns. Twilight murmured her threats of night. A chaos of bats swooped and whirled, while dark clouds of shrikes squealed and hurried to find their roosts.

Harpagos dismounted and stepped slowly towards the main entrance of the temple. Two of the Companions brought up the rear. They climbed the steps, flagstones so immaculate they looked as though they were perpetually polished. But by whom? The Letoon was deserted. As the Persians entered the grand, marble portico, the mighty Leto fixed her stone eyes on them – eyes devoid of irises and pupils, phantom's eyes. Simultaneously, all three men felt the skin between their shoulder blades prickle.

Dusk swam through the temple like a grey oil. It filled the corners, smearing the walls and the mosaic-covered floor. Harpagos strode through the forest of marble. He spied a large altar ahead guarded by three more statues. Leto, Artemis, Apollo. The statue of Leto glowered. The spikes of her gold crown pointed like a ring of accusatory fingers. And the cobra was there, coiled around her right arm. Harpagos gaped at the gold platters covering the huge altar. Dried fruits, nuts, carobs, and quinces were piled high in them. There was someone here, there had to be, or the gold would have been stolen long ago. And the fruit? It was as fresh as though it had just been picked.

For some reason, or no reason, Harpagos' heart began to race. He whirled around to scan the temple, but it was hard to see. Leto and her abode were fast sinking in shadow. The decorative carvings above the altar, on the walls, over the arches, began to contort as darkness snaked over their contours. It made the temple look alive, like an almighty vine or topiary garden. The general's mouth tightened into a straight line. He eyed the fabulous yellow quinces on the platters. They looked almost too good to be real, which was why he stretched out his hand, just to see. He couldn't help it. Those orbs were so golden, they almost glowed. It was plain and simple curiosity.

The voice came from the left-wing of the temple, from one of the inky gaps in the columns.

'Get your thieving little hands off that, *right now!*'

Harpagos yanked his arm back as if he'd been bitten. One of his bodyguards reached for an arrow, the other his sword, and both spun about wildly trying to find something to aim at. And then she appeared. She strutted out from between the columns, a white-gowned, white-haired crone. A bizarre-looking headdress made from bird feathers and laurel leaves was perched on her head. Harpagos squinted to get a closer look at her. Then he waved at the Companions to lower their weapons. She was old enough, with a husk of a face, a beakish nose, and a neck as wrinkled as a tortoise. But she walked with poise. Harpagos wasn't quite sure why, even at his age he suddenly felt like a disobedient adolescent. The woman drew up opposite the general, scanning him up and down. She had the eyes of a hawk. Piercing and grey.

'We've been expecting you. Now, there's a lot to do. Follow me. Chop, chop! You're late.'

Harpagos took a step backwards and gawked. But the words were Elamite not Lycian, and the woman's mouth wasn't moving. Someone else was doing the talking. There was a shuffling and some animation in the shadows. A band of seven or eight white-gowned women drew up to the altar. It was a mishmash coven of womanhood, with females of all ages and all appearances. One of them, dark and handsome, stepped forward and positioned herself between Harpagos and the old, bark-skinned woman.

'I'm here to translate for my Lycian sister. She is the guardian priestess of the sacred Letoon, and the president of the Lycian Federation. You'd do well to listen to her. Now follow us.'

Harpagos raised an eyebrow. Since when exactly did *he* have to listen to or follow anyone other than Cyrus? He was partly irritated, partly amused and partly curious. Many were those who came back with tales of Lycia, of their unorthodox, outmoded practices, of their witch magic and their incredible 'democracy'. And of course the free women. Now, here he was in the middle of it. He turned to the two men beside him speaking with gusto.

'Companions! Gather ten men, forthwith! Let's discover what this strange Letoon is all about.'

The translator and the older priestess drew together. There was something of a kerfuffle. It was the older woman who fixed her eyes on Harpagos. She stepped across to block his path.

'You can't bring them. The prophecy is clear. You are to come alone. Now hurry!' The translator said.

Harpagos blinked. His face drew itself tight into a frown. 'What prophecy?' he gnarled. He took a step back, as if to retreat. The old priestess drew herself up. She roared something in Lycian and grabbed his arm, yanking him. Harpagos yanked it back.

'Look here, Madam! I am General Harpagos, commander-in-chief of the Persian forces. I'm not sure if you realise, but Xanthos now belongs to Persia, which means Lycia belongs to Persia, which means your sacred Letoon is also now a part of the great Persian Empire. So, unless you are about to do battle with us, then you need to swear allegiance. I'm here on a mission of diplomacy. Persia makes no demands on you to change your religious practices, you are free to worship who and as you wish. That is all.'

Harpagos now had eight pairs of female eyes on him. The weight of their stares made him uneasy. It was as though something unpleasant inside him was leaking out, and they had spotted it. Was the blood oozing from his eyes and nose? Or through the roots of his hair? Harpagos checked his fingernails to see if it was visible. He noticed the tips were not quite steady.

'We know who you are, and we know what you've done. We know all about Xanthos. We knew about it before even you did,' the translator said.

And Harpagos saw it all again, careening through his mind, ploughing up the firm soil of his convictions. He bowed his head and began to study his sandals.

'You need to be cleansed before it all begins.'

He looked swiftly up. 'I *beg* your pardon?'

'Follow us. But you must come alone.' The translator twirled about on her feet and headed into the columns. She briefly flicked her head behind her, eyes catching the flagstones to her right. 'But if you are afraid for your safety, tell your soldiers we shall be at the nymphaion.'

Harpagos cocked his head and thought for a moment. Nymphaion? He'd heard the word before, in Lydia or Ionia. Nymphs. Nymphaion. Wasn't it some sort of mystical baths for nubile maidens to frolic about in? Yes. He

238

was sure of it. Aha. Now they were talking! The old crow with the headdress was hardly anything to write home about, but the translator? Now, *that* was a fine-looking woman. Ah well, perhaps it was altogether better he went alone. He didn't want his Companions gawking at his every move if he was about to share a bath with these ladies. And after all, after everything he'd been through, well, he could definitely do with a good cleanse, couldn't he?

So it was, the great General Harpagos, spirits lifting a little, trotting gamely out of the temple with the high priestess and her team of Leto sisters. They filed under the myrtle tree, along a winding path and to the spring beyond.

They arrived at a large, marble bath. It was a basin deep enough for a grown man to stand up in. Harpagos saw a wide cord of water running into it. He also noticed the high priestess was clutching a copper bowl. She paced at the edge of the nymphaion, eyes darting left and right. Suddenly, she halted and crooked a finger at him, beckoning him to kneel at the side of the pool. The last flickers of light were being extinguished one by one. The spring water gurgled like a mysterious night-filled potion. Harpagos looked about. He couldn't see any nymphs, which was a bit of a disappointment. Perhaps they were lurking in the bushes or something, just waiting to come prancing out in their semi-transparent nymph wear. The translator knelt beside him. He could feel the tight springs of her riotous hair brushing against his face. He hoped with all his heart his ablution might include her at some point.

'Close your eyes.'

Harpagos closed one eye. The other eye he kept open, scanning left and right. It occurred to him, his Companions might not even know what a nymphaion was, let alone be able to find the damn thing.

Abruptly, from behind him, came a high-pitched wail. The crone priestess had begun to chant. It was a howling sound. The kind of cry a wolf or jackal might make. The other priestesses joined in, and the wailing turned into a deafening feral cacophony. Then, night dropped its starry veil over the Letoon. That was the exact moment Harpagos felt an icy rush of water over his head.

'*What the . . .* ?' The rest of his sentence was lost in gurgles. He rubbed his eyes and whipped about, face twitching. 'What the *Devil* do you think you're playing at?'

But the high priestess had already filled a second bowl. She deposited it straight over his head again. His hair now lay plastered to his scalp, and it gleamed like a basket of river eels. The water ran in dark rivulets from his beard and over his tunic. He spluttered and gasped before hurriedly moving to pull himself up.

'Don't move! There's one more. Be still. Be quiet!' The translator had put her hand on his shoulder. It was surprisingly soothing, almost as though her palms were full of cool mint, or even moonlight. So, although Harpagos grimaced, he stayed put.

The last bowl of spring water was hurled over him. The high priestess then replaced the copper vessel on the rim of the bath. Next, she began waving her hands over Harpagos while she chanted. Meanwhile, the translator lit a sprig of dried sage from a torch a girl in the entourage was holding. The high priestess grabbed the wand of sage. She used it to draw circles and symbols over his head. The other priestesses looked on. It smelt a lot like the hemp the Scythians burned in their portable sweat-lodges, and Harpagos began to cough.

Finally, it was over. Ancient Persia's greatest general pulled himself to his feet, bedraggled and fuming. He could see neither hide nor hair of his Companions, and looked as though he'd inadvertently slipped into a bog. He felt a fool. Were these witches trying to humiliate him? Was that the name of their game?

'Now, come quickly. We need to make our way to the temple. Quickly!'

He turned to the translator and glared. 'I don't need to do *anything*! Agh, I don't have time to muck about with this lunacy. Now, if you don't mind I've got business in Patara to attend to, boats to dispatch. I shall be taking my leave. Be thankful I don't round up the lot of you!'

The women began to chatter and witter. Then they formed a circle round him. Each one looked panic-stricken, the high priestess gravest of all. She whispered to the translator who immediately relayed the message.

'My elder sister doesn't beg. But you must understand, you *have* to come with us.' Then the translator lowered her voice, and her beautiful black eyes. She spoke quickly sensing Harpagos was reaching the end of his not inconsiderable patience. 'There is a secret, a divine and most important secret. The secret of Leto, and the reason for this Letoon. We are the keepers. But the prophecies have made it clear. At the end of Lycian time, on a night when the moon hides half her face, the new keeper will ride in from the East. His hands will be dripping crimson. There shall be twenty by his side, all with rainbow colours and eagle spirits.'

Harpagos glanced down at the Faravahar on his purple tunic. The Zoroastrian symbol could pass for an eagle, even if it wasn't. The night was now thick and impenetrable, the half-moon almost swamped in the sky above. He was exasperated. Yet, when someone speaks of secrets and prophecies and divine purpose, which one of us isn't affected? Even Persian warlords are susceptible to curiosity. Even the greatest of the great wonder whether magic and destiny could be true. These women were perhaps mad, perhaps they were even white witches, but as Harpagos scanned their faces he found no trace of trickery in them. And that is why, against all odds, just as the prophecy had predicted, General Harpagos followed the line of priestesses back along the path towards the temple. His twenty Companions were lingering in front of the great portico. He ordered them to wait.

ಬ೦ಆ

Ayşe knew the moon had sunk behind the Ak Mountains. She felt the pitch deepening all about her. The heat from her rock and the heat from her body had mingled, the two merging to create a warmth that radiated beyond them. It was a heat the agama lizard could feel, and the pit viper not so far away could see. The agama would have made a good supper for her, had Ayşe not been present. The serpent would move no closer, however. Her diapsid intelligence didn't cognise it as a human's would. But she sensed in her own reptilian way the connection. The rock, the lizard and Ayşe. For the human had awakened to the Earth. She had felt her soul and her grace. In return the Earth would protect her. It was a rule as old as the hills and the stones, and the reptiles that crawled among them.

ಬ೦ಆ

Eventually, I managed to sleep that night, though hardly for long enough. Before I knew it, the lining of the tent was ablaze with the silver of morning. I was on the move again within half-an-hour.

If truth be told, the previous night's adventure had shaken me a little. I suddenly felt vulnerable. The soldiers rattling my tent had brought home to me just how easy it would be for someone to attack me out here, and this was why I started to walk quickly. I wanted to get away from my thoughts and fears. I suppose I had been doing that from the beginning really, hadn't I?

The first section of the day's trail took place on a pathway bristling with thorns. It was a scarifying scramble uphill, the talons of the bushes tugging at my hair and my pack. In the end, I made it to a flattish earth plateau. It was a baking expanse of clay without a scrap of shade, not that I cared. You see, I was in dire need of a rest. But, before I could rid myself of my pack, I spied a quivering somewhere up in front. Peering closer, I saw a mouse scrambling. It looked rather like a miniature horse galloping desperately through the grass. Yet there was something untoward about it. Its tail was unusually long.

I blinked. Oh dear. It wasn't a tail, was it? I noticed the henna brown lariat of what I later learned was a Taurus whip snake. And the most alarming component of this discovery was, both the mouse and its pursuer were headed undeviatingly in my direction.

I turned on my heel and broke into a run. I fled with nineteen-and-a-half kilograms bouncing upon my still-injured back. It was a ludicrous canter spent with my neck craned behind me so that I could monitor whether the rodent-reptile team was still in pursuit, or not. All of a sudden, our three-in-a-line conga scattered. The tremors caused by my boots must have frightened the snake. It fled right, the mouse left, both disappearing into rocky mounds either side of me. I wondered whether the mouse had realised my fortuitous appearance had saved it. I didn't wonder long. This was clearly the most dim-witted mouse in Lycia. It promptly scuttled out of its rocky hiding place and back into the fray. As chance would have it, it scurried precisely to the huddle of stones the snake had slithered into. I heard an 'eek' and a decisive crunch, followed by a rather horrible silence. That was that.

I left the plain and went on, but I was already suffering from the sun, and the next eight kilometres involved the most miserable trudge imaginable. It was a dried-out riverbed. There was a smattering of water springs, but I saw no shepherds, no other help, simply eight kilometres rasping along a barren path. It doesn't matter how many times one does this kind of thing, one always forgets these never-ending stretches of trekker torture. The memory is marvellously selective, choosing only moments of magic, incredible panoramas, or drama, which it then strings together to create an enticing, and altogether misleading, mental log. And this is why we keep doing it to ourselves. It's a lot like giving birth, if you ask me. Anyway, I hereby note for posterity, it was a dire stretch of road, and the longer I walked, the more my pack drove me into the ground. The word 'help' started to roll round and round my head. It became bigger and bolder with every step until it was a large, capitalised exclamation.

Plod. Plod. Plod. On and on. I stopped and stared at the stones on the road. They were round river stones and they made it look like the sides of the riverbed were bubbling under the heat. I muttered to them to do something, call someone, or rescue me. Whether it was the stones or not, I don't know. No one knows in truth, do they? But soon after, help did, in fact, appear. Actually, I was about to stumble upon a love story, perhaps the most unlikely romance I have ever heard, right here in the arid centre of nowhere-at-all. Now, you weren't expecting that, were you? And neither was I, I can tell you.

A man appeared in front of me. Well, he was more of a gremlin really and looked about as old as the Lycian Way itself. He was skinny and dressed in a shirt, a woollen waistcoat, and full, brown trousers. Honestly, I marvel at the way these village folk bundle themselves up in mid-July. I was in no more than shorts and a T shirt, and I seemed to be on fire. Nimbly for such an age, the little old man trotted towards me.

'Hanımefendi! Are you alright? You look bushed! My wife's at home with a pot on. Come and have a glass.'

I took him up on his offer with no hesitation. I followed him back to his home, nearby. It was a charming stone house raised upon struts. There was a large veranda, and cows were chewing and lowing beneath. Then his wife came out, and I have to admit, I swallowed quite hard when I saw her. She was a giant, and a hunchback to boot. She must have been at least one-and-a-half times the size of her husband, and he looked a bit like her child to be honest.

I couldn't take any more tannin, so the old woman brought me a glass of ayran *instead. Then, the pair began to talk. I listened to their chatter, and it gurgled into me like water into a rocky cave. Ah, now that was a story! I think about it even these days. You see, the little old man was besotted with his giant wife. He told me about how they had fallen in love, and how the families for one reason or another had disallowed the marriage (and it wouldn't have been on the basis of anatomical proportions, I'd put money on that). So the couple had eloped. They ran into the forest and built this house with their own bare hands. As time went by they had three children, children who were now long grown up and establishing homes elsewhere.*

As I sat in their shack soaking up their story, I saw the thousands and thousands of lives being lived, glittering strands of existence winding and growing and intertwining; wondrous and colourful pathways stretching from who knows where to who knows where? Nereden nereye. *The trail. It is within us all.*

Having listened to so many villagers on my journey, I started to conclude it must be nature that pushes people to walk the trail. Only in the cities of the organised modern world with our mortgages, job security, pensions and other plans, have we forgotten how to walk, how to let life move us, how to risk touching the chaos within.

Late afternoon slipped into evening. I was served a dinner fit for royalty. Mahmut and Fatima cared for me as though I were their prodigal child returned from afar. They cracked open nuts for me and spoiled me with extravagant treats like Turkish delight squashed between biscuits.

But I was grateful to these two hobbits for more than their hospitality, because they taught me something quite profound. Both of them radiated pure love for life and each other, and their happiness replenished me. It made me realise how superficial we moderns can be. How important physical appearance and status is in the supermarket of romance, even though it brings none of the happiness or depth the love of a soul can bring. Yes, our list of wants on the relationship shopping list (the lists those self-help gurus will tell you to write) is banal. It's all about conquest, and what others think, never about what we deeply feel; age, body, job, money, what have any of these got to do with love? Nothing. They are only concerned with egos, and egos, as I am learning, always end up shrivelled and empty in the end. Souls, on the other hand, grow forever, like vast unstoppable trees.

That night I accepted the offer to sleep there in their gorgeous mountain hut. I curled up on a handmade eiderdown feeling the soft hand of Lycia rocking me.

Ayşe closed her eyes. So did Mahmut and Fatima. One by one the cows below them dropped their haunches and plonked heavily onto the floor. Their breathing became deeper as all of them, animal and human, slid further and further into nothingness. That pure, empty space where we began, and presumably where we will end up. The house, a house built of courage and love, breathed alongside. It gathered about its dwellers, each stone convening to hold them. The stones housed a crew of minerals. The minerals in turn sheltered elements. Every element was home to a family of atoms, and each atom lodged its own posse of minute particles. Deep within every single thing in Lycia, a mist of electrons spun wildly about their various nuclei. The aura they formed created their respective homes. It was a remarkable system. In every case and at every level, it was the trails of the inhabitants that transformed their worlds into what they were.

There is much folk don't know about rocks. They have a secret life humans rush by in such haste, they miss completely. Each stone in Mahmut and Fatima's house had its story. Every single one had been on the move since the beginning of time. If you had asked those stones to speak, what would they have said? What would have been their trail?

Now that is a story I know . . .

The story of stones began long ago. Long before Mahmut and Fatima. Long before houses. Long before Lycia. It began back in a time before stones had even emerged as entities in their own right. A time when the essence of rockness had swum as one great magma in the belly of the Earth. It was an enormous melting pot down there, and no one rock was any different to any other. Then one day the volcanos erupted, and suddenly rockness was hurled out into the sky and onto the surface of the planet. It fell to become the mountains, the granite and obsidian. It rose as the peaks of the Ak and Taurus range. Rocks now ruled Lycia from on high. But, day in, day out, millennia after millennia, the sun beat on them. The snows and rains rushed down. Bit by bit they were broken. Shard by shard they fell. Thus they were driven ever further downwards, eventually rolling to that spot somewhere between Çukurbağ and Patara.

One day Mahmut and Fatima found those pieces of rock and picked them up. They stuck them back together, made them something new. And for now, there the stones would stay. Until the wind and the rain came, and they continued their tortuous downward journey, under the surface and into the Earth once more.

It takes millions of years for one revolution of this rock cycle. But what is a million years without a human mind? Those rocks held their trails and their stories. They clutched them in their lumbering bodies far longer than anything else on the planet. In the dead of the night, when everything temporarily collapsed into silence, when human minds became still, and the forms they created faded away, all would become temporarily one. Yet, with no one to witness it, who would ever know?

Every night the humans slept. They thought nothing of it when they laid down their heads. They were so sure they were existing. Yet, as they went under, they were losing themselves, journeying to a place close to death. On the way to the great melting pot within and beyond it all, the rubble of their trails would come floating momentarily to the surface. Fragments of what made them themselves. Shards of their lives. They would bob and drift, carried by the downward current. Until they too were finally subsumed into the great churning ground of everything.

༄○ञ

Istanbul 2004

Ayşe sat smoking by her office window. She'd well and truly had it with being a city slave, with being a mother that couldn't seem to get it right. The sun pierced the glass. It highlighted the veil of dust on her monitor. She wanted out. The state, however, had just put the kybosh on the idea. Thanks to the government tightening the screws on what were until then superbly generous Turkish retirement laws, laws enabling women who had worked all their lives to retire at the age of thirty-eight (and yes you read that correctly, *thirty-eight*) Ayşe now had three more years on the treadmill in front of her. It was a massive blow.

At that time, for the majority of Westerners – obliged as they were to have their noses to the puritan grindstone until they keeled over from a coronary – complaining about waiting until you were forty-one to retire seemed capricious, to say the least. Yet, there is no tablet of universal rights etched up on high. What humans feel they deserve comes from the rights they see about them. Twenty years prior, Ayşe may have been unaware she had a right not to be married. But she *had* known she was entitled to free-time, to a life outside work, and to something the Turks termed *keyif*. *Keyif* was one of the greatest words in the Turkish language. It was a word which encapsulated the essence of Turkish culture. A culture of leisure and well-being. A culture where saying hello and goodbye were more important than being on time, and where families and friends were more important than work. Eating, sleeping, sex, friendship, wine or *Rakı*, or tea. Relaxing legs outstretched with a book. Lolling in a hammock. It was all one big *keyif*.

In the world of the moderns, the idea that free-time and rest could be a 'right' had become an anathema. All the way from the bustling techno-metropolises of east Asia to the achievement-addicted populaces of North America, and from there to the prim, work-ethic morality of northern Europe, work was the be all and end all. It was left to South America, the Mediterranean and the Middle East to stoically hang on and preserve the sanctity of chilling out. Siestas, mañana, *çay mola*. Lounging in French cafés with a Gauloise, or lounging at your desk with a Turkish-American blend and a bag of sunflower seeds. Respect for all manner of torpor was the trademark of any self-respecting once-great bygone civilisation. How else could they have invented the wheel or the art of writing? It wasn't by selling their souls to the corporate anti-Christ, that's for sure. Such flashes of genius have always required careful incubation. They bloom somewhere within an afternoon of restful sloth while reclining under a palm tree, aimlessly watching the sun set and spitting out date stones.

In years to come, humanity would look at the workaholic insanity of the moderns much as they regarded slavery or live sacrifices. Barbaric. Entire lives swallowed up in largely meaningless occupation, in the name of keeping a 'system' functioning. Horrible wasted existences. Gems flushed down the pan. Ayşe, who'd broken far more serious cultural rules in the name of living life, was ahead of her time.

Three years. Three whole years before she could escape. Those 1095 days stretched out before her like a jail sentence. This wasn't where she wanted to be anymore. Istanbul with its bustle and clamour, its high streets and back streets, its subways, tramways and ferryways. Its retail was no longer therapeutic. Its dynamism no longer relevant. But she had a house, a car, a job, a son, and even just recently a husband – because she married the young man in the end. Haven't those, or some amalgamation of those, been forever the excuse for not living a dream? How many times have I heard it over the millennia? A click of the tongue on the roof of a mouth 'Ooh you're so lucky! I'd *love* to do that, but . . .'

If Ayşe had a life philosophy, it was this. If you want it, want it enough. Know it's going to cost you, be prepared to foot the bill, and then take it. She'd saved a bit of money in the last few years. She also had her car, and cars did very well on the Turkish second hand market. So she sold it. The young man (being still young) was on the verge of his military service. There was teenager Umut. But Ayşe had to face facts. The boy idolised his father. He was convinced life was better over there. So, with all that in mind, perhaps it was time for a change.

One day, a day which on the outside looked much like any other, Umut packed his bags and moved in with his Dad. Then Ayşe left Istanbul. She went to the one place on the planet she was herself. Olympos.

Selfish? Find one person on the planet without dreams. Just one. And the word selfish might just become meaningful. The dreams of humans were like the torches on the chariots of their souls. They could burn those torches and charge round the hairpins, or they could blow them out and stumble through the darkness forever lost. They could even get right out of the chariot and spend their life polishing it, whinging at every passing horse throwing up a bit of dust. But no one could deny it. Chariots needed torches because they were meant to be driven. YEEE HA! It meant someone had to take the reins and choose which way

251

to go. It meant there'd be the odd accident and people were injured. But, given humans didn't choose what their dreams were, and given when they didn't follow their dreams they turned into mean-spirited guttersnipes who called everyone selfish, given all these givens, selfish was a redundant word.

It was the end of the twentieth century. Ayşe became part of a ragged thread of tourists that had found their way into the ancient city. Perhaps they came out of archaeological curiosity, perhaps riding on the plush, wide wings of tales from other explorers. Whichever it was, one way or another they came.

When she first arrived in Olympos, it was almost undiscovered. The nights were silent and lightless. The days as open and pure as young Leto herself. The great beach was dotted by no more than a handful of visitors, even in mid-summer. There were no more than a couple of pansiyons. They were ramshackle bungalows catering for low-budget backpackers. Ayşe spent the evenings lolling on the stones with a bottle of *Doluca* red. The great Mount Olympos surveyed from on high. Its white peak glowed in the pitch of Aphrodite's night eye. Clouds of phosphorescence detonated like stardust grenades as the sea plopped onto the stones. And the whispers of the ancient city were almost audible.

Time went by. It click-clacked over the years. And as it rolled, things changed. Other land owners in the valley, sniffing the enticing whiff of both foreign currency and foreign women, copied the original two guesthouses. By the late nineties a wooden village had been created. The Bull Bar had opened up at one end of what was now almost a street. The 1970s rock stars poured in. And the valley began, quite literally, to boom. Mainstream Turkey still had no idea this place existed. It was like a secret enclave of the flaky and funky, the foreign and alien, the offbeat and artistic. In an about-face, it was the Olympians who were now the ostracised. It looked like Leto's bastard children had created an alternative home of the gods. And it wasn't on a mountain peak in heaven. It was in the cool dark valley of lost time.

Day Ten

Dead-end

Mahmut umca and Fatima teze's house, 2008

The early hours fell on the forests of Lycia. A late-rising moon hauled itself higher and higher into the eye of the sky like a dilating, white pupil. Each day the pupil opened wider. And more and more light poured in.

Ayşe slept on, as did Mahmut and Fatima. The old couple hugged each other as they slumbered. The tenth morning had arrived. Dawn was crouching in the east. Waiting. Waiting for her time. The stones in the house shivered. The moon's pearly fingers prodded them touching their plodding cores. They knew something was shifting, and things were coming to light. The trees in the forest knew it too. Their thick winding roots spoke to them of a new day on the horizon. And all of Lycia held her breath, as she remembered what lay hidden below.

Lycia had been one of the last places on Earth to bury her sacred axioms. Her independence and separation had always protected the keepers. Until finally, back in 545 BC, she too was breached. And her story, like all the others, disappeared underground. The grub of that story had hung motionless in its grey-brown chrysalis for a long time. Year after year. Century after century. Now, something had changed. Perhaps it was nothing more than the deadline of mortality prodding it. Perhaps it was on a mystical timer. Whatever the reason, inside the cocoon the tale was unfolding. The soil and the rocks sensed it snaking through them, moving minutiae from one place to another. They whispered fragments of the tale into the night, hoping someone somewhere might just catch their words.

ಬೊO೦ಚ

'Shhh.' The translator turned to Harpagos. She had her index finger perpendicular to her mouth. Night swam through the temple of Leto. Everything, from the columns to the carvings, was awash with it. The procession of priestesses trailed through the pillars, torches in hand. Meanwhile, Harpagos was revelling in his prestigious new role as 'the chosen one'. The white serpent of women slid behind the altar and to the farthest wall of the building. Marble towered in front of them. He wondered where they might go from here.

The high priestess, still toting her outlandish bird's nest of a crown, pointed at one of the marble slabs, her finger a nobbled hook. It was a slab that appeared just like any other; white and oblong and massive. Three women came forward and positioned themselves in front of it. Then they pushed. Harpagos looked on doubtfully. No one could just shove one of those hulks of rock. It was impossible. Yet, when the women put their shoulders to the stone, it grumblingly gave way. It was then he noticed. The slab wasn't even a tenth of the thickness of the others. From the inside of the temple it looked like just another brick in the wall. It was, in fact, a thin stone door.

Now there was a gap, if only knee-high. One by one the priestesses crouched and crawled through the aperture. Harpagos squinted, bent down and peered dubiously inside. He saw a large hidden chamber with eight torch-bearing women bunched up, waiting.

'Hurry up, will you. This isn't a sightseeing tour!' The translator hissed.

The Persian commander swallowed a retort. He was the chosen one, after all so he would rise above it. Dutifully, he squatted down and shuffled through the gap.

Once he was inside, the three women replaced the slab. It was claustrophobic in the tiny cubicle, and the heat from the blazing torches was making Harpagos sweat. But before he had time to complain, his attention was grabbed by something else. The old priestess was sliding underground, and she sank like a statue into a fog-covered mire. It took a minute or two for him to realise what was happening. When Harpagos looked closer, he saw she was descending a flight of steps. Within minutes everyone else had followed suit, except for the three stone pushers. They stayed put, presumably on guard. Harpagos walked slowly to the hole in the ground and put his foot in.

Soon, he reached the bottom of the marble steps. He found himself in a subterranean cavern. Blinking, he stared through the darkness, absorbing the flickering space. There were magnificent statues here of Leto, Artemis and Apollo. All were laden with gold trinkets, diadems, anklets and bracelets. Earthenware jars, pixides, oil lamps, and intricately crafted drinking vessels lined the multiple alcoves in the walls. The floor boasted a fine mosaic of a goddess and a cobra. Scores of tall amphorae lined the edges, carefully sculpted arms bowing onto their wide clay hips. In the centre stood a large marble altar. Harpagos was standing in a crypt.

Two of the women went about lighting the oil lamps, while the high priestess and the others collected around a small water pool at one end of the chamber. The old woman eyed Harpagos witheringly and sighed. He was a little put out, but ignored her. She put a hand on her hip and muttered at the translator, who turned.

'Listen. We have to be quick. Let me explain.'

'Well, get on with it then! I've got a rabble of troops all wondering where I am, I can't dilly dally here all night.'

257

The translator stopped for a moment, her big dark eyes turning as black as a moonless night. The high priestess glared at him as well, her hooked nose forming a vulture's profile. There was some muttering. Harpagos got the distinct impression it was something along the lines of, 'Are you *sure* this buffoon is the one?'

Out of the corner of his eye, he noticed one of the younger girls lifting the lid of an amphora. She put her hand into the terracotta neck and pulled something out. He couldn't see clearly, but it looked like a herb or dried fungus of some sort.

'Here, under our holy Letoon rests the Motherstone,' said the translator. 'It holds our history in its entirety. For, one day in the future our story will be needed. Take heed General Harpagos. There will be a great war between Mother Earth and the corrupt forces of humanity. Our children's children have called to us through the passageways of time. Someone must hold the secret and bury the Motherstone. That someone, it seems, is you.'

Harpagos scratched his beard and shifted his feet. Passageways of time? Future wars? Children of children? What was all this mystical palaver? What did it have to do with him? He had no children, no lineage. It had been stolen from him, hadn't it? And why was the hag with the headdress now gawking at him like that? Anyone would think the wrinkled, old goose had just seen a ghost.

'*That's* why you are full of despair Persian!'

The words boomed through the crypt, and Harpagos nearly jumped out of his perspiring skin. His heart bashed against his ribcage. The voice was coming from the high priestess. Only, something had happened to it. Where was her high-pitched warble now? He didn't know which language she was speaking, but it wasn't Elamite, that was for sure. So why did he understand it, word for thundering

258

word? It was then he noticed the women had begun drinking something. They were knocking it back as though it were honey mead.

The maiden by the amphora reached for Harpagos' hand. She pulled apart his fingers and promptly pressed a silver vessel in them. He was parched. But he peered in at the liquid sceptically and shook his head. He had enough woes without being poisoned to boot. The girl must have read his mind. She quickly grabbed the chalice out of his hand, tipped it towards her mouth and swallowed a gulp. Then she handed it back and indicated he should do the same. He shrugged, slugged it back, and grimaced. It was bitter. It was peculiar.

ಬಂO೦ಣ

The threads of the past coiled back. The story paused in its cocoon. For a moment anyway. And as the modern world returned, the earth of Lycia rocked a little. But only a little. Night was pulling away, step by cool dark step. And if you strained your eyes the tombs of the Letoon were just about visible.

A short way off from the sacred city of Leto, over the Esen River and the plain of Patara, along the coast and up in the hills, was Mahmut and Fatima's house. The house of light where Ayşe was still asleep. Yet, even a space as bright as Mahmut and Fatima's can have its shadows. Darkness finds its home in the crannies no one inspects, the holes they refuse to acknowledge. It hides under carpets, inside closed cupboards, and behind the pictures hung to cover up the cracks.

Ayşe didn't see the visitor, because he had been murdered by the time she opened her eyes. Even so, at about three O'clock in the morning, he was dashing this way

259

and that over the wall beside her bed. Scorpion. His small body was encased in a mahogany exoskeleton. When he ran, he flummoxed his adversaries with his bizarre sideways scuttle. The diehard of the arthropod world swaggered and strutted over the cracks of Ayşe's room. He was a stalwart survivor, almost impossible to kill. You could pull off his legs, stab him, starve him, poison him, throw acid over him, and radiate him, and he would still raise himself up, shake off the damage, and laugh. As Scorpion darted from left to right, his brown, beaded tail was curled in anticipation. Someone was about cop it. The only question was who?

Who in Lycia could ever love Scorpion? He was irredeemable. It made you wonder why he had ever been created in the first place. Well, there was an answer to that. It was all Orion's fault, or at least that's how the story went. The myth had been related through Lycia, Ionia and beyond. The myth of the cocky hunter. There were many variations on the theme, but Hesiod, the Greek poet, explained it this way:

One day in the ancient past when the gods and goddesses walked the Earth, Orion went on a hunting trip to Crete with Artemis and Leto. He was a great hunter, but a conceited one, never missing a chance to spout on about his virility. In the end, he threatened to kill every beast there was on Earth to prove the point. Gaia heard this and was furious. She sent a great scorpion down, a creature near unslayable. Scorpion soon stung Orion, and he quickly perished. Zeus, at the prayer of Artemis and Leto, made a memorial of the two. He placed them among the stars, though at opposite ends of the sky, to prevent them from fighting again.

Gaia grows and she decays, she births and she dies. It's her dance. And dancers are known for their balance. She holds that balance within her. When someone somewhere becomes a little too arrogant, a little too despotic, she will bring forth something new to keep them in check. She always has and always will.

Scorpion pranced along a dark patch of Ayşe's wall, finally reaching the lip of the windowsill. He had seen an injured moth, and the sight of it puffed him up ready for the kill. Little did he know, he wasn't alone. There was a lady in the room. And it wasn't Ayşe. Her stalk of a body swayed slightly in the breeze, and the green of her multiple spines was so bright she was chartreus. Praying Mantis. With those odd, ungainly front legs of hers, folded as they were in sinewy supplication, she looked an unlikely predator. But for many of Lycia's smaller inhabitants those legs were the gruesome face of death itself. She was queen assassin of the insect world, striking terror into the hearts of crickets, small lizards and scorpions. She should have petrified any male mantis as well. She was notorious.

Not many of Gaia's creatures go as far as to eat their own kind. But Earth likes to keep us on our toes, always creating an exception to any human-made rule. Like the black widow, having seduced the male of her species, Praying Mantis would often ingest him post-coitally. Strangely, this never put the suitors off. More often than not they would sacrifice themselves willingly.

Scorpion inched over the sill. Had Praying Mantis possessed the ability, she might have smiled. She knew her own power and her ruthlessness. Scorpion was almost invincible, but almost is never enough. He stepped very slowly about the corner of the ledge. His attention was absorbed by the floundering moth. He was absolutely confident he would snare it. No one would have seen what happened next. Praying Mantis' raptorial legs lashed out at

261

such phenomenal speed they could snatch up their pray in fractions of the time it took a human to blink an eye. All anyone would have seen was Scorpion sitting ready to pounce one minute. And Scorpion being ingested the next.

ॐ O ☙

Ayşe awoke a little later than usual, unaware of the murder that had occurred next to her in the night. The sunlight streamed into the window burning a white square onto the wall above her bed. She pulled back the sheets and swung her legs out of bed. Sitting, she looked through the rectangular opening. It was a gateway from the inside to the outside, from sleep to being awake. The window was a splash of vibrant colour on the grey wall of her room. It was a living picture of forests and flowers and rocks. And a world where everything was intertwined.

Ayşe moved to the window. She placed her hands on the sill, and stared out. The track gleamed in the early light. The stones were smooth crystals as the sun slid off their backs. The cicadas had begun their daytime strumming, the birds their morning twitter. The handsome shadows between the trees raised themselves up. They prowled under the great boughs, standing on guard behind the rough old trunks. They stood proud here in this place, because they knew before the sun even reached a quarter of the way up the sky, everyone would be running to them for salvation.

ॐ O ☙

I ate a simple breakfast with Mahmut umca and Fatima teze; goat's cheese, fresh eggs, unleavened bread, and milk. I left reluctantly. I could have stayed, so why didn't I? Yes well, old habits die hard, as they say. I was restless, and isn't that so often our ruination?

So I said goodbye. And then a two hour hike began. It took me onward and upward, before the trail plunged back down into the fields. It was an odd space of land there. The large glade was encircled by a necklace of enormous, round rocks. Actually, I should mention, this spot has since become a part of the Lycian Way I have come to dread, and the reason for my trepidation is human. You see, there's a shepherd who takes care of sheep and goats there, but the trouble is, he's so bothersomely talkative, and it's something of an ordeal to get away from him. He has the most astonishing memory, as well. This is an unfortunate combination, because if you've run into the fellow once, he will never forget you or your story again. You are, in a manner of speaking, cursed. Anyway, I daresay I was cool with the man. I brushed him off and strode on, attempting to indicate I was in a hurry. It was all rather a foolish act though, for where could I have been hurrying to in this wilderness? The chap followed me for quite a while, annoying me to the point of exasperation. But eventually, he tired of me, and I walked on in peace. I began to descend an earthen road. And then other mischief appeared.

The road wasn't particularly strenuous. That wasn't the problem. The trouble started when I turned one corner, and what should come bounding towards me, but a dog. This is perhaps the worst enemy of the Lycian Way hiker. Forget all the prattle about wild boar and snakes. They are generally harmless and leave a hiker well alone. But dogs . . . some of them are so poorly trained or badly treated, or both, they have obviously come to hate humans. Once, on a later Lycian Way hike, I was bitten, and I had to limp fifteen kilometres to the nearest hospital for help. But let's not get on to that story.

The dog in question here was a nasty piece of canine work, all fangs and saliva. It's a vicious circle, isn't it? One knows they smell the fear, which only makes one all the more anxious. I screeched at it. The owner – a village woman – heard me. She rushed out of her house and pulled it off. I was a bit worked up I suppose, which was why I shouted at the woman, as well. Then, I flounced off feeling both silly and righteous all at the same time. Well, why do these people keep such dogs if they can't control them?

Four to five kilometres later along the road, I spied a sign-post claiming to point in the direction of Bezirgan. Kalkan was just around the corner. I was reaching the Xanthos basin. But I was stopped in my tracks. To my dismay, the pathway had completely disappeared. It had vanished under the tracks of some monster of a machine, bulldozered into non-existence. What little had been left of the trail had washed away in previous floods. I stood with my hands on my hips and muttered a few words. I hate that this is what is happening to our beautiful land, and I feel powerless to stop it. As I stood there, I shivered as I thought about those machines reaching my dear Olympos, ploughing through her forests, ripping up her roots. It might be a national park, but that doesn't seem to count for an awful lot anymore, does it? I closed my eyes tight at this point to expunge the images. Olympos. Beautiful, mysterious Olympos.

As I stood there considering my next step, I remembered how I had come to live there in the lost valley. I smiled as I recalled my early adventures; the winding turns that had brought me all the way to this very spot, where I would in turn recall them.

⧇

It was the end of 2004. Ayşe had quit her job and left Istanbul. No one was going to applaud her. She was criticised from start to finish. But she wrestled with her conscience, pinned it down, fixed a wad of duct tape over its mouth and did what she wanted. She went to Olympos. Hurling herself from the precipice of the righteous, she skidded headlong into the land of lotus-eating, wanton mothers. Little did she know, it would be three years before she would return to the country within a country that was Istanbul.

Ayşe arrived in the Olympos valley on the cusp of winter. A cool mist wafted out of the mountain crevices. As the small bus veered along the snake of broken tarmac, the smell of wet pine seeped through the chinks. Hectares of orange groves banked the slopes, their bright fruit bobbing. The valley was beautiful in its winter isolation. Tourist free, the peace was interrupted only by birdsong or the rush of fresh water torrents dragging over the riverbed. A lyrical backdrop of crisp skies and an empty beach drew in many a romantic.

Ayşe stepped out of the bus and hauled her bags up the steps of her favourite tree house pansiyon. She spotted Olga, the fatigued Russian émigré who'd been ensconced in wooden reception since the good old days. The woman was still young, but boredom had eaten away her freshness. She already had faint bags under her eyes. Ayşe leaned over the pine wood counter to get her attention. 'Hi, I'm staying until summer. Can I have a room?'

Olga pulled herself away from her magazine and raised an eyebrow. 'What, a cabin? Or you want one of the new ones with a bathroom?' She yawned, and made no effort to hide it.

'Just a cabin, the one at the end if it's free.'

The Russian stared at Ayşe unwaveringly. Then she yanked a key from a white board of nails on the wall behind her. 'Does it look like we're overbooked? You see any other guests here right now other than Halil's in-laws?' Then she half-muttered, half-breathed, 'Till, summer like hell! I'll give you till February'.

Olga had a point. The expanse of time from New Year to April in Olympos was elastic. It could rain for days on end. And the options, when you were squatting in a three by three wooden hut, were scant. Unprecedented upheavals of nature would occur. Rivers burst, bridges were ripped out, and the one road in would become impassable. Then you were cut off. Nothing came in. Nothing went out. You found yourself reduced to a strange and sickening diet of citrus fruit and chicken. Squawk, squawk, squaaaawk, Chop!

Days were short. Nights closed in cold and early. Then the power would fail for a couple of days – and worse, nights. Reading by candlelight held the nostalgic ring of bygone eras. Modern romantics imagined glowing hearths with Dickens and Chaucer, and piping suppers on trays. Reality was different. Reading by candlelight proved nigh impossible unless you'd developed night vision. And who had lit that hearth? No one ever imagined the tribulations involved in fire-lighting when the wood was soaked and they'd used up the last of the newspaper.

Following your dream, there was *always* a price to pay. But it was a price Ayşe could afford. As the days trawled by, Ayşe's old routine soon sank into the recesses of the past. Life flowed anew on its unpredictable course. It was the unstoppable pumping of human essence. It moved like stems twisting through cracks in tarmac, or new neurological pathways being soldered.

After a week or two in Olympos, Ayşe noticed other trails on her daily jaunts to the beach. Soon she tried them out. Wading into the leafy darkness, she found herself up banks, in old castles, lost on cliff edges. She wasn't physically up to it, though. Years of sedentary office work had resulted in a cardio-vascular system utterly unused to the stress and strain of hill walking. But as the days went by, Ayşe's forages into the wild grew increasingly ambitious. Her heart and lungs adapted to the challenge of each climb. And when the sun sank, and darkness put pay to her walks, she spent her evenings crocheting tops she thought she could wear when the heat of summer returned.

One evening she sat by the campfire, needles chattering along at a fair clip. Olga, who was secretly impressed with Ayşe's longevity in the Olympos winter survival stakes, spoke up. 'So what are you going to do with all this knitting? And what are they anyway, dishcloths?'

Ayşe held up the low-cut backless number she was currently working on. 'I'm going to *wear* it! Why do you want me to make you one?'

Olga nearly choked on her tea. After wiping her eyes, she grabbed the garment and fingered it dubiously. Then she thrust it back in Ayşe's hand.

'There's hardly enough here to cover a tit! Nah, I couldn't wear something like that, Halil wouldn't have it. Still, the students in summer would love them. Why don't you set up a stall out front and sell them? You could make a bit of money, I reckon.'

The click-clack of the needles slowed pace. Ayşe let the top rest on her lap. She stared at the flames of the campfire voraciously licking the night air. Hmm. Why not? Sell her creations. Yes. She could do with a bit of extra money now she no longer had a source of income. Good idea. She'd open a stall.

Before long, winter packed his heavy cases. Hurriedly, as is always the case on the Mediterranean, he took off out of town. He had business elsewhere – other hemispheres to thunder about it. In his stead, spring took up residency in the valley. One by one she unpacked her knick-knacks of orange blossom and frog orgies.

The first of the foreign travellers filtered into the pansiyon. Many were hikers or long-stay backpackers hoping for a job. By now, Ayşe had discovered nearly every finger of trail in the valley. The human body is unparalleled in its capacity to transform itself in the face of on-going challenge. Not one being in Gaia's kingdom can adapt at such speed. The human is unique. How strange then that back in those days they were so reticent to move out of misery. How odd they had forgotten just how powerful they were. For within the space of two months, Ayşe was someone new. She could charge up a mountain face without even pausing for cigarette.

෮○ෘ

The heat of the sun brought me back. I sped from Olympos, from the past and the starting point of this expedition. And at long last it dawned on me. Since the beginning of the trek, I'd been desperate to shed my history, hadn't I? And that yearning had been fuelled by a library full of books, all written by New Age gurus banging on about living in the Now. So I'd been striving for that place, as if it was my salvation or something. And here on this bulldozed piece of trail, I suddenly wondered why I was mindlessly following these self-proclaimed teachers instead of working it out for myself, because the past wasn't leaving me, and perhaps that was not altogether a bad thing.

So here, for what it's worth, is my take on the whole Now/Living in the Present shebang. As I see it, if such a thing as Now exists, it can only be something not quite of this world, something not comprising rocks and atoms and genes, and the like, because I think our Earth, and all it's made of, necessarily holds time, just as a wellspring holds water. At least, that's my opinion.

I was tottering on the edge of Bezirgan. The large expanse of the Xanthos valley was next door. All kinds of events had brought me to this point, and they were all in the past, some farther away, some nearer. Even my DNA had something to do with it. The choices and actions of my ancestors, the food they had eaten, the environments they had lived in. Well, they had created me, hadn't they? It was thanks to them I was able to walk this trail, and in Turkey at this particular point in time. I, in turn, was creating with every step as well, wasn't I? This is what I see as the significance of the present moment. It's not that the past or future are irrelevant, that one should toss them away and grin inanely for eternity, smoking marijuana and listening to The Eagles on repeat. It's that Now is the extraordinary place in the flow of time where one might begin a new path, change timelines, or create a brand new day, so to speak. And because, here on planet Earth, the present moment is made out of the past, it helps to know just what brought one to one's present predicament, if not, we humans tend to repeat our mistakes on and on.

Anyway, I was headed for Bezirgan, wasn't I? Only, a mountain of earth rose between me and my destination. I faced the obvious. My trail had been ploughed up by one of those things cunning marketers branded Caterpillar (Nature Destruction Module, or Environmental Apocalypse would have been less catchy, but more accurate), and I would simply have to create a new pathway. Unfortunately, it wasn't quite as straight forward as it sounded. I set off up the trail-less slope, my feet falling in and out of the machine tracks. The midday sun dripped from the sky like hot oil.

269

What a dire climb that was! One can't even begin to conceive the extent of verticality I struggled up. For every ten steps I took, I had to sit and rest. I vowed there and then never ever to attempt that incline again. The only reward was the view. The touristic hamlet of Kalkan was squashed into the walls of the bay, its nearby cake batter islands swimming in a pan of ultramarine. You could see the sea floor even from my distance.

When finally, I stumbled on to the summit, I discovered a shepherd's hut. There was a well in front of it, too. I stopped, dropped my pack and went to the stone circle. Yanking up the tin can, I caught it in my hands. Then I poured the contents directly over my head. It all but sizzled as it rushed over me.

I heard a noise. The door of the shepherd's house creaked open and a middle-aged mountain man stepped out. I flinched and wondered if I had trespassed. The man had his back to me, so I shouted to attract his attention, but there was no response. I shouted again. Still no reaction. How rude! I thought. So I grabbed my pack and left him in front of his hut collecting his sheep.

But then, as I rambled onwards, I heard him running to catch me up. He yelled, 'Hellooo! Hellooo!' How strange. I stopped and turned. He reached me and grinned.

'I just called out to you twice back there, but you ignored me,' I said. Again the man said nothing. He stared at me blankly, as though I were speaking a foreign language. Then it dawned on me. The reason he was unable to hear was because he was quite literally deaf! After that, there was a short, and not wholly unsuccessful, foray into sign language on my part. We both descended the slope to Bezirgan in partial comprehension.

By the time we arrived, evening was threatening everything. The man waved, and continued on his own silent way. How is the world when one can't hear? *I wondered. No music and no language, no bulldozer noise, no cars roaring, no bird chatter, just a lake of silence one swims through day after day, each stroke as noiseless as the last. Is that silence rich and profound, or empty and lonely? There are so many worlds within this one, aren't there? And each of them is unique.*

I looked at the last remaining flares of daylight striking out over to the west. Kalkan was just over the hill, and next to her was Patara, both my destinations for tomorrow.

Quite soon, I found an apple orchard. It was sheltered and flat, so I pitched my tent there. (At least I'd have something other than birdseed for breakfast, I reasoned.) I crawled under the tarp and sat on the groundsheet with my feet outside, so that I could untie my boots. I could have done with a blacksmith, it was so difficult to remove them. They stuck to my flesh like hooves.

Evening floated over the orchard; a smoky veil that hid the world. The apple trees became black shadows, and then vanished. I slid inside the tent and arranged my sleeping bag. Then I lay on it with my torch and the Lycian Way map. At the beginning, back in Olympos, it had been Fethiye I had seen as the end of my journey. But now, as I studied the places I'd trekked through and looked at where I still had to walk, I realised I desperately wanted to make Xanthos, Xanthos and her sister Letoon, with those bizarre airborne tombs, and those sunken columns. Flashing my torch over the photo, I stared into Letoon's lagoon again. Why had it flooded? *I wondered.* Where had the water come from? And why was I so poorly informed about it all?

ൟ☉ങ

The cicadas had long made way for the warbling of the nocturnal crickets. The darkness was hot that night. Aphrodite was sullen, and her eye was a haze of disinterest. Not a breath of air made it through the mosquito net. Ayşe stared into the folds of her map. And into the mire of Letoon. The more she stared, the more she wondered. The rows of broken underwater columns looked as though they had come from a temple. But the floor was invisible, hidden under latter day Letoon's filmy swamp. Ayşe's eyelids fell lower and lower as she mused on the submerged temple. *Who had worshipped who? Why did they build all this stuff, and how did they find the time? And under the floor of that temple? What . . . ?*

Too late. She was asleep. The thought remained as buried as Lycia's secret. Because under the floor of that temple was a crypt no one had seen in over two thousand years. One of the last people to lay eyes on it had been General Harpagos back in 545BC when the priestesses had taken him down there.

ತ⃝Oಛ

The oil lamps flickered and wobbled. Harpagos looked into his empty cup unimpressed. He stuck his tongue out and coughed. It had been the worst drink he'd had in quite a while. His stomach was turning.

'*Despair*! You are full of despair Persian!' It was the high priestess who bellowed.

Harpagos jumped. That such a colossal sound could be expelled by the scrawny, old hag before him was staggering. It reverberated around the crypt rattling the amphorae.

'Despair? Well, I might be a bit off every now and again, and who wouldn't be in this world? But despair? No, that's over-emphatic. I think I'd describe myself more as realistically pessimistic with the occasional flash of idealism,' he said.

It didn't look as though the high priestess cared too much about Harpagos' self-analysis though. She was staring through him, as though he didn't exist.

'And you never drop your misery! The parasite of the past is crawling all over you! You're carrying it everywhere like a tortoise carries its shell. It's crippling you, Persian!'

Harpagos' eyebrows began to writhe as he grappled with the idea.

'Because you don't know the secrets of Gaia. Not even *one*! The rocks, the trees, the soil. You have to drop your memories into them, Persian! How can you bring forth a present moment otherwise? How can you ever truly 'create' *anything?*'

Harpagos rubbed his temples. He was starting to get a bit of a headache, one way and another. He noticed the high priestess was dipping her hands into the basin. But she carried on speaking. Her strange, deep voice echoed about the torch-lit walls.

'You have lost a son, but you will gain more. Your descendants will remain here in Lycia. It is so. We have seen it.'

Harpagos proffered the old woman a look of complete incredulity when he heard that. The front of his eyebrows rucked up his forehead. 'Remain in this dusty crater of insanity? Hmph! I don't think so.'

The high priestess glowered. 'I saw it in the Motherstone, and so shall you!'

273

Harpagos shook his head. He brought the corners of his mouth down into doubtful pout. 'I couldn't care less what you've seen, dear woman. I'm off to Phoenicia, the centre of the damn world,' he said. Then he stepped closer and tapped his right temple with his index finger, adding, 'Do you know something? You're insane, the lot of you.'

The high priestess lunged towards Harpagos and slapped him square in the face. Her hand was cold and wet. It was like being walloped with a freshly caught trout. Harpagos gaped. He was so utterly taken aback he couldn't even muster outrage. It shook him out of his thoughts for just long enough that the high priestess and the translator swiftly managed to take an arm each and pull it over their shoulders. They dragged him to the back of the crypt. His heels bumped up and down over the floor all the way.

It was then Harpagos noticed things were not altogether as they should be. Why, for example, had his arms turned to dough, and why was the mosaic on the floor undulating? He could see tiny currents in it weaving through the patterns. And there was something amiss with the walls too. There . . . Good *God!* There were faces in them!

It took a while for Harpagos to notice he was standing in front of an enormous vault of smooth, uncarved rock. And it was bubbling with a thousand human features. It was . . . well, it looked to be . . . alive. He heard the old crow speaking again. She was pointing at the ceiling, jabbing at the darkness with her forefinger.

'Up there, they inscribe rocks. These days, that's what they do. They engrave them as they never have before. We Lycians were some of the last to begin the great cage of deceit that is the etched word. They write on the stones to fool the future, to spread the lies. Words are the great tricksters. They distort and disguise.'

The high priestess abruptly reached forward. She pulled Harpagos' hands to the rock in front, and pressed them over the cool stone. As soon as his palms touched its nobbled hide, he gasped. The sensations almost took his breath away. Coursing through the stone there was fear, excitement, grief, joy, anger, hope, courage and much, much more. It was as though the entire spectrum of human emotion had been trapped inside waiting for some unsuspecting victim like him to let it out. Harpagos had become a porthole the rock could pour its heart out into. The gale rushed through him. It drew out wheezes and splutters. His eyes began to water. He winced. He bent double. Still both his hands remained stuck to the rock face.

Then he began to see things. There were processions of people; faces, many, many faces. They were marching fast, as though something was pursuing them. But they were fearless. Their eyes were uncannily bright too, ablaze even, just like the eagle eyes of the high priestess. Although the landscape and the people were unfamiliar to Harpagos, he knew without a doubt they were whatever the Lycians had been before they arrived here.

The procession of people wore headdresses. He had never seen anything like them before in his life. They were traipsing over a coverlet of sandy desolation. Some gripped staffs with cobra's heads engraved on them. None of them looked to be armed. It was an exodus. Eventually, they reached the seashore. Harpagos saw them board ships. These were not the cutting-edge triremes or even the more dated biremes littering the length of the Mediterranean in his day. These were ancient vessels propelled by a single row of oarsmen only.

The images tailed off for a moment. All grew dark, as though the rock were consolidating itself, gathering its story together and pulling it up by the bootstraps. Harpagos blinked. He was starting to feel decidedly sea sick, listing to and fro as he was on a leviathan of a floor. Then the body of limestone in front of him rose up. It swelled and rolled like a grey wall of water. It grumbled. It roared. Then pulled back, reared its stony head, and crashed all over him. Harpagos wailed. Where were his Goddamn Companions? *Where?*

Now he saw other images. The Lycians appeared in bizarre costumes. They were carrying out strange practices, performing what seemed to be magic rituals of some kind. He watched magicians moving the soil and rocks without touching them. He saw them speaking to the winds and the trees. He watched their fires dance, the flames becoming wild amber spirits. There were wolves in their midst too, great magnificent beasts they were, but they wandered about with the humans as domestic dogs would. And there was happiness. And wonder too. Harpagos could feel it streaming into his hands, reviving him.

But it changed. The stone began to shudder. It shivered in such a way he began to dread what was coming. Sure enough, the next pictures playing on the rock face were of dark colonies of warships. They multiplied on the horizon, a plague of waterborne insects. The Lycians boarded their own boats. Harpagos watched them ploughing through the deep blue waves until they reached a sandy shore. They left their vessels, and trudged towards the neck of a wide river. They followed the river on foot with the eagles as their guides and bands of lions, leopards and wolves as their consorts. Everywhere the wildlife bowed towards these people. It was as though they were casting unseen spells into the air around them.

The last thing Harpagos remembered from the great Motherstone was seeing the Letoon. Only it was empty space. There were priests, priestesses and a special circle of folk who were neither male nor female. Or perhaps they were both. This inner circle was swaying and writhing, the faces deep in trance. Meanwhile, the priestesses and priests sat behind them quite still. They had their eyes closed. They seemed to be listening. Suddenly, the inner circle arose. It swayed and danced over the dust and rocks, until it finally came to a standstill. The place was, without doubt, right here where Leto's temple now stood.

The next thing Harpagos knew, he was slumped on a cold, hard surface, legs splayed and prostrate. Both the translator and the high priestess were peering down at him. There was something cool on his forehead. Someone was holding a poultice on him. He still felt queasy, and hardly dared look about for fear of what he might see next. There were stones everywhere, after all. How could you tell which ones were alive?

Slowly, he picked himself up.

'Hurry up!' The curly briar of dark hair bounced as the translator grabbed Harpagos' wrist and began to yank him off the floor. 'Your men will start to wonder, and they will investigate.'

'I should bloody well hope they do!' Harpagos sat up and winced.

The translator bunched her mouth up and stared at him intensely. 'Listen Persian, and listen well! No one must ever know about here. You must bury the place. Bury it so deep it can never be found . . . until the day arrives.'

Harpagos scowled. He pulled back his arm and slowly levered himself up. He was feeling as though he'd been set about by a band of Scythian mercenaries. His head was throbbing, and the crypt was a blur of sneering flame and stone.

'And which day might that be I wonder? The day angels flutter down from the heavens, cast gold nets of harmony over mankind, and save us all?' he muttered.

The translator was perspiring. Harpagos could see the damp gleaming on her forehead.

'The day when enough of humanity realises it can overthrow darkness.'

Harpagos stared at her for a moment. He was still rubbing his head as he took it in. Dropping his hand, he opened his mouth and guffawed. The hollow laugh left his body to slither about the crypt. It found the cavities and the niches and settled there waiting to snicker at any unsuspecting passerby.

'Overthrow darkness? We *are* darkness for God's sake. Don't you see? The powerful have always spilt blood. The weak have always been the fodder of the strong. It has always been that way, and presumably it always will. Look at the beasts and the birds, look at that old witch, Mother Nature.'

It was the high priestess who moved. She stood in front of Harpagos, hands on her bony hips. Her eyes cut sharply into him, and he tried to dodge them by side-stepping. As she spoke, the lines about her mouth became ravines sinking fathoms deep into her skin. Harpagos thought for a moment he might lose his footing and fall headlong into them.

'And *that* is their greatest power over you. They have all but succeeded in putting out the fire of your hope. Without hope a human has only fear. It is a sheep or a mule, easy to control. But this is all your own doing! The few can never control the many if the many know who they are. It has not always been so. That is one of the many great and terrible lies, and it has been spread over stone, on parchment, and more.

'We Lycians have chosen not to write. And yet even the Greeks notice we are civilised enough to create freedom for our people. There will come a time when the moderns will wonder why we stayed so silent. There is a future where the flame of self-belief flickers anew, when the lights one by one begin to illuminate Mother Earth. That tyrants win, ha! It has not always been so Persian, and neither will it always be so in the future.'

Harpagos narrowed his eyes and raised himself up a little. He looked down at the old woman. 'And how should I know any of your predictions will come to pass? How should I know this is anything but rot and superstition?'

There was an answer, of course there was. The high priestess sighed. Perhaps she was finally getting weary. Her nostrils flared as she exhaled.

'Because the Goddess will visit you. You will see her clearly. You will see her precisely two-and-a-half times. And when you do, you will know I speak the truth.'

With that she clicked her fingers. The elegant translator straightened. That was apparently that. Without further ado the women made for the steps at the back of the crypt with Harpagos weaving a dizzy anguine path behind them.

Day Eleven

Step by Step

And so I woke to my eleventh day on the road. Now, every morning we wake up without the slightest notion of what lies in wait, and that's how I got up, just as if it were any other day. I cursorily brushed my teeth with a slosh of water from my bottle. I ate nuts and apples for breakfast. Then, I packed up my clothes and took to the trail exactly as I had every morning until then. If I had known this was the day I would meet my maker, what would I have done instead? I can tell you what I wouldn't have done; I wouldn't have rushed out of Bezirgan as though I was late for my own wedding, nor would I have hurried to the main road and tried to 'save time' by catching a dolmuş part of the way. What I would have done is phoned my husband and my son, and I'd have told them I loved them. I might just have told my husband to check the bathroom wastebasket, as well.

The nether-ends of the Lycian Way were drawing in by this point. Letoon and Xanthos were close. There was only one major ancient city left between me and my final targets; Patara, the destination I had set my sights on that day.

Patara is a beach endeared to skin bronzers and the Caretta Caretta turtle alike. I can only presume the Lycians were fond of the place as well, because the trail wriggles along the coastline to and from its now crumbling cities. At the far end of the ruins, seven kilometres of sand curl lazily along a dune-speckled ridge, and to this day it is spectacularly clear of 'development'.

I walked briskly taking up one of the most oblique sections of the trail. I lost count of the times I drifted wayward. The sun was vicious, and there wasn't a single tree or drop of water. Eventually, the track squirmed into a *plot of olive groves, and from there, it snaked out onto the seashore. It was only by snatching every opportunity to leap into the water that I staved off heat stroke at all. When I reached the end of the seaside pathway, I began to notice a rather distinct odour; the smell of smoke. I hardly acknowledged it. Our ancestors would have done, wouldn't they? In those days everything meant something. Anyway, for better or worse I ignored the smell. Finally, I reached the ascent to Patara which crawls around the peak of Eren. I braced myself for another gruelling adventure in the uphill and inhaled. The burning smell became obvious; it brooded in the air like an invisible culmination of the ominous. Then, I saw it. Oh dear. Over the ridge of the summit, small flames poked at the horizon. Well, it appeared to be some way off on the horizon at least, which is why I buckled up and forged on regardless.*

I remember there was a tail wind, and it blew with such searing ferocity it felt as though it was singeing my cheeks. A tail wind. It didn't occur to me what was happening until it was too late. All of a sudden, the wind turned, and I realised it wasn't just a hot breeze, but a giant bellows. I watched in horror as from over the top of the hill enormous waves of fire began to roll and thunder in my direction.

I stopped for no more than a fraction of time and gaped. The speed of the fire was phenomenal. It was a seething, roaring behemoth. I took a deep breath. Then I collected my wits, executed an about face and began to run for my life. Oh my good God! In no more than a split second, I forgot all about the twenty kilos of freight I was carrying. I forgot my excruciating backache, my broken feet. I forgot everything, as my life compressed itself into a single moment. Now. I ran and ran, and when I could no longer run, I gasped and staggered until I could run again.

Thirst came and went as I dragged myself, step by step, back along the very same path I had come.

Forest fires are conscienceless monsters. They devour everything in their way, from the smallest insect to the largest mammal. And the trail of a fire is one of pure consumption. Where oxygen and fuel prevail, the flames proceed. Nothing is spared; aging cedars, scorpions, guileless hedgehogs, wild boar, one callow human, it was taking us all without so much as flinching. And then my mind began to wander, and it disappeared down the most irrelevant alleys. I kept thinking of my apartment in Istanbul and worrying about whether I'd left it in a mess. I suddenly felt the most irrational pressure to tidy up all the loose ends.

I could hear the fire behind me as I scrambled over the rocks. Panicking, I stumbled the length of the track, skidding and sliding. At one point, I tripped over and plunged smack onto my face. After spitting out a mouthful of dirt, I hauled myself up onto my knees scanning the area for a rock or branch to lever myself up with, because I just couldn't find the power to lift my pack with my knees alone. I saw a boulder five metres in front, so I crawled over to it, grabbed hold of a couple of nobbles on its side and groaned as I yanked myself into upright position. Then off I loped again. Over and around, up and down. One hour passed like this. I was wheezing, and my legs began to shake. There were so many wretched rocks to negotiate, so many protruding tree roots and branches. The wriggles and bumps of the trail turned from annoying to downright threatening, as I gradually started to run out of power. The smell of pine sap and smoked wood billowed steadily towards me. I felt sick. It was all starting to look rather desperate.

On that day, day eleven, I believe I walked 17 km and ran 8 km back again, and this was all in temperatures easily surpassing 45 degrees and with broken shoes, no water, and nineteen-and-a-half kilograms on my back. As evening slowly came for me, it bore a distinct resemblance to the Grim Reaper.

I reached an earthen track. I was crumbling there with the fire licking its lips behind me. Now, you might find this odd, or even vain, but I reached back into one of the side pockets of my pack and pulled out a comb. Hastily, I began to tug it through the jungle of my hair, before tying it back with an elastic. You see, I thought I could make out the end on the horizon galloping in my direction, and I just wanted to meet it looking half-way respectable.

I took one last look behind me. The trail I had trodden wound straight back into the fire; it was devoured by it. As I stood there, I watched my pursuit going up in smoke. Perhaps they were right. Perhaps this is where chasing your dreams took you. Was I not at last getting my comeuppance for having veered from the straight and narrow and out into something resembling freedom? Spluttering a little, I rested my hands on my knees. Tears burned at the back of my eyes. I could feel myself giving up. And then I sat down, not caring if it was earth or grass or rock I collapsed upon. I threw the comb onto the ground, and then I bit my lip and closed my eyes, because I couldn't straighten all the raggedy edges of my life out. There just wasn't time.

It was then a memory of my first day on the Lycian Way occurred to me; the memory of perching deliriously thirsty on a razor-edged rock just before Gelidonya lighthouse. I'd apprehended death for a moment there too. And here I was again, only this time something had changed. Yes, in less than two weeks a lot had changed.

People spend their lives in aimless wandering, never really knowing what they want, or where they're going. Learning what you love, unearthing what it is that takes you to That Place, can be a lifelong pursuit in itself. Here I was, fleeing from a forest fire at the edge of Patara, frightened, broken-backed, and rasping for air. My past was still clinging onto me with the determination of a beginner cragsman on a climbing wall. Yet, without even realising it, I had arrived quite unprecedentedly at my destination. The penny had dropped with a clink, clunk, clank, and it was a nice dirty penny, like one of those ancient, earth-devoured Lycian coins they dig up and hawk illegally at the bazaar. I saw I wanted to do nothing else but walk. I loved trekking. And I loved Lycia too. Better late than never, as they say.

Moods are fickle things, if you ask me. One can leap from despair to hope in seconds, and there's little tangible basis for any of it. It's all completely in our heads! I collected myself. Standing up, I looked at the road ahead. The pack went on again. Then, I put one foot in front of the other. One. In front. Of the other. Because that is what a hiker does, isn't it? They walk their path to the end, and well, if I was going to die, I might as well die doing what I loved.

The fire was gaining. Every now and again, when the wind turned, I would be hit by a wave of heat. I would never outrun it, that much was clear, but I plodded on regardless, over dirt, rock and scrub.

I kept up the walk for a good ten minutes, no longer looking behind me, nor with any idea of what was in front. Map reading was out of the question, and there was no one to ask the way, so my attention was entirely consumed by the piece of track I was stepping on plus three metres ahead of that. I got into a steady rhythm and even started

285

to feel soothed by the regular tramping. And then, a noise ripped through my equilibrium.

Every single muscle in my body tensed in preparation for disaster. But, it wasn't the sound of fire. Once I had calmed down, I noticed the noise had a genial purr to it. I glanced behind, and I have to say, I just couldn't believe my smarting eyes. There, as if falling from the heavens in answer to prayers I hadn't thought to utter, was a lad on a motorbike. It really did happen like that. It was as if he'd come from nowhere, like a spirit. He pulled over, stared at me with a mixture of concern and disbelief, and advised me to return to Kalkan straight away. Remember what I said back near Kekova about the power of discrimination, and not jumping onto any maniac's bike that happens to drive your way? Well, you can scratch a line through that sentence if you're about to die, because you just won't care. I had no idea whether the man was well-intentioned or not, but I flopped onto the bike, anyway, and off we sped. My pack still lurched behind me. Even through all of that, I'd refused to leave it behind.

The young man left me at a small market on a street-corner of Kalkan. I remember the rest quite well. I peeled off my pack and staggered into the store. Quite spontaneously, I purchased two bottles of soda. Two. I collapsed into a chair placed next to a middle-aged fellow. Stretching out my arm, I offered him a bottle. Why not? Everyone else had offered me plenty during the last ten days. It seemed perfectly ordinary. We chatted, I relayed my story, and he relayed his. Next, almost predictably, he explained I could overnight at his daughter's house. I wasn't up to refusing.

The daughter and mother lived together in a two-storey white-washed village house overlooking the bay. We ate, and we chatted, and as we did we solemnly watched *the peak burn. It was horrible to be honest. Gradually, the flames retreated, but the hill was gouged red with the wounds of fire. It glowed like a beacon to the whole of Lycia throughout the night. Was it a warning, or a memory? I couldn't decide.*

The daughter, a young woman probably in her twenties, was curious about me. She pulled her chair up next to me on the balcony and pushed a cigarette packet in my direction. It was Tekel 2000, a classic Turkish brand. I pulled out one of the cigarettes. She asked me how I'd ever decided to walk the Lycian Way alone, and why I hadn't taken a friend. I was nursing a glass of tea with my feet raised up on the balcony wall. It was still early in the evening, and though my body was exhausted, my mind was a skein of activity. I lit the cigarette watching the end glow as I inhaled. It was a tale I had repeated many times already. But so what?

ஐOஐ

'How will I *ever* finish this?'

It was a year earlier, 2007. Ayşe was crouching in her wooden cabin in the Olympos valley, knitting. Perched on a mattress and wearing no more than a bikini, she frantically moved the needles back and forth. Her hair was slicked back, and her arms were glistening. It was probably forty degrees in the hut. A naked bulb had been squashed through the roof panels. It bobbed above her on a few inches of cable wiring. She had two full bikinis to knit for a pair of Russian tourists, and they had to be ready by nine the following morning.

The hut was a grotto of elaborate creations. There were strappy tops laid out on the bed, lollipop coloured anklets, bikinis hanging on hooks, and clothes' hangers draped with rainbow designs. Spools of every colour of thread nestled like precious eggs in Ayşe's lap. Time had passed, and her stall was becoming lucrative. In the beginning of the season, Ayşe had made a promise to hang on until her money ran out. Yet every week she just sold enough of her knitwear to keep on paying for her room and board. It was August, and she was still in the valley.

Three years had come and gone since Ayşe had first moved into Olympos. The valley was quickly mutating. Rather than hiding a small itinerant mis-match tribe of freaks, in a quirky turn of fate, Olympos – a hamlet of farmers and village folk – was fast becoming Turkey's beating heart of alternative youth culture. Its reputation had spread through the veins of the land. As soon as school was out, a contagion of student revelry would swarm down the hillside in a bid to escape the tight collar of conservative parents. The valley became a jamboree of sex, drugs, and music. It was a wonder the government hadn't shut it down.

The next morning, Ayşe stumbled out of her hut, bikinis in hand. Bleary-eyed and stiff-fingered, she presented her handiwork to the awaiting tourists. Then, she strolled out of the pansiyon and made her way down the track. She walked in the direction of the yoga platform. The sun picked at the dirt road. Its hot dry fingers scratched up patches of dust.

Arriving at the forest-edge platform, she looked for signs of life. It was cool and quiet, except for the odd squawk from the chicken coop behind. After a boisterous summer evening in the Bull Bar, most Olympians rose late. They struggled to crawl down to breakfast, never mind hit the wooden boards of the yoga platform. Ayşe was by far the most regular participant ever to grace the morning session.

She unfurled her mat and began warming up. It was just as she stretched on tiptoes, she spied someone approaching from between the trees.

'Allo!'

It was a young, cheeky-looking foreigner. Her long blonde hair flopped over the lobster red of her arms.

'Is this where the yoga happens?' The young woman climbed onto the platform and stretched out her hand. 'My name's Lisa.' Her face had a knack of contorting into the most bizarre expressions. Her eyes were bulging while her mouth twisted into a wry pout.

'Take a mat. The teacher's on her way.' Ayşe surveyed the newcomer. The financial-advice-selling smile snuck across her face.

Lisa spread a mat on the boards. She sat on it. Her skinny, pink legs stretched in front of her like two sticks of Brighton rock. She began limbering up. With each forward bend she girned. 'Aw me legs! Bloody hell! I'm going to need this.'

It was too bad Ayşe didn't play poker. Her face gave nothing away. She sat with the exterior equanimity of the Buddha. But inside the analysis was over, and the conclusion reached. It was going to be one of those sessions. She could hear it already. The teacher was going to be talking a lot about inner calm and acceptance.

'I'm as stiff as a board. I've walked all the way from Fethiye on the Lycian Way. You know it?' Lisa grinned as she reached for her toe.

Ayşe stopped mid warrior pose. She craned her neck over her shoulder. 'You've walked the Lycian Way?'

'Yup. Just me and my sleeping bag. Had some superb open-air sleepovers on cliff edges. The bit around *Yedi Bur* . . . Seven whatchamacallits . . .'

'Yedi Burunlar. Seven Nazes.'

'Yeah, that's it. That bit's flipping gorgeous.'

Ayşe gave up on the warrior. Now it was her turn for her eyes to bulge.

'You did it *alone?*'

'Yeah. Aw people said it was a no no. Scorpions, snakes, the men . . . you know. It's all bullshit I reckon . . . well, except for the men eh?' Lisa winked. 'I've had a few run-ins with them.' She began to chortle.

Ayşe raised an eyebrow, and then nodded understandingly.

Perhaps the most valuable thing one person can do for another is to live their dream. What can compete with the power of a vision brought to life? Who knows how Lisa came to walk the Lycian Way? That was Lisa's trail. And she cleared the way for someone else in the process.

Ayşe sat down and crossed her legs. She tried to come back to the meditative present moment, but her mind didn't want to know. It had grabbed Lisa's torch and was charging into the future with it. It threw down a gauntlet or two in its wake. *If that snippet of a foreign woman can find her way to our land and trek our paths, then I'll be damned if I can't!*

The switch was flicked. The headlamps were trained on the road ahead. It was only a matter of time.

છા૦ભ

I pulled my feet from the railing. I was horribly tired by then. The lights of Kalkan glimmered orange beyond the balcony. They drew watery, broken lines over the waves in the bay. I yawned and retired to my bed assuming I would sleep instantly. Fatigue is a curious creature, however.

There are times when it paces the length and breadth of one's mind, obstructing all efforts at rest. I remember that night in Kalkan well; the clean, white floors, the proper mattress, the neatly finished skirting boards. I was hovering between two worlds.

On the one hand, I was desperate to complete my trail. You see, I'd set my heart on Xanthos and Letoon. I was now so close that it didn't make any sense to give up. Xanthos was perhaps 25 kilometres away, a day hike at most. Yet, I was also missing Olympos. I had reached my physical limit, and when one feels a little desperate, as I did that night, one always wishes for home. Yes, I realised Olympos had become my home over these past few years.

As I tossed and turned in my white sanctuary, I fell on and off a thread of incoherent dreams. I sped over the Ak and Bey Mountains, over their bony heads and the green fur of their backs. All the time, I was looking for Olympos. Only, I couldn't find her. Each time I thought I was in the valley, I would search for my wooden bungalow. I cantered in and out of the orange groves, but could never locate my cabin. In fact, there weren't any wooden huts at all. And then I would realise, I wasn't in Olympos. Over and over again, I kept finding myself under a huge stone gate, in a river full of rocks . . . or were they skulls? I would wade along the dry gulch, dragging my legs through the cold, white orbs in a feverish attempt to get out. In the distance a mountain burned. And then it would dawn on me. I was lost in Patara of all places, just over the hill.

&Oങ

Night. The dark cavalier. The Romans called him Pluto. The Greeks and Lycians knew him as Hades. And he had the power to extinguish anything and everything. But the darkness hides many secrets, not least that elusive spark, the timeless Now. Hades was known as the God of riches, as well as king of the underworld. Perhaps that's why.

The present moment evades all in the material world. It soars out of reach, winging just close enough to brush a person's skin. Only when humans take off their earthly disguises and sink naked into the timeless valley of sleep, can the Now embrace them. They need the Now just as they need water. Without sleep, folk are mad and deranged. Because only the timeless can make sense of time. Only the Now has enough space for memories to be heard, wounds to be healed, and a new day to enter.

Night had long drawn into Lycia. He had started his journey in Olympos. His chariot of darkness had rolled across Aphrodite's starlit eye, and she had winked at him to come closer. But night didn't want the sky. He wanted the Earth instead. He trundled over the hills, his black cape swirling in the bays. The ancient cities fell under his spell. One by one. Phoenicus, Aperlae, Kaş, and Kalkan. Finally, he swept through Patara, ancient port of the Xanthians. Darkness rushed across the wide, sandy beach. It demolished Patara's roads. It stole the temples. Even the huge, old amphitheatre was lost under the hooves of his ebony horses. There in the emptiness all time was one. All paths were joined.

As Patara slumbered in a vale of nothing, her history found room to breathe. And just like everywhere and every when, her buried memories rose up. They might have been Lycia's dreams. They could have been ghosts from the past, or blips on the ribbon of time. But whatever they were, they crawled out of their holes, because they wanted resolution.

Had any one soul been aware at that darkest of hours in Patara, had anyone seen the city's arched gate disappear, they might have noticed how still the air was, how the temperature plummeted. Had there been a clairvoyant, or even someone under the influence of the psilocybin mushroom, they would have glimpsed it; the silent procession of sixty thousand heads or more rolling through the road. For though much of Patara lay submerged under years of sand and dirt, the torsos of yesteryear were still there, clawing their out.

⁝O⁞

'We're here Sir!' One of the companions called up.

Harpagos cupped his hands over his eyes and looked ahead. A large, brown plain spread before him. It was squashed between two low-lying mountains. It looked like the flat belly of a woman sinking between two raised hips. He could see the bowl of the amphitheatre to his right, and a thickening collection of wooden and stone houses. This was Patara.

The Persians paused on the road, camels snorting, horses shuffling and flicking flies off with their tails. The afternoon sun cast yellow nets over the army. The sombre regiments shone like an autumn catch of fish. They were still reeling from the suicide of Xanthos. Harpagos, on the other hand, was reeling from a lot of things.

There was only one thing he had decided to bring with him from crackpot Letoon; the translator. True, she was somewhat flaky, but she could translate. She would prove useful as a diplomat. Besides, the satrap had a few other, less altruistic designs, as far as she was concerned.

The great gate of Patara stood proud as the Persian troops approached. Harpagos had sent an armed convoy with his new ambassador ahead. Xanthos was essentially

Lycia at that time, so he didn't foresee too much resistance. His conditions were anything but harsh – allegiance to Cyrus and unhampered use of the harbour, that was the extent of it. Yet who could tell with these Lycians? They were wholly unpredictable.

It was early evening when the horse-back regiment of Companions returned. They were a striking sight as they galloped, clouds of dust rising in their wake. Their vivid caps and tunics were visible from a distance. Harpagos waited up in his chariot. The horses of the small convoy snorted, their muscles rippling under their gleaming coats. Finally, they drew to a tail-swishing, hoof-clopping halt in front of him. The Companions shifted aside to allow the translator to come forward. She sat astride a sable steed. As she walked it forward, she drew alongside Harpagos. Raised as he was in his chariot, they were both exactly the same height. He shielded his eyes from the setting sun to get a better look at her.

'They have accepted. You may enter the city, but tell your hordes to break nothing, steal nothing, hurt no one.'

Harpagos nodded and expelled a sigh of relief.

Within ten minutes, the long body of the Persian war dragon picked itself up. It heaved forward, scale by colourful scale. Harpagos stared up when he rumbled under Patara's great gate. As his chariot entered the citadel, folk stood by the side of the road staring. Some wept, some sulked, most were simply shocked into muteness.

Within an hour, the Persian encampment had settled on Patara's fringes. The sun slumped out of sight. Harpagos' scarlet tent was one of the first conoids to grace the evening skyline.

As soon as his quarters were furnished, Harpagos walked inside and stretched out on the divan. He closed his eyes. But his mouth was tight, the muscles as taut as an archer's bow string. Night was coming, and he dreaded it. Because nowadays, when he turned to his bed, his mind was never peaceful. Xanthos would scratch at his soul. The fires. The screams. And when he did finally drift off, he was assailed by rocks with mouths, female sorcerers and other visitations of the grotesque.

'Dinner, Sir!' The drape of the tent twitched. The guard drew back the woollen doorway, and a manservant walked in holding a round silver tray of food. Harpagos opened his eyes and sat up. Then, he reached for the chalice of wine. He felt the warmth of the red grape as he tipped it into his mouth. After knocking back a cup-full in one gulp, he indicated to the servant – who was now lighting the censers and oil lamps – to bring him the whole jug. The man disappeared outside.

Night had arrived. A voluptuous moon was rising outside. The general picked at the barbequed bass on the platter. He pulled the soft, white meat from the bone and rolled it in strips of unleavened bread. His head was bowed so he didn't see the drape of his tent move, nor the figure slip in between the shadows cast by the lamps. It wasn't until he heard a panicked cry outside that he raised his head. There in front of him stood the translator. Her white robe fluttered gently in the night air. She was quite a sight. It was like looking at a statue brought to life.

'Hey! What do you think you're playing at! You can't just wander in here, woman!' The guard rushed in, followed by the servant with the jug of wine. For the first time in a long while Harpagos smiled. It was a crooked old grin, but under the circumstances it was the best he could do.

'Ah. Another chalice is in order,' he said. He grabbed the jug from the servant and waved the guard away. The soldier and servant looked at each other and swiftly made themselves scarce.

The Lycian translator had tied part of her wild mane back. The rest of it sprang out about her face and neck like a dark shrub in need of a prune. Harpagos could smell jasmine wafting from her. It was a good smell, a smell he wanted to get closer to. He thought he saw the sun of good fortune rising. This certainly beat another lonesome night of bad dreams and suppressed guilt.

The translator didn't wait to be asked. She sat down on the divan and gave Harpagos a long, hard stare. It was clear she was expecting his full attention. And he was more than willing to oblige. 'I want to say something about the road ahead,' she blurted. 'It's important.'

Harpagos screwed up the bridge of his nose and handed her a circle of flat bread. 'Do you *have* to? I've had a belly full of the past, and the future is hardly any more inspiring. Don't you think the present might be rather nice for a change? Anyway what's your name? I'm getting a bit tired of referring to you as The Translator.'

She shot him a sideways glance. The corner of her mouth curled in amusement. 'It's Eleftheria, not that it's going to make any difference to anything. You Persians, honestly!'

Harpagos turned to her and lowered both his eyebrows in mock consternation. 'I'm not Persian, I'm a Mede. If you must make crass generalisations, then at least get my ethnic roots straightened out.'

The translator laughed out loud. It was a full-bodied guffaw and it shook the Persian, slightly.

'Elef . . .' Harpagos frowned as he wrestled with the name.

'theria.'

'Aleft-hairier? My God, it's not exactly snappy is it? And I thought 'translator' was unwieldy.' It was a rare

296

occurrence, but it happened all the same. Harpagos had a glint in his eye. And he could feel the glint tickling him somewhere under his ribcage sending tiny shivers of unsubstantiated optimism through him. 'Anyway, what does this unutterable name mean? "Earth Goddess?" "To hell with the Persians?" '

'Liberator.'

'Ah. To hell with the Persians, then. I was right.'

The manservant appeared with another drinking vessel. He filled it for the priestess. Harpagos raised his cup to hit Eleftheria's.

'Now Mede, listen carefully!'

'You're rather bossy, you Lycian priestesses, aren't you?'

'Oh, you mean we have ideas of our own and voices? Now, if you'll let me finish . . .'

The satrap sighed. He half-listened. The other half of his mind was darting about, scavenging for ideas of how to get from here to where he wanted to be, which was closer, in a place where someone as exotic as a Lycian priestess would actually like him, would see something worth falling for. Harpagos might have been the living pinnacle of Cyrus the Great's military achievements, but he was lonely, lonely as hell.

Eleftheria bent forward. She lowered her voice to a conspiratorial whisper. 'You will proceed through Lycia with speed. Nothing shall stop you, the prophecies have foreseen this. However, there is one place where we cannot see anything. It is a place not yet fully Lycia, not yet fully a city even. Because it is on the edge, and also because it is one of Gaia's special spaces – a rift where chaos washes freely in – we . . . we don't know what will happen.'

Harpagos did his utmost to look interested. But it was an effort. Right now, he didn't care two hoots about prophecies. He wanted to get his woes off his chest, enjoy a smidgen of closeness in his wretched excuse for a life, and perhaps even take her to bed. 'And where are we alluding to exactly?' he said

'Olympos. The secret valley. The home of the formidable Chimera.'

The satrap somehow managed to stop his eyeballs rolling upwards. 'The Chimera? Oh. This must be another one of these phantasmagorical Greek myth-beasts. I'm afraid I don't believe in them.' He swirled the wine about his chalice and watched the blood-red whirlpool spin round and round. His eyes sank to the food trays. Picking up another piece of flat bread, he ripped it clean in half before lowering his voice to add, 'To be quite frank, I don't believe in anything at all. I don't believe in belief.'

Eleftheria drew her black eyes into concentrated slits, and studied Harpagos for a moment. A gust of thoughts scudded across her face leaving momentary traces on her skin. Silence fell on the tent like the flat side of an iron hammer. Harpagos kicked himself for his bluntness. But what was he supposed to say? That he believed in Leto and the rocks and all of that? He just couldn't bring himself to be that inauthentic.

Slowly, the priestess nodded. Then, her strangely attractive face cracked into a grin. She clenched one fist and shook it, as if to say, 'By Jove!' Harpagos looked up to find her pointing a half-eaten cucumber at him.

'Now, I must admit while the high priestess is the most able clairvoyant in the land, I was less than convinced regarding her choice of you. I mean, you looked so completely hopeless. But I see it now. She's right. You are indeed the one!'

Harpagos squinted. His war-worn brow wrinkled as he tried to work out how in the ancient world she'd leapt to that remote conclusion. He looked at her and noticed the mole just below her mouth. It was the kind of imperfection he could end up being fascinated by. Seeing as the tide had turned, and not one to waste such an opportunity, he edged a little closer on the divan placing one arm strategically behind her.

The priestess became very still, the chewed cucumber poised in her hand. She turned away, and looked at the door. 'You need to understand, that's not why I'm here. Some things are not actually about that. Some things are a lot more important.'

Harpagos wasn't imperceptive, but he was exceptionally dogged. This was all looking a lot like a campaign. Years of experience on the field told him there was nothing like a bit of persistent slog to get you what you wanted in the end. Which was why, despite every indication to the contrary, hope flickered tenaciously on. For a short while anyway.

'Oh, that's a shame. What would it take to change your mind?' Harpagos did his best to look charming when he said that, but the sentence fell in a sleazy heap between them. Even the fish on the dinner tray seemed to wince. He gritted his teeth, and briefly considered nailing his tongue to the tent post.

Eleftheria raised an eyebrow. 'What it would take is something extraordinary.' She shook her head, her eyes flicking up to the tent roof.

Not one to let a second chance go untaken, Harpagos pulled himself up and cut to the chase. 'Well, I'm a free-thinker and a genius. I invented the earth ramp. I'm the first warlord this side of Phrygia to use dromedaries on campaign, and the second most powerful man in the Persian

Empire. I hold more wealth than Lycia, Caria and Lydia bundled together. Just how much more extraordinary did you think it was going to get, Priestess?'

You had to hand it to the man, he had a point. Eleftheria's mouth did an unorthodox little dance as she swallowed that extensive inventory of accomplishment. She barely stifled a titter. But it only took seconds for the humour to vacate the moment. A lightless silence drifted in. It muffled any suspicion of amusement. She sighed. It was a long, weary sigh, the kind of sigh which sank so deep it could never be picked up. She looked away. 'I'm sorry, you don't understand. I don't mean extraordinary in a worldly manner. I mean . . .' She recoiled. Then frowned. 'You just don't see, do you? Not everything is a question of winning and losing, of competition and power. Those are just the glasses *you're* wearing. And do you know why you're wearing those lenses? Because you're scared and you think dominance is the only way to counter your fear or manifest what you want. The window of power is a coward's window.' She stood up and made to leave.

It was then it all tumbled apart. And when you posit yourself as high as Harpagos had, tumbling hurts. He was rejected. He felt it collapse inside him like a castle in an earthquake. All that was left was the miserable hole of repudiation. But as he himself had said, he was one of the most powerful men in Asia Minor at that moment. He could have given her some tough choices to make. He could have summoned any one of the paid professionals touting their wares outside, as well. But, although he was in many ways asleep, Harpagos was sentient enough to see power for its own sake wasn't doing it for him. Nor was sex, nor drink, nor anything. Nothing at all was doing it for him. A more obtuse man would have been satisfied with the status, but Harpagos wasn't. He had it all and was still depressed. His world was full of sycophants and phonies, and he knew it.

Now even this priestess, the first person with any genuine passion for life he'd spoken to in a long while, didn't want him, no doubt because he was old and worn and cynical. And it felt like the last insult to a lifelong injury.

Eleftheria set the chalice down on the tray. Staring down, she murmured into the gloom. To an outsider it would have looked as though she were conversing with the decapitated fish-head on the platter. 'It's true, we are priestesses of Leto and therefore guardians of Gaia. But the earth and the rocks and humans are brought to life by something beyond all that. Something outside the web of time. Something you might call a soul.'

Harpagos didn't bother to disguise his contempt. He sniffed, and looked the other way. 'I don't believe in souls either. They're nothing more than fantasies humans invent to keep themselves going,' he said.

Eleftheria stared at the floor.

'Look around you! Everything struggles to survive, and a bit of optimism is helpful in that department. So we pull out these figments of hope, things like Gods and Goddesses and souls and destinies and other claptrap, and we clutch at these illusions as we wander through the dark, as a child clutches its mother's teat.' He glanced around hoping he'd dented something precious inside her.

Standing up, she brushed off her skirt. Then she threw him one last half-smile. 'You believe in nothing, and that's fitting. Belief kills truth and magic and love and all that is incredible within us. It is opinionated, inflexible and blinding. So you see, there's hope for us all, isn't there?' With that, Eleftheria turned and swished in the direction of the exit.

Harpagos brooded. He hadn't heard a word of it. All he had heard was that she didn't want him, and that he had lost a conquest. The defeat sidled through his thoughts, leering and gloating all the way. Soon enough it found the old, grubby door in his mind it was looking for, the door labelled 'Failure'. It swiftly knocked on the rotten, worm-ridden wood and waited smugly for fear and shame to come slithering out.

The commander of the Persian forces sat sullenly as the priestess reached the door. He was nursing the wounds of a lifetime without even knowing where they were. His scowl remained long after she had disappeared through the flap into the night. And when the sulking was over, he just felt mean instead.

Day Twelve

Home

As the peak near Patara burned, Ayşe turned this way and that in her clean, white bed in Kalkan. She was dreaming. And she dreamed of her wooden bungalow in the lost valley. Whether Olympos knew of Ayşe's homesickness is hard to say. The ancient city had other things to deal with. Back in the valley, things were moving. The Olympos of 2008 was beginning her ritual midnight dance.

A strobe felt its way through the darkness. It pursued the ripples and crags in the steep limestone walls. A steady rhythm pounded through the rocks and the earth. It jolted them more profoundly than anything had done since they were formed. Things had changed. The moderns were here. And they were shaking things up and out. When the clock struck midnight, and Lycia had her back to the sun, the Olympos valley strutted out for a night on the dance floor. It rollicked to its Mediterranean heart's content. It wasn't until the first glimmers of dawn, the carousing would lay down its head.

Lights played on the sky like titanic fireflies. Even Aphrodite blinked as they span over her sultry eye. The new Olympians bopped and swayed as the Gods of entertainment cranked up the party. Bodies glistened in the darkness. Tourists gaped. Young Turkey indulged in its forbidden epicurean dream.

The bass thundered through the valley. It stormed through the forest thumping into the rocks. Stones shook. They convulsed. One by one the fragments of the past they were holding were loosened. Like the layers of an onion, stories slid off and out into the air. Olympos opened her mouth. She began to mumble. She began to speak. Yet with all that racket going on, who could hear her?

Back then, deep in midsummer, no one could sense the antiquity around them. The hordes of visitors drowned

304

out the voices of the past. Yet, if you waited until the tourists left, the parties died down, and the fresh autumn rain cleaned away their footprints, you might just have heard what the stones had to say. Because the spirits in those rocks are still buried deep enough that even when they shout they but whisper.

As Olympos returns to silence, as the agamas dare to sunbathe, and the wood pigeons coo through the laurels, take heed. For there are tales abound. Tales no one has heard. Tales of lost cities, lost generals, and lost hope. Tales of destinies transformed. Transformed just by the touch of a stone.

The leaves of time are folded back. The hands of the gods turn the pages. Two. One. Zero and beyond. Xanthos is faraway now. Patara is days behind, too. Even Letoon has sunk into the past. General Harpagos has finally reached Olympos. And Olympos will never forget his visit, even if the history books and inscriptions do.

঩Oଔ

'No one's left!'

The two Persian scouts scrambled up through the thorny undergrowth. They stood before Harpagos dripping in the late afternoon sun. He was holding the reins of his steed and feeling the beast breathe beneath him.

'The place is deserted.' The first scout puffed. The second nodded in agreement behind him.

Ridges appeared on Harpagos' forehead as he fumbled through the possibilities of where the Olympians might have vanished to. Had they fled in panic? Or could they be skulking in the shadows of the vale, waiting to ambush? Surely, after Xanthos the Olympians would acquiesce. Surely.

305

Harpagos dismounted. He walked a little way along the narrow, thicket-ripped pathway. He reached a slice of rock crashing along the side of the path. Pausing, he placed his hands on the stone and listened. He waited. He had no idea why he did it. Perhaps he just wanted to try. He was surprised how much it reminded him of the flank of his horse, just cooler.

'Forward!' He yelled. And the war train heaved into action. The soldiers gathered their arms, stood and prepared to move into the lost city. When the last of the men had filed past him down the swarthy, bracken-strewn slope, and towards the main agora, Harpagos breathed. He walked slowly on. He was surrounded by his usual mob of Companions. But he had to think. He spoke to his officers. Within moments they had trailed away to a safe distance.

Now, before they could enter Olympos proper, the trail circled through the necropolis. The tomb-garden clustered there, grey and cold. As Harpagos trotted through the arch and into the small plateau of graves, the sun sank behind the peak. Shadows yawned in the tomb crevices, and a light breeze picked up. It whispered over the stones, making the bushes skittish. Lycia. There was so much time strewn about, people were tripping over the stuff. Myths oozed out of the crevices. Spirits pushed and slid through the cracks.

Harpagos sat on a boulder staring into the valley. He watched his men swarm into the market place down on the bank opposite. One by one, his thoughts began to unravel. They unwound like a bobbin of cerebral thread. Soon, his entire life lay before him in a straggly, misshapen heap. Damn Lycia! From the beginning of this campaign she'd been dragging it out of him, coil by decomposing coil. He saw it all – the sum worth of his existence. He had swallowed fury, suffered loss, been betrayed and betrayed others. He had silently hated. He had so many chips on his shoulder they were toppling off and littering the wayside. It was a wonder people didn't trip over them or pick them up and hand them back. He had tried to right the wrongs. He had killed and ordered killings. He had done it all because he believed it was a means to an end, the end being something better. Here in this nothing place in the middle of nowhere it suddenly dawned on the general. The end wasn't coming. And without a finish in sight, all he was left with was the means.

It was then Harpagos noticed the chill. It crept ominously into the darkening air. The wiry, black hairs on his arms began to spike up. One by one. It was quiet. Far too quiet. Suddenly, it hit him like the heavy, hard fist of a Cyclops. He wasn't alone. Harpagos stole a glance to his right. He sucked in his breath and sat tight. For there, right next to him was . . .

Leto was staring ahead into the valley. Her skin shimmered faintly in the dusk. She looked like moonlight, or an effigy, or something. Harpagos had no idea what to do. Move? Kneel? Run? In the end, he was so consumed by fear he did nothing at all. He just huddled there, sitting hard on the urge to shiver. He watched her watching his men gobble up Olympos. And as he did, the realisation stumbled and limped over the plain of his awareness like a slow, incapacitated animal. Leto was stalking him, and Harpagos had no idea why. What did she want? Should he leave Lycia to the next tyrant on the horizon? Get the hell out?

Against all odds, it was there on a rock in the necropolis Harpagos finally glimpsed a snippet of truth. He was miserable. In fact, he was hopeless. The despair was a gulch so wide, he'd been wading across it forever. And he was tired of it. Sick of it.

He closed his eyes and breathed. The burial stones of the dead were scattered about him like half-open doors. He sensed the spectral light of the apparition by his side wafting about him. The cool silence of it made his teeth chatter. The fear shook him so hard he fell out of the cold, lumpy bed of his self-pity. In the space it left behind, something utterly new and unexpected fluttered in. It landed on the floor of his thoughts gracefully flapping its kaleidoscope wings. Some might have called it grace, others divine light. Whatever it was, Harpagos felt it fill him up like a rhyton of sweet honey-mead wine. It was a moment he would remember for a long time, a moment he would draw on later to imbibe its timeless power.

The general sat and watched in distracted surprise as the best of him got itself together and began to clean the windows. Lycia. He could whinge and grumble all he wanted to. He could sulk all the way to his grave. But there was no getting away from it. Harpagos was, in spite of himself, more fascinated by the place than he let on. Her craggy beauty nudged the Wildman in him. Her nights were witchcraft. But most of all it was the people. They had been to the outer-most edge for freedom. They were real. They were alive. And when Harpagos scraped the vitrified surface of his self-image and fumbled underneath he knew, regardless of his genius and worldly success, that wasn't something he could currently claim about himself.

His profile slumped on the rock, shoulders rounding, head falling, until he looked like another of its stony bulges. The bulge shrank further as he sighed. He had to change, or . . . or move or something. Hell! Somehow, he had to find the other man crouching inside him, the parallel Harpagos waiting for a break. The real one. The one that hadn't sold out. He blinked. Then he threw Leto a sidelong glance. She was still sitting there with that tranquil smile on her face. Change? Harpagos sat with the Idea wondering for a moment where the devil it had come from. Where do Ideas come from? *Where?* Change. Move on. It was a lot easier said than done. He'd been bitter and grumpy for years. He

308

was used to it. It was who he was. And anyway, weren't happy people dim? Wasn't that why they felt content, because their intellects just couldn't penetrate the gruesomeness of the truth?

None of this mattered in the slightest though. Harpagos was in the valley of Olympos, the vale of sinners, the home of the exiles. A fissure in time and reason. Special spaces on the Earth where the inside comes out, where the past touches the future. Spaces where anything is possible. Even the impossible.

ဆဝဝဝ

It was the twelfth day, and I was recovering in Kalkan. Mother and daughter had prepared my breakfast on the terrace. Boiled eggs, feta cheese, olives, butter, honey, homemade jam, and tomatoes covered each inch of the plastic table. The quality of the stay was worthy of a paying hotel. I looked out onto the tiny harbour as I finished off my tea. Everything hurt. My legs, my arms, my shoulders all ached beyond belief, but I had made up my mind. I was going to attempt Xanthos. And within the hour, I had put myself back on the road.

The Lycian Way drops south from Kalkan to fall onto Patara beach. That was the route I had followed the previous day. It then loops about the peak of Eren, through ancient Patara and its crumbling aqueduct, and then stretches back up and onwards to Xanthos. Due to the forest fire that loop was now impassable, so I took a bus to a place called Akbel instead.

The minibus left me near a Lycian Way entrance. I clambered out and pulled my trusty old pack from the baggage compartment. Mustering every gram of effort I could, I executed a near perfect squat-straps-push up manoeuvre for one last bash at the trail. I paused just before setting off. The weight of that rucksack was just unbearable, and I felt all but staked to the ground. I wondered, would I really hike with twenty kilograms on my back again? There had to be another way. I mean, one can't walk without any baggage at all, well, I suppose one could, but it would be just as exhausting. Think about sleeping without a tent, and every bug in a square kilometre swarming in for a free supper. Or imagine wearing the same pair of clothes for two weeks on end, or never using soap!

Then, finally, the answer drifted down like manna from the sky of good ideas. No, I didn't have to get rid of my entire baggage, I just needed to make it work for me. There were lightweight equivalents for everything on the market: special tents, sleeping bags, and clothes; so now that I was a hiker, I'd just have to invest in some new gear, wouldn't I? In fact, later I would learn, the backstreets of Istanbul are littered with Aladdin's caves for the outdoors, and they sell everything a hiker could want: torches that fit in a matchbox, trousers made of magic fabric that dries in an hour, towels the same weight as a teacloth, and tents one can carry in a one's handbag. Happy to have sorted that dilemma out, I marched determinedly off.

I rambled in the direction of Xanthos. The trouble was, the exploits of the previous day had gouged red holes into me too. I hadn't noticed in the panic of my flee, but my feet were now in an appalling condition; excruciating, raw lumps of flesh. I gave Lycia what I had trekking a good twenty kilometres (yes twenty, it has been said, I was perhaps a little unhinged) before reaching the Xanthos aqueduct. Walking the length of a cliff, I looked down onto that remarkable achievement of ancient engineering. It stood, a giant stone caterpillar, crawling and crumbling upon the plain floor. There I walked where ancient water had once flowed. Yet there was no escaping reality, with every kilometre the torment of my feet intensified. In the end, it felt as though I were stumbling upon shards of shattered glass.

Then something odd occurred. It was particularly strange given the season and the previous day's deathly dry wind. Clouds began to blossom in slate-coloured blooms. They thickened rapidly, lathering up the sky. Then, approximately five kilometres from Xanthos city, it started to rain. It was unthinkable. It never rains in July, and certainly not like that! The water rattled down in loaded beads drenching me. It might seem paradoxical given the fact I had spent the previous eleven days crawling along in perpetual thirst roasting under a blazing sun, but the rain signalled the end. In minutes, I was soaked; my hair stuck to my neck in sodden wedges, and my belongings were steadily taking in water.

I reached a main road crossing the Lycian Way. I stared out at the pale gloom gobbling up the mountain tops, and I took stock and listened. A fire had stopped me yesterday, and today it was rain. Perhaps Earth was speaking. I listened to the rocks and the trees. I listened to the air and the soil. I listened to Lycia. As the valley disappeared into the drizzle, and it seemed she was saying, 'Go home.'

Xanthos and Letoon vanished into the mist beyond. There they lay waiting. Waiting for another day. It was time for Olympos now.

৪০Oભ

The water-laden sky above Ayşe churned and moiled over western Lycia. It sent the beasts underground. It washed the outstretched boughs of the trees, and put out the flames on

311

the Pataran hills. In another realm, in a space wide enough and boundless enough to see a much bigger picture, something somewhere had apparently received the message it had been waiting for. A certain level of something not quite quantifiable had been reached. The balance had been tipped.

The rain flowed down the mountainsides like the rivers of the past, present and future. The streamlets intermingled. One swelled another causing their courses to change. The streams joined the rivers. And the rivers pushed on out into that great, old basin of blue called the Mediterranean Sea. Currents sent the sea water out from Patara. The water forged a path in the direction of Crete. That ancient brine would swirl and eddy before it hit the island. From there, it would begin its long homeward journey. It would arc back towards the Egyptian coast and loop around to Israel, Lebanon, Syria. Then it would return into the southeast of Turkey flowing past the ancient cities of Antioch and Tarsus. Finally, it would slide into the bay of Antalya. The bay would hold it for a while. Then it would release it along the Turquoise Coast to shimmy past the fire-breathing mountain of Çıralı, and on to that mysterious groove in the Earth known as Olympos. There it would flow along the pebbled beach, around the flocks of swimmers and the large wooden gulets. It would hold the Caretta Caretta and float around one of the last five hundred monk seals on the planet. It would absorb the new sewage churned out from the explosion of pansiyons too. It would roll over the shore and try in vain to carry off the hills of cigarette butts. It would envelop the plastic bags and bottles the moderns were leaving behind. But no matter how much it gnawed at them, it would fail to digest them. A certain level was being reached, and the sea would carry the message on down the coast. It would tumult over the rocks and howl at the shore, until someone heard its calls.

In fact, there was someone who heard. She stood bare foot at the foamy lip of the sea. Her eyes were closed. As the water curled and hissed, she accepted its complaint letting the waves of all times rumble within her. There was fear and trouble. She didn't turn away. Dark, oily spectres coiled beneath the waves. She remained there and watched. Opening her arms, she embraced it all; the good news and the bad. The woman inhaled with her mind and her heart combined.

Eventually, the future was dragged beneath the rolling breakers once more. The crest of the present rippled over the top. Eleftheria snapped her eyes open and stared into the beautiful, black eye of the night searching out its soul. The moon was full and hung above the sea. It was an orange iris scanning the beach.

An unexpected breeze hurried in. It carried a flutter of utterances from the canyon beyond. The murmurs floated through the narrow gorge. They skimmed the surface of the river water as it poured into the sea. Gradually, a smile spread over the priestess' face. She sensed it, unequivocally. Something extraordinary had happened, was happening, was going to happen. She wasn't entirely sure of the outcome. Who is? But one thing was clear. The stakes had changed. For somewhere within the Lycia of all times, within a few individual souls, truth had decided to put up a fight.

಄O೫

Only a few hundred metres away, Harpagos opened his eyes and surveyed the necropolis. The rock was boring into his rump. His backside was killing him.

The sky had turned dark silver, and the moon was climbing over the peaks. Every now and again, a Lycian full moon would swell beyond all belief, causing anyone who saw her to stop and stare. Tonight she was fantastic. She floated above the necropolis, above Harpagos, like an enormous copper gong.

Harpagos glanced over his right shoulder. No one would believe him, but he clearly saw Leto smile. It was a smile real enough and beautiful enough to light up an entire underworld of darkness. With that smile, the Olympos valley opened its wide, earthy mouth and beamed.

Then all of a sudden, she disappeared. Just like that. It was as if the fingers of the forest had come up and snatched her away leaving the necropolis empty and dark. Harpagos looked left and right. He looked up and down. He heard his steed snort from behind the small stone temple a few feet away. But there was something else. Another noise. It sounded like the whinnying of a new-born foal, or the whine of air escaping from a crevice.

The satrap lifted himself up from his rocky perch and stretched his legs. Slowly, reluctantly, he moved towards the noise. It seemed to be coming from within one of the sarcophagi. Harpagos' innards twisted. He'd had enough of the supernatural for one day. The Persian was about to grab his mare and make a run for it before other worlds and other times chanced to waft through the cracks. Yet the sound was palpable. It was real. It was here and now. Harpagos stopped for a moment and realised he knew it well. It was the stifled bleating of human distress.

Inhaling and cursing all in one gulp, Harpagos strode over to the tomb. It was half-open. The heavy, marble lid had been pulled ajar leaving a small rectangle of night gaping. Inside the hole of the dead huddled the scrunched-limbed body of a child. The figure was shivering. Harpagos

314

squinted. He bent over and held out his hand. It was immediately gripped by the smaller, colder fingers of what turned out to be a boy.

The lad, encouraged by the warm solidity of the grasp, scrambled from the grave. He was clearly relieved to be out of the murk. He stood in front of Harpagos and stared at the general's road-worn feet. Harpagos studied the boy. And then it dawned on him. He'd seen him somewhere before. Recently. My God! What were the odds? This was the street urchin he'd seen counting the boats in Phoenicus.

'Who are you?' The general's voice was a warm rumble through the necropolis.

The boy spoke the tongue of Lycia. Harpagos spoke Elamite. The languages clattered in confusion as the two tried to communicate. Consonants and vowels bumped in mayhem. Even so, from the frantic gestures and the bridge between their eyes, Harpagos guessed the boy was an Olympian orphan. He was their scout or long-distance runner. He also understood the reason Olympos was empty was because the townsfolk had fled.

The warlord laid his capacious, old hand on the boy's head and smiled. It was a good, deep smile. A smile that warmed the ground and the air and everything in between. He opened his mouth and spoke.

'Go find your people,' he said. 'Tell them they have nothing to fear. Tell them General Harpagos is in Lycia, and he personally guarantees both their safety and prosperity.'

ഇ⟠ഌ

Some hours later, back at the shore, Eleftheria was staring at the flames of the Chimera. Their lithe, orange bodies flirted with the night sky a little way off on the hills. The sea splashed and trickled by her in alternation. The pebbles rolled to and fro in time. She listened to the dragging of feet over the stones somewhere behind her, feet which were steadily approaching.

'Priestess, High Translator, Eleftheria! However you prefer to be addressed . . . I've been looking for you. I have to ask you something. *Immediately!*'

Harpagos was huffing slightly as he waded through the beach. He wiped his forehead with the back of his hand. Eleftheria cocked her head to one side. Listening. Waiting. The outline of her hair was as clear as day under the moon. It looked as though it had enough spring in it to attempt a leap for freedom. For a moment, Harpagos could have sworn he saw those dark spirals twist and turn ever so slightly in his direction.

'That great rock in Letoon. I shall see to it that it's buried.'

'Shhh! You don't know who's listening!' She hissed at the sea.

Harpagos grinned. There was nothing like being part of a good conspiracy. By the time he reached her, she had turned to face him. Her robe was picked up by the breeze and flowed behind her, a white flag in a moonlit wonderland. He cupped his hand about his mouth and dropped his voice to a mock whisper. 'But there's something I don't understand. What difference will burying the thing have on the future anyway?'

Eleftheria stepped closer. She looked him up and down circumspectly. Harpagos lowered his head to catch her words. 'We don't really know. There are signs, but nothing is ever certain. In all truth, we didn't know you would agree to bury it in the first place.'

'You didn't *know*?' Harpagos' eyes bulged in disbelief. 'You mean to say you threw me into a nymphless nymphaion, dragged me to your lair of Leto, and set about my mind with all sorts of despicable herbal sorcery, you traipsed from one end of Lycia to the other as my ambassador, and you didn't *know*?'

Eleftheria shook her head and chortled. Her hands were on her hips and she folded slightly in two as she laughed. 'Well, there was what you might call a potential, a hope. Let's just say we tried to improve its chances.'

Harpagos pursed his lips. A slightly larger wave had gathered back in the throat of the sea. As it crashed it sent a thin film of water scudding over his sandals. He hopped back, and ruffled the gold-embroidered hem of his purple tunic to stop it getting wet. 'Well, while we're on the subject of improving probabilities . . . This Motherstone. Now, I realise it's all very romantic to have this one great rock, source and keeper of everything, but . . . '

Eleftheria glanced at him now, hitching up the front of her eyebrows.

'Well, I think it might pay to be practical. You should make a back-up.'

There was a sharp intake of breath. The priestess looked as though she'd accidently bitten into something sour. 'A *back*-up?' She spat.

The air was moving faster now, gusts taking her hair and whipping it this way and that. Harpagos got his speed up. He nodded briskly. 'Yes! Who knows what might happen in the future? You said there will be a war. Well, I've seen a few wars in my time, and if there's one thing I've learned, it's this; *never* put all your eggs, be it blood-line, history or career, in one basket. It's a recipe for disaster.'

Eleftheria folded her arms tightly over her chest and threw Harpagos a hard stare. 'That's not how we do things, General. We are a people of faith.'

Harpagos blinked and sighed. He turned to contemplate the silvery outlines of the mountains, the curve of the bay, the soft, slow pull of the sea against the stones. The orphic warble of the crickets achieved the seemingly impossible. It brought him a sense of enlivenment and peaceful meditation, all at the same time. You had to hand it to Olympos. It was scintillating.

It was then, from nowhere, both of them heard a roar. It rumbled through the pewter bowl of the midsummer night and echoed along the upturned sides of the land. The pair stood stock still as the noise ripped along the beach. It was the unmistakable growl of a big cat. Harpagos turned to see Eleftheria's eyes trained on a ledge jutting high over the sea some distance away. It was then he glimpsed it too; the heart-stopping outline of a male lion as he stalked the frontier of his domain.

Harpagos smiled to himself. Lycia. She was speaking. He waited a moment for the beast to settle. Then he gathered himself together in unison with it. 'I'm just saying, that's all.' He murmured to the back of Eleftheria's head. 'Kings can get the oddest ideas into their heads. Even the best ones turn surprisingly aggrandised once their backsides hit a throne.'

Eleftheria spun around, leaving the lion's shadow to slink back into the dark arms of the forest. She studied Harpagos intently.

He moved closer, speaking even more quietly. 'Seeing as you've entrusted me with the entire history and survival of your people, I suppose I might let you into a few confidences of my own. Don't get me wrong, Priestess, I am always loyal to the great Cyrus. But even he has his moments. He ordered the army divert an entire river once. Completely absurd! I tell you, the world is full of maniacs.

What if some simpleton pulled down every temple from here to Xanthos? What if they found the stone?'

Harpagos paused and watched Eleftheria's eyes widening like circles of dough under a baker's rolling pin. Her mouth followed suit. She stared up at him in astonishment. 'General Harpagos . . . Are you . . . ? Are you hearing voices through the passageways of time? Are you clairvoyant?'

He winced, before continuing. A pained expression dragged on his rugged Mede face. 'No for heaven's sake! I'm being facetious. I'm simply saying, you never know with life. Why not make another Motherstone? Hell! Make as many as you can, just in case. I mean how difficult can it be? What do you do? Gather a few eccentric Lycian women together and chant around a rock a few times?'

Eleftheria sucked on her cheek. Her mouth moved from one side to another, while her forehead twitched and shifted. She looked out to sea, then back to the land, then back to Harpagos. She rubbed her chin with her index finger, and exhaled quietly. At long last, the corners of her eyes wrinkled as her mouth cut a grin into her cheeks. 'Well, well.' She patted Harpagos' arm. 'You're not Cyrus' right-hand man for nothing, are you now?'

He almost managed to contain the swell of his pride, but not quite.

'A back-up. Yes. We can make a whole trail of them. Why not?'

Harpagos scratched his nose as he pondered on the practicalities of a trail.

'The only trouble is, I'd have to bring the High Priestess, and she's dreadfully old now.'

Harpagos scoffed out loud when he heard that. 'She looked spritely enough to me! The damn woman dragged

319

me half-way across a crypt as I recall. How old is she in your book then?' he asked.

Eleftheria's half-smirk was almost drowned by the night, but the moon caught the right side of her face just in time. 'If I told you, you'd give me one of those looks, General, just like you did when I mentioned the Chimera.'

Harpagos drew himself up and adjusted his tunic. He jutted his chin forward slightly as well to accentuate the point. 'Hmph. Try me! I've undergone a radical transformation since Patara. I've seen the light, the Goddess and a host of other things I don't believe in. I think you'll find I'm a lot more open-minded.'

Eleftheria paused for a moment, before letting it out. 'One hundred and twenty-three.'

Harpagos threw his hands up and yelled out to the wind. 'That's preposterous! You can't seriously believe her.' He lowered his arms and turned back to the priestess. 'Look here, you have many powers I know nothing about. You possess a sharp mind and an obvious flair for languages. I can quite see a successful career in diplomacy ahead of you. But . . . you have to be a little less trusting. She can't possibly be a hundred and twenty-three. No one is a hundred and twenty-three. This is exactly the trouble with these spiritual teachers, isn't it? They hoodwink the gullible with their nonsense. Take our priest. Just the same. Full of complete hogwash!'

Harpagos was bemused to find Eleftheria chortling loudly, her face covered by her hands. She shook her head and gave his arm and affectionate squeeze before moving past him. She was still laughing as she made her way up the pebbled beach towards the towering incisor of rock that dominated the entrance to Olympos. Harpagos strode out after her, shaking his head, nonplussed.

When they reached the jutting protrusion of limestone, the priestess winked at Harpagos. Then she swung about and placed both her hands on the rutted surface of the soaring protuberance of rock. The Persian commander scratched his head thinking what an erratic bunch of idiosyncrasies this woman was. Eleftheria's eyes closed. She tilted back her head. She looked to be drinking in the moonlight. Harpagos glanced about hoping no one was watching this embarrassing display of cult sortilege. From then on, everything became extremely pointed. It was as though the air was expanding, and a great power beamed in. Then, she began to speak. It was a voice Harpagos had heard before, back in the Letoon. The verses were from another place and another time. They reverberated about the stones and rang over the pebbles in haunting cadencies.

'Heed all of you! Pray heed!
You in the future.
Heed!

Your trails are lies.
Your paths mislead.
And wayward you wander.
Lost and
        In vain.
Delusion
Confusion
        Reign.

Yet just as the darkness obscures
The light,

The life,
Finds its course.

Once again you will walk her roads,
Lycia.
You will ponder,
The Past,
The Future.
Contemplate her secrets.

The ones who walk her may hear her,
And be granted a gift called grace.
They will return from their journeys
Exuding,
Emitting,
Such wonder.

Stories will be written,
Lightways will be walked,
And when they are,
        The rocks will sing,
So even the deaf may hear.

The earth will carry our words you see,
And our hearts and our feelings within.
There will be those that hear them.
Those that write them.
And those that read them too.

We know not what you will do with our stories,
That is not for us to say.
But there is a potential,
Such a potential,

Then Lycia the balance shall sway.'

The crickets trilled, and the sea splashed on. Yet it was as if the entire shore, from Olympos to the fire breathing hills of Chimera, was there and then embalmed. Even the white peak of Mount Olympos seemed to glow in the distance. The light was palpable. The power of the Earth and beyond had lit a great torch and held it for all to see. Harpagos watched, bottom lip lagging somewhat, as Eleftheria gently removed her hands from the rock. He stood in baffled silence absorbing the sweetness in the air. No one wanted to break the spell. Not even the lion watching from his concealed perch on the hilltop. Not even the six Companions who had followed their commander to the beach, just in case.

Gradually, time shuffled on. Harpagos exhaled and quietly stooped. He didn't know what to make of any of it, except it felt good. And good was something valuable, something worth making an effort for. He knelt on the shingle, stroking the lumpy epidermis of the beach. Gently, resting his hands on the small egg-like pebbles, he felt their smoothness under his fingers, their perfectness in his calloused palms. He sensed something else too. They were drawing something out of him, slowly, patiently. The past, his dark, dark past was moving. It was shifting. Good Lord! Was that possible? All these tiny miracles scattered everywhere, what had clouded them from him before? It had been despair, hadn't it? Despair any ultimate good would ever come of anything. And of course good doesn't come of anything. It just is. Lying about all over the place. Waiting. Waiting for the day humans just stop all their schemes and look and feel.

Eleftheria hunched down beside him. She stretched out her hand and touched his face. He felt her fingers moving through his beard, fingers full of light. Hell! If he'd had any inkling it was going to be such a momentous night, he'd have changed his damn tunic, wouldn't he? He wondered if he should do something. Or whether it was better he wait. Perhaps it was a trick, or a test. Ah, perhaps she was going to turn round any minute now and slay all this good-feeling by telling him he wasn't extraordinary enough yet. Hmm, he could get even now, couldn't he? Yes. She could learn a thing or two about how it felt to be rejected. That would show her. Ha! Harpagos felt the stab of nastiness twist inside him.

And then he saw he was doing it again. All these strategies and plans. This exhausting, convoluted effort to win. And for what? Who cared about the victory if it meant you trampled every drop of happiness into the dust to get there? All this needless analysis. All this bitterness about what had already happened. The struggle and the worry. And he was missing it, completely missing whatever good was glowing in front of him. And it *was* glowing in front of him. It was glowing brighter than the damn sun! Why wasn't he acting on it for God's sake? What the hell was he doing?

What Harpagos was doing was waking up. In the half-darkness, he saw the whites of Eleftheria's eyes. He felt her hands reach into his hair and pull his face towards her. It was then ancient Persia's greatest warlord finally took a stand. He looked his mind firmly in the eye and told it in no uncertain terms to go find a rock to talk to, because right now he had happiness to attend to.

The moon beamed. The sea gurgled. The breeze held its breath. The six companions turned away. They groaned in a huddle. It was going to be a long night for them, that was for sure.

And the stones . . . ?

They trembled. Then they rocked. They rumbled and they rolled. They shuddered and shook, danced and shivered, and moaned. And those stones didn't give up their jiggling and jolting, until they had sucked in every last drop of the story.

Onward Bound

Three days after the rains had stopped, Ayşe was spotted. Recip spied her from the mini market that demarcated the entrance into the Olympos valley. He noticed she was hobbling like an old woman, every step requiring an almost insurmountable effort. He trotted outside to see if she needed help, but she waved him off.

'I'll tell you later!' She called out breathlessly behind her and staggered on her way.

This scene was repeated again and again as she stumbled the last three kilometres along the road to Olympos. Her back now forced her into an ungainly stoop. Evening was floating down from the sky, ready to save the Olympians from the dreaded fire of the day. But the steam of midsummer still choked all those in its grip.

Ayşe trudged on, stubborn until the end. She passed the tattoo stall squatting ramshackle on the corner and the Ala Turca Pansiyon sitting over the riverbed. She pushed on through the guest houses, past Cafe Cactus. She noticed the painted rocks that lined the cactus garden – turquoise, purple, and red, and she smiled. The orange trees chattered in their groves, their thick leaves bunched into sprouting green globes. She trudged breathlessly on past the clothes stall run by the Turco-Australian couple, and she waved at the owner who had lent her the sleeping bag. The young woman waved back from behind a rainbow rail of cotton trousers.

'Ayşe! You're back!'

She grinned. Then she dropped her head over her right shoulder, stooped and mouthed the word 'tired', before making a final lurch over the dry riverbed to home.

The next morning, Ayşe was to be found lounging in a *köşk*. Everything was pretty much just as she had left it. The seventies rock stars littered the garden in various states of lethargic repose. Dave Gilmore now had his tousled head in Cher's lap. One of the Freddie Mercuries was checking his moustache in the mirror. And Sami the cook, whose T shirt still stuck to his paunch like a badly pasted hoarding, had just placed a tea in front of Ayşe. She swirled the ruby brew about the belly of her glass and picked at a plate of watermelon in front of her. It was still early for the Olympians. The citrus garden was quiet. Quiet enough for the rocks to whisper. Quiet enough to hear your thoughts, and may be even your soul.

જ⦿ℭ

I had always imagined a state of enlightenment like my icon of the Buddha floating on a blob of cumulus high above the dirt of the world. I imagined it to be some sort of escape from trouble and woe. I imagined it was a place in time and space, something you could mark on the map of your life with an esoteric cross. Well, perhaps that's how it is for some people. How should I know? But in all honesty, I think these maps of spiritual journeys are at best useless and at worst misleading. I mean for one thing, the terrain (our world and our lives and the universe) is in constant flux. I know some people claim even though our paths are different, we are all climbing the same mountain, but if you ask me, it's a little desperate. There is no 'one' mountain because it's continually evolving, and for all we know it might even be multiplying. Anyway, even if there were one ultimate truth, in reality, this earthly reality, one can only ever talk about one's own trail and one's own mountain, and one's own connection to everything else. Perhaps there are infinite mountains to climb. Perhaps every individual's universe is unique, and probably the reason people are so adamant there is one mountain and one source of all, is they are afraid to stand alone and grasp the full extent of their power.

On my trail, the only trail I am qualified to comment on, rather than gliding on wisps of heavenly ecstasy, the magic comes from connecting with the dirt, from the soles of my feet conversing with the Earth, from exchange. And it is in that connection, that moment to moment flow, I gain my strength and my power. Every moment is a chance to see something new, to become more than I was the day before, to move deeper into myself, care less about what other people think, and stop looking at their outdated maps.

As for the past, I have no urge to get over it, or run away from it, or spend hours on a couch analysing it. It lives in me, each year bunched on top of the one before like the rings of a tree. My trail made me who I am, and I actually like who I am, even if the rest of the world doesn't. Yes, dear World, you may well think me a bad mother because I ran away from my son. There will be many in my country who think I'm a bad wife because I don't sit at home and bake börek, but go off on adventures instead. And I haven't even got to the oodles of others for whom I'm wickedness incarnate because I am divorced and have remarried a younger man. Everyone has their own trail. And because no one else has ever trekked with exactly my history, my culture, my mind, or my idiosyncrasies, judgements simply don't make sense.

As for cartography, I can't see me making a map of my journey, anymore. What would be the point? Because I will never walk the same path again, and neither will anyone else.

It was only just over a year later. Things had morphed beyond recognition in the ancient city of Olympos. There were those that failed to sense the limits of the valley, or the consequences of the changes afoot. Some pansiyons had burgeoned out of hand. Their shacks propagated like pinewood parasites. Their air conditioners sucked the juice clean out of the local grid. The backpacker, the traveller and the student were all steadily being engulfed by the mainstream. And no one was careful with their refuse. Everyone wanted more, only there never seemed to be enough, especially where space on the beach was concerned. A proliferation of shoddy *kokoreç* stalls and ice-cream sellers clogged the banks of the dry riverbed. Meanwhile, the cars poured in. In the space of a single year, Olympos had transformed into a honking, fume-belching runnel. The die-hards from another era looked on forlornly. Was this the inevitable fate of every paradise on Earth?

Little did they know, but the rocks in the riverbed were hearing it all. They drew in the clamour and inhaled the exhaust poisons. They chewed them up, and digested them. Gaia was listening. The Earth was awake. And the odds were not what they appeared. For whenever a human soul touched her, Lycia gained in strength and power. The moderns were vaguely aware their words and intentions touched the plant world. But who knew of the sensitivity of the earth and the rocks? Yet the walkers and the meditators, the nature-lovers, the shamans, the shepherds and shepherdesses, were growing in number and depth. Their affection was balm to the Earth. Their devotion was life in her veins.

There were those who would call it 'an act of God'. Others would shrug and call it a random anomaly. Only

Lycia knew the truth, with her mouth of silt, clay and stone, her eyes of water, her ears of pine.

The season had just drawn to a close. The guesthouse owners and stall holders were shutting up shop for the winter. It was a day which on the face of it looked just like any other of the gruelling revolutions the Earth makes on its axis. Morning yawed into noon. Midday lolled into afternoon. It was then it began to rain.

Afternoon became evening, and it was still raining. The showers thickened into muddy, grey downpours. On and on it went. Medusa had long closed her eye, and Aphrodite had no intention of looking. Instead of an eye, the sky was a gaping blank. And without a celestial observer, the valley began to disappear. That rain fell like no other for many years, and it fell peculiarly and particularly on Olympos. It fell on the channels far upstream. In a matter of minutes they had bulged into almighty torrents. Then night swept in. He kidnapped the trees and the mountains, abandoning the vale to the darkness.

Water hurled itself upon the slopes of the mountains. From one hour to the next, the gulches swelled into a liquid monster of silt, rocks and wayward branches. Soon enough, the monster gathered itself. It rose up.

'*Heed* all of you!' It roared, before rolling over the edge for a night-long rampage. It ripped out trees and boulders tossing the enormous slabs of limestone out of its way like marbles. Oh how it bellowed as it hurtled downwards. It burned a direct trail for no other than the Olympos valley. The home of the Gods no more.

It was the early hours when the Olympians, startled by the gushing outside their windows, awoke. They clambered to their doors wondering what could be the matter. They stood in horror as they watched the river, for it was two metres higher than when they had gone to bed.

Dawn was evading the valley. She skulked the other side of the mountains. Perhaps that was just as well. No one could see the train of destruction that tumbled through the darkness, as livelihoods were swept along in the flood.

The next morning the extent of the damage became obvious. The Olympians blinked in disbelief. In one night, sixty odd cars, a couple of buses, tractors, trucks, bungalows and entire guesthouse forecourts had been washed through the neck of the ancient city and out to sea. Two or three guesthouses all but disappeared, and at least one wooden home was never seen again. Of the vehicles remaining in the valley, most were piled one on top of the other. They were bizarre totem poles of wrangled iron. Brand new BMWs could be found squatting awkwardly in *kösks* as though waiting for breakfast. And the shoddy food stalls were now well on their soggy way to Cyprus.

Yet, strangely, miraculously, despite all this material havoc, not one soul was taken. This was Gaia's little warning. And she wondered if they'd hear it. For three days, the Olympians huddled, unable to move in or out. Water supplies were cut off. Electricity died. And the folk waded through the days in desperate delirium. It was curious, because the two neighbouring villages were untouched. It took a staunch rationalist not to sense a deeper meaning.

In the years that followed, the Earth waited. She listened, tasted and sniffed the air. She watched and wondered. Olympos stopped expanding, but would it clean itself up? Would the Olympians – all of them, from the locals to the tourists, from the partiers to the traditionalists to the government – would they take their rightful place as the guardians of the valley, and feel her rocky magic? Would they know the riches that lay under their feet, the beauty and meaning neither money, nor drugs, nor a suntan could buy? Would they become Gods again? Lycia and Leto and

Gaia knew only too well; that was something only their old friend time would tell.

Yet there was a potential.
Such a potential.

꙳○꙲

And what about old Harpagos? The ancient history books said, having conquered Phoenicia, Harpagos finally settled in Lycia. They said his descendants ruled it too, until a Macedonian called Alexander wandered in. Many a modern historian scratched their head and wondered: Why would Harpagos choose to end his days as satrap of such an insignificant quadrant of the Persian Empire. He had hotspots like Babylon and Phoenicia to choose from. But I know only too well the reasons, because I was there.

꙳○꙲

Twenty odd years after he had first set foot in Olympos, the old Persian satrap known as Harpagos was to be found staring out over the valley. To his right were humped, craggy ridges. They were stacked one behind the other like dinosaur backs. Over these, the man who'd conquered it all could – at least in his mind's eye – see Xanthos. To his left, even further back beyond the snowy splendour of Mount Olympos, were the old lands of Media – the home of Astyages, and the birthplace of Cyrus and his first son. Whether these two points in space and time existed outside Harpagos' mind is anyone's guess. But, as he sat at the cliff-edge, strong gusts whipping his face and hands, the two sides seemed to him to be in perfect equilibrium. And he was at the centre of it all. The fulcrum

Nothing would ever bring back Harpagos' first son or suture the gash in his heart. But the further back the satrap stood, the wider his perspective stretched. Eventually, the landscape of mental relics rolled into different shapes and hues. Nowadays, when Harpagos trudged back to those places in his mind, his son's murder sat side by side a dethroned Astyages. Both these images were embedded in the pyre of Xanthos, which lay at the heart of the Persian Empire of Cyrus the Great. It was an empire where, for the most part, peace flourished. Mints punched out more coins than a field of slot machines. People spent lifetimes without invasions, sackings, war, without despotic rulers crushing them under colossal taxes. It was a world where communities were free in their beliefs and their art. Even Cyrus' enemies, the Greeks, couldn't help but sing his praises. Alexander the Great modelled his leadership on the man. By the end of Cyrus the Great's reign, the Achaemenid Empire would be the first truly multi-ethnic empire in the world. Harpagos' trail, known or unbeknown to him, had laid the foundations for a good few years of freedom and decent living, from the Aegean sea to the Indus river. And that, in the ancient world of yesteryear, was as close to utopia as you were going to get.

But those were only the things the history books wrote of. Far more significant were the quiet deeds no one saw. The nocturnal activity around the Letoon, for example, went completely unnoticed. Harpagos organised a band of his most trusted Companions to carefully fill in the crypt. It was a significant job, and I remember it well. First they covered me in a generous layer of bone-fragments and gravel. Then came the earth. Shovel after shovel, the soil rained down on me, until only my neck and head poked out. The priestesses circled me. They laid their hands of light on my rocky crown. They whispered under the moon and the stars. I took it all in, because that's what a rock does. It absorbs and holds and stores, until the day it is no more.

And then they did something unexpected. Those wily priestesses heeded the words of General Harpagos and created a trail of Lycian lore. It was more of a web than a path – a network of interconnected power stones scattered throughout the land. Each rock communicated with each other rock, and those pathways of wisdom grew thicker and stronger with every story they absorbed. Things moved from inside to outside. From outside back within. And each time they did, history shifted. Changed. Evolved.

The old temple was taken down. A new one was built in its place. And no one was any the wiser that I was sleeping below holding the archives of Lycia deep in my limestone belly. There I sat, slumped in rocky silence, waiting for the day. The day when the secrets of time finally rose out from the darkness. Because the past is never static, nor the future a game of die. Time is not a line moving from one place to another, either. It is a living, breathing network of information, like neurons and synapses, or even a landscape of old Lycian stones.

Finally, one day, a day that looked like any other of the gruelling rotations of the Earth on its axis, my moment arrived. The future became the present. And the present transformed into the vortex of all times. Humans knew of their power and their place. They began to understand the web of time and uncover the secrets of the Earth. I remember my rediscovery well. Gaia was joyful that day, dancing her impossible dance. It was then that I heard a scratching above my nobbled, old head. At last human hands, hands of flesh and blood, touched my craggy body. And as soon as they did, I started talking. Ah how I poured my tales back into those fingers! My burden of memory was finally absorbed into the people from whom it had come. It moved from hand to head, from head back to hand. Always changing. Always evolving. Everyone adding something and taking something away.

The story you are at the edge of was but a shiver of the slab of tales I have heard. But it was a powerful splinter. It was the tiny, unheralded actions of goodness that rendered it vital. History books rarely write much about love and kindness, as though only bloodshed were worthy of the effort. But in truth, it's only in the heart humanity can be victorious. Power and wealth are in the hands of fate alone.

ಬಿ O ೮ಽ

Old Harpagos stood near the large cone of rock at the entrance to the beach. He stared through the small archway nature had created in it, and watched the river meet the sea. He saw a rat-haired man approaching, chisel in hand. Harpagos smiled. Jason had grown to be a strapping fellow in his thirties, and a sculptor to boot.

The shadows of evening left black imprints. They carved up the cliffs into striking grooves. Meanwhile, trees glowed auburn. The pebbles shimmered ultramarine, onyx, and pearl under the steadily darkening dome of a rayless sky. Nothing stayed the same. The dark patches would be light by morning. The crags where the sun now shone would soon sink into shadow. And in evening, or at dawn, when the contrasts were at their strongest, the picture was always at its most beautiful.

Jason reached Harpagos and paused. 'I'm just finishing a new one. Want to come and see it?'

Harpagos patted the man on the shoulder. Then he followed him away from the seashore to a nearby glade.

There, a lump of white marble towered over them both. The feet, gown, and torso of the statue had already been carved. Only the head was missing. The old general watched as Jason hunched in its shadow and closed his eyes, moving his palm over its skin. Because it *was* skin. Rocks were alive and they moved, albeit slowly, in perfect harmony with their surroundings. Each one had a personality, and woe betide you if you were too insensitive to notice. Harpagos had taught him well.

The rat-haired sculptor took up his hammer and chisel. A fig tree was winding its way up from the ground beside him, its fat leaves chattering in the streaming air. As he stood before his heavy, stone canvas, the man was remembering his old leader Licinius. The statue had been the nobleman's last wish. It was in his honour. He recalled the story Licinius had told him, of praying to Leto back in the dark days, and of how the great Mother had listened and answered him. How Olympos had been saved.

Jason looked up at the hulk of rock and let it speak to him. As the light turned slowly over its wrinkled, grey body, he began to see something shimmering through. He laid his hand over a higher part of the epidermis and felt the heart of the rock. Peaceful. It was so cool and peaceful. His core gently began to vibrate with the rock. His mind became quiet. His heart became full. And then, only then, he saw her face. Lifting his chisel and hammer Jason carefully lifted off the first shard.

Glossary for Turkish Words

Allah Allah 'Oh my God!'.

Abla Older sister. Used as a term of respect for a slightly older woman.

Ayran A traditional, salted yoghurt drink.

Bey efendi Sir/gentleman

Börek A classic Turkish savoury pastry, usually filled with cheese or minced lamb.

Dul Widow (also a traditional euphemism for 'divorced'). In mainstream Turkish, the term 'divorced' when used in relation to a single woman, has only become acceptable within the past two decades.

Erikli A popular brand of local bottled spring water.

Gözleme A type of savoury pancake made without eggs and cooked on a large flattish metal surface.

Hadi arkadaşlar! Translates loosely as, 'Hurry up folks!' but in other contexts means, 'See you later guys' or 'Come on!'

Helva Tahini based dessert usually bought in slabs.

ipad Mypad yok yani. In colloquial Turkish an 'M' is often added to a noun to create a rhyme (e.g., ipad Mypad, yoga moga) and adds the meaning of 'and stuff like that'. The entire sentence can be translated as: 'So no ipad and stuff.'

Jandarma The Turkish gendarmerie, a section of the army whose duty it is to police rural areas.

Jeton Token used for public transport instead of cash.

Kervansaray An Inn on the old Silk Road with a large courtyard for horses and camels.

Keyif Pleasure, enjoyment, amusement. The concept of *keyif* can be perfectly conjured up with the image of someone reclining in a *köşk,* drinking tea, smoking, and laughing with friends, with no aim other than relaxation. This kind of activity can go on for hours in Turkey.

Kızım My girl/my daughter.

Kokoreç Barbequed lamb's intestines. Small stalls selling *kokoreç* can be found in any self-respecting Turkish food street. Often served in bread, *kokoreç* remains unloved by foreigners, but a favourite of locals everywhere in Turkey.

Köşk Raised wooden platform with cushions to sit on. Usually constructed in gardens, restaurants or anywhere with a view, this eastern gazebo is designed for the sole purpose of *keyif* (see above).

Limonata Homemade lemonade.

Leblebi Dried chickpea, a staple part of a typical Turkish pick and mix nut snack.

Memur Any paid government official. This group includes a host of government posts, from doctors and post office workers, to teachers and tax officials. Traditionally, *memur* posts were coveted as they offered safety (a memur never used to get fired), ample bribe-taking opportunities, and little in the way of hard-work. In recent years, clamp-downs on corruption in low-level government posts have become widespread with cameras installed in *memur* offices and penalties for taking backhanders. Bribing a police officer or paying off the tax inspector is no longer the simple banknote-in-driving licence it used to be. The high-ranking offenders in government fraud naturally remain unaffected by these anti-corruption measures.

Pişmaniye A white candyfloss type dessert.

Şalvar Very baggy trousers worn by village women and sometimes men.

Şaman Shaman

Serçe Type of car (see *Tofaş*)

Simit A sesame bagel sold by street vendors and often eaten for breakfast with cheese.

Tekel 2000 A well-known Turkish cigarette brand.

Tofaş Turkish Fiat. These are hard-wearing no nonsense Turkish-made cars with superbly cheap spare-parts. They are always favoured by rural folk for their durability on roads that make mince-meat out of most European, US and East Asian motors. *Tofaş* chose to name all their models after birds. The smallest is the *Serce* (sparrow) and is Turkey's answer to the Trabant of former East Germany or the UK mini. This is followed by two simple saloons; the *Şahin* (buzzard) and the *Doğan* (falcon). Finally, comes the *Kartal* (eagle), an all-purpose estate car, short on elegance but high on usability. These cars have incredibly long life-spans, typically running for thirty years or more, after which they are recycled for the parts. Tragically, all but the *Şahin* have been discontinued as city Turks turn to the sleeker-looking but far less sturdy Western car.

Tulumba A Turkish fried dessert, drenched in syrup and guaranteed to improve your chances of a heart attack, diabetes, or both.

Vallahi By jove! I swear...

Vapur Istanbul ferry.

Yenge Literally means sister-in-law. Used as a term of respect for a slightly older woman.

Yok No, an absence of.

Yurtdışı Abroad.

Epilogue

Ayşe Metin 1968 –

Ayşe hiked the Lycian Way for the first time in 2008. The account of that first trek is based on her own detailed description, with names changed. Her life story remains as close to the chronology of her history as possible, although names and sometimes settings have been changed for privacy.

Lycia was only the beginning. To date, since that initial hike, Ayşe has completed the Lycian Way eight times, once trekking from Fethiye to Olmypos in 14 days. She subsequently went on to hike the trickier St Paul's Way in central Anatolia twice, the Kaçkar in north eastern Turkey, and circumnavigated the island of Lesbos on foot. In 2011 she set her sights on Nepal and walked to both base camp Annapurna and Everest. Lycia remains her favourite.

At the tender age of 42, without having stepped anywhere near an educational establishment for over twenty years, Ayşe sat the notoriously competitive Turkish university entrance exam. She passed and was offered a scholarship to study Spanish at four universities in the country. She is completing her degree at Fatih University in Istanbul, and is currently on an Erasmus placement in Spain, where the Cordillera Cantabrica awaits her.

The Lycian Way

The Lycian Way is a 509 km hiking trail in southern Turkey, created and waymarked by Kate Clow in 1999. It starts 20 km from the city of Antalya and finishes in Fethiye (or vice-versa). Following both ancient footpaths and goatherd or mule trails, the trail wends its way through a number of important archaeological sites and constitutes Turkey's first official waymarked footpath for walkers.

Notes for the historically interested.

Olympos

With regards the ancient city of Olympos, its early days are still a mystery. What we do know is, by 168 BC Olympos had become a major Lycian city. It held a massive three votes in the Lycian League giving it the same political clout as the ancient Lycian giants of Xanthos and Patara. Earliest documentation and coinage from the city date back to almost 200 BC. Although it is unclear when Olympos sprang into existence, there are many indications that it must have existed as some sort of metropolis long before the 2nd century BC. The Roman orator Cicero (106 BC to 43 BC) describes it as 'a city of high antiquity, and copiously supplied with everything both for ornament and defense'[4] which indicates that Olympos was at the very least a few hundred years old by then. Given its strategic position, its protection from the elements, its perfectly located river, and the mythical flaming hills of Çıralı right next door, it seems unlikely that there was no civilisation at Olympos when the Persians entered Lycia in 545BC.

Lycia

---

[4] "The Orations of Marcus Tullius Cicero against Caius Cornelius Verres" translated by James White Esq. (II, 1,4 p.51)

Lycia is another historical enigma prior to the Persian invasion. Few records were kept in the local language. Lycia's political structure is also still under much debate. Inscriptions from the second century BC imply that Lycia was the first democratic union of city states in the world[5]. However, many historians think the union may have begun up to three centuries earlier[6]. So, by 545BC was it a fully functioning democratic republic with senators? Or were the people ruled by kings or some sort of nobility? Homer talks of lords, though the names of these dynasts are conspicuously absent from Greek texts. George Bean, among others, makes a case for federalism based on inscriptions found. Herodotus records that it was a matriarch, and Aristotle says the Lycians were ruled by women[7]. Modern historians such as Antony Keen hold that it was likely the Lycians were dynasts rather than elected senators, though he admits this is but an educated stab in the historical dark.[8] All in all it is a mystery.

How far back the Lycians go is debatable. They are mentioned in Egyptian, Hittite and Ugaritic texts dating back as far as about 1500 BC (apparently the Lycians fought on the side of the Hittites against the Egyptians during the battle of Kadesh in 1295 BC)[9]. It is generally thought the Lycians were much older than that, however, and may date back as far as the fourth millennia BC.

---

[5] Bryce, T. Zahle, J. p.102.
[6] This was documented in The Fethiye Times 18 March 2007, and Hurriyet Daily News Dec 14th 2009.
[7] Keen, Antony G. p35-36
[8] Keen, Antony G. p31-60.
[9] Bryce, T ; Zahle, J. p.5

Lycians were known as Lukka by foreigners (the Hittites, Egyptians and Greeks in particular). What that term meant to those who used it is the subject of much historical confabulation. According to Herodotus it is thought to originate from the Cretan, Lycus son of Pandion. The word Lukka could also come from the Greek 'Lykus' which means wolf. At the time of printing the UNESCO website maintained that Lukka meant 'The Land of Light'. The Lycians never referred to themselves as Lukka. They called their land *Trmmis*. The Lycians had their own language with its own alphabet. It was in the Luwien subgroup of Anatolian languages, but died out sometime from the Persian invasion to the arrival of Alexander the Great, and was ultimately replaced by the Ancient Greek language.

Regarding spiritual belief, Lycia was one of the last places in Asia Minor to maintain some sort of mother worship. Leto was daughter of Coeus and Phoebe, lover of Zeus, and also the principle deity of the Lycians, along with Apollo and Artemis, her children. It is widely presumed that Leto was a manifestation of the mother-goddess Kybele of Anatolia. By the first century AD, however, she was under threat. The anti-pagan (and possibly misogynistic) bishop St Nicholas, had the temple of Artemis in Myra razed to the ground. The power of the rocks has been thought to be another aspect of Lycian belief. The rocks were thought to symbolise the strength of the Gods[10].

Lycian society, and in particular the position of women, is another subject of controversy. Just how much of a matriarchy was Lycia? Herodotus and Aristotle paint pictures of varying degrees of female domination, possibly

---

[10] Theory put forward by Professor. Fahri Işık, lecturer at Akdeniz University in Antalya and head of excavations at Patara.

with the aim of making the Lycians appear heathen or promiscuous to the patriarchal Greeks[11]. According to Herodotus the Lycians took the mother's name, and if women cohabited with a slave the offspring became citizens, while if the situation was reversed with a Lycian male and a foreign mistress, the children were 'without honour'[12]. In fact, actual inscriptions in both Greek and Lycian don't appear to support these claims and describe a man as the son of his father. Herodotus might have been referring to earlier Lycian customs, no one really knows. The infamous female warriors, the Amazons, were also supposed to have been found in Lycia according to Herodotus (although as Trevor Bryce points out, in other traditions they are located further north.[13]) Nicolaus of Damascas wrote that 'they left their inheritances to their daughters, not their sons.' Plutarch also refers to a matrilineal society in Lycia. Tomb-building shows that women definitely appeared to be in charge of their own finances. Some tombs have clear inscriptions describing them being commissioned by women using their own funding. There is even a small tomb in the Antalya museum that a woman had built for her dog.

Regarding their appearance, the Lycians were singular in that the men appear to have had long hair. There are two references to this in historical texts. Aristotle writes in his 'Oeconomica' that Mausolos' hyparch taxed the length of the Lycians hair, and the 2nd century Macedonian writer Polyenus writes about a man managing to escape through Lycia by disguising himself with false hair[14]. This seems to be backed up by images on various artefacts such as coins and engravings.

---

[11] Keen, Antony G. p34 – 35.
[12] Herodotus. 'The Histories' Book 1.
[13] Bryce, T ; Zahle, J,
[14] Keen, Antony G. p35.

General Harpagos (Harpagus)

The story of general Harpagos is reported in detail by Herodotus of Halicarnassus in the first book of the Histories *Clio*. Paul Kriwaczek's summary of the tale is delicious as well, and well worth reading[15]. Due to the exaggerated fairy-tale nature of the account many historians presume it to have been made up, or at least embellished, perhaps in order to explain why Harpagos betrayed Astyages in favour of Cyrus.

Harpagos is credited as having put Cyrus the Great on the throne. He has quite a resume and his list of achievements includes successfully taking over the conquest of Asia Minor after the death of General Mazares, the inspired use of dromedaries on the front line against the Lydians (the smell of which panicked the Lydian horses), engineering innovations such as earth ramps and mounds which were later used by Alexander the Great, and the neat idea of utilising mountain climbers to scale walls in sieges.

As a result of Harpagos' reputation, the Phoenicians didn't bother to put up much of a fight and fled to Carthage before he got there. Although he was an almost invincible opponent on the battlefield, he was also known for his mercy and implemented Cyrus' policies of tolerance and freedom of religion. Despite the Xanthian's dread of Persian domination and their subsequent mass-suicide, Lycia entered her heyday right after Harpagos' invasion in 545 BC.[16]

---

[15] Kriwaczek, Paul. P174-176.
[16] Keen, Antony G. p36 – 60.

The Harpagid theory, put forward by the British archaeologist Charles Fellows, has it that Harpagos died in Lycia, and created a dynastic line of satraps. The theory is based on the discovery of the Xanthian Obelisk, which according to the inscription in Lycian was erected for the son of Harpagos (Arppakhu). There is other inscriptional evidence of a certain Arppakhu, but whether it is a descendant of General Harpagos or another Persian who married into the 'noble' blood-line is unclear. Although Herodotus says that Lycia was part of a satrapy[17], Persian satrapies were not usually dynastic. Antony Keen raises the question as to why Harpagos would settle in Lycia rather than somewhere more prestigious[18]. There are any number of possible reasons why a powerful satrap might have selected a quieter province in which to end his days. Given the choice of bustling Babylon with all its politics and pressure, or the idyllic shores of Lycia, the latter is quite plausible as a retirement option. Nonetheless, the Harpagid theory is for the most part rejected by present day historians.

The Achaemenid Army

Herodotus and Xenophon both describe the Achaemenid army in detail. Other information comes from illustrations on various monuments. The Greeks exaggerated the numbers of the army. Historians have made estimates for the Persian forces based on topography and logistics. Xerxes' 3000 000 Persian warriors has been estimated more in the region of 70 000 infantry and 9000 cavalry, for example. The number used here (60 000) is an educated guess only.

---

[17] Herodotus. 'Histories' Book 3, ch 90.
[18] Keen, Antony G. p 61 – 71.

The infamous 'Immortals' were an elite regiment that acted as bodyguards to the commander, as well as a highly-trained warrior force. The word 'Immortals' Herodotus uses, however, is probably a translation mistake (Anusiya = Companions, as opposed to, Anausa = Immortals)[19]. The conditions for this elite were good; regular pay, and permission to bring wives and concubines along on campaign. The Persians had a highly organised military set up using regiments based on the decimal system. 10 men formed a *dathabam*, ten companies made up a *satabam*, ten battalions created a *hazarabam* etc. It was a characteristic of the Achaemenid period that Commanders in Chief fought on the battlefield alongside their subjects.[20]

The Xanthos Poem

The Xanthos poem came to me when I was working on the book in Taiwan and was written in less than an hour. At the time, I had never visited Xanthos. All I knew was the grizzly story of how it fell to Harpagos. Months later when I was rewriting the story for the umpteenth time, I researched Xanthos more thoroughly. While looking online, I stumbled across an ancient Lycian poem that had been inscribed into the rocks. The Turkish archaeologist and translator Azra Erhat had made a beautiful translation of it into Turkish. I was quite startled when I read it:

Evlerimizi mezar yaptık
Mezarlarımızı ev
Yıkıldı evlerimiz
Yağmalandı mezarlarımız

---

[19] Lendering, Jona, 'History of Iran' Iran Chamber Society.
[20] The Circle of Ancient Iranian Studies, 'The Achaemenid Imperial Army'

Dağların doruğuna çıktık
Toprağın altına girdik
Suların altında kaldık
Gelip buldular bizi
Yakıp yıktılar
Yağmaladılar bizi
Biz ki analarımızın kadınlarımızın
Ve ölülerimizin uğruna
Biz ki onurumuz ve özgürlüğümüzün uğrun
Toplu ölümleri yeğleyen bu toprağın insanları
Bir ateş bıraktık geride (Hiç sönmeyen ve sönmeyecek olan)

Here's my translation of her translation.

We made graves our houses
And houses our graves
Our houses were destroyed
Our graves looted

We climbed into the mountains
Dug ourselves into the earth
We were soaked to the bone

And still they found us
They burned and destroyed us.
They plundered us.

For the sake of our mothers, our women,
And our dead
For the sake of our honour and our freedom
We people of this earth chose our own death
And we left a fire in our wake (never to be extinguished and everlasting).

While the words of my poem in chapter six are different, the rhythm and 'feel' of the poems are strikingly similar. It was for this reason, I almost omitted the one I wrote in Taiwan from the book. In the end, I changed my mind, because it seemed Xanthos had written the poem, not I.

Bibliography

Aristotle and Gillies, John. *Aristotle's Ethics and Politics*. London: A Strahan; and T Cadell Jun, and W Davies, in the Strand. 1797.

Atsma, Aaron J. *The Theoi Project: Guide to Greek Mythology*, Web 2007.

http://www.theoi.com/Titan/TitanisLeto.html

Bean, George E. *Lycian Turkey*. John Murray, 1989.

Bryce, T., and Zahle, J. *The Lycians in Literary and Epigraphic Sources*. Denmark: Museum Tusculanum Press, 1986.

Butler, Samuel. *The Iliad and the Odyssey by Homer*, MobileReference, 2007.

Clow, Kate. *The Lycian Way*. Turkey: Upcountry, 2009.

Caldwell, Richard S. *Hesiod's Theogony – Translated, with Introduction, Commentary and Interpretative Essay*. United States: Focus Classical Library, 1987.

Cotterell, Arthur. *The Pimlico Dictionary of Classical Civilisations, Greece, Rome, Persia, India, China*. Great Britain: Pimlico, 1998.

Herodotus, Marincola, John M., and De Selincourt, Aubrey. *The Histories*. Penguin Classics, 1996.

Kriwaczek, Paul. *In Search of Zarathustra: The First Prophet and the Ideas that Changed the World*. New York: Alfred A Knopf, 2003.

Keen, Antony G. *A Dynastic Lycia: A Political History of the Lycians and Their Relations with Foreign Powers, c.545-362 BC.* BRILL, 1998.

Lendering, Jona. Livius Articles on Ancient History, Web. 18 Jan 2014
http://web.archive.org/web/20040206222050/http://www.livius.org/home.html

Lendering, Jona. "The History of Iran," Iran Chamber Society, Web. 18. Jan 2014
<http://www.iranchamber.com/history/achaemenids/immortals.php>

Ragozin, Zenaide A. *Media, Babylon and Persia.* United Kingdom: Read Books, 2006.

Roberts, J.M. *The Penguin History of the World.* Penguin Books, 1990.

Ovid and Melville, A.D. *Ovid Metamorphoses (Oxford World's Classics)* Oxford: Oxford University Press, 1986.

Peak, Harold and Fleure, Herbert John. *Priests and Kings.* Oxford: Clarendon Press, 1927.

Roller, L.E. *In Search of God the Mother: The Cult of Anatolian Cybele.* London: University of California Press, 1999.

Strabo. *Geography Book 14.* Published in Vol. V of the Loeb Classical Library edition, 1928

White, James esq. *The Orations of Marcus Tullius Cicero against Caius Cornelius Verres translated from the original by James White Esq.* London: T. Cadell, 1787.

Atulya K Bingham was born in the U.K. in 1971 and has lived in Turkey since 1997. As well as a writer, she is a natural building enthusiast and lives in her hand-crafted mudhouse in the Turkish hills with her dog, Rotty.